GIFT TO THE GODS

The attendants gently stroked the woman's hair out of her face, then laid her across the altar. Torches threw a bright and rosy light over the sacrifice. She seemed dazed, scarcely frightened—a good sign, Yetecuan thought.

He drew his knife, a long, wide triangle of flaked obsidian, so old that no one knew who had first used it. For a sacrifice Yetecuan would use only glass: its edge allowed a quick, deep incision and the removal of the heart before the victim even felt pain.

"The True Gods love you, my daughter," he said, smiling. He bent over her, looking forward to the sudden burst of energy that her death would give him as he gave her to the Gods. The veins in her breasts were blue traceries of beauty, and Yetecuan revered the power of life he saw pulsing in them. Ah, how this one would please the Gods!

By Crawford Kilian
Published by Ballantine Books:

GREENMAGIC

REDMAGIC

Crawford Kilian

A Del Rey® Book
BALLANTINE BOOKS • NEW YORK

A Del Rey® Book
Published by Ballantine Books

Library of Congress Catalog Card Number: 95-92019

ISBN 0-345-38370-2

Manufactured in the United States of America

First Edition: June 1995

10 9 8 7 6 5 4 3 2 1

For Michael Butler and Christopher Trumbo
who listened to the first stories long ago in Mexico

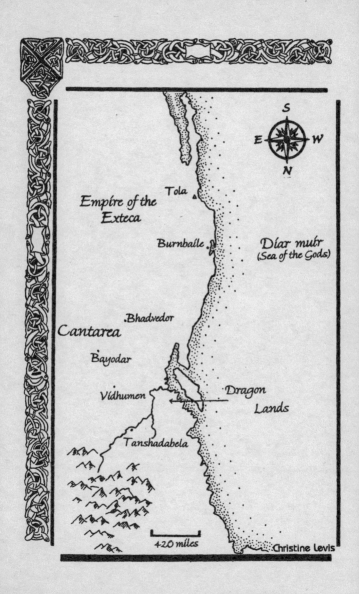

One

Eastward rose the hills, tawny with dead grass and mottled with stands of oak and pine. Streams flowed down from them, watering the fields and gardens of the Airn; then the streams lost themselves in the marshes on the edge of Siar Bagh, the Bay of the West.

Burnbaile stood on a little shelf of land between its fields and the reed beds, overlooking the bay. On this last day of summer the land was warm and the air was cool. Usually that would mean mist or even fog, yet today the sun had shone in a clear sky.

Across the bay, Deir could see the two peninsulas, Donbein and Dubein, reaching toward one another. Between them was the gap that opened westward to the Diamuir, the sea of Gods. A long ribbon of fog had finally entered the bay, stretching eastward and covering some of the islands where the Airn gathered eggs and oysters. Under the westering sun the fog gleamed white, almost too bright to look upon.

The house that Deir shared with her mother, Sivon, was on the southern edge of the village, beside the River Clachwisgy. Its first floor was of mud brick faced with stone, its second of timbers and planks; Deir's father, Bron, had been a fine carpenter, and never better, everyone said, than when he built his own house. Behind the house lay Sivon's kiln, a well-tended garden, and a small orchard of apple trees. The front of the house faced south, sharing with a dozen other houses a lane shaded by oaks that ran along the northern bank of the Clachwisgy.

Beyond the house the lane went a little distance west to a rough bridge over the stream; beyond the bridge the Clachwisgy ran between reeds and mud flats and at last into the bay itself. The lane was always a busy place, but this afternoon it was crowded; clusters of townspeople sat along the banks, drinking and singing the old songs called summonings.

Deir and her mother sat on wooden stools on the little porch before their doorway, drinking mead that Sivon had made the year before.

"Don't *gulp* it, girl. A sip at a time, as your father took it."

"Yes, Mother." Sitting in her finest smock, embroidered with threads of twenty colors, Deir felt herself a grown woman at last; it would not do to drink like a child swigging a mug of New Year's ale. A breeze brushed through the leaves of the oaks and carried a strand of her fire-red hair across her face. Her lips tightened as she pulled the strand back in place and wished for a mirror. On this afternoon, of all, she would want to look composed.

At their feet lay the candleboat that held the bones of Deir's father. Deir had woven it of reeds she had cut herself, making it long and wide—almost as large as the reed boats the men used in hunting waterfowl through the marshes. Its bow and stern rose in peaks adorned with flowers, and the bones themselves rested under a cloth that Sivon had embroidered for months.

"It will be the best of the candleboats," Sivon said, her blue eyes glancing across the lane. The groups of singers were also gathered by candleboats, and Deir thought her mother was right. Only one or two of them were as large or as well made. Some had only plain linen cloths, with flowers but no embroidery.

"Father used to say the custom was dying out."

"He was right in that, if not in some other things. Had he not been so stubborn in following old ways, he might be here today, scorning those boats and with none for himself for many a year."

Deir said nothing, but thought about that day in late spring. Her father had been building a cabin; in levering the roof beam into place, he had somehow slipped and let it roll back down upon him. Her mother and uncles had not let her see his crushed body; not until they had exhumed his bones this morning had she realized how quickly he must have died.

Her mother was right. Other carpenters used the clever bronze pulleys sold by the pochtecky traders of the Plume People, but Bron Mac Conal had stubbornly held to the old ways of muscles and levers and sweat. He had used only the usual geases for wood, though his talent for magic was scant.

"I don't trust the Fabarslúa," was all he'd ever say when people praised their wares: their fine fabrics, their jewels, the amazing feathers they wove into capes and mantles. He would have none of their pots in his wife's kitchen, though she—a potter herself and a good one—admired the Fabarslúa art with clay and glaze. And though their bronze tools were beautiful, he scorned them and kept his wooden mallet and stone chisels.

Well, thought Deir, he had trusted his own magic, and much good had it done him. Two years now—no, three—since the pochteckies had first arrived from the south. Strange they'd seemed then, and many besides her father had mistrusted them, with their loincloths and bare legs instead of proper trousers and smocks, their golden jewels in lip plugs and earrings that pulled their lobes almost to their shoulders, their flat hairless faces and straight black hair braided with the feathers that earned them their common name.

Yet they had been humorous and gentle, as fascinated as clever children with everything they found in Burnbaile and the other Airn villages. Their bright black eyes saw everything, their quick fingers studied and treasured everything that came into them. Apples delighted them; salt fish and fresh oysters delighted them; the fine work of Airn goldsmiths delighted them also. Yes, and even the woodwork of stubborn carpenters who would not buy pochtecky bronze.

More people were coming down the lane, families bearing candleboats and singing as they came. All greeted Sivon and Deir as they passed, with waves and smiles that would not interrupt the summonings. Others came, who had lost no one in the last year but who wished to show their respects. They often stopped and took a sip of mead from Sivon, exchanged a word of courtesy and went on.

The sun was low now, hanging on the shoulder of Dubein, and a chill had crept into the air. Though everyone sang, all kept an eye on the sun as it sank behind the peninsula. When it was fully down, the sky above Dubein glowed red and orange; the first of the families put twigs into a little pot of fire taken from their hearth and lighted the four candles set into their reed boat. Still singing, they lifted the candleboat and waded into the Clachwisgy; they were sending the boat and bones of a child off to the Diamuir, to the Happy Islands of the West, yet the mother wept all the same as she stood hip deep in the cold water and clung to the edge of the boat.

The candles burned oddly bright in the deep twilight beneath the overhanging oaks; the boat bobbed on the current and glided downstream, under the bridge, and out between the beds of reeds beyond.

Sivon and Deir made no move while boat after boat set off down the darkening stream, each with its candles burning while the high, sad keenings of the living bade farewell to the dead. *How few we are, yet how many of us die in a year.* Deir realized she was weeping only when she felt spots of dampness on her smock.

"What a good man he was," Sivon murmured, in tears as well. "Ah, what a good and funny man. For every time he vexed me, a hundred times he made me laugh." She stood, a sob shuddering in her throat. "Come on, Deir, let's send your father to the Happy Isles with his women's songs warming his soul."

She stood up in obedience, feeling her self—the Deir within her head—shrink to a tiny point behind her eyes: cold, silent, observant. They took up the candleboat, which was light for all its size, but after three or four steps Sivon paused. She stopped singing and gently lowered her end of the boat to the cobbles of the lane.

"What is it, Mother?"

Sivon's eyes gleamed under the sunset sky. A strange smile tugged at her lips. "Do you not feel the call?"

"What call? I feel . . ." She did not know what it was, only a restlessness, a kind of distant pulling at her, as if she suddenly yearned for blackberries or the company of a friend. But it was nothing to stop still for.

Smiling, Sivon turned to look eastward up the lane. "Ah, Deir, they've come! The lovely men have come! Quick, girl, let's go to them!"

"Mother?" Deir saw people around them, some walking, some hurrying up the lane. One family waded dripping out of the stream and ran laughing into the growing darkness. Someone bumped Deir's shoulder in his rush to get past.

The songs had ended in laughter or in silence. Now Deir heard only the quick slap-slap of sandals on the lane, and then she saw a blur of motion: something bobbing toward them. Closer: men, wearing red and yellow plumes on their heads, clubs in their hands. Pochtecky traders? But all had gone at summer's start; why would they return now?

Something loomed behind the plumed men, something big yet silent of foot. Deir felt a tremor of fear, though her mother seemed to notice nothing. The older woman took a step, then another, toward the advancing men.

"Come, love—come and embrace them." Deir held her mother's arm and would not let go. Sivon only smiled and pulled the harder.

The men were closer now, close enough for Deir to see that these were men like the pochtecky, but garbed in plumes and odd quilted tunics that seemed stiff and thick. They carried short clubs with heads of bronze, and spears, and shields. They were many, forty or more, walking in good order, and behind them came a monster.

It was a great four-footed beast, twice the height of two tall men—and indeed it bore two men easily on its vast back. Where its nose might have been, a long snakelike appendage waved and curled between two curving tusks adorned with gleaming gold and fluttering feathers. A kind of mantle hung over its back, looking much like the quilted material that the men wore.

The first of the families reached the advancing men. The villagers were reaching out to embrace them, but the men without a pause lifted their clubs and struck down all as they approached. The Airn cried out in surprise and pain, yet still more of them hurried toward the Fabarslúa.

Sivon broke away from her daughter's grip and ran lightly to meet the men, her yellow hair flying behind her. Deir cried out, began to follow, and then saw one of the invaders club her mother to the ground. The blow had not been deadly; Deir saw her mother turn and writhe upon the cobblestones. But the Fabarslúa kept up their advance, leaving their victims where they lay. The snake-nosed monster picked its way delicately among them.

Now a crowd swarmed before the men, as if each Airn wished to be their next victim. Deir turned, gripped her father's candleboat by its upturned end and dragged it into the darkness under the oaks. The river ran silently beside her; with scarcely a moment's hesitation she walked into the water, pulling the candleboat with her. Even if she could not light her father on his way, she could at least send his bones safely to the gods. Then she could cross the river and run down the road to Kiltarra for help. The boat seemed eager to be gone downstream, but she clung to it as she waded deeper; when she reached the center of the stream, it covered her almost to her chin.

She looked eastward, across the stream and up the lane, and now saw torches gleaming and flaring. More men were coming, some holding torches while others bound the Airn who had fallen. The first group of Fabarslúa, and the snake-nosed monster, swept past Deir's house. A noise behind her made her glance downstream; more Fabarslúa were hurrying across the bridge, joining the first.

If they were south and east of the village, Deir thought, then she could now escape only to the west and then to the north. If she could swim down the stream, into the bay, and then make her way along the shore to one of the other Airn villages. But the water was so cold, even at summer's end, and she was a good enough swimmer but not for such a distance and not at night.

The candleboat tugged at her, and she waded farther across the stream, to where it shallowed out on the far side. Her smock clung to her, tangling in her legs as she clambered shivering onto the reed boat. The embroidered cloth that had covered her father was gone, already swept away or left on the far bank; her father's bones gleamed whitely, digging into her flesh as she embraced them to cling to the sides of the candleboat.

Free at last to obey the current, the candleboat swung and drifted toward the bridge and the reed beds beyond. Deir shuddered with cold and with something else as she watched the two groups of Fabarslúa meet at the end of the lane and salute one another with raised clubs and spears. Behind them, their captives seemed to be rousing from a sleep, moaning and calling out to one another.

"Mother," Deir whispered. "Oh Mother, Mother. Oh—"

The candleboat was moving faster now, sweeping under the bridge. If the men looked down, over the wooden railing, they would surely see her; her white smock would gleam in the torchlight. Yet they seemed interested only in the village before them and in greeting their comrades; none troubled to glance down at the water.

Just before she went under the bridge, Deir saw two men starting across it. They were unlike the others, whose pale cotton tunics and feathers made them glow even in the darkness. These two men were in black robes, and their faces were darkened or smudged; their hair rose in stiff disorder and fell about their shoulders. Had they not walked amid torchbearers, she could not have seen them at all. One seemed old, or walked as an old man might, in little steps; the other strode with a young man's strength, yet stayed a pace behind the other.

The old man she had never seen before, but the young man's sharp features were unmistakable: he had been one of the pochtecky traders last summer, smiling and laughing and looking at everything.

Then she was past the bridge, gliding with awful slowness amid the reeds. As they rose around her, she lost sight of the houses and people; yet she still could see the torchlight flickering on the branches of the trees.

Before long she was on the waters of the bay, feeling its little waves splash playfully over her as the candleboat went out on the ebbing tide. She remembered swimming out here when she'd been a little girl, sneaking out with her friends against their parents' warnings; but those adventures had been on hot summer afternoons, with someone's fishing boat or dugout always close in sight. Now the surface of the bay was like the black glass the pochteckies sold, under a sky already filling with stars though the sunset smoldered in the west. And in the stillness, carrying easily over the water, came a dreadful trumpeting cry, a bellow that could only come from the monster, and then a short, agonized scream.

Deir felt the rasp of reeds under her hands and smelled the odd, earthy smell of her father's bones mixing with the salt smell of the bay. The silence from the shore was worse than more screams would have been. Was this what the old legends called a war? It seemed too quiet, too ordinary. Wars were noisy businesses, men stamping about and screaming war cries as they struck at one another with maces and spears. Or so they had been when Airn had fought Airn in the long-ago time. Had they ever simply walked into one another's villages on Candleboat Night and clubbed those who came to greet them?

And why had all gone mad as the Fabarslúa came down the lane with their great beast? Why had none cried out in surprise at the sight of that snakelike nose, or the sheer size of the creature? Why had her mother, her sensible mother, gone as mad as the rest? And what had happened to her?

I should have stayed. I should have pulled her away, escaped with her. And how would she have managed that, a slim girl of sixteen overpowering a woman half a head taller and with strength enough to knead clay like bread dough? Would they both have fit on this candleboat, and would it be better if both of them drowned in these freezing waters?

Outward the tide pulled her, as the stars shone down and the lights of the Airn villages gleamed along the shore. How small they seemed in all this darkness. The lights of Burnbaile were as bright as the others: Kiltarra, Barnachy, and on up the bay. Were they, too, overcome now by the Fabarslúa? Was she the only Airn left alive and alone?

She shivered so hard her father's bones rattled and rasped together. Strange, to be so cold on a summer's evening. She scarcely felt her hands and feet now, and a kind of dizziness held her. The shoreline was out of sight now. All around was darkness flecked with glints of light, and she could not have said which were the stars and which their reflections in the bay. One light glowed brighter; she lifted her head a little, looking over her father's skull, and saw another candleboat. One of its candles still burned. Even as she watched, it guttered down and set the reed boat afire. Flames licked around the cloth, then swallowed it in a bright orange flash. The whole candleboat burned now, fire dancing among the blackening bones. Deir smelled smoke, and half wished her own craft would catch fire from a stray spark. Then at last she might be warm for a moment.

The other craft burned itself out and sank with a hiss. Its last embers hung for a moment on the water and then went out.

Now I am truly alone. She felt the candleboat sinking a little as its dry reeds absorbed water. Her weight unbalanced it, keeping her tipped a little into the water, but she would not move: to do so she would have to push her father's bones into the sea, and it would gain her only a few more minutes of painful cold before the boat sank under her in any case.

"Come on, Deir, let's send your father to the Happy Isles with his women's songs warming his soul."

If only a song could do that. Well, it would be a song for both of them, and she would go hand in hand with her father Bron to those Happy Isles in the west. There they would wait for Sivon, and perhaps not wait long, and from her learn what had become of Burnbaile and all its people.

So she began again the words of the summoning that she and her mother had been singing when the Fabarslúa had come down the lane out of the darkness. Her voice was a whisper, a moan, yet the words consoled her:

> "We summon you back, summon you back
> From dark and silent earth;
> We summon you back, summon you back
> To sail the sea and sky
> Our love will abide, our love will abide
> When sun and stars are gone . . ."

And only then did Deir ni Bron the daughter of Bron Mac Conal know that the bones she sang to, the bones she embraced, were all that remained of her father—that he was dead beyond all recall, beyond all justice, and whatever might lie out in the Sea of Gods, no Happy Isles awaited him nor any other of the Airn. She felt a grief hard and sharp enough to cut a stone, and it cut her soul and heart before she even knew it was coming; in her anguish she sang again, not in a whisper but a cry that rose out of the dark within her like a whirlwind:

"I summon you, I summon you!"

Two

Yetecuan walked into the foreigners' village without help, shuffling across the bridge with Nezaual close behind. Yes, he was old, and the invocation of the spell of love had exhausted him. It would be a pleasure to sit, even in one of these wretched little hovels, and then to sleep. But not yet.

Torches burned up and down the dirt path between the stream and the first houses. The teteuctin had done their usual efficient job of taking prisoners and then selecting which ones would go south as slaves and sacrifices. Some were now binding the foreigners' hands. Others were punching a hole in each captive's nasal septum and threading a fine cord through it to link them all, ensuring that none would try to escape on the long march south to Tola. A few were searching the houses, making certain that no one was hiding.

Yetecuan walked a little way up the path and saw a couple of wooden stools in the doorway of one house. That would do as well as any other place. He sat down on one of the stools. Torchbearers flanked him, keeping back a little so that the light would not hurt his eyes. Nezaual squatted close to Yetecuan's right knee, eyes on his master.

Sitting down was absurdly pleasurable. The weariness after making magic was almost sensuous, but he could not let himself yield to it. Not yet.

A clay jug stood on a little table beside the chairs, and two cups. One still contained a dark liquid with a pleasant smell: this must be the intoxicating drink the pochteca had reported. He picked up the cup, ignoring Nezaual's alarmed look, and allowed himself a sip. His senses were intensified by the sacrifice he had given before the attack—a slave and blood from his own arm—so he could see a residue of the magic that had gone into making this liquor. The magic might be simple, but the result was not bad at all; this drink would fetch a good price in Tola, and the foreigners would find it a useful tribute item. A barrel of this would be worth a foreigner's life.

Colotic emerged out of the darkness, yellow plumes waving around his hard features. The commander of the teteuctin knelt before Yetecuan.

"Honored father, we have secured the village. We took two hundred and ten prisoners."

"The pochteca counted well. I believe they said this place had two hundred and five."

"Yes, honored father. We have selected forty women as slaves, and fifteen men as sacrifices. The rest we leave in place."

"For now," Yetecuan murmured, and Colotic smiled. The old man turned to Nezaual. "You remember these people's language."

"I do, honored father." The young priest's grin was a white flash in his smudged face. "When I came as a trader, I took care to learn it. Shall I speak to the ones we leave behind?"

"Yes, my child. But not tonight. They will be dazed from the spell, and from Colotic's clubs. Let them sleep. In the morning, before we go, you will speak to them."

"As you wish it, honored father."

"For now, then, we have only to consecrate this place as a new tributary. After that, we rest."

"Are you well, sir? It was a strong spell you cast; I felt its power."

"Quite well. Colotic, find me one of the handsomer of these people—not one of the captives. A mature person . . . a female, I think. Yes, a female."

The warrior knelt again, then rose and hurried into the night with his attendants close behind him. Yetecuan was vaguely aware of the sounds of the village: moans, shouts, even someone's laughter. Very much the behavior of those recovering from the spell of love.

He was relieved that it had gone so well. This far north the people had no knowledge of the True Gods, or of how to placate them. That was why they lived in squalor, lacking anything beautiful. Sometimes, if the raiding party's priest failed to cast the spell of love properly, the people would resist. They would run from the teteuctin, or even attempt to fight them. Then the priest would have to find the strength to cast a spell of terror, and if he failed in that as well, the warriors would mock and jeer him.

The old man smiled a little. That had happened to him once, when he had been a young priest—younger even than Nezaual. Afterward he had scourged himself with a glass claw, cutting deep scars in his chest and belly and thighs until the True Gods saw that his blood gift was enough. They had blessed him then with great gifts, and he had used them humbly for the Gods' glory and that of their greatest people—the Exteca, the Blood People, lords of Tola and some day to be lords of all the world.

But it takes so long, and the Gods are so hungry . . .

Long ago he had thought only about the immediate task, the details of the raid and the spell before him. Now he saw the pattern that he and his people were making as they did the Gods' bidding. In learning redmagic, the Exteca had made themselves masters of their southern deserts, and the Gods had blessed them with water and fertile fields and many children. But every child needed a blessing also, and that blessing meant a blood gift. The more children, the more sacrifices; so the Exteca swept out from their deserts to seek captives and tribute. Gratefully, the Gods sent more children, so the Exteca must go still farther in search of yet more sacrifices, more slaves, more tribute.

And priests like himself, masters of redmagic, were the key to it all. The pochteca traders would scout ahead, finding barbarous tribes like these pale-skinned swamp dwellers; then the teteuctin would strike, exploiting the spells of love or terror cast by the priests. Later the officials would come, to set up a garrison and depot, ensuring a steady flow of tribute and sacrifices, but by then the priests were in search of the next tribe, the next miserable village.

Tonight, as always, Yetecuan marveled at the Gods' wisdom and kindness. Never could the Exteca grow dull and lazy with success, and they served as the Gods' net to snare the wild tribes into civilized, religious life.

This place, he knew, was one of several villages of this tribe. The traders had seen no need for a major assault; this village would serve as an example, and the others would surrender quickly. That was convenient, but not always the case. He was exhausted, and Nezaual was too young and inexperienced to cast great spells; if these people with their frog-belly-pale skins chose to resist, Colotic's warriors would have to fight without the aid of love or terror.

Only give us enough priests, oh Gods, and we will feed you with the hearts of all the world.

Colotic and his men were back, escorting a woman in a filthy smock. Her yellow hair fell in confusion over her face, but she seemed healthy and handsome enough. Yetecuan nodded to the warriors, who gently removed the woman's smock. In the torchlight her body was pale and strong, and Yetecuan was pleased to see stretch marks on her breasts and belly. She was fertile; her blood would ensure this land's continuing prosperity under Exteca rule.

"You have chosen well, my child. Let us give her to the True Gods as a token of this land we have given them also."

Colotic clicked his tongue at two of his men, who promptly knelt side by side on hands and knees. Yetecuan smiled affectionately at them: they were just boys, and clearly stunned with the honor of serving as an altar. They would feel blessed by every drop of blood that fell from the sacrifice's flesh onto their own.

Colotic and Nezaual gently stroked the woman's hair out of her face, then laid her across the backs of the kneeling teteuctin. Two warriors gripped her ankles, two others her wrists. Torches rose on all sides, throwing a bright and rosy light over the sacrifice. She seemed dazed, scarcely frightened—a good sign, Yetecuan thought.

He drew his knife from the pouch at his belt. It was a long, wide triangle of flaked obsidian, so old that no one knew who had first used it. Bronze knives and spears might suit the teteuctin in the routine business of war, but for a sacrifice Yetecuan would use only glass: its edge allowed a quick, deep incision and the removal of the heart before the victim even felt pain.

"The True Gods love you, my daughter." He smiled. Only a little surprised, he recognized her as the maker of the drink he had sampled; he had seen the touch of her soul in it. The Gods must indeed love her, to guide him and the teteuctin to her so that she was now about to join them.

He bent over her, looking forward to the sudden burst of energy that her death would give him as he gave her to the Gods. The veins in her breasts were blue traceries of beauty, and Yetecuan revered the power of life that he saw pulsing in them. Ah, how this one would please the Gods!

Something hurled him violently backward, and for a moment he thought one of the teteuctin must have senselessly hit him. The knife fell from his fingers and shattered on the cobbles. Yetecuan sat down, curled up on one side and wrapped his arms around his head. Some fragment of his awareness knew he was wailing in shock and fear, but he could not control his own cries.

What is happening? Are the Gods coming for me? Have I offended them in some way?

Once, years before, he had fallen into a rushing stream that had tumbled him over rocks and logs for a hundred paces before he had regained his feet and escaped. This was worse. It went on and on, until it seemed it had always gone on, that he had only dreamed a life before this one. Consciousness whirled away into a state he had never known before. Vaguely he was aware of Colotic shouting something, of Nezaual sobbing close by, and after a time he realized he and his young disciple were in the grip of magic. Someone had cast a spell, a violent and powerful spell, and anyone with a talent for magic would feel it as he and Nezaual did.

When at last the violence slackened and he could think again, his first thought was surprise that it was still night; surely many hours must have passed. His arms and legs were twitching uncontrollably, and his bladder had emptied into his blood-crusted black robe. Colotic was holding him, calling his name in anguish; Yetecuan smiled faintly up into the warrior's frightened face.

"I still live," Yetecuan whispered. "Thank you, my child. Your arms are strong and warm. Are you well? Did you feel it?"

"Feel what, honored father? You were about to consecrate this place, and then you and your disciple fell as if the Gods had possessed you."

"Perhaps they did." He saw the woman still sprawled over the backs of the two boys who formed a living altar. Her eyes, strangely blue, met his; she was no longer dazed, but shuddering with terror. Yetecuan shuddered also, knowing that divinity had come as close to him as his shattered knife had come to this woman's heart.

"Release her," he said. "Dress her in fine robes and plumes. Keep her warm and fed and clean, and look after her every need. Let nothing and no one harm her. She is a special gift, to be given in Tola." He looked at Colotic and Nezaual, and smiled so joyously that they smiled back. "Always they guide us, dearest children. They guided us here, and they guided me in my choice of a gift, and now they guide us in calling this precious person to their temples in Tola. *That* was the message of the Gods."

The endless buzzing of the flies seemed suddenly louder, until it was a roar in Ometollin's ears.

The heart in his hand, hot and beating, slipped from his fingers. Absently, the Chief Priest saw the heart fall into the pool of blood around the altar and lie pulsing there.

The sacrifice's body was still twitching and evacuating on the curved stone block. The assisting priests, who should by now have flung the body down the steps of the pyramid to the butchers, were standing around the altar like blind men. One of them, his eyes wide and unfocused, was vomiting.

Ometollin bent down to pick up the heart and place it on the glowing coals with the rest of the sunset offerings, but found himself on his hands and knees in the blood. Hundreds of flies and other insects were trapped in the coagulating puddle, many of them still buzzing and struggling to escape, and for a moment Ometollin imagined himself one of them. He heard his breath whistle in his throat. The heart beat a few more times and then went still. In the light of the great torches it was a shiny purple-red lump, already crawling with flies.

He wondered dreamily why any God would want such an absurd offering. Why not a gall bladder, or a colorful length of bowel? He giggled. Perhaps he had been drinking? The weariness in his limbs was like that of drunkenness, but he was certain he had drunk nothing. More likely he was dying, of a stroke or heart attack. If so, he was blessed to die in the very act of sacrificing to the Gods.

Yet he did not die. Gradually his strength returned. After a few deep breaths he gripped the still-warm arm of the sacrifice and pulled himself upright. The other priests were still dazed; Ometollin saw warriors crowding up the steps but reluctant to step onto the holy platform where only sacrifices and priests might go. Beyond and below the warriors were the maceuali, the common people, gathered at the foot of the pyramid to witness the special gifts due the Gods on the last day of summer. And beyond the commoners the lights of Tola stretched far away into the night.

His senses were returning, and his memory. *I have felt this before,* he thought. Two winters ago. The shock of a great magic, like an earthquake, far away to the north. This was not as strong, but it was closer. Much closer.

Gently, he touched the arm of one of the priests.

"Please, my child, dispose of this body." His voice was a whisper, barely audible even to himself. "And then send the rest of the sacrifices back to their pens until the time of the sunrise gifts. I must go and meditate. The Gods have sent us a message, and I must think about its meaning."

Ignoring the young priest's stuttered commands to his fellow, Ometollin walked slowly to the rear of the temple, through a bare doorway, and down a narrow flight of steps. It was completely dark, but he knew every tread and riser; in moments he was within his cell, fifty-two steps down inside the pyramid.

A small lamp burned in the windowless cell, its flame swaying in the breeze from a vent to the outside. Grunting, Ometollin sagged onto the pile of rags and skins he used for a bed. An anxious servant looked in; he waved her away, too tired to be polite.

The walls were black with the soot of lamps that had burned here for sheaves of years. Here he had lived for all the thirty-seven years of his life as Chief Priest; for twenty years before that, he had slept in cells much like this one, or out under the stars when he had gone raiding with the teteuctin. He preferred the cells to the stars; here the Gods came closer, made their will known. Now he blew out the lamp and looked into the darkness for the face of a God, listened in the silence for the voice of a God.

Nothing came except the whine of hungry mosquitoes, but Ometollin was not disturbed. The Gods spoke as often in silences as in words or images, and he understood them tonight as always.

North was mictlampa, the evil direction, the realm of savages who did not know the True Gods. Now, somewhere in that realm, magic was at work on a scale no Exteca magician had ever dreamed of. It was a human magic, not a deed of the Gods; even at this distance, Ometollin had recognized human voices and souls.

One great magic was an omen. Two were a threat.

The long days of summer were ended, but twilight still lingered above the pines and spruces that stood among the cabins of Tanshadabela. Tilcalli was shaping disks of hardbread at a table by an open window, glad that she did not yet need candles. Across the room, Dragasa was drawing the latest batch of hardbread out of the oven. Its aroma filled the cabin.

"It's worth putting up with winter," he said to his wife, "just to have this bread to smell."

"I'll remind you of that in a couple of months," Tilcalli said, "when you're complaining about 'hardbread yet again!' " She imitated his deep voice, and they laughed together.

Ah, how beautiful she is. He caught himself a hundred times a day marveling at her. Too often he regretted the lost years when she and their son had lived among the Badakhar, but then he cursed himself for a fool who could not savor the good moments when they came to him—and this was another good moment, a time that a sensible man would prize above any glory. He was in his home, with the woman he loved, and she loved him.

"At least when winter comes I won't be able to complain about all the outsiders," he said, glancing out the window. Two stocky blond Badakhar traders, more than a little drunk, were swaying down the street toward Svordo's inn.

"I know how you feel," Tilcalli said, following his gaze. "They still make me uncomfortable when they're drunk. You never know when their mood will change and they'll want to quarrel."

"Well, it's the price we pay for peace. At least they're not coming at us with swords and spears."

"No. Not yet."

He looked sharply at her. "What? Do you suppose they'd try to be our masters again?"

"Nothing so simple. But life is still so hard in Cantarea, and the Badakhar aren't used to sharing power—least of all with their former slaves. I see the traders coming here, and I see their eyes. They respect us, as they never did before, but they don't like us. And they don't like living as poor people must."

"Would they blame us for that? They ruined the land with their mines and herds, and if Calindor had not renewed the soil after Callia's wrath—well, they'd be dead of starvation by now."

She nodded. "The wiser ones understand why it happened, and some are even glad. But many still remember how it was in the old days. When they lived well on our suffering."

"The next generation will be better," Dragasa said, putting the next batch of hardbread onto a long-handled wooden paddle and then sliding the disks into the oven. "They won't remember how it used to be; their parents won't tell them much because then they'd have to explain how their own folly brought the storms and floods. But for now it's harder than I expected."

"Calindor will know what to do."

"If he knows what to do, then why is he off in the dragons' land all this time? We've been expecting him for weeks. By the time he and Callishandal get back, the snow will be here. He won't be able to get out onto the prairie to see for himself how things are going."

She smiled. "You forget how easily he travels."

"Yes, yes . . . he could walk in the dead of winter from here to Ghrirei or Kormannalendh." Dragasa's mouth twitched at one corner. "Something else to dislike about them. Our old lands still have their names. We should—"

Dragasa dropped the long-handled wooden paddle, letting it clatter to the plank floor. He drew a deep breath and groped as if suddenly blind for the chair by the hearth. Tilcalli, leaning over the table, sank into the chair behind her. She too gasped for air, her eyes wide.

Dragasa recovered first. Pulling himself out of his chair, he stumbled over to his wife and put his hands on her shoulders. Tilcalli looked blankly at him, through him. Moments ago a smudge of flour had stood out against her brown cheek, but now she was so pale the smudge was almost invisible.

"The hardbread's burning," she said.

"Let it, let it. Are you all right?"

"Yes. Get the hardbread."

They took a few minutes to compose themselves. Dragasa

poured them each a mug of beer and then sat across the table from her.

"Magic," he said.

"Very strong magic. I've stood next to Badakhar sorcerers, and next to our son, for that matter, but I've never felt anything like that. Except perhaps when Callia overthrew the Badakhar."

"But it was so far away—was it Calindor?"

"I don't think so. You can feel his spells. They're not like anyone else's, because he's learned so many magics. This was . . . like the Stony Falls."

Dragasa nodded, thinking of the white cataracts not far up the Cantabela River: powerful, chaotic, obeying nothing but the wild energy of the Gariba within their waters. Yes, this had been similar.

"Well," he said, draining his beer. "No doubt he sensed this also. I wonder what he makes of it."

Tilcalli looked worried. "Tonight we shall go into the Open Dream and seek him."

Three

All day the sea had been in turmoil. A wind from the southwest had stirred waves that rose and fell against one another as they blindly sought the unseen coastline far to the east. Above, the sky was clear and cloudless; below, the sea tore itself to spume.

Yet Calindor's boat glided in the center of a circle of stillness like a mirror of the sky. As every wave surged in from the west, it seemed to pause, part, and swirl around the boat as if it lay sheltered in a landlocked harbor. Now, at twilight, the sinking sun filled the west with pink and gold; the wind abated, the fog began to form to the south and east.

"I don't know what to do," Calindor said.

"Start a fire," his wife Callishandal told him. Obediently he snapped his fingers over the firebowl in the stern of the boat. A disk of dragonfire blazed white-orange within the bowl. Callishandal put a flat iron pan over it and laid fish fillets upon it. While they sizzled, she placed an iron pot full of soup beside them.

"And some light?" she added.

A thin, bright ring of dragonfire sprang into being above the stern deck. Twilight fled; the boat cruised on in a circle of daylight.

"It's the end of summer," he went on as their supper cooked. "We should be turning back; my parents expect us soon."

His wife smiled at him. "But you are too happy here."

"Much too happy." He looked around, loving everything he saw: his wife, his boat, the darkening sea, and the flaming sky. The boat moved steadily on, rising and falling a little on the swell.

None of their people had ever seen the sea before, though Calindor had glimpsed it once in a vision. He and his wife had journeyed by longboat down a great, nameless river to the western lands where only dragons lived. The dragons had made them welcome, though Calindor had sensed in them something like the feeling of householders finding two wandering wolf pups on the doorstep: the humans were a pleasant diversion, but perhaps a nuisance if they made themselves too much at home and attracted their kin.

"As if humans could ever feel at home among dragons," Callishandal had said when he spoke this thought. "And none of our kin will come seeking us here, will they?"

It had not mattered; they would not stay long. Calindor had been at once delighted and amazed by the sea beyond the great river's estuary where the dragons had built their strange city. It was like an enormous lake, studded with forested islands and bounded on the west by a far larger island. But to north and south, Calindor could tell, the sea opened onto something far vaster; and he had at once determined to venture out upon it.

He had studied the Powers in the landlocked waters of the inner coast before building the boat. These Powers were much like those of the streams and lakes of Cantarea, but their strength and diversity gave them a personality of their own—if beings without self-awareness might have personality. He had shaped his boat accordingly.

They had made *Tilcalli* from the trunk of a great cedar; from stem to stern she was seven spans long—seven times the height of a tall man. Calindor had felled and carved it with dragonfire, decked it over, and with Callishandal he had built a log cabin upon it much like those in Tanshadabela. They had named the boat for his mother, who in a far smaller boat had led them to safety when Calindor lay mute and entranced and a whole kingdom sought his death.

Together Calindor and Callishandal had launched the boat on an overcast day while dragons watched from the pebbled beach. The Powers of water had found it amusing to bear up this odd creation and to propel it along the surface. The Powers of air had played with the boat as well, but Calindor had built no mast and hung no sail; he preferred to surround the boat with the circle of calm, a bowshot wide, and to let it cruise easily while the waters all around it heaved and crashed.

Once out in the true ocean, they had turned the boat south, moving usually within sight of the coast. Each night they had pulled into some silent cove, some beach piled high with driftwood logs, to hunt for meat and fruits; each morning they had ventured south again, Calindor half dazed by the world they had entered.

He had not expected to be so caught up in the beauty and mystery of the sea. Even the surface was the study of a lifetime, but beneath it were even greater wonders. Calindor had seen the Powers of the deep, seen them moving far below the surface, and revered them without calling to them.

But now he had gained both confidence and curiosity, taking the boat farther out from shore and letting it cruise both night and day. From the stern, or from the prow, he watched the Powers at play in the great deeps, and in the slow-flowing stone that underlay them. The Powers of earth focused themselves in abysses where the stone had fractured and would fracture again. The Powers of water sank and rose in the lightless depths, moving in strange rhythms he almost understood. Within their silent streams and fountains also moved creatures of the deep, cold and great; they were ancient cousins of the dragons who had preferred sea to land, and now swam far below the light. Calindor heard them call to one another, though not with his ears. Their rumbles were too low for human hearing, but he sensed the disturbances they made in the Powers, and knew the sea dragons were the source.

Calindor loved the beauty of the Powers and the hidden creatures that dwelt in the deeps, but he drew back into the world around him: the sky, the sea, his wife who had no magic talent yet often saw more than he did.

He watched the fish cooking on the pan. "It'll be snowing in Tanshadabela in a month or a little more," he said. "And in the spring I must go out onto the prairies again, to help with the planting."

"Yes. And I miss them all—Tilcalli and Dragasa, Svordo, all the people of Tanshadabela."

"I miss them too. But I miss the prairies more." He thought of Cantarea, the Big Prairie where he had grown up in the grimy city of Aishadan. The Badakhar kings, in their folly and arrogance, had half destroyed the land; Callia, the goddess of Cantarea, had used him to blast their castles into rubble in a storm that left the land scoured and bitter. Yet thousands of Badakhar and Cantareans still lived there, trying to rebuild. Without the aid of his greenmagic, little would grow on the prairies for generations to come.

"Very well," he said. "We will go south until noon tomorrow, and then turn north again. If we don't stop, *Tilcalli* will take us home in just a few days."

Callishandal smiled teasingly at him. "You don't want to stay again among the dragons for a time?"

"I would love to stay among them all my life, and to sail this sea all my life, and to live in Tanshadabela all my life." He shrugged and smiled back at her. "This world has too many wonders in it for a single lifetime." He reached for the wooden plate that his wife held out to him.

In that moment the ring of dragonfire flared yellow, then blinding white. Calindor sprang to his feet, knocking aside the plate of fish, and then crumpled to the deck.

The dragonfire dimmed again, until it was no brighter than before; to Callishandal's dazzled eyes, it seemed scarcely visible. She went to Calindor's side in two quick strides, calling his name; her hand reached out and delicately touched his throat.

The pulse was there, strong as always but quicker than when he slept. He was alive but shocked by something. Callishandal remembered how he had been when they fled the vengeful warriors of Aishadan almost two years ago; first struck mute by a hidden spell, he had then barely survived an attack by Mekhpur the Firelord. For days after he had lain in a trance while his companions had paddled upriver to Tanshadabela. Now his face had something of that same pallor.

Callishandal felt a shiver of dread. Two years ago she had been only one of a group that included Calindor's mother Tilcalli and eight young men whose strength had taken them all to safety while the Badakhar warriors pursued them. Now she was alone, with neither magic nor much strength, and out of sight of land.

At least the spells of calm and light were undisturbed. The boat was cruising as it had all day . . . no, it was not. It had changed course. Looking back, she could see the curve of the boat's wake:

it was turning east and gaining speed, heading into fog and darkness toward an unknown coast.

Callishandal half carried, half dragged Calindor into the cabin and put him to bed. In the dragonfire light that fell through the windows, his face seemed pale . . . much as it had when he had lain entranced in the longboat. *But now I have no Tilcalli to rely on, no Svordo, no Minukhi—only myself.*

She went out through the forward door and onto the foredeck. The sea hissed and foamed about the prow, but beyond the circle of calm she could see nothing but thickening fog. Shivering, she went back inside and sat on the edge of the bed, holding Calindor's hand.

The boat had never moved so swiftly before. Clearly some great magic was at work, so great that its exercise had hurled Calindor into unconsciousness—just as Calindor's spells had once stunned lesser magicians like her old master Pelshadan. She prayed to Callia, but felt no reassurance. Even thinking of the time when Callia had spoken through her, made Bherasha the slave girl into Callishandal the Voice of Beauty, gave her little courage. Then, at least, Calindor had stood beside her, the channel into the realm where Callia lived.

She looked out the window beside the bed. Fog was thick now around the circle of calm. The only sounds were the slap and hiss of water along the hull, and the rasp of Calindor's breath in his throat.

This had really been their only home, she realized. Even when they had married and built a cabin in Tanshadabela, they had traveled too much to feel settled. The mountain villages of the Cantareans, the prairie towns and cities of the Badakhar and their former slaves—how many had they visited, so that Calindor could work greenmagic and help the survivors of Callia's wrath to build new lives together? And then he had followed an old urge to go west into the dragon lands, and of course she had gone with him.

With him she had built this little cabin on the boat; she had adapted their travel gear for it, so that they slept in a bed and stored their clothing in a closet. The windows even had curtains, woven of thin reeds from the estuary marshes. Here they had returned from their explorations of the beaches. Here they had slept, laughed, talked night and day, made love. Now perhaps it would all end here.

I don't think I'm ready to meet Callia, she thought. *I love this man too much. I love this world too much.*

She wondered what Tilcalli would do, and then laughed softly at herself: Tilcalli, one of the greatest magicians of the Siragi

Aibela, would doubtless have fallen entranced just as her son had. Sometimes a great talent for magic was also a great weakness.

Sometimes too, she reflected, a talent for magic concealed other weaknesses. Magicians were often abstracted, their true attention always on the Powers that they alone could see and control. That was why they usually made poor warriors; Calindor was a rare exception, for he could fight better than most Badakhar warriors. So if some magician had cast a spell upon *Tilcalli*, and was drawing them to himself, perhaps he would not expect a physical defense.

That kind of defense she could certainly offer. She lifted the top of a bench built into the wall opposite the bed and found there a fine ax and a scabbarded sword, both of Staldhuno steel. Calindor used them for clearing brush when they went ashore, and he had kept them clean and sharp.

She pulled the sword strap over her head and shoulder, so it hung by her left side; the ax she kept in her left hand. Then she went out onto the foredeck again and untied a long pole. It was no spear, but it might serve to fend off an attacker for a moment.

Glancing back into the cabin, she saw Calindor still motionless on the bed. How beautiful he was! How strong and gentle—

Enough. She would defend him with her life, and if they must go to Callia, then they would go together. Perhaps, though she was not a magician of the Siragi Aibela, Callia would allow her into the Open Dream, where the sun hung always at noon and Calindor's ancestors spoke without sound while they danced the past and the future.

The fog was thick now, a curve of grayness that never grew closer—like the melting ice that had given them passage on their return down the river to Aishadan. But something seemed different now; she thought she could almost detect a distant rumble, perhaps the thump and boom of surf. Could they be at the coast already?

Without warning the fog vanished; the boat glided into clear air above black water. Callishandal gripped her ax in one hand and the pole in the other. She wished it was the staff of Pelshadan, which she had wielded like a club on that grim day in Aishadan when the old magician had stolen Calindor's voice.

But nothing emerged out of the darkness. The ring of dragonfire, still suspended over the stern, threw light ahead onto dark water. Far ahead Callishandal could see the darker loom of hills and a few lights glowing at their feet. Looking to left and right, she glimpsed more dark hills behind and realized they must have come into a great bay or inland sea. The lights must be those of towns of cities along the shore.

So this would not be herself against some lone magician; warriors would be there, quite capable of dealing with a frightened young woman.

Even at this speed they would not reach the shore for some time. She relaxed, sagging back against the wall of the cabin.

An instant later the boat halted as if it had struck a reef.

Callishandal pitched forward, scrambling to regain her balance and swinging the butt of the pole before her. It struck the deck and kept her from falling. She muttered an old slaves' curse as water snarled and splashed around the hull; then she turned to see if Calindor had fallen from the bed.

But before she could look in the door, the noise of the water grew louder, as if cascading down a fall. And indeed it was: just off the right side, water fell gleaming from a height of a span or more, all the length of the boat. It gleamed in the light of dragonfire and seemed to rise yet higher. Callishandal squinted, unsure what she was seeing: a waterfall? a fountain?

The sound of falling water died away. Something moved in the darkness, turned toward her—

The light of the dragonfire ring caught it at last, and flamed in its eyes as it looked down upon her.

"Callia!"

The creature's head was a span and a half long, perhaps two spans. The eyes rose far back behind a muzzle like a great spearhead. The jaws, fringed with scaly barbs, parted to show teeth as long as Callishandal's fingers. Black it was, yet the dragonfire sparked every color from its dripping skin.

A dragon of the sea: Calindor had spoken of them, his voice thick with awe. He had sensed them moving far down in the deeps, and now this one had risen out of one darkness into another. Compared to it, the dragons of land were sandpipers scuttling along the strand. And humans were mere fleas.

The head sank and extended until it brushed the gunwale and rested on the deck. Was it going to sink the boat? It could do so as easily as a cook might crack an egg. No; it placed no weight on the deck. Callishandal might have reached out and touched its muzzle, or an eye as large as her head and alive with strange fires. The smell of it was rich, salty, like the sea wind itself. And on the broad, flat expanse of its skull lay a young girl.

She was gripping two of the many spikes that formed a kind of crown on the beast's head, jutting backward to protect its neck. *O Callia, against what greater creature might this beast require such defense?* A sodden garment clung to her, and wet hair fell in fiery strands all about her. Her eyes met Callishandal's; the girl seemed dazed, a little frightened, but mostly sad.

For a long moment they looked at one another. Callishandal drew in a low breath, then another, before she trusted herself to speak.

"I think it is giving you to us," she said.

The girl looked at her without understanding. Callishandal shuddered and laughed, casting aside her pole and ax, then pulling off the sword as well. Then she stepped forward, close enough to touch the great beast, and lifted her arms to the girl.

"Come on, then. Come on down." How could the dragon be so hot? Steam was rising from its skin.

The girl hesitated; then she let go of the spikes and slid slowly down between the dragon's eyes. Half falling, half leaping, she stepped from its muzzle and into Callishandal's arms. She was as cold as the dragon was hot, her hair and garment as clammy as kelp. The hair was indeed red, a color that might have seemed a trick of dragonfire.

"All right, then, you're safe. You're safe." Callishandal held the girl tightly, patting her shoulder as the girl shuddered and then cried out.

The great head lifted from the deck, its teeth and barbs glittering, and then it was gone. Water ran one way and another across the deck, the only sign of what had been there.

Silence. Wavelets lapped at the hull. Callishandal patted the girl a little longer and then said: "We must get you warm and dry. Come in. Come in—it's all right."

They went into the cabin. Calindor still lay there, but he had turned on his side and seemed to be sleeping normally. The red-haired girl glanced at him with little interest. She allowed Callishandal to pull her wet dress over her head and to wrap her in a blanket. Then she sat on the bench, staring at nothing.

Callishandal sat beside her. "Well. I wonder why a dragon would want to give us a skinny young girl with red hair and whiter skin than a Badakh's. And with little brown spots on her skin as well. Why would a dragon summon us for this? I wish you could speak our language."

"The dragon didn't summon us," Calindor whispered. "She did."

The fish was cold but edible, the soup a thick, overcooked paste. From a cupboard in the cabin Callishandal drew out some flat, unleavened bread she had made on the pan the day before. The girl sat on the bench, dipping her bread in the soup and then eating in small, dainty bites. Calindor and Callishandal sat on the bed, watching her and eating very little. The boat was drifting; Calindor seemed not to care.

"What was she doing?" he muttered.

"Sitting on its head, soaking wet."

"No, I mean what was she doing in the water? Was she fishing, or traveling like us?"

"A human, going traveling on a dragon of the sea? That seems hard to believe."

He shook his head, not even noticing her irony. "She wasn't traveling on it. She summoned it too. It held her up until we came."

Callishandal laughed without much humor. "And that's harder still to believe."

"Yet it is true. The dragon told me, just before I woke." He finished a piece of fish and licked his fingers. "Somehow this girl cast a spell that called it from the sea, and called us as well. When I felt the spell, it was like nothing I have known before. Not even like dragons' magic."

"She doesn't seem like a great witch."

"She isn't. I don't think she even knows what she did. But I can see she has suffered a great fright, and great grief. Perhaps some terrible shock released the talent within her."

"What shall we do with her?"

"Try to take her back to her home. I thought no one lived on this coast, but obviously I was wrong. I was too busy studying the deeps, and paying no attention to the land." He hesitated for a moment. The boat swung about and cruised slowly toward the distant lights on the shore of the bay. "Good. I was afraid I wouldn't be able to do that. Perhaps this is what other magicians feel when they have cast a great spell and exhausted themselves."

"The girl doesn't look especially tired. She's still cold, but she's alert." Callishandal got up and offered her more bread. The girl took it with a nod and a whispered word that surely meant thanks.

"My name is Callishandal." She pointed to herself, and then to Calindor. "Calindor."

"Cali-Calisanda? Calindo? Deir."

"Day-eer." Callishandal smiled at her. "A pretty name." She pointed out the doorway at the lights on the shore ahead. "Is that your home, Deir?"

"Burnbaile." And then a few stuttered words that choked off in sobs. Callishandal sat beside the girl and put an arm around her.

"Something bad has happened," Calindor said. "We'll find out tomorrow, when it's light. I don't want to go ashore now, even with dragonfire to light our way."

"Why not? What could harm us?"

He frowned. "Some other magic is at work nearby. I don't like the feel of it. It's like the magic Pelshadan worked to invoke the Firelord ... I feel death in it. This is a strange country. I don't want to take foolish risks."

His words made Callishandal fearful again. If Calindor, the greatest of the great magicians' clan of the Siragi Aibela, was alarmed, then something truly dangerous was at work.

Tilcalli stopped. Calindor murmured a few spells of protection. Then he pulled a couple of blankets from the cupboard and put them on the floor. "I'll sleep here," he said. "You and Deir can share the bed."

"Sleep?" The events of the last few hours suddenly rushed in upon her, and she began to shake uncontrollably. "Dragons and witches and strange magic all around us, and you tell me to sleep? Calindor, you must be—"

"Sleep," he echoed her. "Sleep, my love. Sleep, Deir."

A delicious weariness enveloped her. Deir stood up and shuffled like a sleepy toddler to the bed. Callishandal felt the girl collapse beside her, felt a blanket drawn over them, and then slept.

Four

In the Open Dream the sun was always at noon in a cloudless sky.

By the banks of a slow-flowing river, the ancestors of the Siragi Aibela danced the past and future. They spoke without speaking, to one another and to their descendants who came seeking guidance. Some had been there for countless generations, others for only a few years. A few had left the river, walking toward the snowcapped mountains on the horizon, and none had ever returned.

Tilcalli and Dragasa walked along the riverbank toward the village of the ancestors. The sun was warm on their shoulders. Sitting on a log overlooking the river was Calihalingol, Woman

Who Laughs, Tilcalli's great-great-grandmother. She smiled in welcome.

I was expecting you, the old woman said. *Come and sit beside me, and tell me all the news. Something has happened in Sotalar.*

Something strange, Tilcalli replied. *Someone has cast a great spell, far to the south, somewhere near Calindor and Callishandal. We have come here seeking my son, to learn more.*

We felt it here, too. Calihalingol nodded, smiling. *It was something like the great magic that your son made to bring Callia back to the world. But it was not his magic this time.*

Do you think he is all right? asked Dragasa.

We feel him all the time, the old woman said through laughter. *He is always casting one spell or another, reminding us he is there. Your grandmother was like that, Tilcalli, when she was a little girl. Always getting into trouble! Yes, he is all right. But something else is very wrong.*

What? demanded Tilcalli.

I am not sure. We are creatures of Callia, and through us she sees and feels and thinks. She is a great god. But she is not the only god.

Calindor stepped onto the foredeck, moving a little stiffly. The shock of the girl's spell had been bad enough; sleeping on the cabin floor had only made it worse. He stretched, then rolled his shoulders and rubbed his face.

The sun was well above the tawny hills to the east. A thin mist was burning off the water, revealing the blue vastness of the bay. Far to the south and north it stretched, bounded by marshes and hills and a few actual mountains. To the west, two peninsulas almost met; instead the sea glinted between and beyond them. He thought of the inland sea where they had launched *Tilcalli*. This was something like it, but the hills here were almost treeless; the Powers of water were rare on the land.

Some other Power was at work, though. He had seen something like it before; the great Badakhar magicians, the Veikar, had invoked it for their greatest spells. It was a magic that grew out of death, that fed on it. Somewhere on the eastern shore of the bay, where the smoke of many fires was rising, someone had cast a spell with a human life.

He had thought last night about going into the Open Dream to consult with his ancestors; perhaps his parents would be there also. But then he had realized how little he still knew—scarcely enough to frame a question, let alone seek an answer. A feeling of hopeless ignorance was an inevitable consequence of learning magic: each bit of knowledge offered glimpses of all that remained yet unlearned. Calindor had come to understand that, but not to accept it. Perhaps, he thought, that was part of the reason for this journey into unknown lands and seas.

Grunting a little, Calindor sat cross-legged on the deck. The sun was growing warm, but he no longer felt it. Instead he focused.

The boat, the water, the sunshine became both more and less real. He could see the stresses rippling through the deck planks as easily as he could see the wavelets on the bay. He sensed the fish slipping through the waters below the hull, and the slow sifting of mud from the marshes into the deeper parts of the bay. The reed beds came alive with all their birds and insects glittering and singing. This was a good place, a place where Callia was strong though humans had long lived here. Deir's people understood how to live as one more thread in Callia's tapestry.

Beyond the reeds, out of sight but not beyond his focus, stood small villages of stone and timber. He sensed terror in them, but also a strange joy.

—There. That village, a little to the southeast: the deathmagic had happened not far from there. Though the spell was many hours old, it still had the power to raise the hair on his scalp.

Most magicians, he knew, would be exhausted by casting such a spell, and would be helpless for days or weeks after. He himself was unique among Cantareans and Badakhar for his ability to do magic without tiring. But the sorcerer here might well have companions equally skilled, and ready to attack—or might be tireless also. Calindor murmured a spell of shielding, and saw it take effect as a shimmer around the boat. A few more words and *Tilcalli* began to move slowly southeast, toward the village still invisible in the thinning mist.

He let the focus fade and stood up. Callishandal stood in the cabin doorway, holding two flat disks of bread. Behind her stood Deir, wrapped in a blanket and looking curiously at him.

"Will you eat now?"

"Gladly." He kissed her, then took one of the disks. "Come out and enjoy the sun."

The woman and the girl stepped onto the deck. Callishandal looked around with interest and admiration. Deir saw at once where the boat was heading, and pointed straight ahead.

"Burnbaile," she said.

"Burn-bay-lee," Callishandal echoed. "Your home?"

Deir did not speak again. She nibbled a fragment of bread, never taking her eyes from the shore. Calindor studied her for a moment. The morning sun, falling on her hair, made it seem even more fiery than it had the night before. It fell in curls and waves almost to her waist, framing a pale, narrow face mottled with light brown freckles. Some blond Badakhar, Calindor thought, had such skin, but never had he seen such hair. Were all her people so strange looking?

Callishandal, standing beside her, looked very different. She was taller than Deir, slender yet strong, and far from Deir's delicacy. Like Calindor, Callishandal's skin was a rich brown and her straight hair was a glossy black. Deir's eyes were bright blue, Callishandal's deep brown. Most importantly, Callishandal was a woman of strength and confidence and Deir a gawky girl.

How could she have invoked such a spell? As soon expect a toddler, playing in the mud, to build a snowcapped mountain. Nothing in her appearance or manner suggested the abstracted behavior of a magician; if she saw the Powers at play all around them, she gave no sign of it. Even a small sorcerer, good for nothing but creating illusions, revealed more of his talent than this girl did of hers.

Perhaps more to the point, why did she seem so calm now? Something had happened in Burnbaile not long ago, something grim. Because of it she had summoned a sea dragon and seized *Tilcalli* from a great distance. Now she was returning there as if from a day's fishing.

An uneasy feeling gripped him. Had *she* been the one who had cast a spell with a human life? It seemed impossible, yet in this southern land, who knew what was true, what false?

"Deir."

She turned to face him. He extended his hands to her, palms up. Hesitantly, she gripped her blanket about her with one hand and put out the other. Calindor took it.

All was well, but that meant something was very wrong. He saw only the Powers that should reside in a healthy young girl. She was still weary from her ordeal, but her constitution was strong. She was even still growing, and would for two or three more years. Yet no sign of magic, cast or endured, lingered in her body. That surprised and perplexed him: when he had become the vehicle of Callia's magic, in the confrontation with Mekhpur, he had felt the residual effects for weeks after. This girl had somehow shattered reality for a moment, yet nothing of that act remained.

He let go and explained to Callishandal what he had been seeking. She nodded.

"She's an unlikely witch, poor thing. But it is strange how she seems unconcerned to be returning. Perhaps whoever cast the spell has left."

"I doubt that. I can sense many people in the village, crowding close to the water. Look, you can see them even now."

In two or three places rough docks extended through the reed beds to the open water; people stood on them, looking westward.

"They've seen us coming," Callishandal said.

"Or sensed us. A good magician would have felt the spells I've put on the boat this morning."

"What do you want to do, Calindor?"

He hesitated. "Perhaps to return the girl to her people, if it's safe to do so. But mostly to see what's happened here. I want to find out how such magic could be done."

His wife smiled at him. "So you might do it yourself?"

"So I might *know* how to do it. The knowing is more important than the doing."

"Of course. You merely want to know how to summon a sea dragon."

He smiled back. "I wouldn't want to summon a sea dragon by accident."

The boat came closer and closer to the edge of the reed beds and the middle of the three docks. It was really just a long, rough wooden walkway, raised on pilings a span or so above the salt marsh, and ending in a tethered raft where several simple boats were moored. On the walkway and on the raft stood perhaps twenty armed men dressed in gaudy plumes of many colors. Calindor saw their spears and bows and realized their weapons were tipped with bronze. Strange: in the north, bronze was used only for the poorest tools and weapons.

"Fabarslúa," said Deir. She spoke a few more words, angrily, then quit in obvious frustration. Turning to Calindor, she pointed to them, jabbing her finger as if it were a spear. Then she drew her finger across her throat.

Calindor laughed briefly. "I'm not going to kill people," he said. He slowed the boat until it just balanced against the pressure of the tide. The plumed warriors were only fifty strides distant. Among them, he saw, were two men in black robes. The older one was probably the leader of the group; he stood slightly apart from the plumed warriors, with his younger companion standing deferentially at his side.

Magicians, both of them. Even a small sorcerer of the Badakhar would have seen that at once. The Powers rippled around them in auras with colors only magicians could see. Yet they were unlike any magicians Calindor had ever known. Their black robes were of an unknown fabric—a plant fiber—saturated with dirt and blood. Their dark hair stood out in stiff crowns, looking almost like helmets, yet fraying into clumps and tassels around their shoulders. The older man's face was a map of wrinkles above a strong jaw and a humorous mouth; the younger man might be any age from fifteen to thirty, so dirty was his face. But the eyes of both men gleamed with a high intelligence.

A focus swept Calindor, leaving a metallic taste in his mouth. It had come from the older man. In response, Calindor probed back, not gently, and saw both magicians stagger a little. He saw too that the older man had cast the death spell; it still glowed in his body.

"And now what?" he murmured to himself.

Yetecuan gripped Nezaual's arm to steady himself. "Thanks be to the True Gods," the old man whispered. "They have sent back the great magician to us."

Nezaual shuddered and tried to compose himself. "Honored father, this is very dangerous. That man on the boat has powers no man should hold. You saw his boat come without sails, with the waves parting around it. You felt his focus. We both felt his power last night."

"Yes, and when did we feel it, my child? When the Gods wished to tell me to spare the sacrifice. She is a gift to the Gods, and the magician is their gift to us."

Nezaual looked doubtfully at the strange craft floating absolutely motionless less than a bowshot away. "What about the two women? One of them looks like us, but the other is like these people." He squinted. "Yes. I recognize her. The girl with red hair. She lives in this village. Her father disliked us, and would not trade. What would she be doing on a magician's boat?"

"I don't know. Why don't you ask her?"

Nezaual looked embarrassed, cleared his throat and called out in the girl's barbarous language. She answered in a clear voice that carried across the water like an arrow. What an angry child, Yetecuan thought. What would a magician want with a creature like that? She must be simply a courier, sent to bring the magician. Perhaps he was the true lord of these seemingly lordless people, a guardian undetected by the spying pochteca merchants.

"She wants to know where her mother is, honored father."

"One of the villagers? Give us the woman's name and we will bring her here."

Another brief exchange. Nezaual repeated the name the girl had called out: "Si-bon, honored father."

"Then my beloved Colotic—" The commander of the warriors

turned instantly to stand beside him. "—send one of your men to find this woman and bring her here at once. The mother of the girl with long red hair."

"You will not have to look hard for her," Nezaual said with a smile. "I remember now who she is. She is the woman the Gods chose last night."

Yetecuan beamed and embraced the young magician. "Of course! They choose the mother, and send the daughter to bring us this splendid gift! Hasten, Colotic. Have the woman adorned in the finest clothes and jewels you can find. Then bring her to us in the main square. Tell some of your men to prepare a feast of welcome."

Colotic nodded to one of his men, who sprinted back along the wooden dock to the shore.

"Tell her they are welcome to join us. She will be in her mother's arms in a moment. We will not harm them."

Nezaual passed the message. The girl shouted back. She was not talking with the man, Yetecuan noted, nor with the woman. If they understood the exchanges, they gave no sign of it. Very strange: if he was the lord of these people, would he not speak their language? Perhaps the Gods had indeed sent him directly here, with the red-haired girl simply a messenger—as she was at the moment.

"She says the man and woman will kill us all if we don't leave at once."

An empty threat, but an enlightening one. Yetecuan knew the man was a great magician, but very unlike those of the Exteca. Forces swirled around him that Yetecuan could sense but not recognize; he was a handsome young man, but even if he had been ugly, his aura would have made him beautiful. The stranger would surely find Exteca magic equally unfamiliar; he would want to learn more because that was what all magicians desired. So he would not kill—at least he would not kill Yetecuan and Nezaual. The girl's threat was personal, uttered without the knowledge or permission of the magician. Perhaps she did not even speak his language, nor he hers.

This was all conjecture. All he really knew was that the man standing out there on that strange craft was the greatest magician ever known. The Gods had been preparing him, making him ready just as the priests made ready a truly beautiful sacrifice. He himself might not yet know his destiny, but Yetecuan could see it plainly: to lead the Exteca in conquering all the world, and putting it at the feet of the True Gods.

Oh Gods, he prayed, *grant me the wisdom to do your will.*

* * *

Calindor could not understand what Deir and the young magician were saying to one another, though the girl's hatred was obvious. One of the plumed warriors spoke briefly with the older magician and then dispatched one of his men back along the dock to the village.

"We should go ashore," Calindor said.

His wife looked at him. "You don't sense danger?"

"I sense a great deal of danger. But I must know as well as sense. Whatever happens, they can't harm us." He murmured to *Tilcalli*, and the boat slid silently up to the dock.

The Fabarslúa, or whatever they called themselves, stepped back to give them room. Calindor read their faces carefully: the warriors were watchful, alert, but far from tense—professionals, very like Badakhar soldiers, whatever the difference in their clothes and weapons. The magicians were almost quivering with eagerness, their eyes bright. Calindor had seen that look also, in many magicians' eyes. *You know all that is worth knowing,* it said, *and I respect you for your knowledge but I would gladly kill you to gain it for myself.*

The dock felt far less secure than the deck of *Tilcalli*; it sagged beneath the weight of so many. The old magician put his filthy hand to his lips and then extended it, palm outward. Calindor returned the gesture, ignoring the sudden intake of breath by Callishandal and Deir. Yes, the old man stank, and his young assistant smelled little better. Their odor was the least of their unlikable qualities: the aura of death around them was far worse.

Smiling, the old man now reached into his black robe and withdrew a small object something like a mushroom. It was made of gold; the cap was set with a polished bloodstone the size of Calindor's thumbnail. He saw that it was a lip plug: most of the warriors wore one set in the space between lower lip and chin. With some, the weight of the plugs pulled their lips down and exposed their teeth in a kind of snarl.

Accepting it, Calindor undid his belt and slid off his sheathed knife. Holding it in both hands, he gravely offered it to the old man. It was Staldhuno steel, far finer than the bronze weapons of these warriors; it would give them something to think about.

The old man drew the knife and sighed to see it catch the morning sun on its gleaming blade. His blackened fingers tested the edge. Then, smiling, he lifted it to his left ear and sliced the lobe. Blood ran down his neck, startlingly red against his skin.

The two magicians spoke animatedly, evidently pleased with

the knife's efficacy. Calindor felt a twinge of uncertainty. The knife had not been such a wise choice of gift after all.

"Perhaps they expect you to wear that plug in your lip," Callishandal murmured in his ear.

He put the bauble in his belt pouch and smiled slightly. It was time to regain the initiative.

Calindor gestured toward the village and then began to stride up the walkway. The smiling magicians fell in on either side of him, speaking softly in a language of liquid cluckings and whistlings. Callishandal and Deir came immediately behind, while the plumed warriors followed in two orderly files.

"Can you tell what they're talking about?" Callishandal asked quietly.

"A compliment sounds the same in any language," Calindor replied over his shoulder, smiling broadly. "They very much want to put us at our ease."

"So they mutilate themselves. Do they mean to kill us?"

"No. I think the magicians know they couldn't do it, and the warriors obey them. Have you noticed that they pay the girl no heed?"

"I notice it now."

"Don't do anything to attract their interest to her." He chuckled and smiled at the old magician, then went on: "This old man and his helper surely felt her magic last night, but they must not realize that it came from her. That's why they're treating me with such attention."

The dock ended in a dirt lane that went more or less straight into the village. Calindor paused for a moment to look around. He liked what he saw: simple houses of brick and planks, surrounded by orchards and gardens. Callia was comfortable here and gave abundant life to this place.

But he did not like what he felt. Some spell hung over the village, as invisible yet powerful as the stench from the magicians. A few people walked the lanes or worked about their houses, but they moved as if in a daze. Plumed warriors were everywhere, usually in twos or fours, as relaxed as their fellows had been on the dock. Evidently they saw no threat from the villagers.

Still, they were newcomers here; Calindor could see that in the curiosity he saw in the eyes of the more intelligent warriors. They moved like trained men, comfortable within themselves, but this village was not a familiar place to them. So they had come recently, and not in peace.

Their weapons were conspicuous: short swords, axes, bows, and javelins. Most were of bronze; some men even carried wooden swords edged with obsidian. A Badakh cavalry squadron, with steel swords and iron-tipped lances, could sweep through the village and leave not one of these Fabarslúa alive.

The tools of Deir's people seemed even clumsier: a woman squatting by her doorstep slowly split firewood with a copper-headed ax, and a man nearby was digging up some kind of root vegetable with a crude wooden spade. Yet there had been no battle here, no unequal combat of gardeners' tools against bronze spearheads. Something else had given the Fabarslúa their victory, something in the deathmagic that the old man had made last night.

Calindor went on up the lane, seeing a kind of open square near the center of the village. The people looked at him with little interest, but when their gaze shifted to the magicians and warriors, Calindor saw a strange longing in their faces: a kind of fear, but also a kind of love.

Surely the people themselves could not be enchanted. To cast a spell on a human soul was the hardest and most dangerous magic any sorcerer could attempt, and few succeeded; Calindor himself had done it only once. To enchant a whole village was impossible, yet the old man's magic had done something like that. A great illusion of some kind? A shadow army of thousands? No; surely that would not have required a human death to accomplish. And what small sorcerer's trick could strike not only fear but love in its victims?

The old priest was speaking rapidly to his assistant and the retinue of warriors. Several men broke away to hasten into some of the huts facing the square. They emerged bearing tables and stools; others carried baskets of fruit and bread. The villagers helped the warriors set up tables and chairs in the shade of an oak tree. When the food sat in piles upon the tables, the old priest turned smiling to Calindor and pointed to one of the chairs.

"They believe in hospitality, at least," Calindor murmured to Callishandal. "Come and sit." He took a chair; his wife sat on his right, Deir on his left. She looked even angrier than before, he noticed, especially when she saw her townspeople helping the warriors.

The two magicians and one of the warriors sat across the table and ceremoniously offered bread and dried fish and apples. But they did not seem offended when Calindor took the food from their hands without eating.

The old magician pointed to himself and said: "Yetecuan." Then to the younger one: "Nezaual." And the warrior: "Colotic." In return, Calindor named Deir, Callishandal, and himself. Soon they had a few words of one another's language: man, woman, girl, village, bread. The younger man spoke again to Deir in what must be her language; she refused to answer.

Nezaual smiled as he pointed to her and several other villagers: "Airn." To himself and the other Fabarslúa: "Exteca."

Calindor repeated "Exteca," and pointed in various directions. When he pointed south, Yetecuan chuckled and smacked his lips. From somewhere inside his robes he pulled out a folded piece of buckskin and opened it up on the table. Calindor tried to conceal his surprise, but Callishandal's gasp spoke for him as well.

Spread across the table was a work of art in many colors. It showed people, buildings, mountains, rivers—and the sea. It was a map, more detailed and beautiful than any Calindor had ever seen. Its maker had written strange symbols that must be place names; after a moment's scrutiny, Calindor found the bay and a string of glyphs that must name Burnbaile. He pointed to it and spoke its name.

Yetecuan laughed again and held up his palms in delight. "Bona balalee," he echoed.

The map faded out not far north of the bay, leaving one end of the buckskin blank. But to the south the map was thick with names of towns along a coast that trended south-southeast and then curved back north to form a long peninsula that trapped a narrow sea against the mainland. A little to the north of the peninsula was one coastal town evidently much larger than the others. Calindor put his finger on it.

"Tola," said Yetecuan, and then spoke a few more words—more to Nezaual, Calindor saw, than to him. The old man seemed very pleased. Tola must be the Exteca capital; a network of roads ran to it from north and south, marked in black on green. Almost no roads ran east, where the land was colored pale brown. Desert perhaps, too poor to support many towns.

Yetecuan pointed to Calindor and Callishandal, then at the map. "Cantareans—Tola?"

"They're inviting us to their own town," Calindor said.

"Are we accepting?" she asked dryly.

"No."

Now the old man was pointing to them and then to the map. Calindor hesitated for a moment: they had showed him where they came from, but should he do the same? Another look at the map gave him a sudden sense of scale; the distance from here to Tola was as great as from here to the dragons' city. The Exteca were on the edge of their known world. Still, he understood too little of their abilities; for all he knew, their magicians could travel as swiftly on land as *Tilcalli* could on water. He pointed vaguely north. If they came seeking Cantarea, the dragons would give them something to think about.

A squad of plumed warriors approached the shaded table, bearing a kind of chair mounted between carrying poles. Seated in the chair was a woman richly dressed, her hair braided with jewels; Calindor saw she was an Airn, but did not expect Deir's reaction.

"Madair!" the girl cried out and sprang up, hastening to the woman.

The bearers gently lowered the chair, and Deir embraced the woman. She returned the embrace, though Calindor saw something distant in her blue eyes. Deir burst into speech, and then into tears. The woman took Deir on her lap, like a little girl, and stroked her long red hair.

"Her mother?" Calindor murmured.

"Surely," Callishandal answered in a whisper. "But I don't understand what's going on. These men have conquered this village, and Deir seems to hate them, yet they cherish her mother. Perhaps she is their Speaker, or like an Aryasha among the Badakhar, and they do not want to anger the people by humiliating her."

"Something is wrong with the woman." He focused on her, ignoring the pained grunts from the magicians across the table.

Yes: she had been under a spell. It had faded, but like a vivid dream recalled on waking, it had changed her. Not a spell on her soul, but something that had thrown her emotions into a tumult. She was not the same person she had been, and Deir could now see it also. The girl was standing, holding her mother's hands and speaking urgently. Once she gestured toward the table, pointing to the Cantareans, but the woman scarcely seemed to care. Her only reply was a bemused smile.

Until she caught the scent of her mother's hair, nothing had seemed quite real to Deir. The arrival of the warriors, the escape on the candleboat, the coming of the sea monster and of the strange boat of the fiosas and his woman—none of it had the substance of real life. To come back to Burnbaile and be welcomed by the pochteckies as if they were the owners—as now they were—that was strangest of all. And now to find her own mother adorned in feathers and beads, being carried about by the Fabarslúa, made her wonder if this were not indeed some dream from which she could not wake.

But that was the scent of her mother's hair, and the strength of her mother's arms about her.

"What are they doing to you?" Deir demanded, weeping as she sank into her mother's lap.

"Hush. A great girl like you, bawling like a baby! It's all right. It's all right."

Deir felt her mother's hand smoothing her hair, but it gave her no consolation. "This is some pochtecky geas they've put on you, and everyone else. Can't you see?"

"Hush, hush. No one can put a geas on another person; you know that. But these are a great people, greater than we ever dreamed. When they came last night, I felt as if some awful burden was off my soul at last. Ever since your poor father died, it lay on me heavier every day. Now I feel free. As you should. What became of you, Deir? Where did you go last night?"

Deir stood up, without letting go of her mother's hands. She looked into Sivon's eyes. Yes—a light shone there that Deir had not seen in a long time. Sivon was happy. But she was not Sivon. *And if she is not Sivon, am I Deir?*

"I escaped. These people came in a boat and rescued me. I think he's a great fiosas, for he makes the boat go with neither sail nor oar. He calls himself Calindor, but I think he's really the ancient wizard Calidin. I asked him to kill the pochteckies, but he would not."

"Kill them? Whatever for?"

Deir did not answer. Instead she asked: "Why have they adorned you like this?"

Her mother laughed, but in a whisper. "I think they are very sorry. Last night the old man was about to kill me on our very doorstep, and then he fell in a swoon—and that young fellow too. When they woke, the old man spoke to the warriors and had them look after me. Just now they came and dressed me in all this. Do I not look strange?" she asked, and laughed again.

"Madair, come with me. Come with me and the magician in his boat. The pochteckies mean us no good."

Sivon shook her head. "They have made us part of them, as a man makes a girl part of his family when he weds her. I would no more leave them than I would have left your father."

"Then *I* will leave, and never come back!"

"Child, listen to yourself. You sound like a four-year-old who doesn't want to take her nap."

Deir looked at her mother, at the sunlight gleaming on her golden hair and the jewels braided into it. *No, I sound like someone I have never known before.* "I will have to go, Mother. I can't stay here. This is not my home anymore."

"Of course it's your home, and always will be. Would you truly run off with strangers, even if they'd have you, rather than stay with those who've loved and reared you all your life?"

Without replying, Deir let go her mother's hands and turned away. She looked around the square: here she had played with other children at the spring festivals, keened with the other women at the funerals, sold apples on market days while boys from Coillyrathad and Kiltarra and Barnachy flirted with her. Could she indeed walk away from all this?

The old magician had left the table and walked slowly over to them. He kissed his fingertips and held his hand out to Sivon. She smiled and returned the gesture. If she noticed his stink, she gave no sign of it.

Yes, she could leave it, because her mother would have fought like a raging sow bear to keep her here. And the woman who had been her mother only sat and let her go.

Deir turned and walked back to the table where the strangers sat. Trembling with sorrow and anger, she knelt between their chairs and took Callishandal by the hand.

Five

The morning sun was rising toward the zenith, and even in the shade of the tree the air was warm.

Calindor smiled at the girl, and then looked at Callishandal. "Have we been adopted?"

"Apparently so. She's quarreled with the woman, who must be her mother or aunt. She hates the warriors." Calindor noticed his wife was careful to use none of the words they had just learned from Yetecuan and Nezaual. "But can we take her back to Tanshadabela?"

"Yes."

"Because of last night?"

He thought for a moment, while Deir patiently sat between them with her freckled cheek against Callishandal's arm. "Because of last night on the boat, and last night here in this village. The girl cast one spell and the old man cast another. I think I recognize what the old man was doing, and the effect is . . . strange. Dangerous. But the girl is completely outside what I know of magic. I want Tilcalli and Dragasa to see her, and Renjosudaldor."

Callishandal nodded. "Then we will take her." She turned and embraced the girl. Deir was past tears now, but she shuddered in Callishandal's arms.

The Exteca magicians were watching with interest while speaking softly together. The woman in the chair, whatever her relationship to Deir, simply sat and waited, showing little interest in anyone but Yetecuan. Other villagers and warriors passed through the square, glancing at the visitors but never pausing.

"We need to take the young magician also," Calindor said.

"*What?* What for?" Callishandal looked up in surprise, releasing Deir.

"To learn what happened here last night. To learn whatever magic he knows."

"He stinks."

"He certainly does. Though a Badakh slave hut usually smelled worse." Calindor touched her shoulder. "I don't much like him either. My mother and father will like him even less. But we need him."

"Will the old man let him go?"

"If the old man can keep me from taking him, that will be a useful lesson in itself. Come, we should leave."

He stood up. Callishandal took Deir's hand, and the three of them walked around the table. The magicians looked surprised. Yetecuan held up a restraining hand and spoke anxiously. Calindor smiled, pointing to Nezaual and then to himself. He beckoned both men to accompany them. Uncertainly, they obeyed. The woman in the chair watched them go with an unreadable expression, and did not stir from her chair.

Calindor set a brisk pace. The magicians, and a retinue of warriors, followed close behind. Sometimes Calindor met the eyes of a villager, and the blankness in the Airn's gaze stirred a cold anger in him.

When they reached the raft at the end of the dock, he waited while Callishandal and Deir climbed aboard; then he turned to Nezaual. With one hand he took the young man's arm; with the other he pointed to *Tilcalli.*

Nezaual looked astonished, and pulled back a little. Yetecuan's wrinkled face showed surprise also, mixed with pleasure. The old man's eyes met Calindor's.

We understand each other, old man. Each of us wishes to know the other, but we know this is a dangerous gamble. More dangerous for you than for me, because you already know I am the better magician. You must give me your apprentice and all his knowledge, and hope that somehow he will steal enough knowledge from me to make it worthwhile.

Yetecuan spoke rapidly and softly, scarcely taking his eyes off Calindor, and allowing Nezaual no reply. At length the young man's arm relaxed under Calindor's hand and he stepped forward. In four strides he was off the raft and onto the deck of *Tilcalli*. Calindor turned, kissed his fingertips, and held his palm out to Yetecuan. The old man smiled and returned the salute.

In moments they were pulling away from the dock while Nezaual waved farewell and Deir looked disgusted. Yetecuan and the warriors raised their hands in salute; then, without further ceremony, they turned and walked back up the dock to Burnbaile.

"Now what?" asked Callishandal as the boat skimmed swiftly into the bay. "Straight back to the dragons?"

"Almost." He pointed to a small island straight ahead. "First we stop there."

The boat glided into a cove with a sandy beach on its southern shore. When the keel touched bottom just a few strides from the beach, Calindor left his seat at the stern. Nezaual had been standing on the afterdeck, looking a little perplexed. Calindor gripped him around the waist and flung him over the gunwale into the water.

The Exteca scarcely had time to cry out before he disappeared under the surface in a splash of foam. Calindor followed, stepping over the side into waist-high water. As Nezaual spluttered upright, Calindor ripped the black robe from him. Naked, the young magician seemed slight. Calindor shoved him toward the beach, until they stood in water only up to their knees. Dipping his hands into the sand, Calindor scrubbed Nezaual's back and shoulders; then he gestured that Nezaual should continue to clean himself.

The Exteca looked appalled, but obeyed. While Callishandal and Deir went into the cabin to give the youth some privacy, Nezaual rubbed sand on his skin until it glowed a surprisingly light brown.

"Cut his hair and he'd look like a Cantarean," Calindor called from the water. "A Cantarean slave. He's covered with scars."

Washing Nezaual's blood-stiffened hair was the worst of it; every time he ducked his head, the clear, cold water turned redbrown. But at last he was clean enough to clamber back on board. Calindor gave him a spare set of buckskin tunic and trousers. Nezaual tied back his hair to keep it out of his face.

Callishandal and Deir came out of the cabin and looked critically at Nezaual.

"He does look like a Cantarean," Callishandal said. "But no

Cantarean ever had that look in his eye. Or earlobes cut into fringes."

Calindor said nothing. He started a fire, mixed bread batter and poured it onto the cooking lid. While it puffed up and turned brown, he steered *Tilcalli* around the little island and toward the open sea beyond the two peninsulas.

"Now," he said, "we learn each other's languages."

The boat was in the strait between the peninsulas of Donbein and Dubein when Deir saw at last that she was leaving the only world she knew.

Looking at the wooded hills to north and south, she left her bench by the rear door of the cabin and walked the few steps to the stern. Callishandal sat there, casting out a fishing line; the magician and the pochtecky priest were in the cabin, learning each other's language. Deir stood beside Callishandal, gazing east past the islands of the bay to the tawny hills on the horizon.

What have I done? What has happened to me?

At this time yesterday she and her mother had been bathing after digging up her father's bones. Then they had sat on the doorstep, drinking mead while other families had come down to the riverbank. No thought had Deir given to what would come next. She had taken it for granted that life would go on as always. She would pick apples in the orchard. She and her mother would harvest the garden vegetables and pickle them for the winter. In the fall they would go to the big markets in Kiltarra and Coillyrathad. Sivon would barter her pots for more wood to fuel her kiln; in the short cold days of winter, Deir would be glad to tend the kiln fire while her mother shaped new pots and the two of them talked and sang. In the spring she might look more seriously at the young men, and someday she would go as a bride to her husband's home . . .

Now all that was gone like a dream in the morning. Now her world was this magic craft, gliding through the water faster than a horse could gallop, yet as smoothly as a twig on the Clachwisgy. Now her mother was a half-mad queen in a conquered town, sea monsters roved the bay, and a magician plucked her from her life as she herself might pull an apple from its bough.

What could have caused all this? The pochtecky magician, the filthy old man who had smiled and bowed to Calindor, had cast some strange geas on Burnbaile and its people. In every story she had ever heard, magicians could no more enchant a human soul than fly to the moon. They could shape wood or clay, hasten a spark into kindling, call rain from a cloud, heal a wound. Yet somehow the old man had enchanted everyone but herself.

Then she should have drowned, and joined her father's bones in the sea. Instead, even as the candleboat was coming apart, the monster had risen out of the water, studied her for a moment, and then lifted her upon its enormous head. And there she had stayed for what seemed an eternity until the boat, glowing under its orange ring of light, had come alongside.

Was it something I did? But what?

She had no gift for magic; few in her family had. Her father's geases with wood had been simple and not always achieved; often, he'd said, it was less work to split a log by sheer muscle than to find the words that would part it into planks. Sivon would talk to her clay, but more out of courtesy to the earth spirits than from any thought of commanding them.

But something had shielded Deir from the pochteckies, something had brought the monster to rescue her, and the magician's arrival must be more than chance—especially when he seemed so concerned about her.

"Golodi," she heard Calindor say, and then Nezaual repeated: *"Golodi."*

"Passa."

"Passa."

Admittedly, he now seemed much more interested in the pochtecky. Perhaps Nezaual was the source of all this strangeness? Surely not, when he was so young and awkward; now that he was clean and dressed in simple tunic and trousers, he seemed just another boy—bright enough, perhaps, but utterly lacking the calm confidence of Calindor. Even his voice was high and thin, while Calindor's was a kind of soft rumble, like thunder far away.

The boat was through the strait now, out in the Siar Muir and turning north. Soon the shoulder of Dubein blocked the view of the bay and the hills beyond it. With a gasp that was close to a sob, Deir sat beside Callishandal. The older woman smiled, murmured something in a sympathetic tone, and put her arm around Deir.

For a time Deir let herself be held. Then she pulled away and looked Callishandal in the eye.

"What is *golodi*?" she asked. *"Golodi?"*

Callishandal looked surprised, and then laughed. She pointed to her own head, then to Deir's. *"Golodi."*

Good—that was one more word. *"Passa?"*

Callishandal touched her own black hair, then Deir's red curls. *"Passa. Fusipassa."* And pointed to the strange fire that burned in the little stove nearby. Deir pointed to the fire also and asked: *"Fusi?"*

"Fusila." And again touched Deir's hair. *"Fusipassa."*

Fire hair. So it must seem to them. She felt a brief pleasure at learning the words, but it passed as she heard the men's voices from the cabin. Whatever Nezaual might be, he was not her friend. She must learn these people's language quickly and well, or go among them as no more than a child while Nezaual—who had learned to speak Airn with eerie skill—dealt with them as an equal.

I will learn faster than you, pochtecky. And someday I will come back and drive your warriors from Burnbaile. Someday.

"We must move with the speed of frightened deer," said Yetecuan. He was sitting with Colotic at the table where, so briefly, the strangers had been. The woman Sivon still sat patiently in his chair, her blue eyes fixed on Yetecuan.

"We have six horses available for courier service, honored father. I could provide several more, but—"

"Six will be quite enough."

"Do you wish to send the woman to Tola on one of them? If she cannot ride, she would slow the others down. I had planned to send her to Tola on the mammoth."

"The mammoth will be quite acceptable. The Gods know what sacrifice we mean to give them; they will be in no hurry. But the priests and nobles must know about Calindor and his people as soon as possible."

Colotic calculated: "A day and a half to the nearest relay post. Tomorrow night. Couriers would switch to fresh horses thereafter at every post. If they ride all night and the next day, they would reach Tola before midnight."

Yetecuan marveled and fretted at once. How wonderful, that couriers could ride from this remote fringe of the empire to its heart in less than three days—yet how small that very achievement made the empire seem. So much of the world awaited the rule of the Gods and the Exteca ...

"Bring me paper and inks, beloved son. I will compose the message while your men equip the horses. Choose your best riders, for they will never carry a more important message."

Writing materials appeared almost at once. Even as the old man dipped his brush in the first ink pot, he heard the courier horses whinny. Someday, Yetecuan knew, young Colotic would be a great general; he was a superb organizer, so that he need only speak a command to see it carried out.

Yetecuan wrote quickly, in the cursive script reserved for the most secret messages between priests. He hummed as he wrote, occasionally glancing up to meet Sivon's eyes. He would smile at her, and she at him, before he returned to his task. Before long Colotic and two couriers stood discreetly behind him.

When he had finished, Yetecuan glanced critically over his text and then turned. The message lay rolled up in his hand, with the stranger's knife bound to it. He was reluctant to let it out of his hands, but it would lend another authority to the message. Even better than himself, the Chief Priest Ometollin would see the spirits of metal and fire shimmering within the knife. Ometollin would grasp the implications at once. *Time, time . . . we must hasten.*

"If you are ready, honored father, you may instruct the couriers."

"Thank you, beloved son. My children, you must ride as quickly as possible to the relay station at Tetlapan. Between here and there, ride at a steady trot. Change your horses often so they do not tire too quickly. When you speak to the horsemaster at the station, tell him that the future of the Exteca hangs upon your news; he must give you fresh horses and a direct pass to Tola. Three nights from now this message must be in the hands of the Chief Priest Ometollin. Do you understand?"

They nodded, their eyes widening just a little at the urgency in the old man's voice and at the majesty of the intended reader.

"I bless you, my children. When I return to Tola, you shall enjoy great honor for this service. You go with the Gods."

In moments the couriers were mounted; their horses, even the four spares, seemed to understand the importance of their mission. They stamped the earth, shook their manes and snorted. Without further ceremony the couriers trotted out of the square.

The afternoon was half over. Yetecuan felt weariness assail him again, as if he had just cast another spell of love. For a time he sat silent at the table, eyes closed.

"Honored father?" asked Colotic hesitantly. "What shall we do with the woman?"

Yetecuan opened his eyes. The woman was still there, looking tired and sunburned.

"Put her back wherever you've been keeping her, beloved son. Tomorrow we leave for Tola with the mammoth and enough soldiers to guard her and the captives." He thought for a moment. "When you have put the woman away, find me a healthy young child. We will give it to the Gods to ensure a safe and swift journey for the couriers and for ourselves."

"I am glad to obey you, honored father."

* * *

No longer did Calindor sit alone on the foredeck, focusing on the deeps beneath him. Now he and Nezaual spoke together almost without ceasing, each teaching the other his language, long into the night. At last they stopped, while *Tilcalli* slid steadily over the dark waters and the stars shone down.

Calindor gave the young priest a blanket and told him to sleep on the foredeck. Meanwhile, Callishandal made a simple pallet for Deir on the floor of the cabin. The girl curled up on it, pulled a blanket over herself, and was asleep at once.

"You and the boy seem to understand one another already," Callishandal murmured as she slipped into bed beside her husband.

"Magicians are usually good with languages. His is a strange one, but I can feel some of its power. I wonder what he thinks of Cantarean. And you and Deir are learning also."

"She wants to learn our language, not teach us hers. But I've gained a few words, yes. She's quick." Callishandal realized he was only half listening, and sighed a little: holding the attention of a magician was not always easy. "What is it?"

"What could call a dragon from the sea?"

Nezaual woke very early and remembered at once where he was. Within an easy bowshot the waves and wind contended; yet the magician's craft moved in its circle of serenity. Nezaual saw and felt, though he could not understand, the complex web of magic woven around the boat and everyone within it.

He wished he could talk with his master. Yetecuan was wise, but he was also quick in his thoughts and perceptions. Unlike many magicians his age, Yetecuan still looked for new spells, new ways to invoke and please the Gods. A more ordinary priest would by now have taken his place in the temple of some sizable town—even Tola itself. But Yetecuan preferred to explore the barbarous lands of the north in the service of Gods and empire.

The north: the evil direction, the direction of cold and bad luck, the direction in which he was going farther than any Exteca before him. While the armies of Tola spread south and southeast long ago, only in the last lifetime had they ventured north. Even though these lands were far richer than the deserts of the south, the Exteca had conquered the north almost reluctantly.

Perhaps we have been right to fear the north, Nezaual thought. He sat up on the deck, wrapping his blanket around him. The first light of dawn was breaking; the peaks of the coast mountains were just visible against the paling eastern sky. *We find only these barbarians, and now a sorcerer who can cast spells like thunder-claps . . . He is young—what if he is only an apprentice, like me?* The thought chilled him more than the cold air. Perhaps Calindor was indeed doing the will of one even greater.

Yet the spell two nights ago had been cast nearby, and therefore it must have been Calindor who had cast it. Surely no magician, however great, could act at a distance. Or could he? Nezaual remembered the shock two years ago, the magical disturbance in the north that priests had felt even far south of Tola.

Fear sat on his shoulders. He considered Exteca magic. The priest-magicians could see far more of the spirits and forces than they could control. What did they know but some healing spells, some invocations of the Gods, and the great spells of love and terror? Out of those few scraps of knowledge the Exteca had built their empire. A few like Yetecuan sought new knowledge, but even he had learned little. Barbarians like the Airn offered only a few crude enchantments. Now this newcomer showed that magic could still the sea and drive a boat.

And it could knock an Exteca magician off his feet like the blow of a war club.

That was a thought worth remembering every moment. He was still young, only partly versed in Exteca magic, but whatever he learned among the northerners could make him a very great sorcerer among his own people.

He had lost his personal obsidian knife when Calindor had thrown him overboard, but his own fingernails were long enough to serve. Nezaual began a whispered prayer to the Gods, and at the end of the first verse he sank his nails into the skin over his ribs. The bloodspell had just begun to take shape, however, when the cabin door burst open and Calindor strode naked onto the deck. His face was rigid with anger. Without a word he swung his open right hand against Nezaual's face.

The force of the blow half blinded him and threw him sprawling on the deck. He would not have thought a magician to possess such physical strength.

"You will make no magic without my permission," Calindor said.

Nezaual said nothing, but thought: *I understand his words. And I give the Gods the gift of the pain he gave me.*

The day went on as yesterday had: the men in the cabin or the foredeck, steadily teaching one another how to frame words into sentences, while the women did the same at the stern. Judging from what the men were saying to one another during the midday meal, Callishandal saw that Nezaual was making good progress in Cantarean—better than Calindor was making in Exteca. Deir, meanwhile, was acquiring Cantarean with a lovely singing accent; the young men of Tanshadabela would be eager to help her learn more. Some of her own language seemed oddly akin to Badakhi; perhaps Deir's pale-skinned ancestors had drifted southwest while their pastoral cousins the Badakhar moved west into the great prairies of Cantarea centuries ago.

So they coursed northward along the mountainous coast, while the sun blazed down through flying clouds and waves swept around the boat under banners of foam. At sunset they ate again, and then sat under the ring of dragonfire to learn more of one another's language. Calindor sometimes wrote down words, while Nezaual watched with interest; Callishandal saw that learning Exteca writing would come next. The map of Yetecuan had been beautiful yet clumsy; the simple letters of Cantarean and Badakhi seemed far more concise and simple. But if magic lived in words, then it lived also in writing; Calindor, she knew, would learn much when he had learned the script of the Exteca.

At last they went to bed, with Nezaual again on the foredeck and Deir on the floor of the cabin. When all was silent, Callishandal whispered in her husband's ear what had troubled her all day:

"You *struck* him. Do you think Callia would be glad?"

"Of course not." His warmth enveloped her as powerfully as his arms embraced her. "But until I know more about their magic, I cannot let him cast any kind of spell—even the simplest. When we have him back in Tanshadabela, and the magicians of the Siragi Aibela can study him, then we can let him show his spells. But he is a captive, not a visitor."

"He frightens you."

For a long time he was silent. Then he spoke: "They are simple people. Even iron and steel are strange to them. But they understand something that we have never learned, or that we forgot before we came to Sotalar. They know how to conquer in ways the Badakhar never imagined. If they come to Cantarea, we could find ourselves conquered forever, and yearning for the whips of the Badakhar."

"Surely they will never come so far north."

He sighed and brushed his lips across her cheek. "We frighten them too. They will come."

Six

Ometollin stood on the broad, topmost terrace of the pyramid, facing west across Tola to the sea. Above and behind him rose the temple where he worshiped the Gods. Falling away below him was the steep slope of the pyramid, gleaming white; at its base, the city was an intricate pattern of red-tiled roofs and whitewashed walls, broken by lines of trees along the main streets. An hour's walk west the city ended suddenly along the cliffs that dropped to the beaches.

At mid-morning the city was cheerfully noisy. The trumpeting bellow of a mammoth rose briefly over the clatter of carts and the cries of the maceuali, ordinary people, selling their wares in the markets. From the pens where the sacrifices waited for sunset, chanted prayers rose and fell.

Looking north, Ometollin could see the palace of the Tecutli Itztlac and the precincts of the pipiltin nobility; beyond were the mountains that bounded the plain of Tola. To the south he saw poorer houses amid countless market gardens stretching into the autumn haze. Hidden in the haze, but not from his magician's vision, stood a cluster of low hills; beyond them the coast bent from south to east and then southeast.

Gleaming with colors under its mantle of smoke and sky, the city was yet more splendid to one like Ometollin, who could see the forces that wove themselves through every structure, every plant, every person. Divinity shimmered everywhere he looked, giving life to everything just as blood gave life to every part of the body. He pitied those who saw only the surface and not the magic beneath it.

How great was Tola, and how beautiful. And now, how terribly threatened.

The message from Yetecuan lay unrolled on a bench, one end weighted down by the weapon of the northern magician. Ometollin was not sure which was the more dreadful object.

He had always loved and respected Yetecuan, and more than once had offered him a post in one of the capital's temples. Now his respect was greater still. The man had been close to the great spell that they had felt even here, and he had recovered quickly. More to the point, he had understood the significance of the spell, and had drawn wise conclusions.

Yes, the True Gods clearly wished the woman sacrificed in special ceremonies here in Tola, and no one would deny them such a gift. The northern magician was surely in quest of his destiny, though he might not yet know it. Ometollin saw, as Yetecuan had, the hand of the Gods in bringing the magician to the little village of the barbarians. And as Yetecuan said in his message, the northern homeland of that magician was both a great danger and a great opportunity.

Yetecuan had shown forethought in giving the stranger a gold lip plug. It carried a seeking spell; even an apprentice magician would have no trouble following the northerner. Nor was it trouble to see the provenance of this strange silvery knife. Ometollin had dangled it from a thread while he murmured a homing spell, until it steadied with its beautiful blade pointing steadily to the north-northeast. A long way away, perhaps, but if the magician had come south, then the Exteca could go north.

And they must go. The magician's arrival and departure had been a clear beckoning from the Gods. However far the magician might go, however strange and dangerous the way, the Exteca must go there also.

But how? A few traders, the usual reconnaissance before sending in priests and warriors? That would be easy enough, even at this awkward time of year when the pochteca usually returned to their homes and warehouses. Show a pochtec this knife, and he would be packing his ponies the same day in hopes of bringing back more such weapons.

But these northerners were far away, much farther than the pale-skinned barbarians whom Yetecuan had just brought into the empire. A small trading party, even accompanied by a good priest, could well find itself trapped in some barbarian ambush, or held up by bad weather. They said that if you went far enough north, ice and snow covered the land all year . . . an unpleasant thought, though surely an exaggeration. Even northerners must plant crops and raise livestock.

No, too much was at stake to risk it all on the good fortune of a priest, twenty pochteca, and an armed escort of ten or twelve. This would have to be a major enterprise—thousands of warriors, thousands of slaves and horses, at least a dozen mammoths, and a cadre of the best magicians in the empire. Nothing must stand in their way, all must yield, and they must reach the land of the magician intact and ready for whatever wealth or war it might offer them.

Ometollin could imagine the impassive faces of the pipiltin at hearing such a proposal. They would smack their lips politely, praise the Chief Priest's wisdom, and then raise a hundred foolish objections: the lateness of the season, the slowness of their slaves to bring in the harvest, the cost of horses and the great cost of mammoths . . . and not one of them would see that without this expedition, all their power and glory might vanish like a hummingbird's feather in a storm.

No matter. The Tecutli Itztlac was still young, and intelligent for a man brought up as a warrior. He lacked any talent for magic—of course, or he would have become a priest—but he respected those who could cast spells and see the Gods. And he had recently encouraged his smiths to experiment with bronze and copper, to find ways to make them stronger and sharper. He would understand, as his nobles would not, that the edge of this northern knife was now pressed against the throat of the empire itself.

The nobles represented their clans, and thus the whole Exteca people; however slowly they might think, they were the voice of the people and entitled to respectful hearing. With encouragement and guidance, the Tecutli would eventually sway the debate until he got his way. But it would take so long, months at the least, before the nobles finally yielded and the expedition could set off.

Well, it would be longer still if he did not stop fretting and get to work. Ometollin called for paper and pen; one of four attendants, squatting in a line nearby, sprang up and hastened into a nearby door. While he waited, Ometollin composed the letter in his mind; with the paper on his lap and the pen in his hand, the actual writing took little time. A small cut on the back of his left hand provided blood for ink: a sign of respect and love for the reader and a courtesy to the Gods.

Folding the paper twice, he handed it to the attendant. "Beloved son, this message is for the Tecutli. Deliver it into the hands of General Yaocatl and no one else."

"Honored father, I obey. I shall place it in the general's hands as you ask."

Ometollin smiled faintly as the attendant sprinted down the terrace toward the stairs on the north face of the pyramid. He was a quick-footed boy, and intelligent; as a servant of the priesthood he was unafraid of the warriors—even of the pipiltin. He would reach the general quickly, and the general in turn would convey it to Itztlac without hesitation.

Success was itself a message from the Gods. Yetecuan's message had come swiftly to this place, and now his own would be in the hands of the Tecutli before the midday meal. Perhaps by tomorrow, if the Tecutli decided quickly, a message would go out to the pipiltin and priests. Another six or seven days to assemble them from their temples and farms . . .

Suddenly he had nothing to do but wait. Pacing the terrace, he saw the forces holding the pyramid together, and the forces that held the very stones together: delicate, so delicate that a mere glance from a God would rip even this vast temple into rubble. Unplacated, the Gods would destroy the world; yet in their mercy they gave humanity the means to preserve itself through the gift of blood.

O Gods, we shall give you gifts greater than any you have enjoyed before. Only grant us this magician as your servant, and his people as your servants and sacrifices.

The sun was warm on his head and shoulders as Calindor walked along the river toward the village where his ancestors danced the past and future. He stood among their simple huts and tents, smiling his greetings to those who sang in silence as they danced.

His great-great-great-grandmother Calihalingol stepped from the dance, her arms held wide and the fringes swinging from her buckskin sleeves. Her long braids, as white as snow, swung also.

How beautiful you are, Calindor! And how far you have come!

Very far, Calihalingol. We are still on the sea, returning to the dragons' land. We will not be home for many days yet. Have you spoken with my parents?

Yes. They worry about you.

They need not. Come and sit with me.

They walked down to the riverbank and sat in the shade of two aspens whose leaves were always golden and would never fall. The river slipped slowly by from its unknown source to an unknown sea.

Did you feel a great spell a little while ago?

The old woman laughed, rocking back against the trunk of one of the aspens, her gnarled hands on her knees. *It is all the same here, Calindor, a long or little while! But the last time your mother and father were here, they mentioned a spell that we felt too. I knew it was not yours, but that you must be close to it.*

You are old, Great-great-great-grandmother, and you remember much from the past. Do you remember any spell to summon dragons? Or any spell that might enchant a whole village?

Her hand rested lightly on his arm. *No one summons dragons, Calindor. And not many can cast a spell on a single soul. Imagine a whole village!*

Yet we saw these things happen. A little girl, who shows no sign of magic, called a sea dragon to her, to keep her from drowning while our boat came to rescue her—and her spell overpowered me. For all her power, she could not save her people from enchantment by a magician of a people called Exteca. It means Blood People. Have any of the Siragi Aibela ever known of such a spell, or such a people?

Never. If our cousins the Gulyaji know of such things, they have not told us. Perhaps the magicians of the Badakhar know.

He shook his head. *They know spells of death, and the Exteca used a death to enchant these people, but it was not the same. And their spell did not affect the girl we found.*

What do you think, Calindor?

I think I am an ignorant boy. You have taught me, and so have my mother and father, and the Badakhar, and the Gulyaji, and even the dragon Obordur. And everything I learn teaches me how little I know.

But . . . ?

But I know that the magic of the Blood People is opposed to Callia, and the Blood People know that mine is opposed to theirs. And the magic of the girl is greater than either. She can teach us, if we can teach her.

And use her against these Blood People?

Or they will use her against us, and we will become slaves again.

Calihalingol laughed silently, her hand on Calindor's. *You are angry and worried, but not so much about becoming a slave. You are angry because you have learned how little you have learned.*

Tilcalli sped north in her circle of tranquility. To the east the coast was sometimes a jagged line of mountains, sometimes a sawtoothed horizon of forests, sometimes a gleaming white ribbon of sand. To the west the sea was sometimes calm, sometimes stormy; clouds swept overhead and were gone.

Callishandal was amazed at how quickly Deir learned Cantarean. By the end of her second day aboard the boat, the girl was speaking in simple sentences and beginning to grasp the nuances of verb tenses. True, she was learning the simpler dialect of Cantarean that the slaves had spoken under the rule of the Badakhar; the free mountaineers and the Gulyaji had preserved older and more complex forms of the language. Yet anyone might have understood her, and marveled at the strange music she put into the words.

Nezaual was much slower; he had to teach his own language as well as learn Calindor's. Yet he was perceptive enough to learn from what he overheard as well as from Calindor. He was good, Callishandal saw, at observing the unspoken language of gesture, stance, and expression. If his accent was strange and his vocabulary slow to develop, still he could mimic Calindor's raised eyebrows and lopsided grin—so well that Callishandal found herself suppressing laughter when she glimpsed them.

"The girl doesn't like him to learn from her," she said to Calindor when they lay in bed on the second night of the voyage home. She spoke in Badakhi, rather than let Deir catch the drift of their conversation. The girl might be lying silent on her pallet on the cabin floor, but she was likely still awake—as was Nezaual, on the forward deck.

"No. And he doesn't care. He thinks she is just a foolish girl, beneath his notice." Calindor was silent for a moment. "He doesn't realize who cast the spell. He thinks I did."

"Then he's a fool."

"Not really. His people don't seem to respect women much. They're like the Badakhar in that. And after all, I arrived just after they felt the spell. Why should they think a girl cast it?"

"They're fools," she insisted. "They used magic on her people, but it didn't affect her. Shouldn't that have surprised them?"

"It might have, if the power of her spell hadn't surprised them even more. Well, we will try to keep our young fellow from guessing the truth as long as possible."

Callishandal sighed. "I suspect that won't be long."

When he had finished with the sunset sacrifices, Ometollin left the altar and descended the long flight of steps down the north face of the pyramid. The sacrifices this evening had of course been in the western altar of the temple; those at tomorrow's dawn would be in the east. North would not be the site of any but minor ceremonies until the winter solstice, when a hundred souls or more would go to beg the Gods to lengthen the days once more. So the steps were clear of fresh blood, and no butchers worked here to carry the sacrifices' corpses away.

He walked alone, unattended at his own command. By the time he reached the middle terrace his knees were aching; it seemed to take forever to reach the plaza at the pyramid's base. A passing squad of pipiltin smiled and kissed their fingers at him, and he returned the salute. What did a little pain matter, anyway? Every ache was another gift to the Gods, and they in turn gave life and joy.

The summons from the Tecutli had come quickly, but without fuss: the same attendant had returned with a brief note from Itztlac himself, bidding him visit the palace tonight. Ometollin had been more surprised than pleased, for the Tecutli usually responded slowly and after deliberation.

Darkness was falling quickly now, but even blinded he would know the way to the Tecutli's palace. Warriors, traders, common people all greeted him affectionately; some lighted his way with torches for a block or two, and would have accompanied him all the way to the palace if he had not insisted they return to their homes and shops.

Those who met him at the open gate of the palace would not be so easily turned away: forty pipiltin warriors, all armed and bearing torches, waited to escort him through the gardens. General Yaocatl himself was there, dressed plainly in a linen tunic and a plain leather poncho belted at the waist; he bore no weapon but the baton of his rank, a carved thighbone. His dark, square face broke into a smile.

"Honored father! Your children are happy to welcome you. I wish you had let us escort you from the temple."

"Beloved son, you would have kept me from greeting my other children. In any case, I will not deny you now. I am in your hands."

"And in the Tecutli's chair," said the general with an even broader smile. The men behind him parted, allowing four bearers to step forward with a beautifully made sedan chair. Ometollin allowed himself to be borne upon it through the gardens, around the east wing of the palace to a small patio screened by trellises. Within the patio a little fountain bubbled and gurgled as it filled a shallow pool. Torches burned on the edges of the patio, sending gleams across the surface of the pool.

Itztlac sat alone, on a low three-legged stool. He was dressed even more simply than Yaocatl, in a long linen tunic split up the sides from ankle to thigh. His hair, thick and black, gleamed in the torchlight. He smiled a greeting to Ometollin, but his eyes were alert. Good, Ometollin thought. This was indeed a serious meeting.

Welcome and response took time, but the ceremonies allowed Ometollin to review the speech he had planned. With more relief than he wished to display, he took a seat on a bench facing Itztlac. A female attendant placed a mug of frothy chocolate in the priest's hands and then slipped into the darkness.

"Honored father, the Gods speak to you and through you."

A common expression, but Ometollin realized the Tecutli had phrased it in the declarative, not the aspirative—it was a statement of fact, not a pious wish.

"Beloved son—"

"Your message is a command from the Gods. I obey it."

Ometollin felt an uncomfortable mixture of pleasure, surprise, and anxiety. His sipped his chocolate. The Tecutli had always been a decisive man on the battlefield, but in council he usually weighed all arguments before acting.

"May I ask you how you will obey it?"

"Much as you requested. Summonses have gone out to the nobles and the greatest of the pochteca. They are to meet with me tomorrow to plan the expedition to Tonaltlan, the Magician's Land. The first detachment will leave within six days. Others will follow as they become ready. We will send five thousand warriors in all, with twice that many slaves and maceuali, five hundred horses, and fifteen mammoths. More mammoths if I can find them."

"This is most astonishing news, beloved son. But surely the nobles will wish to debate the matter first."

"They can debate all they like, once they are on the march north. We have no time for idle oratory. Now, I decide."

Ometollin frowned, his mind darting to seek out the implications. "They see you as their leader, beloved son, not their master. They will resist a direct command."

"If they resist, they will die—and not under your loving hands as a gift to the Gods, but as common criminals."

"My beautiful child, you honor me with your frank speech. I breathe with your breath on this issue, and my soul rejoices that you have understood so quickly what we face from the land you call Tonaltlan. I speak now not to block you but to assure myself that I understand you. The nobles chose you as their Tecutli because you have always been quick of mind and bold of heart, and because you understood them. You are quicker of mind than they, and bolder of heart. I am not sure they will understand this threat as quickly and fully as you have. To them, Yetecuan is already at the edge of the known world, among barbarians of no importance. A threat from still farther away will hardly seem worth such an effort—"

"Honored father, excuse my interruption, but that is precisely why I must move quickly. I love my brothers and cousins too much to see them destroy themselves in empty babble. Better that a few die at the butchers' hands, so the rest may obey me and live."

"This ... is a new thing in our life—a Tecutli who wields power without the informed consent of the nobles."

Itztlac held up the foreign knife so that its blade gleamed in the torchlight. "*This* is a new thing. The northern magician is a new thing. I cannot use the old ways to deal with them."

For a long moment he studied the knife, turning it this way and that. Then he put its point under his left eye and drew it sharply down over his high cheekbone to his jaw. Blood welled from the cut like a long red teardrop. Itztlac repeated the incision under his right eye. Blood ran black down his neck and spattered his white linen tunic.

"I give my blood to the Gods, honored father. Are you with me in this?"

Ometollin drew a long breath. Two gifts of blood from the face made this a serious matter, more serious even than a gift of blood from the penis. The Tecutli shimmered in the torchlight like one of the Gods in the temples, beautiful and terrifying. He would indeed be master and not merely leader, and the Exteca would not remain the same people. Change: the very word carried a charge of fear. But the True Gods had changed the Exteca from a wandering band of nomads, had led them north out of the deserts to this place, and had made them lords of the greatest empire ever known. Now they must change again. So be it.

He put out his hands as a beggar might ask for cornmeal. "My beloved son, only lend me the knife for a moment and I shall give my blood also."

Seven

Nezaual woke well before dawn. The darkness did not matter; he could see everything in the auras of the magical forces that filled the boat. The deck, and his blanket, were wet with dew. Stars shone down through ragged clouds. The only sound was the slap of water against the bow of the magic boat. From the cabin came the sounds of the northerners breathing slowly in their sleep.

He had lost track of the days. The boat had moved steadily, day and night; the sun had risen and set, clouds had crossed the sky. Calindor had spent almost every waking moment with him, learning the tongue of the Exteca with amazing speed; Nezaual had mastered the rudiments of Cantarean, though he understood it better than he spoke it. That was convenient: if the northerners thought him a slow learner, they might speak more freely in his hearing.

Meanwhile Callishandal and the barbarian girl had spent their days together, and Deir too was learning quickly—quickly enough to understand jokes and to make them as well. The black-haired woman and the red-haired girl seemed to enjoy each other's company.

The east was brightening behind dark and rugged mountains. Nezaual heard a light footstep, then the sound of the cabin door opening onto the afterdeck: Deir's morning piss. Sometimes she went back to bed; sometimes she stayed up, watching the night turn to day. Nezaual stood up, clutching his blanket around his shoulders, and pissed over the side of the foredeck. He felt ashamed not to be offering the Gods a drop or two of his blood in thanks for the dawn, but Calindor would sense the gift and punish him again. No one had ever struck him before; the magician's slap had been a dreadful humiliation that Nezaual would not willingly seek.

The sky was growing lighter, a few wisps of cloud turning pink. When he looked again at the shore, Nezaual saw it end in a steep, cliffbound cape; to the east a great inlet ran beyond vision, and another shore now loomed to the north and northeast. The boat began to turn, curving eastward to enter the inlet.

The girl had not gone back inside. Nezaual stepped along the narrow deck between the cabin wall and the railing until he reached the afterdeck. Deir sat on the bench at the stern, wrapped like himself in a blanket. She glanced at him and looked away, toward the forested cape.

Nezaual squatted not far from her, close enough that he need only whisper. In the girl's rough language he asked: "Why do they bring you with them?"

"They choose to."

"They bring me because I am a magician and a priest. They want to learn about the True Gods and the spells they have taught us. Do they need a servant? A slave?"

"I am neither."

He ignored the contempt in her voice. "You do not love the Gods, or us. You threatened us with death at the magician's hands, as if he were *your* servant. You want to make him our enemy, when we want only to be friends with him and his people. He does not know about us, or about your people. So he brings you along to teach him about the Airn, and about us. Am I wrong?"

She would not reply. He took her silence as an admission; it was logical, after all. In Calindor's place, knowing nothing about the Airn or the Exteca, Nezaual imagined he would have done the same. Though he would have chosen someone besides a girl—one of the village leaders, a man in any case. Someone who could talk about the resources of the Airn, the geography, the number of men who might serve as warriors and women who might grow food and weave cloth for a rebel army.

Then again, the Airn had been no warriors at all. The idea of an army of those pale-skinned weaklings was absurd. Surely Calindor, who seemed no fool, would not think for a moment about enlisting the Airn as allies against the armies of Tola.

Putting himself in Calindor's place brought understanding at last. Realization struck suddenly, clear and unquestionable: the girl was to be a gift to the magician's gods, just as her mother was to be a gift to the Gods of Tola. Nezaual grunted with annoyance at himself, making the girl look briefly at him. How could he have been so stupid? How could Yetecuan have entrusted such a fool with such a mission, one who could not even understand such plain messages from the Gods?

Well, at least he had finally understood. He would treat the girl with more respect and gentleness now; if the Gods desired her, no priest should question them.

"I have been impolite," he murmured. "Please forgive me."

"I'll never forgive you, or any of your people."

He smiled. When she was with the Gods, she would understand and forgive.

All that day the boat cruised east and then southeast through the great inlet. To the south and north rose distant forested mountains, their peaks gleaming with snow. The Cantareans seemed restless, and for once did not pursue their language lessons. Instead they talked quietly between themselves and watched the coasts slip by.

Nezaual watched also. He had never seen such forests, or so many rivers and creeks. Surely the Gods enjoyed great gifts from the inhabitants of these lands, if they gave in turn so much water and wood. In Tola, in years of drought, the priests had sometimes given thousands of lives to draw water from the wells and springs.

Yet something about the landscape troubled him, and it was

close to noon before he understood it: the forces that shimmered and glowed in Tola, fed by the knives, were invisible here. In their place he detected other powers, great spells buried deep in stone and sea and forest. And as he sat on the foredeck in the warm sun, he began to feel afraid.

Simply to contemplate the auras of those spells was to feel dizzy and sick. Surely no magician could be so powerful; but if these were the work of Calindor or someone like him, then all the lore of the Exteca was children's prattle. Perhaps Calindor himself was a God and this was one of the heavens. Better that, better to be dead, than to contemplate the Exteca contending with a whole nation of human magicians such as this man.

He listened to the Cantareans, understanding just enough to realize how much he was missing. They were talking about a people called Dragasasu, whose land the boat was approaching; the Cantareans' land was somewhere beyond, up a river. Were the Dragasasu enemies? Calindor seemed to worry about them, which in itself seemed strange: what could he fear from anyone? Could these unknown people be the magicians who had cast the spells underlying this land? Might they be even greater than Calindor?

The warmth of the sun and the beauty of the islands in the sea at last put such thoughts out of his mind. What would happen was out of his hands; the True Gods still looked over him, even in this unlucky northern realm.

For most of the day their course was south of east, running swiftly down the middle of a great gulf or channel. At last it divided into two branches, something like the bay of the Airn but on a far grander scale. To north and south, islands studded the gulf; to the east, yet more snowcapped mountains rose on the horizon.

The day was waning, and Calindor seemed tired at last of being at sea; he murmured a spell that sent *Tilcalli* leaping ahead, cutting through the water until spray rose from the bows like wings. His course wove among the islands, sometimes so close to shore that deer turned and fled at the sight of the boat. Then the islands fell behind and open water stretched to the near horizon; beyond, mountains caught the last light of the sun.

This was nothing like the sea at Tola, Nezaual thought. There the surf rolled in from the infinite west, breaking on empty beaches of fine white sand beneath the brown hills. Here the waves were small, the shores were stone, land and sea were in more complex contention, and those strange underlying spells seemed to live in everything—especially in the greens and blues and grays that filled this world.

Now the sun was down behind the great mountainous spine of the largest of the islands, and a single light gleamed in the twilight to the northeast. Nezaual sat eating bread and fish with the others, listening to the northerners speak again of the Dragasasu. *If they slay me, may I be a gift for my own Gods, and not those of Calindor . . .*

"Will they be angry if we don't stop?" Callishandal asked quietly. The light of the tower beacon was brighter now, and its reflection made a path for the boat to follow to the mouth of the river. Overhead the sky was full of stars.

Calindor answered in a murmur: "Dragons don't have feelings as we do. Or if they do, they don't choose to let us know them. I will greet them, and we will go on."

"I wonder what our young friends will think of them," Callishandal said. He glanced at Deir and Nezaual, who sat on opposite sides of the foredeck; they too were watching the beacon.

"The girl will probably find them dull. Sea dragons are much more impressive."

Callishandal could not suppress a shudder, recalling the sight of Deir on the great head of the sea dragon.

"The boy will probably compare them to the mammoths he's always talking about," Calindor went on. "I wish I'd seen the one his warriors brought to Burnbaile."

"The girl talks about it all the time. It must be a frightening creature—look."

The mouth of the river was a delta of salt marsh, sandbars, and bogs. *Tilcalli* was now gliding up a winding channel whose banks, thickly wooded, were just visible in the light of the dragonfire ring over the boat. Now and then other lights glinted back: the eyes of raccoons, deer, or wolves. Ahead glowed the beacon, fiery orange above the trees that lined the banks. But now, on the southern bank, another circle of dragonfire glowed in a grassy clearing. Under it stood three dragons, so still they might have been statues twice a tall man's height, facing the river.

Long and massive tails balanced their heavy heads. Intricate patterns of scales—red, blue, yellow, green—adorned their muscular torsos and hind legs; their bellies and forelegs were creamy white. They stood upright, the forelegs held close to their ribs, like birds' wings. Frills of spikes stood out from their muzzles and around their gleaming eyes.

Calindor stood on the afterdeck with hands extended. Without words he greeted them and asked their leave to journey home upon their river.

Their focus swept over him, rocking him back on his heels. Nezaual, standing nearby, choked and fell from the bench to his hands and knees. He rolled onto his side, shuddering convulsively.

Then the dragonfire over the boat flared brighter, brighter, until the humans squinted and covered their eyes. For a moment they stood or knelt in a painful glare; then the light returned to normal. On the shore the three dragons turned and slipped among the trees with surprising lightness. Darkness fell over the clearing where they had been.

Tilcalli continued upstream. Callishandal rubbed her eyes. "What happened? Why did you make the dragonfire so bright?"

"I didn't. They wanted to see Deir."

Callishandal looked at him, ignoring the stubborn afterimages in her vision. "Why?"

Deir herself, untouched by the dragons' focus, understood enough to echo the question: "Why see me?"

"I don't know," Calindor answered them both. "But I think I caught their feelings."

"You said they don't show them to humans," Callishandal said.

Her husband sat on the bench and rubbed his face. "They do when they're frightened enough."

Colotic's men had moved, systematically and without hurry, from Burnbaile to the other villages of the Airn. Yetecuan had worried that some of them might resist, and force him to cast a spell of love or terror before he was fully recovered from the first spell. But the people of Burnbaile themselves had done it, going with the warriors from one settlement to the next and assuring their neighbors that the Exteca would be kind and generous masters.

Now he found himself in Kiltarra, northeast of Burnbaile and high enough in the hills to command a splendid view of the bay. The autumn afternoon was warm and clear. An Airn attendant brought him a cup of the pleasant honey drink called mead, and Yetecuan sipped it as the natives did.

From the dooryard of the house he had occupied he could see tiny triangles of red or white on the bay: the fishermen's boats, their sails filling in the breeze. Siar Bagh, they called it, Bay of the West; he murmured the foreign words, tasting them like the mead. The Airn had been fortunate, he thought, to have this bay; it had encouraged them to explore its waters and gain skill as sailors. The Exteca, for all their knowledge, were no mariners.

Another reason to worry about Calindor and the people he came from. Their mastery of the sea was clearly enormous; imagine a whole fleet of their boats, sweeping south with no care for wind or current, and appearing one fine morning on the beaches of Tola.

He put the thought aside and took up the message that lay unfolded on the table beside him. No matter how many times he read it, Ometollin's glyphs filled his heart with wonder and awe.

Somehow the Chief Priest had persuaded the Tecutli to mobilize the greatest army seen in the empire since the civil wars of a century ago. Already its vanguard was on the march north; the cavalry would arrive within the waxing of the moon, and the first foot contingents would see Siar Bagh by the next new moon. More would arrive over the next month, but none would pause for long among the Airn; they would push on north, and Yetecuan was to be their chief magician.

He tried to imagine what the army would look like, and how it would appear to Calindor's people. *Am I the man to choose, old and weary as I am? Should not some younger man take on this task?* He thought of Nezaual, somewhere far to the north and now apparently moving eastward with the northerners: the gold lip plug was still detectable, though it now lay farther than any such object had ever been before.

The True Gods had chosen them both, he reminded himself. The youth's was the greater responsibility, going alone into a mysterious peril. Yetecuan himself would be within the protecting arms of a great army, whose warriors would love and cherish him as their own father. All would happen as the Gods wished, and he would be their hand—better said, he would be the blade within their hand, cutting open the heart of a new land as a gift for them.

Only do the Gods' will, and he would have nothing to fear.

The tower beacon was the tallest of a group of stone structures lining a precipice overlooking the river. They were not houses, or fortresses, and they did not make a town. They were simply what dragons chose to build, and where they sometimes chose to live. As *Tilcalli* glided past, the structures seemed deserted.

"They know already," Calindor said. On the foredeck nearby, Nezaual lay wrapped in a blanket. He had fallen into an almost-normal sleep after recovering from the shock of the dragons' focus. Callishandal and Deir sat on the bench beside the front wall of the cabin, looking across the water at the tower with its crown of dragonfire.

Gradually it receded and the only light was that of the boat's own ring of dragonfire. It shone now on a long canoe, lashed to the roof of the cabin; it had borne them down the river last spring, and waited all summer in a sheltered place near the dragon's tower.

"Deir, I would like to talk with you," Calindor said.

On the long journey up the coast, he had spent most of his time with Nezaual; sometimes he had helped Callishandal in her language lessons with Deir, but he had spent little time alone with her.

"Yes, I will talk."

"Tell me about your people," Calindor asked. "Have you always lived in Burnbaile?"

"I don't know. Mother and Father say we come faraway place. Gods bring us to Siar Bagh long time. Our towns old."

Calindor nodded. He had learned in his confrontation with Mekhpur that a god—*the* god, the Great God Bha—had brought people here to Sotalar from another world. Many peoples still retained some vague memory of that journey, and Calindor himself, in a vision granted him by the dragon Obordur, had seen his own ancestors arrive in Sotalar. But why Bha had willed this, no one knew.

"You live in peace with your land," he said.

Deir stared at him, evidently not sure she understood. "Yes. Land and water, they feed us. We don't hurt them."

"And you do not fight each other."

"Oh yes. Children fight, many times. Then they grow up, don't fight more."

"Villages don't fight each other?"

"Only Fabarslúa fight," she said contemptuously. "Long time, Airn fight Airn. Man fight man. Then woman say no more, stop fight."

"Who was the woman?"

"*All* woman. Girl, mother, mother of mother. Tell man stop fight. Maybe they do wrong. Airn don't fight Fabarslúa."

"But you wanted me to fight them."

"You are not Airn. Also, magic kill is not fight. Magic kill is clean mess."

He suppressed a smile: Callia, the goddess of beauty and love, had expressed a similar view when she had spoken through Callishandal in the overthrow of Mekhpur.

"Do many Airn know magic?"

"Many, some, maybe. We know geas, spells to make help in work."

"Can you see the Gariba, the Powers that obey magic?"

She was silent for a moment. "Some say they see. My father Bron, he sees nothing. He learns geas for wood, says geas, wood listens maybe. But wood kill him. We send bones to gods in Diamuir."

He nodded. Callishandal had told him already that she had been consigning her father's bones to the sea when the Exteca had come, that she had escaped them on a reed boat that had sunk just as the sea dragon had arrived.

"But no gods are in Diamuir. Gods all gone away."

"Why do you say that, Deir?"

"I learn that on candleboat. Gods are gone. Maybe Gariba still here, but no gods."

Calindor said nothing. All around him the night shimmered and glowed with the Gariba of earth, air, and water; those of fire rejoiced in the blazing circle above the boat. The Powers rejoiced also in his body and those of the others. True, they were not gods as Callia was, or Bha, or even Mekhpur, who had once been a man. This girl did not seem to see the Gariba as a magician could, yet she spoke with calm certainty about that which no magician could see except in the deepest spells and invocations. She was the one who had summoned the sea dragons, and who now drove their land cousins in terror from their own river.

Watching light gleam in her red curls, Calindor felt a kind of dread. Yet beneath his fear he felt also the constant hunger of the magician for new knowledge, at whatever price. *You do not know yet what you have to teach me, Deir. But it will be a great vision.*

Eight

Are we still in the world?

Nezaual was unsure. The ocean had been strange yet not entirely new; the same waters, after all, fell upon the beaches of Tola and the shore of Burnbaile. Now the northerners had brought him deep within a terrifying land guarded by monstrous reptiles capable of magic. This river ran broad, sometimes so broad that the dragonfire over the boat could not illuminate its shores. The current ran deep and muddy and strong. Though Calindor's spell still kept calm water around the boat, Nezaual sensed that the Powers in the river were more tolerant than obedient: they might choose for now to allow *Tilcalli* to pass upstream, but on a whim they could crush her and her passengers to bits.

First the boat had cruised east, through a vast plain of bog and forest glimpsed by dragonfire; then, long before dawn, they had turned north. The land had risen on either side into the steep slopes of a canyon; where the water plunged white and roaring, the boat glided upward like a seabird somehow advancing into a storm. The circle of calm around the boat had shrunk to a mere film, and the air itself was a storm of spray. Calindor and Callishandal had seemed unconcerned that instant death raged all around them, and Deir sang songs not even she herself could hear above the crash of water. Shamed by his own terror, Nezaual had crouched against the wall of the cabin with his hands pressed to his ears.

Now it was day and the boat continued northward. The rapids, for now, were behind them. The banks of the river were tangled with logs half buried in avalanches from the steep slopes of the canyon. Again and again Calindor diverted yet more logs, drifting like giant spears into the boat's path. Impossibly far above, the cliffs blazed in the light of an autumn sun that was too far south. The air was chill.

He listened to the northerners speaking together, comparing the size of the river with what it had been last spring. Surely he was misunderstanding them—it could not have been even higher and stronger then. And had they really descended this raging flood in the simple canoe now lashed to the cabin roof, and built this boat under the gaze of the giant reptiles?

While the northerners and the girl sat on the foredeck, he preferred to sit against the stern wall of the cabin. The sun was warm, until it slipped westward behind the cliffs, and he did not have to see the next series of oncoming rapids; he only had to brace himself as the boat tilted upward and shot through the roaring spray.

After a few hours of such travel, it seemed impossible to believe that a world might exist beyond this river and canyon, a world where the land was flat and water ran slowly.

How could we conquer these people? We have no spells for calming water. If we did, it would take a hundred of our greatest magicians to carry a simple canoe up this river. Somehow another way must lie open, something to the east . . .

Another night passed while the boat ran north. Now the air was truly cold, and Nezaual shuddered all night under three blankets. By next day's dawn, the river was different: it ran a milky blue, not brown, and though it ran swift, it was only half a bowshot wide. Along its banks rose thick stands of unfamiliar trees: pines of some kind, and golden-leaved trees that shimmered in the sun like the feather cloaks of the Gods. On every side, forested mountains rose against the sky. They seemed to Nezaual like pyramids not yet consecrated—or perhaps, he thought grimly, consecrated to the gods of monsters like the Dragasasu.

Late in the afternoon they came to a narrow lake at the foot of a steep-sided mountain. *Tilcalli* glided across its blue-green surface to the far shore, where a cabin stood—the first human-built structure Nezaual had seen since leaving Burnbaile. As the boat drew near, he saw it was not a house but a kind of steep-roofed shed, open at either end.

Calindor guided *Tilcalli* close to the shed, until the keel bumped the pebbly lake bottom. Then he leaped from the foredeck into shallow water and waded onto the beach.

"Nezaual, beloved son, come and help me."

"Of course, honored father."

Nezaual marveled at the magician's speech: his fluency in Exteca was limited, but from his accent, Calindor might have grown up in the south quarter of Tola where Nezaual himself had been born. Jumping into the water, he gasped at its coldness and hurried onto the shore to join Calindor in the shed.

"We built this here before we went down the river," Calindor said. "I didn't know then that I would build a seagoing boat, but I knew we would want shelter when we came back. We'll portage the canoe and our supplies, and leave *Tilcalli* here. No doubt she'll take us back to the sea someday." He looked a little sad as he spoke, but Nezaual could only rejoice at feeling solid ground under his feet at last.

While Callishandal and Deir prepared a meal, the two men waded back and forth carrying the boat's contents into the shed. Though it did not take long, Nezaual was shuddering with cold by the time the job was done and he could sit by the cookfire. The meal was a simple pot of boiled grain, but he ate it with impatient greed and then lay down on a luxuriously soft bed of reeds. For a few moments he listened to the northerners talking cheerfully about their destination: Tanshadabela. He knew enough Cantarean to recognize the meaning of the name—Two Streams. But before he could tell what the others were saying about it, he was asleep.

The portage was long and very steep, a winding trail through dense stands of pine singing with mosquitoes. First Nezaual helped Calindor carry the canoe; it was surprisingly light, and very strong, but by the end of the portage Nezaual's shoulders were aching and his legs trembled.

They had come out of the woods onto the shore of a blue-green lake. Two birds paddled across it, crying out; other than that, the only noise was the wind in the trees. Calindor left the canoe upside down on a moss-covered bank and headed back without pausing to rest. Without complaint, but without joy, Nezaual followed.

The next time up the trail, the women came also; everyone carried a heavy pack of clothing and food, though most of the cooking pots and utensils stayed behind in the cabin. Nezaual was interested to see that Calindor used no magic to ease their burdens; perhaps even he had his limits.

And through his weariness Nezaual sensed also a shift in the Powers around them: this endless mountain trail crossed from one watershed to another, and the blue-green lake was a source of a river that would never see the great ocean in the west. Where its waters would find the sea he had no idea, but this little lake was a frontier: they were now within the true realm of the Cantareans.

The day was almost gone by the time they had loaded the canoe, but the Cantareans were eager to leave. While the sinking sun struck fire from the peaks above, the canoe slipped silently down the lake and into a shallow, noisy stream: Sanibela, Calindor called it, Green Stream, though here it was white and blue.

Nezaual sat uncomfortably, gripping the gunwales and trying to avoid looking at the rocks just below the surface. Behind him knelt Calindor, steering the canoe; Nezaual could see the spells shimmering in the paddle and in the one Callishandal used. Deir sat just behind the Cantarean woman, chattering away happily and asking the name of every tree and shrub along the banks.

Night fell, but Calindor showed no interest in stopping. The stream grew deeper and quieter; the mountains became black pyramids against a starry sky. At last, almost absentmindedly, Calindor put a ring of dragonfire above the canoe. In its light a nightmare creature looked up in surprise from the riverbank: long-legged, with an enormous rack of antlers above a grotesque head. Then it plunged away into the forest.

"Moose," said Callishandal, and Deir repeated the word, laughing.

Nezaual shivered in the cold and wished himself back in Tola—even Burnbaile, anywhere but here in this strange northern land.

Long into the night they ran down the river; Nezaual dozed and then woke suddenly at the sound of water roaring shallow over stones. Callishandal sang out, a single clear note that filled the night; her husband sang it also. The single note became a complex antiphony in which words slipped and darted like fish in the stream beneath them. Though Nezaual could not understand it all, he knew it was a song of greeting and return. For all that Cantarean music was utterly unlike the noble chants of the Exteca, he felt its beauty.

A third voice joined in the song, and a fourth, a fifth—

The canoe slipped under a bridge, invisible in the darkness until they were between its pilings. Calindor steered them over a short patch of white water; beyond it the river merged with a greater one. This must be Cantabela, the Great River running through the enormous mountain valley the Cantareans often spoke of. The canoe stayed close to the left bank, which rose abruptly into a bluff perhaps ten times the height of a man. Horses whinnied in the distance. Lights glowed along the top of the bluff and at its foot, where a dock jutted into the stream. Men and women stood at the end of the dock, singing their welcome; Nezaual suddenly remembered the arrival of *Tilcalli* at Burnbaile: strange, he thought, how water seemed to love and obey this magician.

Calindor steered smoothly around the end of the dock, into its lee, and reached up. Hands took his and held the canoe. Before he knew it, Nezaual was on the dock himself, surrounded by the wizard's people. This was Tanshadabela, home of the greatest threat the Exteca had ever faced.

Something was wrong, but Calindor could not tell what it was.

He sat on one of the crowded benches of the Meeting Hall, with Callishandal on his right and his parents on his left. The hall was one large room; three rows of benches ran down each long side, with a great fireplace at each end. Flanking the hearths, cedar columns rose to hold the roof. Great carvers had shaped the columns into images of bear, wolf, and dragon; in the firelight they seemed to move and listen.

He remembered how the first time he had seen this place, he had been exhausted and enchanted—a magician deprived of his voice and therefore of his powers. Yet for all his weariness and despair, this had seemed a place of strength; so it seemed tonight as well.

But it was also a hall of strangers. Since the fall of Mekhpur and the Five Kingdoms, he had spent little time in Tanshadabela. These were his kinsfolk, he knew their names and their relationships to him and his parents, yet he was still an outsider here. So he felt himself, and so he saw himself in their eyes. It did not help that he and Callishandal had been alone for so many months; Calindor was unused to so many people in one place.

The floor between the benches was strewn with white sand. There stood the keeper of the hall, an old woman named Tulucuingol. She wore a plain blue wool cloak, and though the hour was late, she regarded Calindor with a clear, alert gaze. Yet she seemed annoyed, he thought.

Equally wakeful were the people of Tanshadabela who had come into the hall to greet Calindor and Callishandal. Not all were there; some stayed home with sleeping children, or looked after the foreigners at Svordo's inn nearby. But most of the adults and youths had gathered quickly.

Tulucuingol's voice seemed too quiet to carry over the murmur of the people, yet when she said "I ask for your hearing," the hall fell utterly silent.

"We welcome you back, Calindor and Callishandal. You say your news cannot wait until morning, so we gather as you asked."

She was annoyed with him, Calindor realized; the village would much prefer to have held a welcoming feast tomorrow, and then heard his news on full stomachs. But his mother and father, sitting beside him, seemed only glad to have him and Callishandal home.

He stood. "We thank you, Tulucuingol, for your welcome. Our news is indeed urgent, but I will try to be brief." He whispered a small spell of illusion, and the sandy floor disappeared into a mist. The mist cleared, and they seemed to look down at *Tilcalli*—no larger than a child's hand—cruising upon the sea. Calindor spoke quickly, describing the voyage down the coast; then the image of the boat appeared within the great bay, with Burnbaile's roofs rising above the reeds in the distance.

"Here a raiding party came from the south to conquer the town you see. Of all the people there, only one escaped the strange magic of the raiders—the red-haired girl we brought with us. She cast a spell that no magician ever cast before, and it knocked me senseless, though I was far from her when she did it."

"We felt it too," Dragasa said.

His son nodded. "Perhaps every magician in Sotalar felt it. Yet the girl has no real understanding of magic, and does not understand what she did. I hope to study her and to learn what her powers are. Equally important is the magic of the Exteca." He created an image of Yetecuan and Nezaual as they stood upon the dock in their black robes.

"These people do not know steel magic, yet they know something powerful and dangerous. It is like the worst magic of the

Badakhar, the kind that springs from blood and death. Somehow this old man cast a spell upon a whole village and made them all willing slaves—all except the redheaded girl Deir." Calindor paused. "To enchant a human soul is the rarest achievement of a magician, yet somehow the Exteca do it. That is why I brought one of their magicians with me, to try to learn from him."

An old man, his hair in white braids, spoke up: "Were you wise to bring such people here? What if they cast their spell upon us and make them us their slaves?"

"It is a wise question you ask, Cantacala. The older magician you see in my spell might indeed do to Tanshadabela what he did to Burnbaile. The younger one is far less able, though I think he has talent. I hope I can learn the principles of their magic from him, and find a way to stop it."

"Why?" asked a young woman. "These people are very far away. They will never come this far."

"I think they will, Sisimingol. Soon."

They looked at him in silent surprise. Above the sandy floor the illusion changed; it expanded, showing the plumed warriors crowding the dock behind the two magicians.

"Perhaps they look odd in their feathers and their weapons seem like toys. But they have a great empire, greater than the old Five Kingdoms of the Badakhar. All the nations they have conquered have been simple people like the Airn. Now they know about us, about our steel, about our magic. They must see us as a great threat and a great opportunity. The old magician understood that. If the Exteca are as wise as he is, they will seek us out and try to conquer us."

"But why?" Sisimingol insisted. "We are no enemies of theirs."

"We were no enemies of the Badakhar in the old days. But we had the land they wanted, and they saw everyone as an enemy—even other Badakhar. The Exteca know only conquerors and conquered. If they see us as strong, they see us as *their* conquerors."

Dragasa spoke: "I grant you all you say, Calindor. But what would you have us do? We can fight, but we are not a warlike people. The Badakhar are fighters, but they are too busy trying to feed themselves."

"Too busy fighting Cantareans," another man broke in. The villagers growled.

"Fighting Cantareans?" Calindor frowned. "What is this news?"

"We have heard reports since late in the summer," Tilcalli said. "Some of the Badakhar are quarreling with the Cantareans."

"They don't like to see us walking free," someone shouted.

"They want us to be their slaves again. Callia didn't teach them enough of a lesson."

Calindor's gaze turned on the man. "You were not at Aishadan when Callia spoke," he said quietly. "She could have slain us all, swept us away and left no sign that anyone had ever lived in Cantarea. Or in Tanshadabela."

An uncomfortable silence fell.

"Whatever the news from the prairie," Calindor went on, "I ask that you think also of what I have told you. We will see the Exteca soon, and not as illusions." The images vanished, leaving only the sandy floor. "If we are not ready for them, they will make us yearn for our happy life under the Badakhar. I thank you for your attention."

He sat down, struggling to control an unexpected anger. His father was right; these mountain Cantareans were not really warlike, though they had held off the Badakhar for centuries. The horsemen of Aishadan and the other kingdoms would have understood the Exteca threat at once, and sent to their stalmaghar for new swords and pikes. With smiles on their faces, Calindor thought.

He felt an odd pang of homesickness. For all their brutish cruelty, their arrogance and spite, he knew the Badakhar as he did not know his own people. He had grown up among them, a dark-skinned princeling scarcely more accepted than the Cantarean slaves he resembled; without the protection of the Aryo Albohar, he would have been a slave himself, like his captive mother. Damn the Badakhar as stupidly evil, but they had the virtues of their vices too: quickness to see danger, courage in facing it, contempt for death and cowardice alike. In their language, *bad* and *weak* were the same word.

Perhaps, he thought wryly, it was a good sign that the Badakhar were quarreling with their former slaves; they must be feeling more themselves.

The meeting ended and the people dispersed to their homes. Calindor and Callishandal walked with his parents across the village to the new inn. It was a large log building, built as three sides of a square around an open courtyard. Though it was late, lights burned in the windows and voices were loud within.

They entered and found the dining hall half full: villagers stopping for a mug of beer, traders from the prairie, and Nezaual and Deir sitting among them. Few took much notice of the Exteca; he looked much like any Cantarean. But Deir's pale skin and red hair, gleaming in the firelight, drew everyone's attention.

She seemed to be enjoying it, Calindor thought. She was sitting at one of the long tables, talking in simple Cantarean with some villagers who seemed amazed that such a person could speak their language. Nezaual, at the far end of the table, sat quietly listening. He understands more than he pretends, Calindor warned himself. Yetecuan would be pleased with him.

"Back at last!" boomed a familiar voice. A stocky, scarred Cantarean in buckskin trousers and a woolen vest was standing by the kitchen door with his hands full of foaming beer mugs.

"Svordo!" Calindor laughed and strode over to his old friend, who scarcely had time to put down his burden before the magician embraced him. The very sight of him was cheering: a prairie-born Cantarean, not one of the mountaineers, and an ex-slave who knew the value of freedom. "You're looking well, and you've gained weight. The inn must be prospering."

"Very well indeed." Svordo passed out beer to the newcomers and commanded the people at Deir and Nezaual's table to make room. "A rare pair of visitors you've brought us. You must tell us everything about them. Were they pets of the dragons?"

Calindor laughed. "No. Just two young people with a desire to see the world. I will tell you everything tomorrow; tonight we simply rejoice to be home again."

Svordo nodded, looked into Calindor's eyes and grunted enigmatically. "And I will tell you everything tomorrow also. Drink up! We have whole barrels of this stuff that'll go bad if we let it sit."

Some of the villagers seemed to want to continue the discussion from the hall, but Calindor only smiled at their comments and turned their attention to Deir. She answered their questions easily enough: where she was from, her name, what she thought of Tanshadabela. Calindor glanced at Callishandal and murmured: "You taught her well."

"Not so well as she learned."

"And what language do you speak among your people?" someone asked.

"We talk Airna."

"And can you say something in it for us?"

She answered with a simple recitation of her name and age, while her listeners smiled and clapped—that mountaineer custom that Calindor was still unused to.

"And do your people sing songs? Like this?" The villager, a little drunk, broke into a few lines of a famous love song while his listeners clapped again.

"Yes, we sing."

"Good, then sing us something."

Deir sipped her beer and put down the mug. She closed her eyes and lifted her chin a little.

The first notes were almost lost in the bustle and chatter around her, but then all fell silent. To Calindor the song seemed to fill the room like smoke, like sea spray flying before the wind, and he caught his breath even as his parents shut their eyes and gasped. Nezaual shivered at the other end of the table.

All listened while Deir's voice rose and sank, and when she was through, the room stayed silent.

"A strange and lovely song," Svordo said at last. "You have a fine voice."

"I thank you. It is just an old song we would sing when we went fishing on the bay. It's about a boy who sailed into the fog and never sailed out again, and the girl who mourned him."

"We hope you will sing us many more of your songs," said Tilcalli, "but now it is late. We must go home."

"Yes," Calindor said. "Deir, you will stay with us. Nezaual will stay here in the inn, if there is room."

"Of course. A fine room, with a proper bed."

"Good. Nezaual, we will meet here in the morning. Until then."

The Exteca seemed a little alarmed at being left among strangers, but he did not protest when Svordo led him off. The rest of the travelers said farewell and left.

"It seems so large, after the boat," Callishandal murmured as they entered the cabin Calindor had built for them. Tilcalli and Dragasa had kept it clean, and kindling lay piled in the fireplace. Calindor lighted it with an absentminded snap of his fingers, and then called up a ring of dragonfire.

"It is like home," Deir said. She looked around at the log walls, the gleaming plank floor, the cabinets and shelves flanking the fireplace and chimney. "It is a very good home."

She began to weep, silently, her eyes closed. Callishandal hugged and rocked her for a long time, and then guided her to the smaller of the two bedchambers. Calindor, sitting by the fire, heard his wife singing old Badakhi lullabies, as if Deir were a tired little girl and not a young woman in exile.

At last she came back into the main room, closing the door behind her. "The poor girl's exhausted. I'm surprised she lasted this long."

"I'm surprised that any of us has." He slumped in his chair, staring at the Powers dancing in the flames. Perhaps he was unique among magicians in being able to cast spells without fatigue, but like anyone else, he could tire after days of travel. "Come, my love. Let us sleep also."

He had half expected that Deir's singing voice would have revealed some hint of her strange power. It had been a beautiful voice—he had been almost as moved by it as his parents had—but it was just a voice.

He mocked himself: *Just a voice! When you nearly lost life and soul together for lack of a voice. When every human magic starts with the spoken word to the listening Powers.*

Women's magic, Calindor thought, was different, hard to grasp. His mother had taught him much, but much had eluded him. The magic of the Badakhar was male, fierce, a coercion of the Powers to do what they would never do by their own nature. In its own way it was simple, comprehensible, a matter of the right words in the right times and places.

When Callishandal had been only Bherasha, a simple domestic slave, she had had no gift of magic; but when Callia herself had chosen to speak, it had been through her. He had been only the medium, the opener of the door. Callia had spoken, and her words had scourged Cantarea to death and then to life again. The door had closed once more, and she who had been the Voice of Callia had become an ordinary woman again: intelligent, loving, full of laughter and anger and foresight—but with no more magic than Deir revealed.

The thought made him shiver, and he put it aside. Callishandal was warm beside him in their bed, and sweet-smelling. While he slept with his arm around her, Calindor felt the pulse of a magician's focus sweep over them: Nezaual, seeking whatever would let itself be found. Calindor smiled wryly and sent back a stronger focus, like a hawk swooping on a chattering squirrel, and then went to sleep.

Nine

They brought in the last of the harvest: late wheat and rye, small red apples, camas root. The fields were larger than they had once been: though the mountains had escaped the worst of Callia's wrath, her storms had brought down countless trees around Tanshadabela and the other villages farther upriver. But the mountain soil, thin and bitter, had never held little nourishment of its own. The Siragi Aibela, the clan of magicians, had learned the spells of greenmagic; without it, the mountaineers would long since have starved, or surrendered to the Badakh slave masters who had conquered Cantarea.

But a spell was a spell, and exhausted the magician who cast it. Even the best of the Siragi Aibela might give life to only two or three fields in a year. So the Cantareans had survived in a delicate balance, a small and scattered population.

Then Calindor had come, the greatest son of the Siragi Aibela, the magician who worked his spells without wearying. The Cantareans had been glad of Calindor's greenmagic; it allowed them to grow far more than in the past, and so to feed themselves and the newcomers who had arrived from the prairies after the fall of the Five Kingdoms.

He worked in the fields and orchards with everyone else, enjoying the warmth of the sun on his back and the smell of ripeness all around. With every sheaf of wheat, every apple plucked from a gnarled branch, he felt his own spells returning ... no, not returning, but concluding, like the last notes of the harvesters' songs. In the spring he and his relatives of the Siragi Aibela would have to cast the spells of greenmagic once again, while the Cantareans sang the songs of planting.

Nezaual worked beside him. The crops were mostly strange to him, though he recognized apples from the Airn's country. But he quickly became an accomplished reaper, delighting both in the power of a steel scythe and in the Powers bound within its blade. Sometimes as he swung it he sang his own people's songs and the others listened. The youth's voice was clear and vibrant, his songs monotonous yet strangely resonant. Before long Calindor was hearing an echo of them in the Cantareans' songs.

"Do you see the Gariba, the Powers in the stalk and fruit?" he asked Nezaual.

"Yes, honored father. They are the same as those in our own crops. But I marvel that they choose to live in such plants, in such cold country."

"Greenmagic gives them strength. Without it, this land would grow little but spruce and pines and wolf willow, and a few flowers."

"I see its effects, and I admire it, honored father. In my own country, in Tola, the land is hot and dry. We must use redmagic as you use greenmagic, to give gifts to the True Gods and gain water and fertility in return."

"And your gifts are the lives of men and women?"

"And children. Many of the Gods are very fond of children."

Calindor said nothing for a moment. "And do your gods have names?"

"Of course. But we do not speak their names unless we seek to give ourselves to them. That is why they are the True Gods, because they come when we call them." He smiled. "They have other names as well, like—like the work they do: Raingiver, and Watcher of Dreams, and—" He groped for the words in Cantarean. "—She Gives Babies. Or from their appearance, like Lady Serpent and Hummingbird Flower. And they send food also, as your spells do for your people. We use the names of their work."

Calindor wondered what kind of redmagic could also be a greenmagic. "So you call on the gods who make your crops grow?"

"And the gods who protect the harvest. I did that three years running in my village, before the priests learned of me and made me one of them."

"How protect the harvest?"

"Against rats, honored father, and against mice and insects that devour our corn and fruits."

"Can you protect this harvest also?"

"With redmagic? But you forbade me to use magic, honored father."

"Now I permit you, honored son, this one time. Can you protect this field against rats?"

"I think so."

Standing in the sunny field, Nezaual called out the words of a spell while the other harvesters gaped and grinned and went back to work. Then, without warning, he picked up his scythe, held it by the blade, and made three quick incisions across his belly.

Calindor shuddered, scarcely hearing Nezaual's words of thanks. Something had appeared within the field, a kind of Gariba; it was silent, invisible to ordinary people, but as real to Calindor as the sunlight on the stubble or the boy standing beside him. He heard a rustling at his feet. Two rats were running for the edge of the field, their black fur puffed out. The Gariba reached out, though it had no limbs, and touched them. They squeaked, convulsed, and died. Crickets leaped into the sunlight, thousands at once, and did not leap again. The air turned black with flies and mosquitoes; then their frantic buzzing ceased and they, too, fell back into the stubble.

Cries from the other harvesters showed where they had also

seen rats and insects die. Far across the field, Calindor saw his mother sway and sink to one knee.

Nezaual grunted and reached out with one hand to break his fall. He lay faceup in the stubble beside the scythe, blood running in rivulets off his belly and soaking into his deerskin trousers. He smiled sleepily.

"I will be back," Calindor said, and ran across the field to where his mother now sat surrounded by harvesters. One of them was giving her a cup of water. Calindor had never seen her so pale.

"Tell me how you feel," he asked her, speaking in Badakhi as if the harvesters crowding around were strangers.

Dully, in the same language, Tilcalli whispered: "I do not feel very well, Dheribi." His boyhood name: she must have been shaken indeed. "I want to go home. I want to get out of this field."

Gently but easily he lifted her in his arms, ignoring the anxious questions of the harvesters. They had felt nothing, seen nothing, yet to his eyes Nezaual's Gariba was as obvious as they were.

His path to the village took him past Nezaual, who still lay bleeding. Calindor looked down at him.:

"When you are ready, go back to the inn and stay there until I come. Cast no more spells."

Nezaual half giggled, half sobbed. "I could not if I wished, honored father." He stared past Calindor's shoulder at the autumn sky.

Still carrying Tilcalli, Calindor walked quickly down a trail that led through a stand of aspen to the outskirts of Tanshadabela. As soon as they were within the trees, he felt the Gariba's influence vanish. *Every rat, every insect within three hundred paces or more—and we felt every one of them die.* A few people looked curiously at them, and one called out: "Is your mother hurt?" He shook his head and hurried on.

His parents' cabin was empty; Dragasa was with a harvesting crew up the river. Calindor pushed open the door, sidled through it, and put his mother down gently on the bed. She shivered uncontrollably. He wrapped a wool blanket around her and sat on the floor beside the bed.

It seemed to take a long time for Tilcalli to recover. At last her eyes opened and she looked at him.

"You felt it." Her voice was scarcely a whisper, and she still spoke Badakhi.

"Yes."

"It is something like Badakh magic."

"Only a little. He said he could protect the field against rats. I told him to do it."

"Yes. I saw a rat die. But mostly I felt the spell, and the deaths." And she shuddered again. "Strange. I wanted you to learn both the magics, Cantarean and Badakh, and you did. And the magic of the Gulyaji also, and even the dragons. But this . . . makes me feel . . . *mela*." Weak. The same word for *bad*.

"I know what you mean." *But do I?* The force of the spell had been astonishing, unexpected, and shocking. But it had also been fascinating. Even the greatest of the Badakh magicians, the Veikar, had never sensed the true power in blood. Their spells were crude and wasteful by comparison with Nezaual's. *And he is just a novice, knowing only the simplest skills.*

Tilcalli said little else, while Calindor thought about the spell. After a while Dragasa came in with Deir right behind him. She seemed more puzzled than anything else, while Dragasa looked grim and frightened. He ignored Calindor and stood over Tilcalli.

"I knew it," he said softly. "When I felt it, I knew it would sicken you."

She smiled faintly and opened her eyes. "I will be all right soon. How are you?"

He sighed. "I feel as if I should cleanse myself in the river. It was the Exteca boy?"

"Yes," said Calindor, though his father had asked Tilcalli. He explained what had happened. By the time he finished, his mother had stood up and walked slowly into the front room. The others followed her. Calindor snapped his fingers at the kindling in the fireplace, and flames sprang up. Dragasa helped his wife sit in her chair by the hearth and then looked at Calindor.

"You can still do magic."

"Yes, Father."

"I tried to cast a spell of protection over your mother when I felt the Exteca's spell. Nothing happened. I felt . . . numb. As if I had already done some great magic."

Deir bustled about, hanging a pot of soup over the fire and setting the table. Calindor turned to her.

"Did you feel the spell?"

"No. Nothing. He cut himself, did he?"

"Yes. Three times. You understand Cantarean very well now."

She ignored the compliment and plunged a wooden spoon into the soup kettle. "I wish he had cut deeper, and sent himself to his evil gods."

Callishandal arrived, out of breath; someone had told her about the incident as she was returning from the orchards, and she had run straight across the village. Tilcalli smiled wanly at her as Calindor told the story yet again.

"Well, you wanted to learn Exteca magic," Callishandal said when he had finished.

"Now I have no choice," he said. "They can make people wish to be slaves, they can kill every small creature in a field, and they can make our magicians weak and helpless. When they come, how will we stop them?"

Callishandal glanced at Deir and away again. The girl blushed, her face turning pink under her freckles.

"I can't stop them," Deir said angrily, ladling out soup. "You think I am some great witch, but I'm not. I couldn't stop them from taking my village, my mother." Her lips trembled. "I would kill them all if I could, but I'm just a girl."

Calindor took a bowl of soup from her. "Serve yourself, Deir, and sit with us. I know you do not see the Gariba, and you do not feel magic around you."

"A good thing, today," Tilcalli murmured.

"But I think Callia has a use for you," Calindor went on. "She called the sea dragon through you, and called us to you as well. When the time comes, she will act through you again."

"I don't know *anything* about your Callia!"

"She knows you and your people. She is strong there, even if you don't know her name, because your people lived wisely with her and within her."

"She didn't save my people."

Calindor dipped his bread in his soup and ate it. "We used to think that Callia was a god of love. We knew that when we fought, when we killed, we weakened her. When we loved, we strengthened her. And she is like that. When we hunt, we seek only the creatures that want to return to her. When we fight our enemies, we are unhappy that we must hurt her. But that is not all she is.

"She is not like a person, Deir, who strikes back at every blow. She is like a Gariba, only very much greater, and Gariba do not know themselves—they only rejoice in their power. Callia does not think as people do, but as a god does, slowly. *We* are her thoughts, and her dreams. When she speaks through us, as she spoke through Callishandal, it is we who give her words.

"I think she has chosen you, as she chose my parents and their parents, as she chose Callishandal, so that we could overthrow those who had abused her. She brought us to you, so I believe I must somehow serve her purpose—not only by saving you in the bay, but by learning from you."

"And from Nezaual," Deir snapped.

"Yes, and from him."

"Well, I have nothing to teach you, and he will teach you only evil."

Silence fell. They ate for a time without speaking. Dragasa wiped his bowl with a scrap of bread and looked up at Calindor.

"Magicians always want to learn more magic."

"Yes, Father. All magicians. That's why Nezaual was willing to come with us."

"But this is a magic I do not want to learn. Badakh magic is rough and cruel, and I do not like it, but I can use it. Exteca magic makes me feel . . . perhaps it is the way a slave feels."

"Worse," Tilcalli said. "It made me *want to obey*. Even when I was a slave in Aishadan, I did not want to be one." She turned to look at her son.

"When we came here and your voice was gone, and the dragon Obordur taught you, you decided to go back to Aishadan, to face the Firelord and all the Badakhar. I wanted you to stay, but your father supported you. You were right to go, and I was wrong to want to keep you here. Now I feel I am going against your will again, but I feel I must say this: do not learn what this boy has to teach. He has already brought a strange Gariba into our land. While it is here, I will not walk in that field again."

"I am listening to you, Mother."

In the long silence that followed, Deir and Calindor cleared the table and put the bowls on a wooden tray; Deir took them outside to wash them on the porch.

"This time I agree with your mother," Dragasa said. "It isn't that the boy's magic might corrupt you. It might corrupt a weaker magician, but not you. Calindor, if his spells affect us as this one did, we will not last long. He will not kill us, but he will make us useless as magicians. You have brought a diseased horse into the herd."

"I am listening to you also, Father."

They heard steps and words on the porch; then Svordo looked in, grinning.

"Good evening to all, and we've been having a time cleaning up that foreigner of yours, Calindor. Never seen anything like it. He came staggering in not long ago, covered in blood and singing some strange song. Said something about a spell he cast at your command."

"Come and sit with us, Svordo," Calindor said. "I'm glad he got back to the inn. What is he doing now?"

"Sleeping in his room. I told him he'd better not cut himself while he's in one of my good beds, or I'd give him the last cut he'll ever feel. I thought I'd better let you know what's happened."

"Thank you. Do people know what the spell was about?"

"Something about killing rats? I didn't pay much attention."

"I'll walk back with you. I want to talk to Nezaual. Callishandal, will you come with me?"

"Of course."

No one spoke much on the walk back through the village. As they entered the courtyard of the inn, five or six people were coming out, a little unsteadily and smelling of beer.

"A mighty spell indeed," one of them said.

"Driving all the rats and insects out of a harvest field," said another. "Now there's a practical spell. The Siragi Aibela never learned how to do that. Maybe they ought to try spilling a little of their precious blood now and then."

The others laughed; none noticed Calindor, who glanced at Callishandal with a faint smile.

The dining hall was busy with late afternoon drinking and gossiping; the air smelled of harvesters' sweat and spilled beer. Calindor, Callishandal, and Svordo walked past the big room and down a corridor. Near its end was a plain plank door. Svordo knocked once, then pushed it open.

The room was small and dim, lighted only by a narrow window. Nezaual lay on his bed, a bandage tied around his waist under a pair of light trousers. His chest was bare. He seemed to Calindor a little dazed.

"How are you feeling, beloved son?"

Nezaual smiled. "I am well, honored father. The spell worked. No rat or insect will enter that field until next spring."

"I believe you. Now I must ask you to allow me to examine your wounds."

"Of course. But they are not serious." Almost casually, Nezaual tugged at the bandage until it came loose. Fresh blood oozed out over darker clots. Calindor heard his wife take a deep breath, but he had already focused. Down on one knee beside the bed, he put his hands over the Exteca's wounds.

Strange Gariba hovered above the cuts, almost like mosquitoes seeking blood. Calindor tried to ignore them, bringing his focus into the wounds and beyond them into Nezaual's body. Many spells had settled in his flesh and bone, and each had left its mark. Calindor studied each in turn, his eyes closed.

Yes . . . he could recognize the function of many spells, but not the method. Nezaual's body was like the strange map Yetecuan had shown them in Burnbaile—Calindor could see what was there, but he could not understand the details.

Scar tissue was everywhere, and much of it ran deep; it glowed in Calindor's focus, shimmering with the unknown Powers that redmagic had called forth and trapped. He did not try to speak to them; once he had called out Powers he had not understood, and had nearly paid with his life.

Nezaual had been right: the three new cuts were not serious, and Svordo had cleaned them properly. Calindor murmured a small spell of healing.

"Beloved son, again I forbid you to perform magic. In time you will show me more of your art, but for now lie still and rest, and do not trouble the Powers or your gods."

"I obey you, honored father." Nezaual smiled affectionately at him, and fell asleep.

They left him and walked back down to the dining hall. Svordo led them through the crowded tables and into the kitchen. He drew three tall flagons of dark beer and carried them into his own quarters—a room no larger than Nezaual's. Callishandal took the single chair, while the two men sat on the edge of the bed facing her.

"What did you think?" Callishandal asked.

"An arrowhead is an arrowhead whether it's steel or copper or flint. I can see spells of protection, spells of healing, but I don't know how they work." Calindor lifted his flagon and drank. "When I think of all we saw when we went south, I begin to think the sea dragons were the simplest. Nezaual's people don't think as we do, and their thoughts are dangerous."

"But you still want to know those thoughts."

"I must."

"You want to," she repeated. " 'Must' is only an excuse."

Calindor laughed. "Perhaps so. I am no magician if I can't even deceive my wife."

"I hear people talk," Svordo said, "and no one seems to worry about these southerners except you. Some say you're just jealous of their magic, or looking for an enemy."

"Looking for an enemy?" Calindor felt a flare of anger; then he sighed and relaxed. "I can see why they might say so. They still see me as more Badakh than Cantarean, and sometimes I think they're right. The Badakhar are miserable without someone to fight."

"And so are you," Callishandal said with a smile. "Drink your beer and cheer up! What are you going to do about learning Nezaual's magic?"

"For now, nothing. Talk with him a little, perhaps, learn the words." Seeing her expression, he smiled. "Don't worry—I'm not going to slice myself. But Nezaual won't be able to cast another spell for days—more likely weeks. And I won't have him cast a spell anywhere near here. You saw what my parents were like."

"So you'll take him away from Tanshadabela?" she asked.

"In the spring, when we go out onto the prairie. I want to talk with Renjosudaldor and the other Gulyaji magicians. And with the Badakh magicians too. They may understand redmagic better than anyone. But until then I need to study Deir."

"Just don't ask *her* to cast a spell!" Callishandal said. "If Nezaual could affect you and your parents as he did, think what Deir could do."

Calindor lifted his flagon and drank. "Yes," he said. "I often think about what she could do."

Tilcalli did not go out to the harvest next day. She slept much of the morning, and then went out in the afternoon to gather firewood. The day was chilly and overcast, a warning of the winter to come. She listened to the Gariba flying on the wind, playing in the treetops, and felt her spirits rise a little, but only a little. The Exteca's spell still lingered in her thoughts like a bad taste on the tongue.

By late afternoon she had stacked a tall pile of firewood beside her family sweat lodge, not far downriver from the village. Then she went home to change her clothes. Deir was there, pulling loaves of bread out of the oven.

"Good," said Tilcalli. "That will do for everyone's supper. I'm fasting today and going to take a sweat bath."

"May I come with you?"

The question caught her by surprise. "If you wish. Is it a custom among your people also?"

"Sometimes."

"I will be glad of your company."

They walked together through the village and along the bank of the Cantabela. The river was low, running in countless noisy streams in its wide bed of rounded pink and gray stones. The path led through open stands of lodgepole and fir, with wolf willow and juniper growing everywhere. From every clearing the women could look up at mountains mantled in new white.

"The snow looks strange," Deir said. "I can't wait until it falls down here. It snowed once in Burnbaile, long before I was born."

Tilcalli laughed. "You will get all the snow you like, and then a little more."

They reached the lodge as darkness was beginning to fall. It was a simple log cabin, really just a lean-to, with a stone hearth and chimney taking up one side. It had no windows, only a narrow gap under the door to admit a little air. Tilcalli started a small fire in the hearth, calling on the Powers of Fire and Air to help her; it was not a spell, only a prayer, but the flames leaped up eagerly as she finished. While Deir went to fetch two buckets of water from the river, Tilcalli built up the fire.

The girl came back and put the buckets inside the lodge. Tilcalli stood outside the door and looked west at the darkening sky.

"Callia," she said quietly, "I am tired and frightened, and I need to cleanse myself of weariness and fear. I have done your will, and given my life to you. I have given my husband and son as well, and I know they are still angry with me for that. A foreign magician has fouled one of our fields, and his magic makes me sick of all magic. I have done your will, but I am not content. I ask that you cleanse me, that you give me some peace, and that you help this foreign girl as well."

She pulled off her deerskin tunic, embroidered with many beads and porcupine quills, and pushed down her trousers. The air was cold on her body. Deir did the same: Tilcalli marveled at the girl's skin, almost luminously white in the twilight. Even in the darkness her hair gleamed like the fire on the hearth. But what a slender, frail child she seemed, scarcely a woman, even if red fuzz grew between her legs and her breasts had begun to swell. Deir shivered in the cold, and Tilcalli pulled open the door of the sweat lodge.

A rough bench faced the hot stone wall; they sat side by side. The sweat lodge was dark, shimmering with heat. Tilcalli crushed juniper berries between her hands and dropped them in the water buckets. Then she cupped her hands in one bucket and splashed the water on the hot wall. Aromatic steam flashed out, stinging their faces and making their eyes water.

For a long time they sat there without speaking, while one or the other threw water on the stone wall. Then Deir spoke softly:

"Why did she choose me?"

"Callia? I don't know. Why did she choose me, or Calindor? Do you know what I did for Callia?"

"Callishandal told me a little. You conceived your son with Dragasa, and then you let yourself be captured by a young prince of the Badakhar. He took you away to his kingdom in the east, and Calindor grew up there thinking he was the prince's son. Then he learned the truth, and became a great magician. He overthrew a god named Mekhpur, and the prince, and then he left this country and came to my country."

"It was a plan. Calindor was right when he told you that gods think slowly. Callia was dying at the hands of the Badakhar, and she took centuries to save herself. First she took us, the Siragi Aibela, the Cold Spring clan, and made a place for us that we call the Open Dream. We go there to speak and dance with our ancestors, and when we die we join them and become mentors to our descendants. My great-great-grandmother welcomed me into the Open Dream when I was a little girl, and told me what I must do to save Callia." She threw more water on the rocks.

"I must marry within the clan, which was a scandal, but my child must be born of two strong magicians. Then I must let myself be captured by the Badakhar so that my child could grow up to learn their magic as well as ours.

"And I did all that Callia wanted of me, and my son did save Callia, and we have tried to become the family we might have been. But I am a stranger to my husband, and to my son as well. Calindor went off to the dragons, and then to find you, and now he worries about Nezaual's people."

Tilcalli did not speak for a time. Then she said: "When I was a girl I was proud of my skill, and I was glad to serve Callia."

"You were very brave," Deir said.

Tilcalli wiped sweat from her eyes. "I thought so too," she said with a smile. "Now I think I was just foolish. All I wanted to do was save my little village from the Badakhar, and now we are in greater danger than ever. If the Badakhar had conquered us, we would at least have kept our souls free. But Nezaual—"

"I know. I saw my mother, and everyone else."

"You are immune to it. And you have some kind of great power, but such power always seems to end in destruction and death."

"So does weakness."

"Yes. So does weakness." Tilcalli got up and went outside to feed the fire. She came back shivering. "Cold!"

Deir's voice was soft in the darkness: "Will I destroy the Exteca?"

"Or yourself, or us, or everyone. No one ever cast a spell like the one you did on the last day of summer. I thought Calindor would be the greatest magician Sotalar had ever known, but you will be greater by far."

"I want . . . I want to punish the Exteca, but I don't want to kill them all. I just want my mother to be herself again, and Burnbaile to be home." She began to cry. "I don't want to be a magician!"

Tilcalli put her arm around the girl, startled by both her slenderness and her hardness. Deir leaned against her, sobbing, and Tilcalli rocked her back and forth.

"I'll sing you a song, and then you sing me one." And Tilcalli began to sing an old lullaby, one she had rocked Calindor to sleep with when his name was Dheribi. How could it seem so long ago, and so recent?

Deir stopped crying, and after a while she began to sing. It was not like the song she had sung before; this was a kind of lullaby too, full of love and sadness and hope. Tilcalli sighed as she listened, and felt her own sadness and anger loosen a little, and then a little more.

Suddenly she felt as if she were sitting on the edge of a precipice she could not see, as if one step forward would send her falling or flying. What was at the bottom? She did not want to know; but she sensed that it was something even worse than redmagic, something deep in Deir's soul beyond all reach of healing. She hugged the girl again.

"It's time to go home. Come."

They went outside with the remaining water in the two buckets. The light of the fire in the hearth threw a flickering yellow glow over Tilcalli's brown skin, Deir's white skin. Giggling, Tilcalli tipped one of the buckets over Deir's head. The girl shrieked at the shock of the cold water and then tipped her own bucket over Tilcalli. Shivering and chattering, they pulled on their clothes and then made torches from long branches. With these they lighted their way home through the woods, hand in hand.

Tilcalli felt a kind of serenity she had not known in a long time. Yes, the girl would bring some kind of terrible new destruction, but it would be part of Callia's will; so be it. The dragons had fled from her, but they had not tried to kill her.

I must serve her as I served my son.

"What's that?" Deir asked as they neared the village. Something seemed to be glittering in the light of their simple torches, like the gnats that sought summer fires.

"It's snow, Deir."

"Snow! Snow! It's snowing!"

Laughing, they ran into the village as the dark path began to grow light beneath their feet.

Ten

The air was sharp, clean and cold. Remnants of the first snowfall lingered in every shaded patch of ground, but the sky was cloudless and the sun blazed down on the mountains. Not far up the little Cantabela River a bridge connected the village with the fields and orchards to the south. This morning Calindor and Nezaual walked down to the bridge carrying backpacks, while Tilcalli, Dragasa, and Deir accompanied them.

At the bridge they said farewell. "We'll be back within five or six days," Calindor promised.

"Be sure that you are," his mother said with a slightly strained smile. "We still have plenty of work before winter."

The two young men trudged south along the left bank of the Cantabela. The going was slow. Elk had used the trail recently, their hooves punching into the snow crust to the mud below. The fields were now carpets of yellow stubble, where horses grazed for whatever the harvesters had left. The Cantabela, though diminished at this time of year, still roared and clattered off to the left of the trail. With the sun low in the southern sky, most of the mountains were black bulks outlined in white fire.

Calindor kept an appraising eye on Nezaual. Just a few days after casting his spell, the Exteca seemed fully recovered. He might not yet be ready to do magic, but he walked with a light step and carried his pack without trouble. Good: they had far to go.

All that day they walked through open forest and grassland, practicing one another's language. The trail was narrow, cut deep into the soil by humans, horses, and elk. No one else was abroad.

"It's *cataval*, harvest season," Calindor explained. "Everyone's too busy storing their grain and vegetables. After they're finished they'll get out and do a little trading before winter truly settles in."

"In Tola the trading never stops. And only on the frontiers do we have empty land between towns. It is strange to think that this valley is full of your people. How many Cantareans live in these mountains?"

Calindor suppressed a smile. He had been a spy himself once; he knew Nezaual was more than idly curious.

"That's hard to say. Some of the old villages are empty now, and others are much bigger than they used to be. When I first saw Tanshadabela, it was less than half the size it is now. In any case, it doesn't matter. We're going into true wilderness, where no one lives."

Nezaual looked puzzled, but did not ask why. He had accepted Calindor's command to accompany him, and had not inquired about the purpose of their journey. Such unquestioning obedience was convenient, Calindor thought, but if it was a trait of the Exteca, it might be used against them somehow.

In late afternoon they came to another trail, angling west along the edge of a creek. By now Nezaual did seem tired; he was sweating in his fur-lined tunic and pants, and his skin was flushed. Yet he followed without complaint as the trail grew increasingly steep. The elk had abandoned the uplands long before the first snowfall, so snow lay thick and unbroken on the tree-shaded trail.

At length they emerged from the forest onto a hillside of exposed gravel, too steep and rocky to support trees. The trail was a treacherous scratch, no more, across the hill. Here they could look north, east, and south over the great valley of the Cantabela. With the sun almost down, the peaks across the valley seemed to float, burning, above the dark river.

Calindor pointed to fine threads of smoke far up the river:

"Hanashar, Shadamidan, Valadan, Supalarea, Faradesta. Those are some of our towns. I haven't visited them all, and there are more still farther south."

"And all have magicians living in them, like your family."

"They have magicians who *are* my family. The Siragi Aibela are the magicians' clan; we are all related."

"Whole families of magicians! This is a wonder."

Calindor looked a little uncomfortable. "Most people in the clan aren't really magicians. If you're a Cantarean man, you're supposed to marry out of your clan, and then your children belong to your wife's clan. My mother and father were both born into the Siragi Aibela, so they should both have married outside the clan. Instead they married each other. It was a scandal."

"But they married so that they might have a child with talent from both parents?" Nezaual asked.

Calindor nodded. "It was my great-great-grandmother Calihalingol's idea," he explained, and carefully kept from smiling at the baffled look in Nezaual's eyes. Let him think his grasp of Cantarean was still weak.

"If men marry out of their clan," Nezaual continued, "then your clan's talent for magic would soon disappear, or else be spread among all your people."

"Perhaps. But if a young man in another clan shows the talent, it's likely that the parents will arrange a marriage into the Siragi Aibela. I think I caused a scandal also, because my parents did not arrange my marriage to Callishandal. We chose each other."

Nezaual looked embarrassed. "Choosing one's own wife? I am sorry, honored father, but among my people that would be disrespect for one's parents."

"Many among my people say the same thing. But do the Exteca encourage magicians to have children?"

"The True Gods send magicians to all our clans, which shows their kindness because our magicians do not marry. Sometimes a family will hide a child's talent if they want him to become a warrior or a merchant, but usually they are glad to give such boys to the priests. A real magician is not much good for any other calling."

"As with us and the Badakhar," Calindor said with a laugh. "But what about your women magicians?"

"A woman can't be a magician among us, honored father!" Nezaual looked even more embarrassed. "Some may have a little talent for healing or easing childbirth, but for real magic we need men."

"Is my mother not a magician, then?"

"Well," muttered Nezaual. "Cantareans are strange people."

I often think so too, Calindor thought. But he felt slightly reassured to hear such foolishness. Nezaual still did not realize who had cast the spell that night in Burnbaile; if he insisted on dismissing the idea of women as real magicians, so much the better. Calindor knew how valuable an enemy's blind spots could be.

But what are my own blind spots? What is it that Nezaual sees that I do not?

They climbed on across the gravelly hillside and came to a broad, steep ridge of stone running southwest to join the forested slopes of a mountain. From here they could look west into a steep-walled valley, and east into the far greater valley of the Cantabela. Every horizon was a jagged line of snowcapped peaks.

"All these lands belonged to the dragons once," Calindor said. "Their ancestors lived here when the mountains were young."

"How do you know this, honored father?"

"A dragon named Obordur granted me a vision once, when I could speak no more than she could."

Nezaual looked baffled again, and Calindor smiled. "Never mind. Up there is a cabin; we'll spend the night."

Hunters had built it long ago, before the Siragi Aibela had taken it as their own. It was more a lean-to than a real cabin, but snug enough: last year, when Dragasa had first brought him here, they had spent a day putting fresh clay between the logs and repairing the chimney. Calindor soon had a fire burning on its crude hearth, and they warmed themselves as they ate bread and butter and dried apples.

"How much farther must we go, honored father?"

"Almost as far as we have come today, and it will be harder travel."

"Why do we go so far from Tanshadabela?"

"I am going to learn some redmagic from you, without troubling my parents or any other magicians in this valley."

He saw a gleam of excitement in Nezaual's dark eyes. "I will teach you what little I know, honored father."

"And I will teach you some magic in exchange. Here is a good spell for the Gariba of water. Your boots are wet; take them off and hold them in your hands."

Nezaual obeyed. Calindor taught him four words, one at a time, and then told him to focus. Nezaual spoke the words smoothly and confidently, but almost instantly looked alarmed. Steam swirled out of the leather with a faint hiss. Calindor put a hand down one of the boots and then handed them back.

"Well done on the first try, beloved son."

Nezaual, panting a little, pulled his boots back on and smiled.

"They are wonderfully warm and dry, honored father! I thank you for your kindness. I never would have thought a spell to drive away water would be so useful—all our water spells are to bring it to us."

"Would you like to show me one?"

"When I have recovered my powers, honored father. I could do nothing now."

Calindor knew from the strength of Nezaual's focus that he still had plenty of ability left. But he did not press the matter. Tomorrow he would begin to test Nezaual's strength in earnest.

They sat companionably by the fire, each in his own sleeping bag, while Nezaual told stories about his people: how the True Gods had led them from the world of the dead into this one, how they had wandered for years in harsh deserts and arrived at last at the shore of the sea to found Tola. In those wandering years the Exteca had known little magic beyond that needed to heal a wound or illness.

"Then the priest Patlikimili, Medicine Bundle, learned the first spells of redmagic in a dream the True Gods sent. They wanted gifts from us, so they gave us gifts also. Tola was a tiny village, with a single spring. When it dried up, people suffered and their crops died. Patlikimili went to the spring, which was only rocks and dry mud, and pierced his own tongue and penis with cactus spines. He invoked the help of the Gods, and gave his blood to them. In exchange the Gods gave back the water, and it flowed up through the rocks more strongly than ever."

"Is it only blood that your gods value?"

"They love flesh also, especially the flesh of the heart. When we feed them, they grow strong, and then they become even hungrier."

"So you must feed them more."

"Of course."

"Tell me, Nezaual: do your gods ever send spirits to possess human bodies?"

"Certainly, honored father! But it is a very rare honor."

Calindor said nothing for a while. "It happens with us sometimes too. The great magicians among the Badakhar can call a spirit from the Black World to possess a human. We call such a creature a jenji, a not-person. But it is not an honor. It is a horror."

"I see you are alarmed, honored father. That is because you do not yet understand redmagic or the True Gods. Tomorrow, I hope, I will show you something of their beauty."

Calindor suppressed a sudden shudder. Nezaual had of course used the Cantarean word for beauty: *callia*. How could the goddess of the Cantareans have anything in common with the bloody magic of the Exteca?

They slept under a ring of dragonfire too dark to see, but hot enough to keep them warm. In the morning they woke before dawn, made tea, and ate dried apples and camas root.

"We are going to a place my father showed me last year," Calindor said as they set out again on the trail. "The Siragi Aibela have used it for many years as a place for learning new magic."

The trail led roughly west, around the north flank of the mountain. Many times they had to cross icy streams, stepping from one slippery rock to the next. Here, shaded from the sun, the snow had partially melted and refrozen until it was hard and slick. Both men fell again and again, but Calindor kept them going.

At last, not long before noon, the trail turned south and followed the edge of a forested valley half filled by a lake of intense blue-green. Islands of ice drifted across its surface, fusing to one another. Calindor pointed up the trail, above the tops of the spruce trees that surrounded them. In the south rose an immense cliff of layered stone, crusted with ice and snow and filling half the sky.

"I recognize the mountain now," Nezaual said. "I have seen it from the village."

"They call it Burdan Atana, the great mountain between."

"Between what?"

"Between this world and the *theala*, the gods."

Once past the lake, they followed a narrow but noisy stream that raged white in its bed. At last they emerged from the forest into a great open space. Nezaual looked up in awe and murmured something under his breath before turning to Calindor.

"Honored father, this is a holy place."

They stood at the northern end of a valley of brown and black stone, where almost nothing grew. Westward, to their right, the valley floor sloped steeply up to a moraine of gigantic boulders; beyond the moraine the mountain rose sheer to an unmeasurable height. Farther down the valley a glacier descended like a waterfall from a great cirque, smothering the cliff. Beyond the glacier the mountain rose again in the great snow-crusted cliff that Nezaual had seen from the village; and eastward, to their left, another moraine rose like a wall. Beyond it was dense forest climbing to an unseen crest that must overlook the valley of the Cantabela.

A dull boom resounded down the valley; the men saw a cascade of ice and snow spill with dreamlike slowness down the cliff at the southern end. As if in answer, the glacier cracked and roared. A cold wind blew through the valley, and Nezaual shuddered.

"Come," said Calindor.

He led the way along a barely visible trail that followed the noisy stream. A dun soil lay thin over huge rocks; here and there a stunted pine struggled for life, but only lichen seemed to belong here.

"Honored father, what is the name of the god who lives here? Please do not speak it if it is a True God," Nezaual added earnestly.

"No god lives here. The Gariba of water made this, before men came to Sotalar. That glacier once filled this whole valley with ice, from one moraine to the other." Calindor pointed west and then east at the parallel lines of gigantic boulders. "The dragons lived here then, and roved across the glaciers. If you focus, you will sense their presence."

Nezaual did so, and immediately fell to his knees on the snowy trail. His eyes stared up at the empty blue sky beyond the saw-tooth ridges that crested Burdan Atana.

"I see them."

"You see their traces only, left where they once played. Sometimes real dragons return from their lands in the west, but not often. When Callia overthrew the Five Kingdoms, many came back to Cantarea for a while, and then went on to the far north.

"Enough, Nezaual, let go your focus. We still have a way to go."

Through the short afternoon they walked the length of the valley until they stood on the gravel shore of a pale green lake. Much of it was ice-covered, and its southern edge was a cliff of ice three times the height of a man. A mantle of scree lay over the top of the ice, extending back to the base of the cliffs. The lake was at the foot of the glacier also. From here the men could see the glacier, a column of ice, descend the cliff like one of the rapids they had ascended in *Tilcalli*. Far up the cliff the glacier spread north and south in two vast blue-white wings, and beyond them rose the harsh walls of the cirque.

"What we see of the glacier is only a part," Calindor told him. "Most of it is out of sight, in a bowl almost as big as this valley."

Somewhere up in that torrent of ice, something broke again. Thunder echoed among the cliffs under the cloudless sky. When it died away, the only sounds were those of running water in the stream and falling water roaring down the glacier.

Calindor glanced about and then sat on a flat-topped stone that had, thousands of years ago, been ripped from the heart of the mountain and carried to this place.

"Now," he said, "tell me about redmagic."

This is not a proper raiding party, Yetecuan thought. *It is more like the years of the desert, when we wandered homeless.*

A raiding party almost never went into unknown country; the pochteca would have done detailed reconnaissance first. A raiding party would stick together, with scouts on all sides, and it would move in precise stages until it was ready to strike.

But this great expedition broke all the rules. Every step took them deeper into lands never before seen or even heard of. Though Tola had sent bale upon bale of supplies, the expedition must live largely off the land, so its divisions were scattered and none followed in another's track; where the Exteca rode or walked, nothing edible remained.

General Yaocatl had fretted at first as his forces arrived in the lands of the Airn and prepared to venture on into unknown country. He had shared his fears, of course, with Yetecuan: ambush, attrition, battles with nameless tribes that might think a single Exteca division too weak to fight. But day had followed day without even the sight of a human being; this was the northern wilderness, still waiting for civilization.

Yetecuan rode one of the mammoths in the vanguard division, a rare luxury and one half forced upon him. The warriors were under command to cherish and protect him, and they forbade him to weary himself when they might need his magic at any moment. Colotic, the ever reliable warrior who had taken Burnbaile, rode a pony beside the mammoth, where he might converse with the priest at need.

The riding hut was really most convenient, Yetecuan thought. It was made of bamboo, with low walls and a waterproof roof. Designed for archers who needed plenty of room and unimpeded vision, the hut now furnished its lone passenger with a comfortable couch upon which he might even nap if he chose. The mammoth driver, a tough young fellow named Mixnal, rode just behind the beast's little ears; he guided the mammoth with soft commands and an occasional tap from a long, ornately carved stick.

The expedition had left the lands of the Airn ten days ago and was now moving north through a great uninhabited valley. It was grassland and open woods, abundant with game animals and wild foods of all kinds. The soil would welcome corn; Yetecuan had already sent messages south, urging the Tecutli Itztlac to send colonists at once.

When he suspended a knife from a thread, Yetecuan could see that the gold lip plug that he had given Calindor was somewhere northeast. Eventually the expedition would have to turn in that direction; but for now they were doing well. Scouts ranging east had found foothills and a forbidding mountain range beyond them; northward the land was increasingly dry and harsh, but permitted quick travel.

The scouts, traveling among the Exteca columns, were also learning about great tracts of land. Every night, when he dismounted from the mammoth, Yetecuan interrogated whatever scouts had come in. Thanks to them he had begun a map of this whole valley, and his dispatches to Itztlac supplied detailed accounts of its resources.

What a province this would make! He could see pyramids rising above its fertile plains and streams, wilderness tamed and given to the True Gods. If not for the threat in the north, this valley would occupy all the efforts of the Exteca for a generation or more.

This evening the column had camped in gradually rising hills; beyond them, still bright in the light of the setting sun, snow-capped peaks rose into the darkening sky. Yetecuan had eaten, moved his bowels, consulted with the scouts and added a little more to his map. He sacrificed an Airn bearer as the evening gift to the Gods, and gave the heart to the campfire of General Yaocatl; the flesh went to the rest of the bearers, mixed with beans and chilies.

Yaocatl was in a good mood, joking with his officers as they spooned up their own beans. But he noticed Yetecuan's worried expression.

"Honored father, something troubles you tonight. May I share your burden?"

"It is kind of you to ask, beloved son. Perhaps it is no real concern, but we will soon run out of sacrifices. It is prudent to use the bearers as we consume the supplies they carry, but soon we will have to preserve them. I never imagined that this land would be so empty of humanity."

"Nor did I. At least we do not have to spend time conquering anyone, and we can keep you and your magicians rested. But I understand your concern. If we find no other tribes between here and the Magicians' Land, perhaps we can promise the Gods a great slaughter when we get there."

"Of course we shall. But I do wish we could end each day properly."

Colotic, who had taken Burnbaile so easily, was sitting near Yaocatl. He gained permission to speak and rubbed his palms thoughtfully.

"Perhaps, honored father, we could ask our beloved Ometollin to make a sacrifice in our name each night in Tola. He will have no shortage there, and it will keep our names in the people's prayers."

Yetecuan beamed. "This is a wise warrior, Yaocatl, and the Gods will look after him with love."

Yaocatl nodded. "Tomorrow's couriers will carry our request to Tola. I think you have helped to hasten us on our way, beloved Colotic."

The warriors around the fire all murmured, "Ha ya, ha ya." Colotic looked impassively into the flames, but then looked up and met Yetecuan's eyes. The priest saw a boyish pride in the warrior's face, and felt yet another burst of affection for Colotic and all the others who had marched for weeks into the unknown.

The True Gods love and guide us every step of the way,
Yetecuan thought contentedly.

No dragonfire, no fire of any kind burned on the shore of the
glacial lake. A few streaks of cloud glowed red above the jagged
ridges of Burdan Atana, and snow reflected it back into the darkening sky.

Calindor sat cross-legged on the icy gravel, hands on his knees,
looking across the half-frozen lake at the scree and cliff beyond.
The wind off the glacier struck him harder than a fist, numbing
him. A few steps in front of him, Nezaual sang to the True Gods,
asking them to recognize him. His voice at last sank away, and
the only sounds were the wind and the water cascading down the
glacier.

Calindor felt the Gariba of water and earth close around him.
Though the glacier had retreated from this valley long ago, its
Gariba had not; they swarmed around him, as if he were but a
stone at the bottom of a lake. The sky was showing stars now, but
he felt as if he were deep in the caverns of the Gulyaji.

Nezaual stepped forward, hands close together and a thin obsidian blade held between left thumb and forefinger. The blade
touched the flesh of his forearm and hot blood spattered on
Calindor's face and hair.

The great ice-carved valley seemed to fill with red light, and
within that light something moved. It was a woman's shape,
heavy-breasted, dancing in a garment of living snakes. However
Calindor turned his head to see her, she kept at the edge of his vision. But he could hear her feet scrape and rattle on the gravel of
the lakeshore.

"We greet and honor you, Cihuacoatl, Lady Serpent," Nezaual
whispered. "We seek the gift of water. May we do you some service in exchange?" His voice faltered a moment. "Please do not
try to look at her, honored father. You might succeed."

Calindor sat unmoving, listening to the goddess's feet rasping
out a dance. He felt a cold very different from the freezing air. He
sensed her close behind him, studying him and then turning away.
A low, humming chuckle came from her. It grew louder and suddenly ended.

The red light was gone; late autumn twilight filled the valley
again. Calindor breathed, breathed again, and sent out a focus that
swept the whole valley. Only the ordinary Gariba were there, as
if nothing had happened. He glanced down and saw something
resting on his tunic where it stretched across his lap: small, white,
delicate. The skull of a snake.

Nezaual saw it also, and leaned forward to see it better. Even in the gloom Calindor could see how weary the spell had made him.

"Ha ya . . . This is a very great honor she gives you, honored father. A skull from her left wristlet. The right wristlet is skulls of men."

Calindor felt Nezaual's blood drying on his face. He breathed twice again before he spoke: "What is the significance, beloved son?"

"She has accepted you as her servant, and she has accepted this land as part of her domain. I think she likes this valley very much."

"I did not ask to become her *servant*," Calindor said through his teeth. "Or the servant of any of your gods."

"Of course not, honored father! That would be arrogant and foolish. The Gods choose us, not we them."

"And this valley is Callia's, not some snake god's."

Nezaual looked at him wearily, without comprehension. "But—Cihuacoatl, Callia—they are the same."

Calindor sprang to his feet, holding the snake skull in one hand. He crushed it, felt threadlike splinters of bone pierce his skin, and hurled the fragments away. Dragonfire splashed from his bleeding hand and blackened the ground until no trace of the bones remained.

"She wanted to *kill* us," he snarled, turning on Nezaual in rage. "Couldn't you feel that?"

"Of course, honored father! Of course she wanted to kill us; she loves all who call on her, and wishes to keep them with her forever. But we still live, and it is her gift to us out of her infinite love."

Calindor did not answer, but turned on his heel and walked away. It was full dark now, but his focus showed him every rock and tuft of moss. He walked west along the shore of the lake and up onto the scree slope that buried part of the glacier. The slow dance of the Gariba in the ice was oddly consoling: they would kill him too, if he let them, but not out of love.

He found a boulder and sat upon it. Below him stretched the lake, mottled black and white in the darkness. Nezaual was clear in Calindor's focus, huddled in a blanket.

Sometimes, in the old days, the Veikar—the chief magicians of the Badakhar—had called monsters from a realm they called the Black World. Once his mother had sent one back, freeing it from a Veik's command. It had been easier than it seemed, for Tilcalli's magic had only helped the creature return to where it belonged.

No Sending would drive Cihuacoatl anywhere, he realized. In the red light, as she danced, he had seen that she belonged here in Sotalar as much as anyone did. He did not believe, could not believe, that she was an expression of Callia. But she inhered in this world, she was part of it, and she wielded power as naturally as the Gariba.

Something hot and wet fell on his cheek, almost like a tear. He looked up and saw the stars had gone, and with them the last light. The sky was overcast, and a warm rain began to patter on the cold stones. Mist rose until the lake vanished. Out of the mist, barely audible, came Nezaual's voice:

"Lady Serpent gives what we ask of her."

Eleven

Calindor sat, unspeaking, in the warm rain and utter darkness. Not until the rain turned cold and then began to fall as ice pellets did he stir himself and walk back to the edge of the lake. The spell he had taught Nezaual served to dry their clothes. A solid disk of dragonfire shielded them from what was now a blizzard. In its orange glare he unrolled his sleeping bag on the gravelly soil and then sat cross-legged upon it.

"I have seen the power of redmagic," he said. "Now tell me how it works."

All that night Nezaual talked. He spoke of the tonalli, the Powers of skin and flesh; of the teyolia, the Powers of the heart; of the ihiyotl, the Powers of the breath. He gave the deep names of atl, water, and tlachinolli, fire. He gave the deep names of nal, air, and tlalli, earth. He spoke of the great cycle, by which tonacayo, "our flesh," went into the soil, returned to life as the corn, and changed once more into flesh.

Without wearying, for he was past weariness, Nezaual spoke of the parts of the body and their value to the True Gods: the gift of blood from tongue, from earlobe, from belly, from genitals and face.

"Ordinary people may give these gifts also, but they will not see a God. The God may grant their wish, or not; these are personal concerns. Priests bargain with the Gods on behalf of all Exteca. We do see the Gods, or as much as we cannot avoid seeing."

"But you and I saw the Lady Serpent. Wasn't your invocation a personal concern?"

"Oh no, honored father! It is a concern of our whole empire that you recognize the True Gods and choose to serve them."

Calindor said nothing. He had suspected that something like that concern had occurred to the old priest, Yetecuan, when he had agreed to let Nezaual go with the Cantareans. After all, that was why Calindor had also wanted Deir: whatever power she might possess, he wanted it safely allied to his own. The Exteca would of course want Calindor serving them and their gods.

He suppressed a shudder. Odd that magicians, who were too obsessed with magic to care about ruling, should worry about magic as it enhanced the rule of their kings. In the days of the Five Kingdoms, the Badakh magicians had maintained an uneasy balance with one another; any who sought too much power would find the others allied against him—and thus against his king. So each king could defend his own land and sometimes snatch a bit of his neighbors', but none could gain power over all.

The Cantareans had no kings, and scarcely any government, but the Siragi Aibela were crucial nonetheless. Without them, no field in the valley of the Cantabela would yield enough to support its owners. The Cantareans would not be free and equal farmers, but bands of hunters and scavengers, ruled by whoever could feed them with spear and snare.

His stepfather Albohar, once the Aryo of Aishadan, had dreamed of uniting the Five Kingdoms into a single empire, and he had been ready to use any magic to achieve that end. Instead he had brought disaster upon himself and all the Badakhar kingdoms. Now the Exteca sought an even greater empire, and would need every magician they could find.

But it's futile. They conquer so they can feed their gods, and every sacrifice only makes their gods hungrier. Surely they see it.

But Calindor saw no point in quarreling with Nezaual about his empire's motives. As soon explain to a Badakh why Callia had overthrown the Five Kingdoms.

"The great spell of redmagic is what Yetecuan cast upon the people of Burnbaile," he said. "In all the magics I know, a spell upon a human soul is the rarest and hardest. How did your master cast his spell upon Deir's people?"

"I do not know, honored father," Nezaual responded at once. "The spells of love and terror are very difficult. Only the greatest, wisest priests can learn them. I do not think so many as fifty of all our priests can cast them."

Calindor reached out and touched Nezaual's face; their eyes locked. "I know you are not lying, beloved son. But I do not know if you are telling me all the truth. You are not an apprentice magician. You called up a True God tonight. Now I ask you to explain the principle of the spells of love and terror."

He saw no resistance, no hesitation in the boy's face. Good: he was not experimenting with treachery. Or was it bad, that Nezaual took for granted that he was now a servant of the True Gods?

"The spells call upon the tonalli, honored father, the Powers of skin and flesh. Sometimes the mind and soul want different things from the skin and flesh, but sometimes they want the same thing. When the skin and flesh want love, sometimes they overpower the mind and soul. When the skin and flesh are afraid, the mind and soul cannot calm them. The spells of love and terror speak to our tonalli. And our minds and souls answer."

Calindor thought about Nezaual's words. It made a kind of sense. He could half enchant himself, simply by envisioning Callishandal's body locked to his, his lips against her breast. Once, in his youthful arrogance, he had ensorcelled the soul of a Badakh warrior, forbidding him from the rape of Cantarean children. Somehow, without understanding his own powers, he had destroyed the warrior's lust. Perhaps, as Yetecuan had inspired love in the people of Burnbaile, he himself had destroyed lust in that warrior's flesh.

Now he would have to move cautiously: to learn the spells of love and terror without a teacher, and then to devise counterspells. A priest like Yetecuan would not simply teach him, but enslave him in the process. Somehow, by the time the Exteca arrived in Cantarea—and they would, he was certain of it—he would have to make himself and his people immune to those spells.

"We have stayed here long enough," he said. "It is time to return home."

"As you wish, honored father." Nezaual lurched to his feet, swaying a little. "I hope I will not slow you down."

"You will not."

The night had been long and still showed no sign of ending. Beyond the orange glow of the dragonfire, the rain of Cihuacoatl had stopped; an icy crust covered the snow. Stars were shining through gaps in the cloud, a sign that natural weather was reasserting itself over the True God's gift.

They set off north up the valley, listening to the creaks and groans of the glacier. The frozen crust squeaked under their boots.

By the time they had descended from the valley to the lake beneath it, the sky was turning purple-blue and mountains were emerging from the night. Calindor called a halt, heated water in a little pot, and cooked grain into a dense cereal. They ate it steaming from the pot, scooping it out with wooden spoons. Then, revived, they went on down the mountain.

The descent was quick. By noon they were back at the cabin, where they stayed long enough to make a proper meal of bread and salted venison. Calindor was eager to be home, and would not rest though Nezaual seemed very weary.

"We will find our way home by dragonfire light if we must," he said. "I have much to do, and little time."

By late afternoon they were back in the valley of the Cantabela, on the main trail. The Lady Serpent's rain had not fallen here, but a night of frost had turned the mud rock-hard and easier to walk upon. They headed north for Tanshadabela, but almost at once a horseman overtook them.

"Callia bless us all!" he exclaimed as Calindor and Nezaual looked up at him. "I believe I've found my goal sooner than I thought. You are Calindor?"

"I am. This is Nezaual, my apprentice."

"Yes, the foreigner—we've heard of you. A pleasure to meet you both. I am Milivo, from Hanashar." He dismounted, pulled off a mitten and shook their hands. He was a broad-shouldered young man, his hair long and tied back. His tunic, of white buckskin, was ornately beaded in red, yellow, and orange. "We have need of you. The speaker of our hall sent me to ask if you would come to help us."

Calindor frowned. "Is it magic you need?"

"It is. We have a blight in our granary, poisoning the wheat and oats."

"My kinswoman Suripi lives in Hanashar. Can she not deal with this?"

"She has tried, and exhausted herself in the trying. She says this is a blight she has not seen before, and greenmagic has no effect on it."

Calindor stamped his feet to warm them. "This comes at an awkward time, Milivo. I have much to do in Tanshadabela."

Milivo smiled without pleasure. "Then you have at least saved me a longer journey, and I thank you for that." He climbed back onto his horse.

"Tell me," said Nezaual. "What happens if the blight does not go away?"

"Then we slaughter our horses and cattle to feed ourselves, and in the spring we will go hungry while we plant next year's crop."

Nezaual turned to Calindor and spoke quietly in Exteca: "Surely, honored father, we cannot turn away from this man and his village. A priest who does not serve his people does not serve the True Gods either."

Calindor gazed coldly at him. "I am a magician of the Siragi Aibela, not a priest of the True Gods." He spoke more harshly than he had intended, and heard the uncertainty in his own voice. *Am I a free magician, or a priest enslaved? If I do not master the spells of love and terror, I will not even be free enough to ask the question.*

"I am sorry, Milivo," he said, "but I have urgent tasks in Tanshadabela. Perhaps later this winter I will be able to visit Hanashar."

"We will welcome you at any time, Calindor." Milivo tugged his horse's reins.

"Wait," Nezaual said, again in Exteca. "Honored father, give me permission to go with him. I have some knowledge of pests and blights. Perhaps I can help."

Cold, tired, and worried, Calindor felt himself losing his temper. "How many human sacrifices will it take?" he asked in Cantarean. Milivo, who had understood nothing until now, stared incredulously at Calindor.

"None, none, honored father! The Gods will need only a small gift."

Calindor went a few steps up the trail, turned and walked back. "Very well, Milivo. We will both go with you to Hanashar."

This time Milivo smiled with joy. "It is not that far, Calindor. We can be there by sundown—sooner, if you wish to take my horse and ride ahead."

"Never mind. Keep us company if you like."

They turned back south on the trail, with Nezaual leading the way. Milivo, leading his horse, walked with Calindor. He seemed greatly relieved at Calindor's change of heart, and talked cheerfully as they walked: of the harvest, of the village gossip, of news from the wider world.

"We had four Badakh horse traders this summer," he said. "Strange-looking men, with their yellow hair and blue eyes. And a strange Cantarean they spoke also."

"They don't know the mountain dialect," Calindor said. "They speak it as they learned it from their slaves."

"Well, a poor language it was in their mouths. But we understood them well enough—they wanted horses and cattle, especially horses. They paid in good steel and wool." He showed them his dagger; Calindor recognized fine Staldhuno workmanship. He could imagine the Badakhar scavenging in their ruined cities for trade goods, desperate to rebuild the herds that had always meant strength and security—even when most Badakhar had abandoned herding for the life of the city. Never mind that the herds had overgrazed the prairie, insulting Callia until she finally punished them. The habits of centuries would not quickly change even under Callia's fury.

"Did they deal fairly with you?" asked Nezaual.

"Fairly enough. They know the value of a horse, and their knives and axes are better than any we can make. But it was strange to deal with enemies out of the legends. Some people said we should drive them away, not barter with them."

"That would be foolish," said Calindor. "We have to live with them whether we like them or not. We would mock Callia if we went back to warring with them."

"No doubt you're right, Calindor. Though I think the Badakhar would profit more than we from your advice."

Calindor said nothing. Ever since their return from the south, he had heard the same message: the Badakhar had not changed, they were reverting to their old arrogance and brutality, and given half a chance, they would restore the Five Kingdoms and enslave the Cantareans again.

Nezaual would have heard much the same during his stay in Tanshadabela, and Calindor had noticed his seemingly innocent question. In his own clumsy way the boy was gathering intelligence for his priests and warriors. The Exteca would be quick to exploit every conflict they found, and they would find plenty.

Well, that was a problem for another day. He turned his thoughts to spells against blights, molds, and rots. The Gulyaji, Cantareans who had lived in caves for centuries, knew some good spells. One or two Badakh spells might work. He would try the Gulyaji spells first; Badakh magic still set his teeth on edge with its crudeness and its ignorance of what living things wanted to do.

The sun was behind the mountains by the time they reached Hanashar. It stood on an east-facing hillside, overlooking the Cantabela and the enormous peaks beyond the river. Callia's storm had blown down thousands of lodgepole pines and aspens around Hanashar, and the villagers had planted many new fields. The village itself was large and pleasant; good carpenters lived here, who had built cabins and barns of simple elegance.

Instead of a large inn like Svordo's, Hanashar had only a small guest house. Milivo led Calindor and Nezaual into its snug common room, which was warm and rich with the aromas of good cooking. The cooks—two women and a man—made them welcome and served them barley soup while Milivo went in search of Suripi and the village speaker, a man named Sedabisi.

"I never thought I could be so cold," Nezaual said as he drew his chair closer to the hearth. Each time he emptied his wooden bowl, the cooks refilled it. When the soup pot was empty, fresh spice bread came out of the oven, and mugs of hot apple cider.

Calindor did not eat as much as his apprentice, but he too felt cold and tired. When Milivo returned with Suripi and Sedabisi, Calindor accepted their welcome with only a nod and muttered thanks.

"I am glad to see you, cousin," Suripi said. She was a small, thin woman with graying hair; she looked to Calindor like Tilcalli without the spark. "Milivo has told you of our problem. The blight is destroying both our wheat and oats. I have tried two spells in three days, and neither worked."

No wonder she looked so pale and weary. Casting the second spell would have been an act of desperation, performed without enough strength. Calindor listened as she described the preparation and casting of the spells. They were good greenmagic, spells to strengthen the resistance of the grain rather than to kill the blight directly.

"Can you show me the blight?" he asked.

Without speaking, Suripi handed him a small pouch of yellow leather. Calindor opened it into the palm of his hand while Nezaual watched closely. The grains were mottled by a powdery black mold.

"This is a new blight," Calindor said.

"Yes," Suripi said without emotion. "It spreads very fast."

"I must focus for a moment." So warned, Suripi and Nezaual did not wince or cry out as Calindor probed into the Powers of the blight.

This was like healing: sinking deep into something very small and complex, where Gariba worked with intricate subtlety. For a moment Calindor felt as if he were falling through a world of stars and spiderwebs. Then he was back in the room, feeling the fire's warmth.

"I see why your spells failed," he said to Suripi. "The Gariba of the blight all turn inward, and they keep the grain from hearing the spells. The Gulyaji have spells that help the grain form poisons that kill the blight but do no harm to humans or animals. But those spells would fail also."

Suripi frowned. "How can Gariba 'turn inward'? They have no in or out, front or back."

"These do. They have arrayed themselves in a way I have not seen before."

"So the harvest is lost," Suripi said quietly.

"I am sorry. If I can take this sample and study it further, perhaps I can find a remedy."

"You will only spread it to Tanshadabela."

"The pouch is sealed already. Nothing can enter or leave it until I lift the spell." He tucked the pouch into a pocket. "I am sorry, cousin. You know as well as I that magic cannot do everything."

"Honored father—" Nezaual spoke softly in Exteca. "I do not know this blight, but when you talk about the Powers turning inward—this sounds like some blights and blasts that we know. We can destroy it."

"I give you permission to try, beloved son."

Nezaual shook his head. "I have no strength. Calling Lady Serpent was a hard task. But you could do it."

Calindor seemed to hear the dry shuffle of Cihuacoatl close behind him. Fear prickled his skin—not fear of the True Gods, or fear of pain, but fear that he was losing control. He was the greatest magician his people had ever known, the man who opened the way for Callia's return, yet now he felt himself caught like a twig in a slow but unstoppable stream that led into unknown danger.

He felt also the magician's insatiable desire for new magic.

"Teach me the spell," he said.

Hanashar's granary was a big six-sided cabin. Its floor was a man's height below ground level, sealed by thick walls of mortar and stone. Lidded wooden bins, one against each wall, held the grain; now each lid was up, and in torchlight the grain was crusted with black powder.

Calindor walked from bin to bin while Milivo held a candle in a lamp. Dragonfire would have cast a brighter light, but Calindor did not want to risk a conflict of magics.

A steep flight of stone steps rose to the granary door. In it stood Nezaual and Suripi, their breaths fluttering in the frosty air. Behind them stood other villagers holding lamps and torches. Night had fallen.

Calindor stripped off his tunic. He realized, now that he saw the bins, that this was a far worse threat than he had thought. If redmagic could not save this harvest, the people of Hanashar would have to abandon their homes and seek help from other villages—but they might well bring the blight with them, and spread starvation all over the valley.

Ignoring the cold, he drew himself into focus. The words Nezaual had taught him began to form themselves in his mind. He held his hands open before him and spoke the Exteca spell:

"Now I call on the True God Huitzil Xochitl.
Now I call on the guardian of our flesh.
Now I call as servant of Cihuacoatl.
Take the blight from our flesh, the black blight.
Make our flesh strong with your strength.
Ca ge cuel. It is coming true."

Taking his knife from its sheath, he drew its edge down across his chest, over the ribs above his heart. His own blood was hot on his skin; he felt no pain.

Milivo's candle lamp went out in a sudden gust of wind.

Sparks whirled around the granary, multiplying into thousands and then into a shimmering banner of flame. Heat filled the room, as if the grain had caught fire, and a deep buzzing made the walls tremble. From a great distance Calindor heard a woman's scream: Suripi, crying out in one long agonized wail.

The burning banner vanished in a spray of purple afterimages. The only light now was a lamp still burning beyond the doorway. Calindor looked up and saw Nezaual descending the stairs, the lamp in his hand.

"Honored father—you still stand!" His eyes were round with amazement. "And Hummingbird Flower accepted your gift."

Calindor looked down. The wound on his chest was a red line, just beginning to hurt, but the only blood was a wet gleam within the cut. The blood that had spilled down his skin was gone.

Milivo came down with another lamp. He and Nezaual inspected the bins carefully, saying nothing. When they were finished, Nezaual took Calindor gently by the hand.

"Honored father, please come and see."

Calindor let himself be guided to one of the bins, and looked into it. The blight was gone. The poisoned grains were gone. What remained, perhaps four-fifths of the original store, was clean and intact.

"Muchiuatiuh," Calindor said in Exteca. "It has come to pass."

The village was suddenly alive. People ran from house to house shouting the news, and learned that grain stored in the cabins was clean also. Four men carried Suripi to her home; she was in a kind of twilight consciousness, speaking incoherently. Others escorted Calindor and Nezaual to the Meeting Hall for a ceremony of thanks.

"You were splendid, honored father," Nezaual said as villagers came into the long hall. "Every word perfect, as if you had prepared for months. And now you still stand, unwearied. The greatest priests in Tola, even Ometollin himself, would be in their beds for a month." Calindor smiled but said nothing.

The ceremony was brief. The speaker gave words of thanks, the villagers clapped their hands in the Cantarean custom, and Calindor replied: "I am glad I could be of help. May you know a gentle winter and an early spring."

Milivo would have escorted them back to the guest house, but Calindor asked to go to Suripi's instead. She lived close to the river with her husband Obasaga and two adolescent daughters; Obasaga met Calindor and Nezaual at the cabin door and welcomed them.

"I am glad to see you, kinsman. We would have attended the ceremony, but my wife needed our attention. I hope you understand."

"Of course. I have come to see her, if I may."

"Please." He gestured to the adjoining room.

Leaving Nezaual to talk with Obasaga and the girls, Calindor stepped into the room. Suripi lay in the bed, a wool blanket pulled over her. A single lamp burned on the wall.

"Kinswoman. My spell harmed you, and I hope I can make amends."

"Your magic can only make me worse." Her voice was a whisper.

"I will not use redmagic. Only greenmagic, and only with your permission."

"Do what you wish, Calindor."

Gently he placed his hands on either side of her head. He sensed the turmoil in her mind, and the weakness it had spread throughout her body. Tilcalli had felt like this after Nezaual's spell. Perhaps redmagic affected all the Siragi Aibela like this; if so, the Exteca were even more dangerous than he had imagined.

Well, worry about that later. For now it was enough to call to the Gariba in her blood, calm them and let her rest.

. . . Blood. He sensed it in a new way now, saw its Gariba as more than just a tribe of the Water Powers. His own blood pulsed with a dizzy joy, as if the Gariba within him had glimpsed their own new might. With an effort, he calmed himself and then Suripi.

"Will I be all right, Calindor?"

"Yes. First you must rest." But he knew what she really meant, and added: "I think you will not want to do magic for a while. But then you will recover."

"I hope so. I'm the only one in the family who can do proper greenmagic. Obasaga's all right for simple spells, but not for making crops grow. And the girls, poor things, have no talent at all. All they see is the gleam in young men's eyes."

Calindor laughed softly. "They have enough magic to put that gleam there. Who is your mentor in the Open Dream?"

"My grandfather Vengalindor."

"Go to him when you are feeling better, as I will go to my great-great-grandmother Calihalingol. But until then, rest and sleep."

She smiled and closed her eyes. The care slipped from her features and Calindor saw the beautiful girl she still was. Callia's daughters were a nation of their own, he thought. Men really knew no more of them than ants knew of dragons.

He went back into the front room, where the family looked up anxiously at him. "She will be well soon. Cherish her. And now Nezaual and I must get some sleep. We must be back in Tanshadabela by tomorrow night."

"You will go on my best horses," Obasaga said. "And you will go with all our thanks."

The girls walked them back to the guest house, through streets noisy with laughter and song. Lights burned in every cabin window, and villagers ran from cabin to cabin to celebrate with impromptu feasting and drinking. Nezaual seemed not to notice the girls' giggles and flirtatious look, but Calindor saw that his apprentice listened carefully to the chatter of passing villagers:

". . . first time a Siragi Aibela's been of real use . . ."

". . . foreign magic really works . . ."

". . . only one in his clan good for anything."

As he pulled blankets around himself in the unfamiliar bed, Calindor worried about how the news would travel: before long, everyone in the mountains would hear that redmagic worked where greenmagic—and the Siragi Aibela—had failed. That would weaken the standing of his whole clan.

But redmagic did work, he thought. *I gave a little blood, and a foreign god saved my people.*

And I have invoked two True Gods.

Twelve

They rode north in a misty autumn drizzle, with an escort of six warriors as a sign of respect. Calindor saw that Nezaual rode well though he was unfamiliar with the Cantarean saddle. If the Exteca were good cavalry as well as good magicians, that would be yet another problem to deal with—though he could not imagine the Exteca, with their crude bronze weapons, surviving the steel lances and swords of the Badakhar.

Unless the Badakhar are under the spells of love and terror . . .

At the Cantabela bridge the warriors of Hanashar turned back. They would not enter Tanshadabela; too much work remained at home, and they were impatient to complete the harvest and prepare for winter. So Calindor and Nezaual crossed the bridge alone and walked up the path to the village. Their journey had been swift on horseback; it was only mid-afternoon. Most people were out of sight, working in the barns and kitchens. The scent of vinegar hung in the damp air: every household was pickling the last of its autumn vegetables.

But the cabin of Calindor's parents was oddly quiet. He called out as he stepped to the door, and his father opened it. Dragasa looked pale and exhausted.

"Your mother is sleeping. I have never seen her so ill." He stood back and let them enter.

"What is the matter?"

Dragasa slumped onto a bench and tossed a stick into the fire. "You may know better than I. Two nights ago we felt something like the spell Nezaual cast in the field. We both fell as if poisoned. Yesterday we recovered, and then it happened again last night. Callishandal has been looking after us." He looked at his son. "Will this happen again?"

Calindor crossed his arms over his chest and felt the sting of his wound. "No, Father. Not if I can help it."

"Sit down, both of you, and tell me what has happened."

Calindor began to speak, but stopped himself when Tilcalli came in. She was pale and slow-moving, her hair falling in a tangle over her shoulders. She sat next to Dragasa, leaned against him and whispered: "Go on. Tell us what happened."

Calindor told them what had happened in the valley at the foot of Burdan Atana; how Nezaual had invoked Cihuacoatl; how the next day they had met Milivo and gone to Hanashar; how Calindor had destroyed the blight by invoking Huitzil Xochitl.

"So you have learned redmagic," Tilcalli said in Badakhi.

"I have used it. I have not yet learned it."

"You will. You learn everything. But now you serve their gods, not Callia."

Calindor felt his jaws clench. "Would it serve Callia to let Hanashar lose its harvest and starve?"

Anger flared in her dull eyes. "Does it serve Callia to shed blood and weaken the Siragi Aibela? If we felt it here, they felt it in Shadamidan too, maybe even in Supalarea. This magic is too strong, too dangerous. If you've stopped the blight, it's only to provide his people—" She did not even glance at Nezaual, who, like Dragasa, understood nothing of what they were saying. "—with well-fed slaves and sacrifices. You have done a terrible thing, Calindor."

He said nothing for a time. Then he spoke while gazing into the fire. "We did not come to Burnbaile by chance. Callia sent us there even as she sent the boy's people." He did not look at Nezaual either. "She wants me to learn redmagic as she wanted me to learn Badakh magic, Gulyaji magic, dragon magic. I look at you and my father, and I feel grief that this new magic weakens you. You know I would not harm you willingly. But sometimes we harm one another in doing Callia's will."

"So we must give up our strength and skill? Will redmagic make the crops grow next spring? How many of us will you have to kill so the rest of us can eat?"

Calindor stood up. "I will talk with you later, when you are feeling better. I hope it is soon."

"What is the matter?" Dragasa asked. "What have you been talking about?"

"Mother will tell you when we have left. I will be back tonight or tomorrow morning. I—Father, I am truly sorry that this has happened. I will have to go still farther away. Until I do, I promise you I will not practice redmagic again. Come," he said to Nezaual. The Exteca followed him obediently out into the street.

Neither spoke as they walked through the streets to Calindor's house. Calindor only nodded grimly when others greeted him, and ignored their puzzled looks.

Callishandal and Deir were cleaning a deerhide under a lean-to behind the cabin.

"What's wrong?" Callishandal asked, standing up and dropping her scraper. Calindor embraced her and took a long time before letting her go.

"Come inside and we'll talk. Nezaual, help Deir clean the hide."

Neither bothered to light a lamp; they sat close together at the table by the little window, while the drizzle turned to rain and Calindor spoke steadily and quietly. After a while Callishandal reached out and took his hands. When he had finished, she looked down at the table. Then she looked up, meeting his eyes.

"I think you are right. Callia arranged for us to be there when Deir needed us. I think you do need to understand redmagic. But I am frightened. Callia—Callia killed how many in her rage? She would kill you too, if she chose. You told Deir that we are her thoughts, but where does a thought go when you stop thinking it?"

"I understand. All I can do is what seems right. But it is hard." He lifted her hands to his face and kissed them. "Why am I doing these things? My mother raised me to do Callia's will, not my own. When we met the Exteca, I felt I must defend Cantarea against them—but why should it matter who rules here, Badakh or Cantarean or Exteca? What is the difference whether people die for Callia in her storms, or die for the True Gods on their altars? What do I owe the Cantareans or the Badakhar, that I should care about them when we could go back to sea?"

She shook her head, smiling. "Someday we will again. But Callia has given us this task, and we will have to do it."

He smiled back, not happily. "Well, I named you Voice of Callia, so I must listen to you. Now I do need to know what to do. I have learned enough redmagic to see that it works, and now I see that it weakens our own magicians. So I must find out why, and find a counterspell. But redmagic works over a long distance, so I will have to go a great distance from here or I will destroy my parents and kinfolk."

"What about Deir? She seems untouched by any kind of magic; perhaps she has something that will help you."

He nodded. "I know, but—she knows nothing, and Nezaual knows a great deal. It's too easy to spend time with him, and learn his secrets."

"Think about it for a while," she said. "Even you must rest sometimes. Your mother's anger has angered you. Rest for a time, talk with people, and think about other things. You'll soon think of what to do."

"And if I don't, perhaps my great-great-grandmother Calihalingol will set me right. Well, enough of this! Let me start preparing supper, and you and Deir can finish the hide."

"What about Nezaual?"

"He can go back to his room at the inn and tell Svordo that we're coming over for some beer and gossip this evening."

The dining hall of the inn was crowded and noisy with people celebrating the end of harvest. The two fireplaces blazed and crackled, and the air smelled rich with simmering soups and roasting meats. From the kitchen Svordo and his cooks brought great wooden trays of fresh-baked bread, the brown crusts still steaming; his guests snatched the loaves, complaining happily about how hot they were.

When Calindor, Callishandal, and Deir came in, Nezaual was guarding a table for them. He had already eaten a bowl of stew and most of a loaf of bread; a half-empty flagon stood before him. The people at the other table were listening to him with interest.

". . . and then my master invoked the True God Huitzil Xochitl," he was saying, "and all the blight vanished in flames that left the healthy grain alone. You do not believe me?" He waved his flagon in the direction of Calindor. "Here he is. He can tell you himself!"

"Be still, beloved son," Calindor said in Exteca. "And do not drink any more beer tonight."

"Of course, beloved father. I hope I have not angered you. No one here yet knows of how you rescued Hanashar."

"They will learn in good time. Now be still." He smiled at the other guests as Svordo brought beer and bread.

"Good evening, Svordo. What news?"

"I would gladly tell you, but I have no time. These good people are just arrived from the prairies; they can tell you."

They were two tall, rawboned Cantareans, clearly ex-slaves, from the scars on their faces and bare arms. If they had been skeptical of Nezaual's boasting, they seemed astounded to meet Calindor face-to-face.

"Welcome to Tanshadabela, cousins," he said, shaking their hands, and introducing Callishandal and Deir. They were brothers, Songo and Sisima—Loud and Quiet.

"So our mother named us," said Songo, "and they say she had reason in my case. Our masters had other names for us, but we've given them up."

"As many have," Calindor said, reflecting that Svordo seemed content with his Badakh slave name. "Where are you from?"

"Tenarvedor," Sisima replied, louder than his brother.

"Still a Badakh name?" asked Callishandal. "I thought the old names were coming back."

"In some places," Sisima said. "But where the Badakhar are more numerous, they vote to keep their names. We are perhaps three hundred Cantareans and a thousand or more Badakhar."

"It was a much greater place once," Calindor said. "The second city of Ghrirei."

"Now it's the first city of itself," said Songo, "and not much of a place. A few foundries, a pottery, a brewery. If you can call it beer." He hoisted his flagon. "This stuff would fetch high prices, if anyone had any money."

"What brings you here?"

"Horses, if we can buy them. And hides for making saddles. The Badakhar are nursing their herds better than their own children, and won't slaughter a cow or horse until it's already dead and rotted." Songo laughed at his own wit. "We'll also buy all the steel blades we can find."

"You won't find very many. Our smiths aren't as skilled as the stalmaghar, and what little steel they make goes into chisels and burins for wood carving."

"We're thinking about carving something softer," Sisima muttered.

Calindor's gaze fixed on him. "Is there trouble with the Badakhar?"

"A little, but more all the time. A fistfight, a kicking, insults. Their electman protects them, so if we go to complain, he just smiles and says he needs more proof. Mind you," he added with a grin lacking a couple of teeth, "we get the occasional strawhair in a dark alley and remind him of the old days."

Calindor said nothing for a moment, while Songo's grin faded. "That's revenge."

"A little perhaps," Songo agreed, "but not much for what they did to us for hundreds of years."

"Revenge is a Badakh idea, not ours. It only hurts Callia more."

"Maybe we need to take revenge on Callia too," said Sisima, anger in his eyes. "She let us suffer under the Badakhar, and then punished us as well as them. Plenty of slaves froze and drowned in her storm, didn't they? And now we're free to scrabble for a living in the mess she left." He did not grin like his brother; his eyes met Calindor's and did not turn away. "I'll say this for her:

she evened the odds. But the game's not over, and it won't be until the Badakhar are gone and we can live as we choose on our own land."

"So you want to fight the Slave Wars again," Callishandal snapped. "And if you lose, will you go underground like the Gulyaji, or move in with us?"

"We won't lose," said Sisima. "Not if we've got enough swords and spears."

"The Badakhar aren't fools," she persisted. "If they think you're planning a war, they'll murder you in your sleep—and thank you for giving them an excuse. They outnumber you three to one in Tenarvedor, and in the old days there were always more of us than of them. Yet they were the masters still."

"They aren't masters now, and they never will be again," Songo replied. Calindor saw that the Cantareans had already had plenty of Svordo's beer. "All they ever understood was the sharp edge of a sword and the hot end of a torch. Give 'em that if they want it."

"Do others quarrel with you when you speak like this?" Calindor asked.

"Some," grunted Sisima. "But most would gladly sweat to bury the last Badakh, and all would dance on the grave. Now, have we offended you, magician, and your wife?"

"Not offended, no. But it worries me that Cantareans should plan war, when war destroyed us once before." He did not look at Nezaual, but he knew the boy was listening closely. "Well, enough of this fierce talk. You say you want horses; what can you offer us in exchange?"

The talk turned instantly to business, with Songo and Sisima eagerly promising gold and silver coins plundered from the treasury of the Aryo of Ghrirei. Calindor argued that such wealth meant little to the mountain Cantareans; they preferred goods of immediate usefulness. Food, spices, fabrics and tools would interest them, not disks of gold or silver.

"We brought little of such things," Songo admitted. "We thought you people in the mountains were Cantareans like everyone else. But if you truly have cattle or horses to sell, bring them to us and we will pay you handsomely in whatever you wish."

"Perhaps we shall do as you suggest," said Calindor. "But this is no time to drive cattle down the river. They'd die long before they reached the prairie."

"Horses would do quite well," Sisima said at once. "They can break through the snow for their fodder, and when you reach us, we have plenty of hay to see them through the winter."

"Let me think about it," Calindor said. "If we can manage it, I might be able to bring a hundred or so horses down before the winter solstice."

"A hundred!" Sisima's insolence vanished. "Oh sir, that would be a very good idea. A hundred horses would make you a rich man indeed."

"Very rich," Songo echoed.

Calindor saw that both brothers had assumed the averted eyes and soft whine of slaves dealing with masters. "I promise nothing, you understand."

"Of course," Sisima agreed. "I only hope that since it was my brother and I who advised you on this, that you will bargain first with us. I can promise you that no one in Tenarvedor could offer you better terms."

"I am grateful for all you have told me. May your visit here be profitable. Now, if you will excuse me, I must go home." He smiled at Callishandal and Deir. "By all means stay on if you like."

"I think we should come with you," his wife said. "It's growing late. Deir, will you stay?"

She shook her head. No wonder, Calindor thought: half the men in the room were staring at her. Even after all this time in Tanshadabela, she was still a red-haired freak. He felt a twinge of sympathy for her: a girl her age should be rejoicing in herself, flirting with men and taking counsel with other young women. Instead she was just one of Calindor's two exotic pets, with no friends outside his own family.

Well, it could not be helped now. Callia took little heed of her servants' private needs.

Bidding good night to Nezaual, they left the noise and light of the inn and walked home in companionable silence. As he opened the door of their cabin, Calindor turned to his wife and let her and Deir enter first.

"What did you think of those two?" he asked Callishandal.

"I thought they were horrible. Forgive me, but their master should have flogged them more."

He laughed, a little scandalized. "Well, if slavery made people better, we would all want to be slaves. But they did us a service tonight. It is worse on the prairies than I'd thought. If Cantareans and Badakhar are already feuding again, they'll soon be at war. Did you see Nezaual drinking it all in? I could almost read his mind: 'Which side should we back? The warriors or the slaves? The steelmakers or the magician's people?' "

"The Fabarslúa can't be your enemies," Deir said. "They have to be friends with your people, so they can be friends with you."

Calindor sat down and stirred the coals back into flame. "Sometimes I wonder who my people really are. The mountain Cantareans? I hardly know them. The prairie Cantareans, like Songo and Sisima? The Siragi Aibela? My own parents are angry with me, and my other kindred don't trust me." He tossed a stick on the fire. "And no one else much cares for the Siragi Aibela. Sometimes I miss the Badakhar—well, some of them, anyway."

He shook his head irritably. "Deir, my people are you and Callishandal, and Svordo, and a Badakh small sorcerer named Minukhi, and a wise magician named Renjosudaldor. Maybe even Nezaual is one of my people. If I am to care for them, I must care for all their people. If they want to fight one another, then I must find a way to stop them."

"I want to fight the Fabarslúa," Deir said with quiet ferocity.

He smiled at her. "Then I will have to frustrate your plans, won't I?"

Callishandal gave Deir a comforting hug and then looked at Calindor. "So what now?"

"I want to go horse trading. But not in Tenarvedor."

"Where then?"

"In Vidhumen."

"Vidhumen!"

"Where my once-father, the once-king, is now the electman. Yes. Vidhumen."

That night rain fell, drumming on the roof. As Callishandal lay warm in his arms, Calindor went into the Open Dream.

There the sun was always at noon, and snow gleamed always on the peaks of distant mountains. In the clearing by the silent river stood the tents and cabins of his ancestors. Between their shelters and the river they danced the past and the future.

Calindor stepped into the dance, taking his great-great-great-grandmother by the hand.

I greet you, Calindor. Your mother is worried about you.

She has reason. I have begun to learn the magic of the Exteca. It is very strong, and it makes other magicians ill.

I think we have felt it here. You made it rain in Burdan Atana.

No, the Lady Serpent did. She is one of the Exteca's True Gods.

Like Callia?

I don't know. I don't think so. But she is powerful enough. If the other True Gods can do so much for a little blood, then the Siragi Aibela will not withstand them.

We could never withstand a god, Calindor. Not even Mekhpur, who was really only a man wanting to be a god.

Should we withstand them? Should we not accept them and their new magic?

Her name meant Laughing Woman, and usually her wrinkled face was full of smiles. Now he saw anger flash in her eyes, brief and dangerous as lightning.

We are not slaves, but some of us sound like fools. Callia did not free us from the Badakhar only to make a gift of us to these Blood People. She freed us so we would be ready to resist them. To resist, Calindor.

But you said we cannot resist a god, and the Exteca have many gods.

You are not listening to me. She led him from the dance, out of the clearing and into silent woods where sunshine dappled the leaves. They shimmered in the breeze, but made no sound.

I said the Siragi Aibela cannot withstand a god. But you are more than just another clansman. You withstood Mekhpur; you opened the way for Callia's return. Perhaps you will drive away these evil gods as well.

Perhaps? And perhaps I will not!

He turned away in anger, and stood utterly still.

The dance had stopped. His ancestors stood unmoving among their tents and cabins while the noon sun shone down on them. All were looking at the only dancer as she stepped gracefully along the bank of the silent river. In the brilliant light her hair blazed and rippled like fire: it was Deir, dancing in the Open Dream.

She wore a white buckskin tunic and soft moccasins; her white legs flashed as she stepped and turned. Her face was calm and smiling; though she danced near the edge of the water, her eyes were closed.

Calindor ran from the shade of the trees, calling her name in the silent speech of the Open Dream. As he drew near she opened her eyes and looked at him—at the whole Open Dream. She smiled.

"Hello, Calindor."

No voice had ever before spoken aloud in this place, and Deir's words struck like thunder.

He was in his bed again, and Callishandal still slept beside him. From the other bedroom came Deir's soft snores.

For a long time he lay awake, waiting for the slow dawn.

Thirteen

Darkness visible: he lay in an endlessly shifting network of Powers that moved and paused, quarreled and rejoiced and took no notice of the humans who sometimes commanded them.

Calindor thought about the lost city of Aishadan, where he had grown up half slave and half prince; he thought about the night he had met Callishandal—then just Bherasha, a sorcerer's slave girl—and had slain a Badakh noble for her sake. He remembered his atonement for that crime, and how it had led him to the caverns of the Gulyaji and the gaining of his true name.

At the time each event had seemed little more than chance; one different word, one different decision, and all would have been changed. Only later had he seen Callia's plan and marveled at how she had achieved her ends.

Callia had not spoken since the day she had scourged Cantarea and overthrown Mekhpur. Then, the whole world had seemed to suffer her rage; now, he knew, Cantarea was very small and the world of Sotalar very large. The Exteca had been untouched by Callia's wrath. Even worse, they appeared to flourish in a hideous mockery of her.

Surely, surely Callia had sent him to meet the Exteca so that he could defend her against them. Surely Deir was part of her plan. Yet redmagic had half seduced him. Deir was just a girl with strange hair and skin; Cihuacoatl, the Lady Serpent, was a True God who had sent warm rain to the frozen valley of Burdan Atana.

But Deir—or her image—had invaded the Open Dream. Even the Gulyaji, cousins to the Siragi Aibela, had no access to it. How could a girl without magic achieve such a thing?

Think! She had not felt Yetecuan's spell of love. She herself had cast a spell that summoned a sea dragon and Calindor's boat, while staggering every magician between Burnbaile and Tanshadabela. The dragons had fled from the sight of her. And now she was in the Open Dream.

He had studied her, but her very simplicity had baffled him and sent him off to Nezaual—the boy was at least a capable young magician, while Deir's secret lay hidden even from her.

... even from her.

Could a talent for magic exist independent of its possessor? Could it act on its own?

In a way, every magician began like that, slowly discovering an inborn talent for seeing the Gariba and using the talent to influence them. His mother, knowing he had the talent, had taught him a little even while concealing his abilities from the Badakhar magicians—and from himself.

Not until the Veik Pelshadan had seen him fight in a state of focus had Calindor realized how great his talents might be. Not until the Gulyaji magician Renjosudaldor had taught him had he begun to express those talents.

So could Deir be acting as he himself once had, without awareness, almost accidentally? Perhaps. Yet after her great spell of summoning, he had found her unwearied, with no residue from a spell that should have left obvious traces.

A raw talent could not do that without conscious control. Some people could walk in their sleep, but no sleepwalker could sweep away her footprints at the same time.

The long night was coming to an end. Callishandal stirred, woke, and drowsily embraced him. They rose and began the morning's chores. Calindor went out to the barn to look after the horses and milk the cow. When he returned, the sky was a twilight blue. Callishandal and Deir were making oatmeal and mint tea. They all sat down to breakfast and Calindor thanked the Powers of Earth for the meal.

"Did you have any dreams last night?" he asked Deir.

"No." She looked perplexed. "I slept very hard."

"Good." He held out his right hand, palm up. "Tell me—can you see anything in my hand?"

"No."

He had called up a small disk of dragonfire, too cool to give off light or heat, but clear to anyone who could perceive the Powers. Deir obviously could not.

"Come with me for a walk this morning," he said to her. "I want to show you the oldest rock in these mountains."

"If you wish." Deir was puzzled but slightly amused.

"What are you thinking of?" Callishandal asked in Badakhi.

"I want to talk to the magician living in this girl. I think I may know how to do it."

"Good luck."

The day was partly cloudy and chilly, but the air tasted clean and sweet. They walked east through the village and out through one of the gates in the palisade. Beyond it the ground dropped steeply away into a bog, but a path led down the slope and around the bog through a stand of spruce and aspen. Before long the path met the Cantabela, just a couple of bowshots northeast of the village. Here the river ran north for a while before making its great turn eastward toward Cantarea, and here it was a shallow braidwork of streams amid islets of rocks. Calindor and Deir crossed easily enough to the right bank, where a steep hill rose straight out of the water. In the lee of the hill was a flat patch of gravel and stones, a kind of beach; beyond it stretched yet more forest.

Calindor led Deir across the beach to the hillside. A path led up the narrow spine of the hill, climbing steeply between two cliffs. On their left was the forest on the river's right bank; on their right was the river itself, and beyond it the village and its fields. On all sides, as they climbed, the mountains rose gleaming into the autumn sky.

Before long they came to a terrace, carpeted with sheep fescue and mosses. The hill climbed much higher, but Calindor was content to stop here. He squatted near a boulder; Deir sat herself upon it.

"That's an old rock," he told her, "but not very old. Long ago, rivers of ice flowed through this valley, and when they melted they left this rock and many others. It's the rock beneath us I want you to look at." He pointed to a bare patch where stone appeared. "The scratches come from the stones in the ice, as they dragged over this hill. When I look at the Gariba, the Powers in this hillside, I can see that they have been here for ... we don't really have words for so many years. Thousands of thousands. We are no more to them than a glint of dust in a beam of sunlight. They will be here long after humans and dragons have vanished from Sotalar. My father showed them to me, just before Callishandal and I were married. He introduced me to them."

Deir nodded, accustomed to marvels. "Did they say anything to you?"

"No. But they stirred in their sleep. They knew I was here. Now I want to introduce you to them."

"But I'm not a magician," she said patiently.

"Someone in you must be. I think she's listening and watching." He stood up and looked down at the bare patch of glacier-polished stone.

"Old Powers of Earth, I greet you. I bring you a person named

Deir who will someday call upon you and other Powers. I ask you to heed her."

Suddenly he lay sprawled across the wet grass, gasping for breath. His ears rang and tears blurred his sight. Not far away he heard rocks rumbling as they fell from the hillside down the cliff and into the forest.

Aching, he got to his hands and knees and then to his feet. A wind had swirled up from the river and over the hillside; it stung his face and tore at his clothes. He looked around and saw Deir staring at him, alarmed. Her hair, lifted by the wind, was a banner of flame against the sky. For a moment Calindor thought he saw actual Powers of fire whirling around her head. His vision cleared and he felt her hands gripping his arm, supporting him.

"Are you all right? What happened? Didn't the Powers like me? Are they angry with you?"

"A moment. A moment." He walked a little unsteadily to the boulder and sat down on it. For some reason he remembered mornings of close-combat drill in Aishadan, with old Demazakh the trainer clouting him about the ears with a longstaff.

"I think I have offended the magician within you," he said slowly. "I did not mean to. I don't think she wants anyone to know she is there, so I did not behave courteously toward her when I spoke directly to her. I apologize to her, and to you for frightening you."

"I don't understand," Deir wailed. "A magician inside me? Someone else?"

He shook his head, smiling. "Not really someone else. A part of you that's closed off. Hiding. I don't know why, and again I did not mean to offend that person within." He looked into her eyes. "Now I must speak to you the magician. I will not speak to you again without good cause. I will serve you in any way I can. In return I ask that you do no violence to me or my people."

The wind died; Deir's tangled hair fell across her shoulders. She was shivering, and not from cold.

"And I will take care of Deir the ordinary girl as well," he added with a faint smile.

Nezaual was working for Svordo, helping clean up the dining hall after last night's drinking and eating. He could scarcely believe what a mess the Cantareans made when they feasted; the floor was as sticky as that of a temple on a True God's day.

Work as an innkeeper's servant had rankled at first, but Svordo was a cheerful master who liked to talk. From him Nezaual learned of Calindor's experience as a slave, sold by his father after the death of a Badakh noble in a brawl; Calindor had found himself in a slave wagon with Svordo, bound for the kingdom of Ner Kes on the eve of its war with Aishadan. Working on the city's defenses, Calindor had spied out the weaknesses in the walls. Then he had escaped, taking Svordo with him, and had found refuge in the caverns of the Gulyaji, Cantareans who had learned to live beneath the ground that the Badakhar had conquered. All this, Nezaual was certain, would be of value to Ometollin and the other great priests of Tola.

As well, Svordo was a good source of Badakhi. Calindor and his wife used it when they wished privacy; it was useful to know at least a little of the language. So as he scrubbed the floor he reviewed some of the words he had learned: *khven*, woman; *pel*, *svordo*, black; *upermanna*, nobleman; *aryo*, king.

The scrub brush fell from his hand as he shuddered, tried to rise, and sprawled in the dirty water on the floor.

True Gods, what a spell! What was Calindor doing? An agonizing pain clamped his forehead, making his eyes water. Distantly he heard Svordo calling him, but an answer seemed pointless. After a long time hands gripped his shoulders and something supported his head. He was looking up at Svordo's worried face.

"I'm all right," he whispered. "I'll be up in a moment. Only let me rest a little longer."

"Rest in this mess? Not likely. Come on, up you get and outside. You look as if you're about to lose your breakfast and your last five meals as well." The innkeeper was surprisingly strong; Nezaual scarcely felt the floor as Svordo carried him out into the courtyard. There he leaned against a hitching post, staring blankly at an incurious horse, while Svordo poured a bucket of cold water over him.

With the second bucket Nezaual began shivering uncontrollably. Svordo and a couple of other Cantareans helped him dry off and got him down to his little room.

"This was magic?" Svordo asked.

Nezaual nodded.

"Yours or someone else's?"

"My master's. He cast a strong spell. A very strange one. Something like the one in Burnbaile. I am sorry, Svordo. I have troubled you. I will finish cleaning up."

"You'll stay on that bed until I tell you. Callia bless us! No wonder they say a magician makes a bad master and a worse servant. Every time I turn around, you're making one another sick. Stay there. I'll go and find Calindor and see what this was all about."

Someone had seen Calindor and Deir walking out the east gate; Svordo went that way and soon found them returning.

"What now?" he asked Calindor. "You look the way you did when they first put you in the slave wagon with me. And Nezaual's good for nothing but being a blanket on his own bed. Moaning about spells."

Calindor took his friend's hand. "I owe you an apology. This town is too small for the kind of magic I seem to be dealing with. Are my parents all right?"

"I don't know."

"If Nezaual's ill, of course they will be too. I must go to them. But the sooner we get out of here, the better."

"Get out? Are you going horse-trading?"

"More than that. We need to talk to other magicians, far from Tanshadabela."

The three of them began walking back into the village. "Who's 'we'?" Svordo asked.

"Callishandal, Deir, Nezaual, and me."

"Take me along too."

Calindor frowned, surprised. "But what about the inn?"

"My helpers can run it for a few weeks. I want to see flat ground for a change, and see what the world is like these days."

"As you wish," Calindor agreed, laughing. "I'll be glad of your company."

They found Dragasa and Tilcalli at the door of their cabin, sitting on the doorstep. Both looked pale and shaken.

"I am truly sorry," Calindor said quietly. "This will not happen again."

Tilcalli smiled faintly. "I suspect it will."

"It's my fault," Deir said. "I did something and knocked Calindor down. I'm sorry, Tilcalli. I didn't mean to."

"I thought I noticed something familiar about it. At least we didn't sicken this time. Does this mean you're making progress, Calindor?"

"It means we've stayed here too long. We leave tomorrow for Vidhumen."

Dragasa nodded slightly. "Perhaps that is best. We will talk with you in the Open Dream."

"And we will be back early in the spring."

"It will take longer than that," Tilcalli said. "I think you will be gone much longer. Come here."

He went to her; she stood up and murmured a spell of protection as she lightly touched his face and shoulders. Then she turned to offer the same to Deir, but paused.

"No. I don't think you need it. It is your enemies who will need protection, not you."

Several villagers were happy to get rid of their horses on consignment before winter, and so save the costs of feeding them. The prospect of gold next spring—better yet, good Badakh steel—was equally attractive. With the greatest Cantarean magician as their agent, they were confident of profit.

By sundown Calindor had fifteen good horses in his parents' corral, as well as his own five. All were tough, sturdy mountain ponies, nothing like the great beasts the Badakhar preferred for combat, but they could carry a rider or a heavy pack for days without tiring. Albohar would be glad to get them.

Deir had never ridden, and Nezaual rarely, but Calindor promised them gentle mounts and an easy pace until they gained confidence. He sent Svordo around the village to buy supplies and packsaddles; they were up late organizing and packing, but all was ready well before midnight. Nezaual, recovered, seemed happy to go; he was eager to see more of the northern lands, and understood Calindor's need for distance from Tanshadabela if he was to learn more about redmagic.

"I wish you knew *nothing* about redmagic," Callishandal muttered as they went to bed. "I wish Deir were just the sweet girl she seems. I wish we were settling down to a quiet winter."

He held her in the darkness, stroking her hair. "Renjosudador named me too well. I truly am the One Who Goes Away."

"And I am the One Who Follows Everywhere."

He chuckled softly, understanding her anger and caressing it away. "You are Callia's eyes as well as her voice. I don't think she wants me out of her sight."

"I don't think Callia wants you wounding yourself so that monsters do your will."

He said nothing, but held her tightly for a long time. In his memory he heard Lady Serpent shuffling over the stones of Burdan Atana, and felt the warm southern rain he had called down upon that frozen valley.

I would rather stay here too, he thought, *even if I feel a stranger here. But the leaf on the stream goes where the Powers of water want it to go. And I go where the gods carry me.*

Fourteen

A dragon's wind blew from the west for three days, bringing warm air from the sea. The snow vanished from the valley and the lower slopes, and the horses found plenty of fodder in the meadows along the Cantabela.

Once, Calindor explained to Nezaual as they rode eastward, Cantarean villages had stood along this river almost to the edge of the prairie. The Badakhar had no use for this forested land; they preferred open country for their herds and their cavalry. But they did not want their slaves thinking about free Cantareans just a few days away, so the Badakhar had made a custom of raiding up the river, burning villages and capturing their inhabitants. After a few generations an empty wilderness extended for many days' ride between the prairies and the easternmost strongholds of the Cantareans.

Now that was changing. Refugees from the east were settling along the river and its tributaries, carving little homesteads. Most were Cantareans, ex-slaves with some knowledge of farming and livestock, but a few were Badakhar. The homesteaders made Calindor's trading party welcome, offering shelter in rough cabins and barns. Though they were eager for news from the mountains, they said little about the prairies: "Always something grim, and usually something false," one old Badakh herdsman grunted.

As the traders left the mountains, the weather turned cold again. They were in what had once been the western marches of the kingdom of Aishadan, but now none claimed it. The foothills had once supported great forests, but they were gone—in part cut down by the Badakhar for timber, but mostly burned to deny their slaves a hiding place. Callia's wrath had knocked down what few trees had remained, and travel was now a slow business of circling bogs and going around blowdowns.

The remains of Badakh farms were scarcely visible. Floods had swept away houses, walls, barns—and often the soil itself. The horses' hooves rang on bedrock even as they passed the shattered masonry that had been some upermanna's keep. Sometimes people still lived in the ruins, and came out to beg or threaten. Calindor gave them sacks of grain and asked them about the cities to the east and south.

"Worth my life to go there," said one half-mad old Badakh. "The slaves would open my guts just for old times' sake. Can't blame them. Do the same in their place. Won't harm *you*, of course." He grinned through his matted beard. "But they'll want to."

At length they left the Cantabela and turned southeast, into rolling country. The homesteads here were little stone castles on hilltops, often built where a stream and an outcrop of coal coincided. The people were almost all Cantareans, living in their masters' halls and complaining that no slaves' barracks was colder than the bedchamber of an upermanna.

While they rode, and when they camped, Calindor and Nezaual talked about redmagic. They cast no spells, but Calindor began to understand how it worked. What he did not understand was how to counter it, and how to protect the Siragi Aibela from its effects.

One night, when Callishandal and Deir were busy looking to the horses, Nezaual asked: "Honored father, why did you bring Deir with you from Burnbaile?"

"Why do you suppose, beloved son?"

"I thought it was so that you could give her to your gods, as we planned to give her mother to ours. But I see now that your people do not make such gifts. Then I thought perhaps you wanted her for a servant, but why choose her when you could have any servant you like? Now I think it must be for some reason I do not understand."

Good; let him stay baffled as long as possible. "You will understand, beloved son, when you fully understand greenmagic."

"May that day come soon, honored father."

The girl, meanwhile, had become an accomplished rider and herder of horses, and an apprentice camp cook who would soon outdo her teacher Callishandal. Calindor himself spoke often and easily with Deir, but would not meet her eyes. He knew that the hidden magician was in there, and he would not idly tempt her to violence again. Nor did he want Nezaual to recognize her. But he yearned to bring that magician out into the world, to teach her what he knew and enlist her in Callia's cause.

One raw afternoon, while dry snow whirled around them, the traders climbed a rutted road to a broad, treeless plateau. The road ran across it to a town of slate roofs and brick walls, half hidden in black smoke: Vidhumen.

Once it had been the stronghold of a great upermanna family, related to the Aryo Albohar and heeded in all the councils of Aishadan. Vidhumen Kes, the castle on the hill above the town, had survived even the great storm; if only for that reason, it had attracted survivors seeking shelter. Now the town was far larger than in the days of the Five Kingdoms, with a skirt of shacks and cabins around the old town of stone and brick.

The road was in good repair, and in steady use despite the lateness of the season. Wagons rolled in bearing sacks of grain, lumber, and coal. The teamsters, most of them Badakhar, stared with open avarice at Calindor's herd. One shouted an offer to buy his horses on the spot.

"I'm offering them first to the electman," Calindor replied.

"You're a Menmanna, a mountaineer," the teamster said. "You don't know prairie ways. The old bastard will cheat you, assuming he doesn't just take your horses and send you home on foot."

Calindor smiled. "I'll take my chances, and thank you for your advice."

He lost his smile when they reached the town and found men working on a defensive wall around it.

"Looks like the good old days at Ner Kes," Svordo grunted. Calindor nodded; watching the crews toil on the wall reminded him of the grim spring and summer when he had been both slave and spy. For all its pain and brutality, that time seemed simple and clear-cut; the present was far better, yet far less secure.

Well outside the walls they pastured their horses. While the rest looked after the herd, Calindor rode into Vidhumen.

He had never been here before, yet all seemed familiar: it was a Badakh town, with quarters for freemen, warriors, and artisans. The houses were of brick with slate roofs, crowded together along narrow cobbled streets; the gutters ran brown with shit, and the air stank as well of coal smoke. A market square, half empty, offered a few colorful tents and booths selling beef and mutton and coarse bread.

People in the streets looked curiously at him, and he soon realized why: he was dressed comfortably in white buckskin tunic and trousers, with a fur-lined cape, while they wore ragged woolens. Badakhar as well as Cantareans were lean and even gaunt; many of them evidently needed the aid of a walking staff.

In the old days every Badakh town had its Cantarean slave police, the arekakhar, their faces scarred with swastikas and bearing truncheons in their fists. Not many had survived Callia's wrath and the first months of freedom. Now Calindor saw mounted patrols of Badakhar and Cantareans, working together in apparent harmony. One such patrol, two Badakhar and a Cantarean leader, approached him as he neared the street leading uphill to the castle. The leader greeted him in Cantarean:

"Good day, traveler. Where are you from and where bound?"

"I'm from Tanshadabela, bound for this place. My name is Calindor and I've come to do some horse trading."

All three riders gaped at him. "The Calindor who brought down the Firelord?" said the Cantarean.

"Well, that was my wife. I helped."

"You are the son of the Aryo—the electman?" asked one of the Badakhar.

"So he always treated me. I am on my way to greet him."

"We will escort you," said the Cantarean; the Badakhar fell in behind, while their leader rode at Calindor's left side.

"We don't get many mountaineer traders this late in the year," he said. "Least of all trading horses. The electman will be glad to see you, I'm sure."

Calindor replied cheerfully and noncommittally to the man's comments. He glanced around as they rode up the hill through quiet streets. A chill wind under a late autumn overcast had driven most people from the streets, but the town seemed busy enough. From the quarter of the stalmaghar came the music of hammers on hot steel, and Calindor could feel as well the spells the stalmaghar used to fix the Powers of fire and earth in each blade. If the air was full of coal smoke, at least no one seemed too poor to afford a fire. The slate roofs were in good repair, and most windows had glass in their panes.

The people were lean and hard, always a little underfed. They wore patched and threadbare garments from the old days, salvaged no doubt from ruined houses; a few also had homespun cloaks of new wool. More important, all carried arms: a sword and dagger if Badakh, an ax or short spear if Cantarean. Even women carried daggers at their waists. Most walked in small groups of their own kind, and those in one group kept their distance from those in the other.

The horsemen reached the brow of the hill, overlooking Vidhumen and the plain around it. Calindor could see his horses grazing, and a small white patch that must be one of their tents; Svordo and Nezaual had wasted no time getting settled.

Once, the approach to the castle would have been through ranks of armed guards; now, two sentries at the gate were all who challenged them. Good: it was the first promising sign he had seen in Vidhumen. Albohar, at least, did not expect an uprising.

The twin doors of the gate were open wide; Calindor and his

escort clattered into a wide courtyard where two grooms took their horses.

The smell hit him first: the mix of damp stone, horse dung, and stale urine. He had grown up in a grim building much like this one, built for bitter defense and not for comfort. Memories struck like blows, and he nearly struck back with a bolt of dragonfire that would have knocked a hole in the courtyard wall. Instead he drew a slow breath and walked into the stinking gloom of the castle.

The corridors were narrow, the rooms pinched and dim. Voices echoed, and Calindor was startled to hear the liquid cadences of Cantarean as much as the harsh bark of Badakhi. Strange to see Cantareans walking easily under such a roof! The Arekaryo Kes in Aishadan had been full of Cantareans, of course—but they had been slaves, shuffling in a perpetual bow, speaking Badakhi only. Here they wore decent wool tunics and leather coats, and bore arms like the townspeople.

Somehow Calindor expected to find Albohar in the Hearing Hall, where an Aryo ordinarily did public business; instead his escort led him to a small chamber on the second floor, overlooking the town. A fireplace in the corner cast a welcome warmth, and the furnishings were comfortably old. Albohar himself was at a desk, dictating to a scribe; he looked up, clearly annoyed at the interruption, and then sprang to his feet.

He was a tall man, still strong and lean in middle age, with broad shoulders and big hands. His pale blue eyes shone with joy and anxiety mixed as he embraced Calindor and then quickly, shyly, released him.

"Is it your mother? Is she ill?" he demanded.

"She is very well indeed," Calindor said with a smile as he returned the embrace. "And sends you her greetings." He smiled slightly. "She sends greetings also to your lady Ghelasha and your son Eskel." Albohar's legitimate wife and son had been deadly enemies of Tilcalli when she had been his concubine. "I'm glad to see you well also."

"I have you to thank for that." Two years before, he had been dying of an ensorcelled wound.

"You're very busy. I should have sent word instead of walking in uninvited."

Albohar grunted. "Nonsense. The chores can wait till you've eaten and drunk and told me all the news. What brings you here?"

"Perhaps we had better talk alone."

"Of course." He turned to his scribe, who was packing up his papers. "Send us some cheese and bread, and a pitcher of beer. I'll call you when I need you."

"Of course, electman."

The chamber seemed larger when it held just the two of them. Calindor spoke quickly and tersely, describing his journey to the south and the events since his return. Albohar said nothing but listened intently. The scribe slipped in with food and drink, and left again; Albohar scarcely noticed.

". . . and now we're here with horses to trade while I see how things go on the prairie," Calindor concluded.

"I'll take them all, and name your price. That's about the only good news you bring." Albohar sat back, arms folded across his broad chest. "New magics, a red-haired witch, people who cut each other's hearts out—this is a hard new world."

"It will be harder still if the Exteca conquer us. The mountain Cantareans don't really believe it could happen, but I know it could."

"I'm sure you're right. I'd like to meet this Nezaual you speak of, see what he's like."

"You'll like him. He's a brave and smart young man. I see much to admire in him and his people, but they will enslave us all if we don't stop them."

"And this witch, this Deir, is the way to stop them?"

"I think so. But she is . . . not in control of her talents yet. I hope to teach her, and to learn from her."

"What will you want from us?"

Calindor thought for a moment. "First, what you have already given me—a fair hearing. Second, a chance to warn the people of Cantarea, in all the cities and towns."

Albohar grinned and snorted as he reached for a lump of cheese. "You can talk to the people of Vidhumen whenever you like, but I'd do it in small groups if I were you. Otherwise someone in the crowd's going to get knifed and we'll spend the next two days putting down a riot. Same goes for the other towns, I expect."

"We've heard as much in Tanshadabela, and I see everyone armed here. Why so much suspicion and hatred?"

"Do those scars on your back ever itch before it rains? The Cantareans remember every blow they ever took, and it doesn't get softer in the remembering. The Badakhar bite their lips to see slaves owning herds and houses, and demanding pay for work. Not all of them want trouble, mind you, but enough do. If I were still Aryo, I'd post the worst ten troublemakers on each side, and we'd have peace for a while."

Calindor vividly recalled the practice of posting rebellious slaves: each one hung by his chained wrists from a tall post, barely touching the ground with his toes, and left there to die of thirst and exposure.

"But as electman," Albohar went on, "I can't blow my nose without permission of my council, and they won't countenance any return to the good old ways." He smiled without humor. "I'll say this much—it's harder work running this little town than it was running all of Aishadan."

"And likely to get harder before easier. Well, if the Exteca take over, these quarrels will end. Everyone will love their conquerors."

"May I not be among the living when that happens. Well, now! You're all guests of the city. Get back out to your camp and bring in your horses and companions. The horses will go in the castle pasture, and you'll sleep here under my roof again."

Calindor saw and understood the older man's awkward affection and the sadness beneath it. *We both thought I was your son, and we loved each other. Love each other still, for all that we are different. Tilcalli changed our lives, ruled our lives—stole our lives. Now we scramble about in the ruins she made of our old world, trying to build something better.*

"It will be a pleasure ... Albohar." *I cannot call you Father.*

Word of their arrival had traveled fast. Townspeople crowded the road to the pasture, watching the Cantarean ponies and their herdsmen. A few recognized Calindor and called him by his old name, Dheribi; he smiled and waved in answer as he rode past. But more were interested in the girl with the flaming hair and pale, freckled skin. The Badakhar were fair-skinned and blond, but red hair was almost unknown among them. They looked at her with mingled fascination and scorn. *You never did like people different from you,* Calindor thought.

As servants escorted them into the castle, he studied Nezaual and Deir. The Exteca said nothing, but Calindor read his face and eyes. He was observing everything closely, marveling at the steel weapons and armor while dismissing the castle itself as bad architecture poorly built—as indeed it was. Deir meanwhile ignored the big, braying men in armor and admired instead the half-rotted tapestries that adorned the hallways.

Their chambers were along a corridor on the third floor of the castle, just below the slate-tiled roof. When a servant showed Calindor and Callishandal into their room, Calindor paused. He had never been here before, yet something seemed familiar.

"Blaidakh," he said, going to the window and looking south across the town and its autumn fields.

"What?" Callishandal looked puzzled. From the next room came the voice of a servant explaining something to Svordo and Nezaual.

"The man I killed, the one who wanted to rape you outside the beer hall. This was his room, when his father Aghwesi was upermanna of Vidhumen. I can feel him here."

"What is it like, to feel such a thing?"

He thought for a moment. "Sad. It feels sad to see the traces we leave, when so much of us is gone forever. There are places where so many have died, in so much pain ... Well, enough. Callia had a use even for Blaidakh."

When they had rested and bathed, they obeyed Albohar's summons to the castle's great hall. There they greeted Ghelasha and Eskel. Albohar's wife looked much older since the days when she had been Aryasha, and Calindor saw something haunted in her eyes. Eskel, however, seemed more comfortable with himself and even with Calindor. His boyish face, with its girlish mouth, was no longer tense and mean; he smiled easily and clasped Calindor's hand with genuine warmth.

It was late afternoon by now, and growing cold despite the great fireplaces at either end of the hall. To warm them all, Calindor put a ring of dragonfire around the table where they had gathered.

"Now that's a useful magic," Albohar said as he carved the roast the servants had placed before him. "Did your mother teach you that?" He spoke Cantarean so that all his guests would understand him; Eskel quietly translated for his mother.

"A dragon we called Obordur. They understand the Powers of air and fire very well."

"I take your word for it, and hope I never meet one. Who wants bread with their meat?"

It was not so much a meal, Calindor thought, as an interrogation. The conversation, with the electman's questions and remarks, kept returning to the mountain villages: their wealth, their livestock, their attitude toward their kinfolk on the prairie. In exchange Albohar dropped a few bits of news about life in Vidhumen and other towns. He was clearly worried about the mountain Cantareans, and feared that they might come to the aid of their relatives in a future civil war.

Nezaual listened attentively even as he gulped down chunks of bread soaked in drippings. Calindor wondered whether Albohar was being thoughtless or deceptive. The Aryos of Aishadan had always been good at intrigue, at manipulating their enemies through an appearance of frankness. To appear anxious about one's weakness was a useful way to hide one's strength. But Albohar's enemies had never been servants of the True Gods.

Deir, meanwhile, was chatting with Callishandal and ignoring the political gossip. She complained in a whisper about how uncomfortable the chairs were and how badly prepared the meal had been. For the first time, Calindor saw boredom in her face. So she didn't care for the Badakhar; well, they didn't do much to make themselves likable.

At last Deir excused herself, saying she was tired and wanted to go to bed. Servants bearing lamps appeared; but as they were escorting her from the table, boots clattered in the hallway and a Badakh in a long cloak burst in. He collided with Deir, nearly knocking her down, but caught her arms before she could fall.

"Amadan!" she blurted in Airn, and then in Cantarean: "Fool! Let me go!"

The Badakh was in no hurry to obey. He was a tall man, his face in shadow beneath a wide-brimmed hat. But the servants' lamps threw light across Deir's face and hair, and the newcomer seemed ensorcelled by the sight.

"And who might you be?" he asked.

Calindor recognized the voice. "Pervidhu!" He leaped to his feet, hands out in welcome.

The newcomer swept off his hat, revealing his face: a short-cropped brown beard around a broad grin, a straight nose and dark eyes. Pervidhu at last let go of Deir and embraced Calindor.

"Hemamagh! Healer! We missed you on our trip to Tanshadabela last summer, and now you're here. And Callishandal, and Svordo! I welcome you all, but first I have news for the electman."

"Speak it, Pervidhu," said Albohar.

"A brawl in the old town. Six men hurt, that I saw, and one of those may die. The Cantareans are coming in from the new town."

Albohar growled as he got to his feet. "Another brawl. This never happened when we had the arekakhar."

Oh yes it did, thought Calindor, *or Blaidakh would still be using my room.*

The electman gave orders calmly, unhurriedly, as he buckled on his sword and let a servant drop a cape over his shoulders: "Call out the evening patrols early, and send them to reinforce the day men. Ten patrollers, all Cantareans, into the old town to keep people in their houses. Another ten to close off the new town. All taverns to close at once. Pervidhu, Eskel, come with me."

"May I be of help?" Calindor asked.

"Maybe so. Can you give me a storm of freezing rain? Something to drive them indoors?"

Calindor paused, hearing in memory the shuffling feet of Cihuacoatl.

"Perhaps some dragonfire," he said at last.

"Come, then. We'll return soon."

Nezaual offered to come also, but Calindor told him to stay. The less he saw of such strife, the better. Svordo had no interest in going, nor did Callishandal or Deir.

The four men strode out into the courtyard, where horses waited; night was falling fast. With an escort of patrollers they rode down into the old town. Doors and windows were shut tight, though a few townspeople were brave or curious enough to peer out to see whose horses were clattering down the street. Not far ahead were the sounds of fighting: steel striking steel, shattering glass, howling men.

Calindor felt a weary sorrow. *What did I expect? That we would all dwell in harmony? The Badakhar couldn't change us; why should we expect to change them?*

The riders came into a muddy market square fast sinking into darkness. Calindor thought a spell as dragons did, and a sphere of fire blazed above the square. Scores of men were fighting in six or seven separate brawls and beatings, and few looked up to see the cause of the sudden brightness; most only fought the harder now that they could see their opponents.

Albohar did not wait longer; he drove his horse into a cluster of Badakhar beating two Cantareans. A long truncheon, its end tipped with iron, appeared in his hand. Wielding it like a saber, he dropped three men before they even knew he was upon them. Eskel meanwhile had ridden up behind and was guarding his father's back.

Now Calindor called up a second globe of dragonfire and instantly made it vanish. The crash of thunder stopped everyone. Glass fell from a few loose panes.

As silence returned, Albohar called out calmly: "The next man who lifts a hand will lose it. Patrollers, arrest everyone here and march them to the castle. Pervidhu, get to the bottom of this. Find out who started it."

"Yes, electman." Pervidhu leaned in his saddle over toward Calindor: "Wish we'd had you here last time. Fifteen wounded, three dead. Hardly anyone left in condition to talk."

Calindor swung down from his mount and went to the nearest casualty, a Badakh with blood streaming down his face. A murmured command to the Powers of water stopped the bleeding, and Calindor went on to put a spell of quick healing on the scalp wound. But he felt as well the Powers of blood that Nezaual had revealed to him, and shuddered a little.

With the riot over, a few townspeople came out of their houses into the market square; they stared impassively at the captives marching or limping away. A flung rock came out of the darkness and splashed harmlessly in the mud.

Calindor mounted his horse again and followed the sad parade back up to the castle. If he intended to heal any more of the wounded, he would have to wait until Albohar had penned them up; but Calindor was unsure that it would do any real good. The market square, the whole town, stank of fear and hatred. In its own way, Vidhumen was even worse than Burnbaile had been on its first morning under the Exteca.

Other patrollers met them, reporting all quiet elsewhere in the town. The patrols had broken a couple of arms and heads, and that had been enough for now. But not for long, Calindor thought.

He caught up with Pervidhu, who rode slumped in his saddle.

"You look tired, old friend," Calindor murmured in Badakhi.

"Do I? I suppose I must. We haven't had much rest. The gods know how we'll get through the winter at this rate. Or is that why you've come, to rescue us?"

Calindor shook his head. "No. I've come to tell you of even worse troubles to come."

Pervidhu glanced sidelong at him, a crooked smile in his beard. "Of *course*. Every time you turn up, life always gets remarkably worse."

Calindor bristled, and then burst into laughter that drew curious stares from the prisoners. "All too true. May I stay with you while you interrogate the prisoners?"

"Of course, hemamagh."

Hemamagh: Badakhi for healer. But its literal meaning was blood magician.

The prisoners went into a brick-walled shed along one side of a courtyard; one by one Pervidhu called them out and demanded their names, residences, and reasons for being in the market square. While he interrogated them, Calindor tended to their wounds. The Badakhar submitted with better grace than the Cantareans: it would be shameful for a Badakh to show fear under the hands of a Cantarean.

Pervidhu got few real responses to his questions. Each man mentioned some recent outrage committed by the other side; none seemed to know the actual cause of tonight's riot, and those who had started it had probably vanished long since. But the captives' sullen hostility to one another was strong enough to taste.

When the last prisoner had returned to his cell, Pervidhu shrugged, stood up and stretched. In the lamplight he looked tired. "Sometimes I think it was better in the old days. At least we Badakhar had a reason for being cruel to you Cantareans. Now we're all cruel for no reason anyone can tell."

Calindor nodded. "I think Callia is trying to tell us something. But gods aren't very good at speech."

"Oh? I remember Callia speaking through your wife, and very clear and eloquent she was too. When she was finished, so were the Five Kingdoms." He smiled suddenly, casting care aside.

"Whatever your goddess has on her mind, we'll learn it eventually. Now tell me about this girl, this Deir."

"Does she interest you?"

"I've never seen anyone quite like her. Red hair, dappled skin, blue eyes, long fingers. Very attractive."

For a Badakh, Calindor thought, Pervidhu was strange. He laughed at what others took seriously, and now here he was interested in a girl whose outward appearance was as freakish as her hidden mind.

Well, he would learn the truth eventually, so he might as well learn it now: "She is a great magician. Probably the greatest ever born in Sotalar."

Pervidhu's laughter was almost musical. "Then I'm lucky she didn't blast me on the spot when I bumped into her."

"Yes, Pervidhu. You are."

"Are you serious? A greater magician than you, Mekhmagh?"

Great Magician: the title they had given him when he had brought Callia back into the world and overthrown the Firelord. Pervidhu was fond of irony, but he used the title with sincere respect.

"When she learns how to control her talent, she will be far greater."

"You mean it. And where does she come from, this great witch?"

Pervidhu found a tall jug of beer in a cabinet and poured some into cups while Calindor told him about Burnbaile and the Exteca, about redmagic and its effect on the magicians of the Siragi Aibela. But Calindor did not tell him about the hidden magician deep within Deir's mind, or how that magician had flung him to the ground like a cast-off garment. Instead he only hinted of talent still untrained.

Pervidhu finished his beer and rubbed his head until his thick blond-brown hair stood out in all directions. "You have a great talent, Calindor, for bringing good things with bad and bad with good. After what you tell me, I don't know whether to rejoice or fall on my sword."

"You might as well rejoice while you can, but keep your sword handy," said Calindor. And both men laughed.

Fifteen

Rain fell next morning, turned to sleet, and turned to rain again. Albohar blessed it for keeping people indoors and out of mischief. Let a day or two pass, he remarked to Calindor, and tempers would cool with the weather.

No doubt the electman was right, but Calindor went out anyway. In an oilskin cape he walked through empty streets down into the new town. The marketplaces were silent, with only a few stalls and shops open; the gutters ran with a stinking mixture of horse dung, human waste, and coal dust.

In a narrow alley he found a small house of brick with a heavy, ironbound door. Calindor knocked and waited.

At last a peephole opened. The man within stared at Calindor, slammed the peephole shut, and swung open the door.

"My lord Mekhmagh! You honor this house!"

"Good morning, Dvoi. I am glad to see you again. Albohar told me you live here with the Veik Sengvakh. I have come to pay my respects."

"I am merely his servant, Mekhmagh. Please, enter and he will make you welcome."

Calindor stepped into a narrow, low-roofed room with a few simple wooden chairs and a square table. A coal fire glowed on the hearth. Two doors led to the rear of the house; Dvoi tapped on one and murmured urgently when it opened a little. Then it shut again and Dvoi turned with a nervous smile.

"My master will be with you in a moment. May I offer you tea? Bread?"

He accepted tea in a simple lidded cup and sat at the table. Dvoi said little until the door opened once more and Sengvakh entered. Dvoi bowed and left.

Sengvakh was a man of middle height, with a grizzled beard trimmed close and long hair tied back in a horsetail. He wore a simple brown woolen robe over a knitted tunic.

"You honor this house, my lord." His name might mean Singer, but his voice was harsh.

"You honor me with your hospitality, Veik."

The magician smiled faintly. "Not many use that title these days."

"You were the chief magician at the Kingdom of Halamor, and now I gather you serve Vidhumen in the same way."

"In more modest ways, I assure you. We have little need here for the kind of spells the Veikar used to cast."

"I have come to ask your advice."

Sengvakh's gravity shattered in a sudden hoarse giggle. "*My* advice, Mekhmagh? I might better ask yours."

"Not in this case. You know I learned Badakh magic under the Veik Pelshadan."

"Rest his tortured soul, yes."

"I could not learn all he knew, and the Veikar were always good at keeping secrets from one another. I want to know if you know anything about women magicians."

The half-mad giggle erupted again. "Women magicians? They say the Cantareans have them, that your mother is one—"

"She is. Please calm yourself, Veik, and answer my question."

"Long ago, long ago," he crooned, "our women knew spells of healing and warding; some kept up the practice in secret, though at risk of their lives, their lives. When the Veikar arose, we banned such abominations."

"Why abominations?"

Sengvakh stared at him—or almost at him. "Too dangerous. They could heal, but they could also kill. Sometimes they drove men mad. That was why we killed them."

"Did the Veikar learn the witches' spells?"

The shift of his gaze sent a sly glint across his eyes. "The Veikar did not become the Veikar by ignoring magic wherever it might be."

"Even the abominations."

"Especially the abominations. When you were Pelshadan's apprentice, did he not tell you that fear of magic is itself a great magic?"

"Not in so many words."

"Then he neglected your education . . . with all due respect," he added, eyes round with mock sincerity. "Respect," he added, giggling. "But it is true, Mekhmagh, as you must know. For a small sorcerer, magic is only illusion and deception, yet men fear even the seribiar, the small sorcerers."

Calindor recalled a time when he had recoiled from a small sorcerer's illusion of a dragon, and another time when the same illusion had saved his life by slowing his pursuers. "The power of illusion is self-evident," he said.

"Oh, very good, very *good*! Not many magicians have a sense of humor among their talents."

"You are trying to divert me, Sengvakh, and it has been amusing but it must stop. I would learn what spells the Veikar learned from the witches."

"Would you indeed. And exactly what might such knowledge be worth to you, Mekhmagh?"

Calindor whispered under his breath, and Sengvakh's head toppled from his shoulders. It struck the table with a bang, rolled back and forth, and stopped. His face framed by his own hair on the tabletop, Sengvakh stared up at Calindor in a shock beyond terror.

"What is your *life* worth, Sengvakh? This is an illusion, isn't it, but a good illusion doesn't feel like one. And someday it might not be an illusion at all. Now you know what the world looks like to a man in the moments after his beheading."

He picked up the head by its greasy hair and shook it gently. "The Veikar had great talents," he murmured, "and without them the Badakhar kings might not have enslaved the Cantareans. You and your teachers and your teachers' teachers put all your skill at the service of enslaving us. Callia herself sickened at what you did, and cast you down, and now you presume to bargain with me. Would you like this illusion to become reality?"

The Veik's lips twisted: *No.*

"Then you will tell me what spells the Veikar learned from the Badakhar witches, especially the spells to do with creating love and fear. You will conceal nothing, not even your hatred for me and my people."

Nothing, nothing!

"I will tell you something else, Sengvakh. Are you paying attention?"

Yes, Mekhmagh.

"When Pelshadan my master needed to call upon Mekhpur for a great spell, he killed a slave. Usually it was a woman. All the Veikar did."

Yes, yes.

"And when I come into a place where they made those sacrifices, or I meet a man who cast such spells, I feel the souls of the dead. I feel them now, Sengvakh, clinging to you. Now listen to me very carefully. You wasted their blood and life. You knew nothing of the True Gods and the power they bestow through blood and death. I cannot even threaten you with them, because you have never heard the footsteps of the Lady Serpent so you do not know how terrible it would be to die into her power.

"You have called me lord and Mekhmagh, Veik, and I have heard the sneer in your voice. But you will do as I say, or you will envy the most wretched Cantarean slave who ever died chained to a post. Will you do as I say?"

Yes yes yes—

Calindor tossed the head back onto Sengvakh's shoulders. The Veik drew breath in a long racking gasp, and let it out in a sob. Above his beard his face was a blue-tinted white.

"Now," said Calindor with a gentle smile. "Tell me about the witches' spells."

Late in the morning, Pervidhu knocked on the open door of Albohar's office. The electman waved him in; Pervidhu resisted the old instinct to kneel before the man who had been Aryo, and instead handed him a leather folder.

"My report on last night's interrogations, sir. Most of the men we arrested are known to us as brawlers and suspected thieves."

Albohar nodded and put the folder on a stack of other reports. "They can go on one of the road gangs until I get around to reading this. Then we'll draft them into a penal company. See how they like five years of fighting instead of just one night's worth. Sit down. Did Dheribi—Calindor—whatever he calls himself—tell you why he's come out on the prairie?"

"Yes, sir. Something about an empire in the south with great magic knowledge. The young fellow with him is from there, one of their magicians."

"Doesn't look stranger than any other magician. If it was anyone but Calindor telling me this story, I'd ignore it. But he seems to think these Exteca people will soon be on our doorstep, and then on our necks."

"We may well lie down to accommodate them, electman. With

all this quarreling and brawling, either we or the Cantareans might turn to newcomers for help."

"It won't be the Badakhar, not while I'm alive. Bad enough to share the land with the Cantareans, but at least they were here first. I'm not going to ally myself with strangers who'll only cast some evil spell on us and then take the land for themselves. And if any Cantarean is foolish enough to seek such a pact, I'll see he doesn't live to regret it."

"We're only one city among many, sir. If these newcomers go elsewhere, they may succeed very well. And then we could face an army of our own people, following these magicians."

Albohar smiled humorlessly. "We Badakhar have always faced armies of our own people. Killing one another is our greatest joy in life, or used to be. Even so, I'm not eager for another war, least of all when we're so disunited with the Cantareans. Calindor suggests I send word to the other cities and towns, to warn them."

"A sensible idea, sir, but not many will take such a warning to heart. Not when they're struggling to get through the winter without massacring one another."

"I agree. Still, we must try. I want you to send out couriers within the next two days to all the larger towns."

"Of course, sir. Are you aware that Calindor sent out a courier of his own this morning?"

Albohar nodded. "To Bayodar."

Pervidhu shifted his weight uncomfortably. "What would he want with the Burrowers?"

"He's very fond of them. I must say they're less frightening face-to-face than they were as ghost stories, and they've traded honestly with us. Still, I know what you mean."

For centuries the Burrowers had haunted the dreams of the Badakhar: they were the Cantareans who had neither surrendered nor fled into the mountains, but vanished into caves beneath the newly conquered land. No Badakh since then had ever gone willingly underground; those who did rarely returned.

"I think he is looking for advice, sir."

"Among all the magicians he can find. I think you're right. He went to see Sengvakh this morning."

"Advice about the girl with the red hair. Calindor says she's some kind of witch, perhaps a greater magician than himself when she completes her education."

"That I doubt, Pervidhu, though I wouldn't say so to his face. But why would he consult with other magicians if this girl is so much greater than they?"

"I don't know, electman. Perhaps I should make myself acquainted with the girl, and renew my friendship with Callishandal. I might learn something useful."

Albohar chuckled. "Didn't you once tell me that the first time you met Callishandal, she led you straight into a trap?"

"And broke my leg, and scared me witless. Now that I think of it, we should have taken *her* with us to quell the riot, instead of her husband. Nevertheless, electman, I think I enjoy her trust."

"It's the trust of the red-haired witch you're really interested in."

Pervidhu cleared his throat and smiled. "If she's as great as Calindor says she is, I would be foolish not to befriend her as well."

"If she's that great, we're probably all foolish not to run away from her. Well . . . join us for noon bread, and then take them riding this afternoon. We haven't much here to entertain them."

"I am at your service, electman."

The rain ended and the overcast frayed into ragged clouds. The sun, low in the south, still offered welcome warmth as the riders set out across the prairie. With an escort of six patrollers trailing them, Pervidhu led Callishandal, Deir, Svordo, and Nezaual east over a range of low hills to the banks of a meandering river. Cottonwoods clustered on its steep banks, their bare branches dark against the sky.

After a time Pervidhu found himself riding alongside Deir and out of earshot of the others. She seemed cheerful and relaxed, enjoying the clean sting of the air.

"You ride well," he said in his awkward Cantarean.

"I'm still learning," she answered; her accent struck Pervidhu as beautiful but almost incomprehensible. "Thank you for bringing us out here. This is pretty country."

He looked around at the distant horizon, the gentle rise and fall of the yellow prairie. "Once it was beautiful. When I was a little boy, my uncle Aghwesi used to take us across these lands. He was the upermanna of Vidhumen. The herds were like the shadows of clouds, and the grass was green."

"Was green? In winter?"

"No, but in spring and summer the grass reached our knees as we rode through it. Then it stopped growing."

"Why stopped?"

"Too many cattle, too many sheep. They ate most of the grass and trampled the rest. We had some dry years and then some floods that washed the soil away. But an upermanna without herds is no upermanna at all, so my uncle grazed his herds where the wheat fields were. That meant the Cantareans and the freemen went hungry, so we went raiding our neighbors. And they raided us."

They rode around a shallow gully choked with bones. "I remember when we lost this herd. I was fourteen. We were driving them to their summer ranges, and a thunderstorm came over us. My uncle was certain one of the Veikar had sent it, from Halamor or Ghrirei. Anyway, we were caught out in the open and the lightning began to hit, and the cattle stampeded. They ran for the gully—it had some trees then—and got there just as the flash flood came down. Two thousand cattle lost in an afternoon."

"It was very sad."

"Oh, yes. But it taught me *not* to be sad. My uncle and father thought the gods were angry with us. They thought we were being punished. I decided the gods were having fun with us, laughing at us. So now I laugh too, while I have the chance."

"There are no gods," said Deir.

"That would make the joke even better," Pervidhu said, and smiled. Then his smile vanished: *I'm talking about myself when I want her to talk. Idiot!*

"Tell me about the land you come from. Does it look like this?"

She began to talk about Burnbaile and the other villages of the Airn, the coming of the Fabarslúa, and her escape from them. Pervidhu nodded and grunted, not sure he understood all she said in her strange accent but eager to keep her talking.

So they rode along, with the others close by, but not too close, while the sun sank low above the horizon. Pervidhu led the riders westward, back to the town across a plain scattered with bones gleaming in the winter light. He was beginning to understand her strange accent, but something else tugged at him: something in her voice that he had never heard before from anyone.

"You must have been very lonely," he said suddenly, interrupting her.

"Lonely? Yes, I am a little lonely. But Callishandal and Calindor are very kind. And many others."

"No, I mean before. You were lonely in Burnbaile."

She turned to look at him, and her eyes were those of a woman he had not seen before: a woman hiding deep within a girl's soul.

"My ... my lady, I greet you," Pervidhu whispered.

"You sensed me," she said in a different voice: deeper, older, sadder. He thought of wind blowing for a thousand years until it found the one tree on an infinite empty plain.

"I heard you, my lady. I am here to serve you in any way I can."

"Ah. Perhaps I will have need of you. Until then, say nothing."

"Nothing, my lady."

The woman vanished from Deir's eyes and the girl returned, speaking slow Cantarean about how cold she was growing.

"We will soon have you back in the castle in front of a big fire," Pervidhu promised. "With hot cider and honey bread."

"That sounds good." Her teeth were chattering and she looked like a little girl.

Not until they were clattering into the castle courtyard did Pervidhu think again about something she had said: *There are no gods.* He had made a joke and forgotten about it.

Now he thought about it again, and about the woman who had appeared in Deir's eyes for a few moments.

What if she is right?

Nezaual was grateful for the excursion; the castle and the town had told him almost too much, without giving him time to reflect. Now he looked across the prairie, trying to ignore the chill wind while assembling his new knowledge for Yetecuan.

The Badakhar looked a little like the Airn, but were utterly different: tall, massive, and loud, they built in stone and brick that echoed back their shouts and coarse laughter. Their fabrics were rough and crude compared to those of Exteca weavers, but they made fine boots and understood leather. Far more important, they made tools and weapons of steel. Nezaual had sensed the spells being invoked by the stalmaghar, and the Powers imprisoned in the steel by those spells. This was a mastery of magic and metal far beyond what the Exteca knew, and it frightened him almost as much as the dragons had.

In an even fight, the greatest Exteca warrior would fall beneath the clumsiest Badakh. Nezaual imagined the Badakhar mounted on their great horses, wielding swords and lances in a charge against Exteca foot soldiers with their bronze spears and obsidian-edged clubs. No, he must ensure that such an even battle never happened.

The spells of love and terror would make the sharpest steel harmless; and where those spells failed, mammoths might succeed. The Badakhar, fortunately, seemed to know nothing of such creatures. Three or four could well rout a thousand startled horsemen.

The black stones they burned were another treasure; in the smithies they gave off astonishing heat, permitting the stalmaghar to invoke Powers of fire and earth undreamed of by the simple smiths and potters of Tola. True, the smoke from such fires was bitter and unpleasant, fouling everything it touched, but that was a small price to pay.

The Badakhar were literate; the Cantareans less so. Still, both peoples would have a great body of lore that the Exteca could take over: medicines, spells, histories, and guides to rich mines and fertile farmlands. A hundred priests could spend the rest of their lives in the libraries of this one small town, and pass on their new knowledge to the Exteca.

Their magicians would join the Exteca as well: the steel-forging stalmaghar, but also a host of others. He had heard of a group called the Veikar, greatest of the Badakh magicians, who would surely make a great addition to the priesthood of the Exteca. The Siragi Aibela might not: they seemed to fall ill in the presence of redmagic. But their cousins the Gulyaji sounded promising; Nezaual knew Calindor had sent a messenger to them, summoning their leader. It would be interesting to see what kind of lore this Renjosudaldor possessed.

He noticed that Pervidhu and Deir had ridden ahead together and seemed deep in conversation. It was offensive that the young warrior should show her such attention without anyone's parents being involved. Morality was a travesty among Cantareans, Badakhar, and Airn alike, it seemed. Well, all that would change when Tola made these barbarian peoples part of its empire.

Had the wind gusted colder? He shivered, then shuddered. No: the sun was even a little warm. But something strange had passed close by and gone away again.

A blight on these lands! Dragons, strange Powers, forces we have never dreamed of . . .

He reproved himself. The True Gods had revealed these lands and peoples as a gift to the Exteca. They had placed him here to serve their intentions. Everything was happening as the Gods willed it. All would be well.

Sixteen

The old man was tall and angular, his face seamed under coarse white hair. His beardlessness showed him to be Cantarean, but his skin was paler than many Badakhars'. Though he had evidently walked some distance in the falling snow, he wore only a simple cloak over a woolen tunic; his feet were bare.

Calindor had sensed the old man's arrival in the predawn darkness and risen from his bed without waking Callishandal. Now he ran across the castle courtyard, a globe of dragonfire above him, to greet the old man with a strong embrace:

"Renjosudaldor! Protector! I welcome you. Thank you for coming."

"I am glad to see you, Calindor." His dark eyes studied the younger man for a moment. "You are well, but troubled."

"Both. I hope my letter explained why I wished to see you." He took the old man's arm and led him across the courtyard to a door. Within, the castle was quiet; few were awake yet.

"Your letter explained very well indeed. You have seen wonders, and brought some of them back with you. I would like to meet Deir and Nezaual."

"And Nezaual will be glad to meet you. I will let Deir know you are here; if she wishes to talk, we will arrange a meeting."

"You truly feel she is two people?"

"One person, divided. The magician hides herself even from the ordinary girl." They were inside the castle now, walking to Albohar's dining hall. A smell of baking bread drifted down the corridor. "The magician does not like attention. She will know at once that you are a magician also, and she may resent your presence."

"Perhaps. Or she may welcome me as a kind of kinsman." He smiled faintly. "We understand the thoughts of those who hide." The Gulyaji were Cantareans who had escaped underground when the Badakhar triumphed centuries ago. They were old rivals of the Siragi Aibela, possessors of another magic; they had lived sometimes within a few strides of the Badakhar, yet concealed behind spells of illusion that even the Veikar had never penetrated.

Their other spells, those that nourished the crops and herds in their caverns, had weakened under the influence of Mekhpur the Firelord, the man become god who now lay imprisoned under a mountain of ice at Aishadan. Calindor, in destroying the servant of Mekhpur who had eroded Gulyaji magic, had also gained his deep name from Renjosudaldor.

Now the Gulyaji lived on the surface again, but apart from others. They had built a town of their own, Bayodar, carved from the cliffs of a small river valley, and were learning the arts of living under sky instead of under stone. Calindor had exchanged written messages with Renjosudaldor from time to time, but still knew little about the Protector's people in this new age. He took the old man into the dining hall and asked a sleepy servant for breakfast. A ring of dragonfire, dropped around the table and chairs, soon warmed them.

Over bread and honey and mead the two men talked quietly: of Burnbaile and Tanshadabela, of Bayodar and the empty caves where golden statues and carved pillars stood in darkness that would never know a dawn.

"We often wish we were back there," Renjosudaldor said. "It is beautiful here, and we rejoice in the sun and stars. But this is a frightening world. We are few, no more than a village, and all around us are people who fear and hate the very name of the Gulyaji."

"Is it the people you fear, or the land itself?"

The old man nodded. "I think it is the land. Our stories remember it as it was before the Badakhar conquered Cantarea, and when we ventured from our caves, it was usually at night. Now we see the land scourged by Callia, and we try to make it green again. But it is harsh and unforgiving." He paused, looking at his long, pale hands. "The wind frightens us."

Calindor reached across the table and put his hand gently on Renjosudaldor's arm. "The Badakhar and the mountain Cantareans are frightened too. This is a frightening world for all of us, and I think that is one reason why so many people want to go back to the old days."

"These new people, the Blood People, are most frightening of all. Tell me more about them."

Calindor spoke briefly, summarizing what he had learned from Nezaual about the history and society of the Exteca. "They have little magic, but the few spells they know are very great. They have found Powers in blood that none of us suspected, except the Badakhar witches, centuries ago."

"And what do you know of the witches?" the old man asked with an odd urgency.

"That they used blood in some of their healing spells, and that they could enchant people so that they loved whomever the witches chose. And that the Veikar crushed them, stole their secrets, and made the spells yet more secret."

Renjosudaldor nodded slowly. "The Veikar were always fools. They preferred a little power, a little knowledge, as long as they need not share it with anyone. The witches gave them scraps."

"How do you know this?"

"One of them did not fall into the Veikar's hands. Her name was Beiasha, Bee Woman, and she fell in love with my great-great-great-grandfather Halasovaldor. It was he who guided the Gulyaji into the caves and started the building of Bayo Bealar. She taught him all the witchlore she knew, and he passed it on to his descendants."

Calindor leaned across the table, his eyes locked on the old man's. "The lore contains spells of love and terror?"

"And much else as well. They were great healers, and closer to Cantarean magic than their menfolk ever were. But I think you already know that. Have you been speaking with the Veikar?"

"With one. He told me everything he knew. You are right, Protector, to say they learned only scraps. Their blood spells need an outright death, when a few drops of blood would achieve the same end. They can't really enchant a soul—they only madden the body, while the soul remains imprisoned inside."

"You would learn more."

"I must. The Exteca will come someday and do to us what they did to Deir's people. I must understand the principles of their magic and devise counterspells."

For a time the older magician was silent, holding an empty mead cup. Then he spoke almost in a whisper: "I know of no counterspells to protect you from the harm you have already done yourself."

"Harm?"

"I sense the scars you have put in your flesh, Calindor. They are the least of your ills. You have learned much, and learned well, but it is taking you away from Callia. And from yourself."

Calindor frowned. "I do this for Callia's sake, and to protect her people."

Another long silence fell. Then Renjosudaldor said: "In the caves of Bayo Bealar you came to us and I taught you gladly. I will teach you again, even the lore that none ever learned outside my fathers' lineage. But one thing I cannot teach you, Calindor; only you can teach yourself to know your own motives. So I can *tell* you that you are as frightened as the Badakhar and the Gulyaji and the mountain Cantareans, but I cannot *teach* you that."

"I will be glad to be your student again, Renjosudaldor. Now here come Albohar and Eskel; let us greet them."

The Badakhar had feared the Gulyaji for centuries, but they welcomed Renjosudaldor as a visiting king. He and his people, foreseeing the wrath of Callia, had ventured from their caves in Bayo Bealar and made their way in secret to the coal mines of Aishadan. There they had prepared a haven for Cantareans and Badakhar alike, saving thousands who would otherwise have died in the great tempest. Albohar and his wife and son had been among those thousands.

For a time the conversation was formal and courteous: an exchange of courtesies and compliments. But soon it turned to the problems of small communities in a hard winter, and how they might help one another.

"While this snow lasts we can't do much," Albohar said. "But the dragon's wind will blow in from the mountains before long, and then we can do some trading. We have sheepskins and good woolens, and plenty of coal."

"We can use them. In return we can offer some good seed grain, early maturing and resistant to blight."

"Our traders will be knocking on your door."

By now others were entering the dining hall, hastening first to the hearth for bread, then to the mead cask, and at last to the long table. Messengers arrived with news of the night patrols, clerks with tallies of foodstuffs and horseshoes; Albohar soon excused himself to deal with their demands.

Callishandal and Deir entered, with Nezaual and Pervidhu close behind him. Renjosudaldor greeted Callishandal with affection, and bowed to Deir. She bowed awkwardly in reply and turned her attention to Pervidhu, who was serving her bread and honey. Nezaual ignored Pervidhu's offer of breakfast and fixed his eyes on the Gulyaji.

"My master has told me of you, honored father. This is a great honor."

"I am honored also. Calindor has told me of the greatness of Tola and its True Gods."

"May we someday walk its streets together, honored father, and sacrifice together to the Gods."

Callishandal had scarcely touched her breakfast, but now she stood abruptly and excused herself. Her face was pale and tense, and she met no one's eyes.

Renjosudaldor glanced at Calindor and spoke softly: "I believe she has summoned you."

"Has she? Well, then I will go and speak with her." He rose and left the table. Renjosudaldor smiled and chatted amiably about the varieties of honey produced in Cantarea.

Calindor found her not in their room, but on the walkway behind the castle parapet. Snow was falling thicker than ever. Callishandal stood unmoving, looking down at the white-roofed town.

"What is the matter?" he asked, standing close behind her. "You are angry with me."

"Not with you—with what you are becoming. Svordo hears in the town that you've made the Veik Sengvakh your servant, and now the Protector comes to serve you also. But whose servant are you? You go off with Nezaual each day, and he teaches you a new spell, and that night I see a new wound. By spring you'll look like a fresh-ploughed field."

He said nothing for a moment. Then: "By spring the Exteca will be here. I'm sure of it. They will make themselves our masters, unless I find a way to stop their magic. To stop it I must learn it, just as I learned Badakh magic from Pelshadan."

Callishandal turned to face him. Fluffy snowflakes glowed in her black hair; her face was hard with anger. "So you have said, again and again, since we met Nezaual and his master. Exteca magic is learning *you*, Calindor. I think it knows you better than I do, better than you know yourself. You may think you can use redmagic against the Exteca, but what if it only makes you its tool, makes you just another Exteca priest? What will happen to us then?"

"It will not happen. That I promise you." He stepped forward to embrace her, but she retreated.

"Do not promise."

He clasped his hands over the small of his back. "Apparently I can't please anyone today. Renjosudaldor is worried about me also."

"Do you think he has no reason? Is Nezaual teaching you simple spells to find water and cure fever?"

"Sometimes, yes. Every spell teaches me something about the principles under it."

"Every spell takes you further away from yourself. And from me."

Was it ice or fire that gripped his heart? "You are speaking of things you don't know. Things I am glad you don't know, because they are more terrible than anything the Badakhar dreamed of. But I will not discuss this further while you are angry."

He turned and walked through the snow along the parapet until he came to the door leading into the castle. Callishandal did not follow him, and he did not look back.

That afternoon Callishandal moved into a small room adjoining Ghelasha's. The former queen helped make the bed and roll out a woolen carpet over the cold floor. While Callishandal silently hung her few garments on the wall pegs, Ghelasha stoked the coal fire.

At length Callishandal sat on the edge of the bed, her hands in her lap, and looked into the glowing coals.

"Can I be of further help?" Ghelasha asked.

"Only keep me company for a while, my lady. I am angry with myself."

"With yourself? Whatever for?"

"I should have stayed with him. I should not have complained. But I have feared for him ever since he first learned of the Exteca and their magic, and today I could not endure it any longer. I should have been stronger."

The older woman sat beside her. Ghelasha's yellow hair gleamed almost as bright as the orange coals on the hearth. "You are loyal to him. You risked your life for him, when we sought to kill him. In his trouble you kept to his side, as I did not keep to Albohar when he lay dying of his ensorcelled wound. I honor you for that, Callishandal. But I honor you more for leaving him."

Tears stung Callishandal's eyes, and she felt a hot droplet fall upon her chilled hand. "Honor? That is not the word I would choose."

"Listen to me. Do you know why Badakhar women are so cruel? Do you know why we whipped our slaves in the old days, why we punished them for nothing? Because we were more loyal to our men than to ourselves. Our mothers and aunts taught us all the old legends about queens who killed themselves so their kings could marry someone who could bear a son, about shepherdesses who died to save their husbands' flocks. Always the woman gave, and always the man took, and the only way we could take back something was to show our slaves that we were at least a little higher than they.

"Now we are still chained to our men, while our former slaves, men and women, treat one another as equals. And when they quarrel and part, they do that as equals also."

"Would you leave Albohar, then?"

"No—he's a good man, and if he does not love me, at least he cares for me and respects me. That's more than many a Badakh wife can say. But if he mistreated me, I would leave him in that instant, though it cost me my life in the next."

"Calindor hasn't mistreated me. He's mistreated himself."

"And you mistreat yourself, girl. If he has not seen your fear and distress, he's been a fool; and if he knows your feelings and does nothing to console you, then he's worse than a fool."

Callishandal shivered. "And if he lets me go?"

"Then wish him well and walk away. Better to be alone with your freedom and self-respect than lose both for the sake of a man under your blanket."

Weeping, Callishandal leaned against Ghelasha's shoulder and took comfort from the older woman's embrace. Strange, that so hard and grim a Badakh woman should understand the grief of a Cantarean.

For three days Calindor and Nezaual spent most of their time in Renjosudaldor's apartment. They came out only to eat and sleep, and did little of either.

No one spoke of the separation. Deir tried to be of use to Callishandal, but the older woman preferred her own company and contrived errands that would take Deir away to remote corners of the castle.

On one such mission, in search of fabrics, Deir encountered Pervidhu. It was a cold afternoon, already growing dark, and the light of Deir's candle sparked glitter on the frosted walls.

"I'm glad to find you," she said to him, her breath fluttering in the chill air. "I want to talk with you."

"You look half frozen," Pervidhu said. "Come into the kitchen and warm yourself."

It was a welcoming place in this cold: a large, low-ceilinged room with a fireplace at either end and two brick ovens between them. The air was warm, aromatic with the scent of baking bread and simmering soup. The cooks—three middle-aged Cantareans—welcomed them with tall mugs of hot tea and then went back to their duties. Pervidhu gestured to a table beside one of the ovens, across the room from the cooks.

She drew out a chair for herself, bumping into Pervidhu in the process, and then realized he had meant to pull out the chair for her, as if she were a toddler. The Badakhar were like that, she'd noticed—insulting when they most meant to be kind. Still, she would not indulge herself in being annoyed.

"I need your advice," she said.

"The best advice I can offer is that you seek it from someone wiser than I."

She didn't laugh; by the time she realized he'd intended to joke, the moment had passed. Still, she was not entirely unhappy to see him look uncomfortable.

"Callishandal is bitterly unhappy since she left Calindor's rooms," Deir said. "You are Calindor's friend. Has he spoken to you about it?"

Pervidhu shook his head. "He is my friend, and I owe him my life many times over. I like him and respect him, but a Cantarean would not consult any Badakh about troubles with his wife."

"Would he listen to you if you talked to him?"

"He listens to his old Gulyaji teacher, and that young Nezaual, and to no one else. I've scarcely seen him more than Callishandal has in the last few days."

"It's not fair. Just because he's a great magician, he thinks he can do anything he likes. If anyone gets hurt, too bad."

"You don't have to be a great magician to think like that; just grow up as a Badakh."

She looked skeptically at him. "You don't think that way."

"I'm a very bad excuse for a Badakh. Most of what my people do strikes me as gloriously stupid. Luckily for me, they also strike me as funny. Now, have you talked with Callishandal?"

"I've tried. She won't talk at all about him, and then she sends me on foolish errands." She glanced at the roll of fabric on her lap. "I like them both, and I want them to be happy. I also want Calindor to destroy the Exteca."

"While Callishandal fears the Exteca will destroy him. Well, Deir, I wish I could help you. I can try to talk with Calindor when I see him next, but that may not be for weeks. I'm leaving Vidhumen tomorrow morning."

"Leaving? You can't! Why? Where are you going?"

"You sound distressed. Don't tell me you're miserable too."

Deir kept her hands around the hot mug. "Only cold. Burnbaile was never as cold as this place."

"We've seen it colder. But a dragon's wind will come soon, and then it'll warm up. I only hope it comes tonight."

"Where are you going?" she repeated.

"Albohar is sending couriers out to the other towns and cities, to warn them about the Exteca."

"Good. I wish someone had warned us. But I'm sorry that you have to go. Will you be long?"

"Fifteen or twenty days, perhaps, if the weather is good. Longer if it turns cold again." He shrugged. "I doubt we'll be very welcome. No one wants to hear about yet more trouble coming."

"I'll miss you."

Startled, he looked up from his tea. The magician was in Deir's eyes, speaking in that strange, womanly voice.

"And I'll miss you . . . my lady." He shivered a little. "This is very strange."

"Is it?"

"To love a woman hiding within a girl, and a girl sheltering a woman. And not even to know whom it is I love, or why she hides."

He glimpsed fear and anguish in her eyes, and then the magician was gone.

"It'll be boring here without you," Deir the girl said.

Does she even realize someone else is inside her? Does the girl sleep when the woman speaks?

"Enjoy the boredom while you can," he replied, hearing a tremor in his own voice. "I'll talk to Calindor tonight if I can find him, but don't expect him to change his mind just because I nag him."

She smiled, and put out a hand to touch his sleeve. "Thank you, Pervidhu."

Seventeen

Forty horsemen, seventy-five horses, and twenty pack mules: enough men to defend themselves and their trade goods, not quite enough to appear a threat. For ten days they had been moving south across the prairie. A dragon's wind had come as Pervidhu had hoped, warming the air and melting the snow. But it melted the frozen soil also. The horses plodded with lumps of heavy, yellow-brown mud clinging to their hooves. Rain fell often, turning the roads into bogs.

Still, Pervidhu thought as they rode into Bhadvedor, the mission had gone well. The towns of the south had welcomed them, though not with bountiful feasts or high prices for Vidhumen's iron and hides. Each electman or speaker had listened thoughtfully to Albohar's warning about the Exteca and their deadly magic. The local magicians had listened also; when they learned that the Mekhmagh Calindor himself was the source of the warning, they had whispered urgently in their masters' ears and the masters had grimly nodded.

The mission need not reach every village on the prairie; news would travel fast even in winter. The Exteca, if they did arrive, would find a hostile land facing them.

Pervidhu remembered Bhadvedor as a busy town, one of the largest in the old kingdom of Halamor. Now it was the capital of a loose association of towns and manors stretching south into the semidesert plains where neither Badakhar nor Cantareans lived. Callia's wrath had leveled the old castle; Elsman, the town's speaker, was building a new one but had completed little more than the foundations and walls.

Nor did the town have room for so many men and their animals. Pervidhu expected nothing better than a patch of ground on the edge of town, and the meadow he got here was quite adequate. Some of his men fed and rested the animals, while others roped off the meadow and pitched tents. Though the sky was overcast, he smelled no snow in the chilly air. A silent crowd of ragged children and gaunt men watched from a distance; no one annoyed Badakhar warriors without good cause.

Some of them will try to steal horses tonight, Pervidhu thought. Everyone else had tried also, but none had succeeded and three had died in the attempt. His men had no desire to walk home in the mud.

Two Cantarean horsemen rode slowly out of the town and into the meadow, one bearing a lance with Elsman's green-and-white-striped pennant. Pervidhu explained his purpose—though the electman doubtless knew it already—and the messengers rode slowly away.

The summons to Elsman would doubtless come before long. Meanwhile, Pervidhu had chores to do: inspecting the horses and mules, buying some coal and firewood, and helping to haul water from a muddy creek for the cooks. Though everyone seemed busy, Pervidhu was glad to see that no one ignored the watchers and the town beyond. His men hadn't lost their edge; if they did, their peril would increase at once. This was the last town. With luck they could ride straight for home and be back in Vidhumen within five days.

Back to Deir . . . He wondered what his parents would think of her. They and his two older brothers had survived the storm, but remained on their battered farmstead rather than seek security in Vidhumen. The whole family were typical upermannar—tough, narrow, humorless save for a rough, malicious wit. He had escaped his kinfolk at the first opportunity, and stayed away; but if anything came of his love for Deir, he knew he would have to bring her to meet them. They would gape at her red hair and freckles, sneer at her inability to speak more than a few words of Badakhi, and laugh if he told them she was a witch.

With any luck, he thought glumly, she would take offense and turn them all into rotted stumps.

His chores done for the moment, Pervidhu unrolled an oiled cowhide on the floor of his tent and then threw his bedroll onto it. He stretched out, hands under his head, and daydreamed: her hair gleaming in firelight, her quick smile, and the woman hiding within the girl. No Badakh woman, no Cantarean, had ever affected him as she did. To be in her presence was to live more intensely, to think more keenly, to taste the sweetness of every breath. For her, he would ride to far Burnbaile itself and liberate it single-handed if he must—and then live there with her into a serene old age with redheaded grandchildren around them.

"Hey, you—you awake?"

A Badakh was standing in the entrance to the tent, staring down at him. He was leaning on a spear bearing Elsman's pennant.

Pervidhu sat up. "I am. You're from the electman?"

"I am. He wants to see you. Alone."

That was typical; not many local leaders welcomed groups of armed strangers inside their walls. Pervidhu walked out of the tent and fell in between the Badakh and another spearman. They walked across the meadow and up the road into the town, under the eyes of scores of quietly watchful people. Well, it would have been no different in the old days: the Halamoris had never liked the Badakhar of Aishadan, even the traders who came with fine steel and good hides.

Rough shacks lined the inner wall of Bhadvedor's new castle. Five or six armed men guarded the largest of them, and stepped aside to let Pervidhu and his escort pass within. A Badakh woman knelt to remove Pervidhu's muddy boots and to replace them with fur-lined slippers; he was grateful for their warmth and lightness.

Elsman, for all his Badakh name, was a short, wiry Cantarean with the swastika tattoo on his forehead that marked him as one of the old arekakhar slave police. Most had died soon after Callia's storm, usually at the hands of those they had terrorized; this one, at least, had survived and prospered. His quarters were spacious, with a serviceable fireplace and comfortable chairs.

The electman was sitting in one of them, his slippered feet close to the fire. He looked up, nodded without expression, and said: "Sit."

Pervidhu obeyed, and smiled his thanks when the servant brought him a cup of mead. Apart from Elsman and the servant, no one was in the room; Pervidhu suspected, however, that others were within earshot.

"Your news travels faster than you do," Elsman said. "Something about a race of magicians coming to conquer us?"

"You have saved me a long speech, electman."

"I'm in no hurry. You can give me the whole longchant."

"As you wish." So he recited what he had told all the other speakers and electmen, while Elsman listened without interruption. The whole account took two more cups of mead, and Pervidhu was feeling pleasantly half drunk as he finished.

"A most interesting account," Elsman said. "I don't believe a word of it."

Pervidhu blinked. "I beg your pardon, electman?"

"It's all too obvious what your master wants. He lost his kingdom, and now he wants to gain power over us. So he sends you out to frighten people into begging for help. Maybe a little garrison of two or three hundred Badakhar? Just to protect us from these evil southerners?" Elsman smiled crookedly. "Albohar was a famous liar and betrayer in the old days, and I doubt he's changed much. As for that half-breed bastard of his, that so-called Mekhmagh—let him come and tell me himself about these Blood People and their magic."

"I'm sure Calindor would be glad to visit you, electman, but he is very busy."

"Busy planning to conquer us. I never believed much of what they say about him, you know. He's more than half Badakh if you ask me, and we don't trust them here."

"I've seen a number of them in your service, electman."

"They know their place. They know we're the masters now. If they don't like it, they can leave."

Pervidhu stood up, a little off balance. "And the same is true of me. I thank you for hearing me out, electman, and for your allowing us the use of your meadow. We will be on our way home tomorrow morning."

"You're not going anywhere. I like listening to you, Badakh. I want to listen to you all night long if I must, until you tell me why you really came here. To spy out our defenses, distract us from the real dangers—isn't that it?"

"Thank you again, electman." Pervidhu turned, not really caring if he was being outrageously rude, and faced three men; the tips of their sabers pointed at his belly, heart, and throat.

For a long instant Pervidhu stood still, looking at the flat dark eyes of the Cantarean swordsmen. He heard Elsman get up from his chair and pad across the floor toward him. Then he flung himself backward, hoping that Elsman was not holding a dagger before him.

They crashed to the floor together, and Pervidhu rolled to his right. The fireplace was close enough to reach into, so he snatched the end of a burning log and flung it at the three swordsmen. That bought him time enough to get to his feet and grasp a long cast-iron poker leaning against the hearth.

Elsman was roaring as he struggled upright; the dagger was in his hand now, too late. "Kill the bastard! No, cripple him only. Now I *really* want him to talk."

Pervidhu smiled bitterly at him. "I'll talk, all right, and you'd better listen. Forty well-armed horsemen are within a few minutes of here, and they'll come through your gates like wind through grass. I may be dead when they get here, but you'll count your own life in ten breaths."

"You forget what I am," Elsman said, pointing to his forehead. "We arekakhar were living dead men from the moment we took the tattoo. The moment of my death is of no concern to me." Then the dagger was no longer in his hand but in the air, a silver gleam.

It will strike me—

He swung the poker up, knowing he was too slow, angry with himself for not expecting this, for talking when he should have battered his way through the swordsmen and made a run for it.

Then blazing light filled the room, so bright he cried out. Somehow he had always expected death to be darkness, not this overwhelming glare.

The light vanished as suddenly as it had appeared. Swirls of shimmering yellow and purple swam in Pervidhu's gaze as he completed the swing of the poker. It struck nothing. He shifted his feet, regaining his balance and preparing for the next assault. It might be something as simple as a flung chair, but more likely the swordsmen would come at him from three sides—and him with the fireplace behind him.

Where's the knife? He dared not even look down to see if it had embedded itself between his ribs; instead he brushed his hand down his chest and felt nothing. Only then did he truly look at Elsman and the three other Cantareans.

Elsman had retreated to a corner of the room, one hand raised as if to ward off a blow. His face was a mask of terror. The swordsmen had dropped their sabers and one man was on his knees, sobbing.

"I'm leaving now," Pervidhu said quietly. No one replied. He stepped slowly across the room, past the swordsmen and through the door. Two other men stood just beyond the doorway, their faces as frozen in fear as Elsman's. Pervidhu nodded to them and walked steadily, not too quickly, down the corridor and back to the gate. The woman there had cleaned his boots, and she helped him put them back on.

"Is there anything the electman needs?" she asked as he pulled on his cloak.

"As a matter of fact, I think he would be grateful if you would attend on him," Pervidhu replied. "And would you tell him I thank him again for his hospitality and not to trouble himself further on our account. We shall be departing before dawn tomorrow."

"Very good, sir."

Ignoring the stares of the townspeople, he walked alone through the streets and back to the meadow. One of his men greeted him.

"Surprised to see you back so soon. What happened?"

"That's what I'd like to know," Pervidhu said.

Yetecuan stepped away from the portable temple. He gave the heart to the coals glowing on the tripod before the idol of Cihuacoatl and felt his spirits rise. Yes, it had been wise and expedient for the priests at home in Tola to sacrifice on behalf of the northern expedition. But a gift to the True Gods was a gift to their priests too, and it did him good to honor them directly.

As well, sacrifices of the northern barbarians would teach the Exteca—and the True Gods—much about the peoples who were becoming their servants. The old beliefs about the north as an empty wilderness had proved wrong; many tribes lived within its mountains and deserts. They were simple people, hunters and gardeners. Their weapons were beautifully flaked stone spearheads and cleverly poisoned barbs of bone. If their ideas of war were simple also, their taste for battle was well-developed. The plumes and bronze weapons of the Exteca had not frightened them, nor had the mammoths charging among them. Yetecuan had twice saved Exteca lives with a spell of terror, driving the barbarians from the battlefield when they would otherwise have stood and died to the last man.

The Gods had other uses for these peoples; first scores, then hundreds, and now thousands of them marched as allies of the Exteca. They called themselves many names, but to the Exteca they were simply Chontalteca, foreigners. They were superb hunters who helped feed the Exteca in country that offered little but sagebrush and thorns. Better still, their women were fine tanners and tailors who could make warm robes against the bitter cold. Without them, the expedition would have lost many men in the snowstorms that whirled across the land.

No such storm now threatened, thanks to the True Gods. A warm wind had thawed the land, and the expedition had made good advances despite the muddy terrain. This afternoon was almost mild. The camp was bustling; smoke rose from a thousand places among the tents and lean-tos. Mammoths carried logs in their curled trunks, fuel for the expedition's insatiable fires. Barbarians carried water from the river just to the north of the campsite. Exteca soldiers sang and danced despite the day's long march.

Yetecuan smiled. The Gods had blessed them all, every step of the way. Foes became servants, desert yielded food and drink, pathways opened through the densest forests. When the time came to write it all down, the historians would call this the greatest exploit in all the centuries of the empire.

Now more good news had come. The latest Chontalteca tribe to join their cause—stocky, gold-skinned people who wore tunics of birds' skins—had used gestures and drawings to describe white-skinned horsemen in the north beyond the mountains. They did not sound like Calindor's people, but doubtless they would make useful allies; none of the barbarians so far used horses as anything but meat.

A servant held up a copper bowl full of warm water. Yetecuan rinsed his hands until the water turned red, then took the bowl and poured it reverently into the muddy soil around the altar. He sensed the soil welcoming the gift, and smiled again.

—Why was he lying on the damp ground? Why did he feel as if he had been struck with a club? Had the servant attacked him?

No. Faintly he heard anxious voices, felt hands grip him and lift him until he sat upright on a decayed log. Servants and priests and soldiers crowded round him, and he saw the fright and concern in their faces. *Beloved children,* he tried to say, but the words would not come. After a time that seemed long he recalled the night in Burnbaile and saw the woman Sivon stretched naked over the backs of his warriors, awaiting his knife.

Magic again. Very great magic. We are getting close.

Albohar had put up gongs of different pitch around Vidhumen, so the deep boom warned of trouble in the main market square again. It was late afternoon, overcast and threatening snow or sleet.

"I'll go," said Calindor. He had been sitting in Albohar's office, talking about the Exteca; the alarm brought them back to more immediate problems.

"Very good. I'll be along shortly."

"No. They shouldn't start thinking you take every squabble so seriously. I'll go with a couple of guards and Nezaual. If I can't deal with a few brawlers, I'll be little use against the Exteca."

Albohar frowned, then shrugged. "You're right. I'm beginning to remind myself of my father, telling the cooks how to make soup. But take more men than two or three."

"As you wish."

He summoned Nezaual simply and roughly, with a sweeping focus that would jolt the boy out of his chair. Then, leaving the office, he heard Nezaual clattering down the stairs.

"Honored father! How may I serve you?" He fell into step beside Calindor, who was already heading for the courtyard.

"Come with me. Another riot in the town. The electman has asked us to end it. This is a good occasion to try the spell of terror."

"Yes, it would be! Not too large a group, I hope—it is hard to control at first, they say. My honored father Yetecuan never let me cast it, though he taught me the words and the means of drawing blood."

"So you keep telling me," Calindor replied with a grin. "I hope I have remembered everything."

Nezaual looked pale. "Oh, so do I, honored father!"

They found horses saddled and waiting—Albohar drilled his stableboys as much as his guards—and rode down into the town with two young Badakh warriors. Calindor rode with his eyes closed, in a deep focus that showed more than sight could. He sensed the Powers all around him; every fire in Vidhumen gleamed like a star in his focus, the coming squall gathered force overhead, earth and water contended in the half-frozen ground. And he sensed also the immanence of the True Gods, residing both in the world and in the souls of men. His spell would rouse them to stir those souls to fear, drive them from the market, and restore peace without violence.

Except to himself.

Four men were down in the mud of the market, two screaming and two lying still. Three others were defending a wagon tipped on its side and spilling sacks of grain: all three were Badakhar, and most of the mob were Cantareans. How many? It mattered. Fifteen, eighteen, twenty-three . . . too many to count!

Nezaual cast an experienced eye over the struggling men. "A hundred and eight, honored father."

"Thank you, beloved son."

Another couple of hundred were bystanders; they might suffer as well, but it could not be helped. Practice with this spell might make all the difference when the Exteca came.

They did not enter the market square or approach the mob. The two Badakhar escorts looked at Calindor curiously, expecting to see some flash and bang of illusion.

From the pocket of his fur-lined coat Calindor drew a small blade of obsidian set in a jade handle no longer than two joints of his index finger. Pulling open his coat and the shirt beneath it, he drew the blade horizontally across his chest three times while invoking the True God of terror, Mitac.

For an instant the market was utterly silent; even the screaming men in the mud were still. Someone dropped a sack of grain he had pulled from the toppled cart and looked right and left. Then a sound arose like a gust of wind in mountain pines, the sound of frightened people scrambling to get out of the marketplace.

Dizzily, Calindor swayed in his saddle. He felt hot blood run down his ribs and soak into his trousers. Behind him came the sound of clattering hooves; he knew it was his escort, riding in panic back to the castle.

Nezaual remained mounted beside him, but his face was pallid and his eyes stared.

"Now it is ended, now it ends," Calindor muttered. The True God enveloped him for an awful moment, savoring his blood, and then was gone.

Snow whirled down out of the featureless sky. All over Vidhumen people were screaming.

The market was empty. Only the two dead men remained; the two wounded were screaming again as they dragged themselves through the mud. One left a streaked red trail behind him.

In one of the houses facing the market, an open doorway glowed orange; a dropped lamp had started a fire. Calindor extinguished it with a thought of dragon's magic and then slowly dismounted. The screams were less loud now, except for that of a baby somewhere near.

"Go and see to the baby," Calindor said. "It just needs some soothing."

"Honored father, I obey. The spell was very strong."

"Too strong. It spilled in all directions, all over the town." In a moment he would have to start making amends, riding in pursuit of the people running blindly out of the town into the teeth of the coming squall. But for a moment he needed to rest, to wait and explore the feelings that the spell had created in him.

He reeled back, too shocked even to grab for the stirrup as he fought for balance. Nezaual, nearing the house with the screaming baby, sprawled facedown.

The spell of terror had been great and beautiful, even as he had clumsily cast it. But the force of this other spell was far stronger, even though he knew it was not aimed at him.

Deir. But what's the matter? Why would she do this?

Nezaual lifted himself onto hands and knees, shook his head and looked back at Calindor. "Honored father? No doubt you know best, but, ah, I do not think the second spell was really necessary."

"Perhaps you are . . . right, Nezaual. Never mind. Go and see to the baby."

Calming the town took all evening. Calindor rode from street to street, calling people out of their houses to tell them that all was well. For all their fear, they obeyed his summons. They stood shivering in the snow, men and women alike, their faces pale in the dragonfire light he cast over them.

"We will have no more brawls and riots," he told them. "Cantareans and Badakhar will live together in peace if not in friendship. Lift a hand against another, and you see now what can befall you."

They nodded and bowed, and some—even Badakhar—fell into the icy mud on all fours as disgraced Cantarean slaves once had when seeking their master's forgiveness. Calindor felt anger rise in him at the sight, but he kept his temper.

Nezaual had found the baby's parents and then caught up with Calindor; now he rode a respectful few paces behind his master, struggling to keep a grin from spreading all over his face.

"Honored father, they will scarcely believe me in Tola," he said as they rode back to the castle. "A first casting of such power! A whole city such as this—well, a town—ensorcelled by a spell of terror! The True Gods love you well, and Mitac is your elder brother."

Calindor said nothing, and when they reached the castle, he went straight to his chambers without reporting to Albohar. The castle was still in an uproar, with women screaming everywhere and men shuddering and staring. He ignored them; the effect would wear off soon, and he was worse than tired.

Was it the spell he had cast? Most magicians could not cast a spell like that more than two or three times a year, if that often; his great gift had always been his immunity to weariness. Was it the shock of Deir's spell? No—he had felt himself caught on the edges of her magic before, and it had not induced this feeling before.

He pushed open the door of his bedchamber and went in without troubling to light a candle. In focus he could sense everything perfectly well—including the absence of Callishandal.

Calindor stretched out on the bed and calmed himself with a few slow breaths. He strengthened his focus, shutting out the clamor in the hallways, and sought the Open Dream. Never before had he felt the need for the counsel of Calihalingol and his other ancestors, and of his mother and father. He was in unknown country now, and if the Siragi Aibela knew no more of it than he did, they at least had wisdom.

When dawn came with a spatter of wet snow against the little windowpanes, he fell into a restless sleep. He dreamed an ordinary dream in which he walked along the silent river with his mother.

I cannot enter the Open Dream, he said to her.

Tilcalli looked at him, her face unreadable, and then walked away toward the little village where the ancestors lived and danced the past and future. But the village was empty, and the sun was setting behind the distant mountains where the ancestors' souls went when they wearied of serving Callia. Calindor watched her walk through the little village, and woke in horror.

Eighteen

The days were growing longer already, though the north wind still cut into the flesh. On this bright cold afternoon, Yetecuan sat bundled in furs in his little hut atop his favorite mammoth. Mixnal the mammoth driver sat behind the beast's ears, speaking softly to it. Ahead stretched a vast plain of white and gold, snow and grass, gleaming in the sun. The sky was clear, an intense blue far different from the milky sky of Tola, and the horizon was as sharp-edged as an obsidian blade.

The approaching riders were visible now, far out across the plain, but he had sensed them since the night before. They were like echoes of the blow he had suffered five days before, like sparks blown into the night from a lightning-blasted tree.

Four sparks, but ten riders. Those touched by the spell had brought companions.

I thank you, True Gods. In all you do, you show your love for us.

It could not be coincidence that spellbound northerners were now approaching the Exteca expedition; the Gods guided them across this empty land to this meeting.

They would encounter an army in good marching order. The days of dispersion were long past, and the army was now prepared for combat at any moment. Without troubling to look left or right, Yetecuan knew that the three columns were in their proper positions, with the main column slightly ahead of those on either side. Most of the Chontalteca allies were in the center, while Exteca teteuctin guarded the flanks. Yetecuan rode in the vanguard of the center column, with a hundred of General Yaocatl's best warriors marching alongside. Colotic rode nearby, dispatching the couriers who galloped between Yaocatl and the columns. The general knew where everyone was: who was lagging, who was wandering off the route of march. Almost five thousand men, another thousand women and children, hundreds of horses—Yaocatl did not so much lead his army as wear it like a great, trailing garment.

Yetecuan looked admiringly at Yaocatl conferring with one of his officers as they rode along; even without the gift of magic, the general knew that riders were coming from the north, and he was already planning how to receive them. No doubt it would be appropriate; Yaocatl had yet to make a mistake. In half a year he had brought a whole world into the empire, and given to the Gods the countless peoples of the Chontalteca. If the Gods chose to take him now, and let him fall dead from his horse, Yaocatl's fame would still be greater and more deserved than any Exteca warrior before him.

And this is but the beginning. When the Magicians' Land, Tonaltlan, becomes part of the empire, then we will give the whole world to you, beloved Gods.

Mammoths, horses, and men marched steadily north across the plain. Sometimes a song rose from the Exteca warriors, and the Chontalteca would answer in their own strange chanting. But for the most part the only sounds were the rustle of feet and hooves in crusty snow, the occasional snort of a horse or trumpet of a mammoth.

The northern riders were closer now, and had paused on a low ridge to await the columns. Yetecuan nodded. That would doubtless be a suitable campsite; he knew the land well enough by now to know that beyond the ridge would lie a shallow, wooded gulley and a stream, where the army could shelter from the wind and spend a comfortable night.

Exteca scouts now rode ahead to greet the northerners. Yetecuan watched as they rode up the ridge and halted. The northerners did not move, though a couple of their horses stamped nervously. This could be critical: not a gentle encounter of smiling pochteca traders and gaping barbarians, but the confrontation of two groups of warriors. Yetecuan thought of the knife that Calindor had given him, of its beautiful sharp edge. If the strangers had such weapons, and chose to use them, the expedition would probably have to fight its way into the Magicians' Land.

When the northerners' horses finally caught sight and scent of the mammoths, they grew frightened; Yetecuan saw the men struggle to control their mounts. It did not take them long, and Yetecuan was now close enough to look down and see the northerners' grim expressions.

The Chontalteca had described these people well, he decided: people of white skins and bearded faces, something like the Airn though far bigger and heavier. They wore clothing of leather and wool, and long cloaks. Their beards and long hair were yellow or brown.

Then Yetecuan looked again and saw that half the northerners were brown-skinned and black-haired, like Calindor and Callishandal, and one of them appeared to be the leader. He was a hard-bitten man in a heavy green cloak, with a scabbarded sword hanging from his saddle. When he looked up at the mammoth, he revealed a strange mark on his forehead, a kind of hooked cross. And beneath that mark were eyes that to Yetecuan seemed half mad.

Three of the other men showed the aura of the spell they had survived, but this hook-cross man had been closest. Yetecuan marveled that he still lived.

The True Gods protected you, my beloved new son. But I think they will soon call you to serve them.

The vanguard of the column reached the ridge and paused before the ten men. The rest of the expedition broke up into small groups and moved to east and west along the river, seeking campsites. Accustomed to this task, the teteuctin warriors made little noise. Their silent efficiency seemed to startle the northerners as much as the mammoths had startled the horses.

Colotic rode alongside Yetecuan's mammoth. "Honored father, would you like to descend to meet these men?"

"Perhaps in a while, beloved son. For now let us invite them to rest and refresh themselves. Do you think someone could look after their horses?"

Yetecuan leaned back and dozed for a while, vaguely aware of the northerners' harsh, deep voices. What an ugly language they spoke! How slow they were to understand the simple words that Colotic and his men tried to teach them. Perhaps being spellbound had fuddled their wits? No, the hook-cross man seemed quickest to grasp what the Exteca were saying, even if he gave off a magical aura that Yetecuan could see even in half sleep.

What could it have been? The aura reminded him of spells of protection, but oddly twisted. Had a great magician, perhaps Calindor himself, sent these men south with some strange magical shield? No. But they had been close to someone so protected. Could they have attacked such a person and incurred the anger of a magician? That might explain the madness in the man with the hooked cross on his forehead.

An uncomfortable thought forced him back to full wakefulness. This could be some northern spell of terror or love, cast not to subdue, but to impel—to drive the hooked-cross man and his companions to seek out the Exteca. If that was the case, Calindor or some other sorcerer had posed yet another challenge.

Sitting up, he opened the little gate of his hut and let himself down the side of the mammoth on a rope ladder, while Mixnal kept the beast as still as a stone. Strong hands steadied him as he reached the ground.

General Yaocatl and his lieutenants were sitting cross-legged on sheepskin blankets, facing the hook-cross man who squatted in a bare patch of ground. With a gleaming steel knife he was sketching a crude map in the dirt. He paused to glance up at Yetecuan and then returned to his task, occasionally growling out some word in his own tongue.

So here we are, Yetecuan thought. *The sun symbol, the horse, the three straight lines: three days' ride north to a city or town named Ba'vedor or something of the sort. More days beyond are other towns. But where is Calindor?*

"But where is Calindor?" he murmured to himself. The man looked up suddenly, his face gray.

"Calindor? Calindor?"

"Yes, beloved son, Calindor. You recognize the name?"

He obviously recognized nothing else, but the name on the lips of an old man from the south seemed to intensify the madness in the man's eyes. To such a man the most innocent act or word might seem a deadly provocation. Yetecuan considered invoking a spell of love; no, it would take too long and would tire him needlessly. Besides, it might react unpredictably if the man did indeed lie under a similar spell already. Yaocatl and his men could handle the barbarian if he grew threatening.

His breath fluttering in the cold air, the hooked-cross man pointed again to the map of his town, then to his knife: "Calindor," he named it, and then held the point above his town as if threatening to plunge the blade into it. Then he pointed to himself, said: "Elsman," and seemed to wrestle with himself to draw the knife back.

Yetecuan giggled softly, repeated "Elsman," and saw the man nod: the Airn did the same when they wished to show agreement.

So this was an enemy of Calindor. If he chose to stay one, the Gods would summon him soon. But for now Calindor did not recognize the destiny the Gods had prepared for him, and he would surely resist the Exteca at every turn. Until he accepted the Gods' will as his own, enemies like Elsman would serve the purpose of the Exteca.

The time of the sunset gift was approaching. Two young priests stood patiently within call, a portable altar between them. Yetecuan glanced over his shoulder at them, smiled, and saw them grip its handles. The altar was wood, a hollowed-out cylinder carved from a tree; for all its bulk, the priests carried it easily enough. They lowered it near Yetecuan, bowed, and hurried off into the bustle of the camp.

Elsman and his partners looked at the blackened, stinking altar and then at one another. *They know,* Yetecuan thought. *They know about us. Calindor has told them. But they are not afraid.*

The young priests returned, chanting a prayer as they led a young Chontalteca boy to the altar. Yetecuan smiled affectionately at him; the Gods would be pleased with such a beautiful and healthy child, a gift from a people new to them. The priests had kept the boy well fed and gently drugged for several days, so he was sleek and obedient. He smiled dreamily at Yetecuan, hardly seeming to notice as the priests lifted him and stretched him out on his back over the curving top of the altar.

Without needing orders, some of Colotic's teteuctin had started a fire near the altar. Flames leaped up in the chilly, darkening air, giving welcome warmth. They turned Elsman's face into a mask that seemed to writhe and twitch without moving.

The heart was out of the boy's chest and crackling in the fire. Yetecuan felt himself revive with the gift, and looked across the altar at Elsman.

Elsman smiled back.

Vidhumen was quiet, so quiet that Pervidhu feared some plague had broken out, or that Albohar had died. The streets were mostly empty, the markets silent. Hearing the horsemen ride by, people looked quickly from their windows and then closed their shutters again. *Sensible enough,* Pervidhu thought, *with this wind blowing.* He imagined the warmth of the castle kitchen, a steaming bowl of stew and a tall tankard of beer. But that would be later, after the horses were safely in their stables.

He had sent a rider ahead with news of their return. Albohar had grooms and stableboys waiting, and extra servants hired from the town to welcome the expedition back. The process of unpacking, seeing to the horses, and paying off the men took less time than Pervidhu would have thought; the servants worked quickly, with little of the chatter and joking they would normally offer.

"Is all well?" he asked a groom.

The man, an old Cantarean, nodded and smiled strangely. "Very peaceful it's been here, sir."

A young warrior escorted Pervidhu to his room, told him that Albohar would see him in an hour, and left. After weeks in a tent, the room seemed dark and cramped. But a kettle of hot water steamed on a shelf, and he was glad of the chance to bathe and change his grimy clothes. In fresh tunic and trousers, his best cloak pinned to his shoulders, he went to the dining hall to meet Albohar.

The electman was sitting in his usual place at the long table, a stack of documents at his elbow. He looked up and smiled a welcome.

"We've some time before supper," Albohar said. "I'm glad to see you back and looking so well. Sit and have some beer, and tell me how it went."

"Did you not get my report with yesterday's courier, electman?"

"Yes, and a good report it is. Now tell me your own sense of how people took the news."

The beer was dark, cold, and good. Pervidhu wiped foam from his moustache. "Most took it well, and promised to resist the Exteca if they come. At Bhadvedor it was another story. You know Elsman?"

"By reputation. A hard man, but no worse than many others."

"Well, he seemed to think this was all your plot to conquer the south, electman. And he thought that I would confirm that if he twisted my arm a bit."

"Fool. Fool."

"A chastened fool. He and his guards tried to kill me, and I'm not sure why they failed. They had me with my back to a fire and nothing in my hand but a poker. Elsman threw a knife at me, and then . . . something happened. A flare of light, I think. Some kind of magic. When it ended, they were all sick with fear, and I got away before they recovered their wits."

"Sick with fear," Albohar repeated. "Magic is very much on people's minds these days." He looked into the fire. "Calindor has learned some Exteca spell from that boy, and it damned near drove this whole city into madness. I thought I was a four-year-old having a nightmare."

"Tell me about it, electman."

Albohar briefly described the riot and Calindor's ride into the town. "Afterward it was . . . ugly. Vomit and shit everywhere, and children who wouldn't stop screaming."

"And this was six days ago, you say?"

"Must have been."

"Six days ago I was in Bhadvedor. Could the spell have reached all that way—no, impossible."

"Anything seems possible these days."

"But you said everyone here came under the spell."

"Everyone I noticed, anyway. Not that I noticed much until the next day."

"Elsman and his guards were terrified by something they saw in that flash of light. Yet no one here saw any such flash?"

"No." Albohar shuddered. "What's gone wrong with the world? Magic was bad enough in the old days, but we could control it. Now it runs wild."

Calindor runs wild, Pervidhu thought, but he did not speak.

At supper Calindor and Nezaual appeared but not Callishandal or Deir; glad as he was to see Calindor, Pervidhu felt a twinge of disappointment that Deir was not there to greet him.

"Damned nuisance," Albohar had muttered as the servants were setting the long table before the magicians arrived. "Callishandal won't see him, and the girl stands by her. So does my wife. So my supper companions are either three grim women or two magicians who mumble at each other in Cantarean—or Exteca."

"Two magicians? What of Renjosudaldor?"

"He's gone home. I don't think he approves of Calindor any more than Callishandal does. Just as well. He's a good man, but Burrowers still make my flesh creep."

Tonight Calindor looked gaunt but alert; his dark eyes gleamed in the candlelight. Beside him, Nezaual looked weary and seemed more concerned with his dinner than with a conversation in Badakhi that he could scarcely follow.

Pervidhu described Elsman's reaction to the warning about the Exteca, and the fight that had ended so strangely.

"It seems to have happened the same day that you cast your spell here," he said calmly.

Calindor nodded, glanced at Nezaual, and said nothing. Pervidhu took the warning: the Exteca still did not understand Deir's powers, and his grasp of Badakhi might be better than it seemed.

"My spell had unexpected effects," Calindor said. To Pervidhu he looked only slightly apologetic. "We spent much of the next day calming the town. The spells of love and terror are a whole new world of magic."

Pervidhu listened to him describe the strange Powers of blood, pausing now and then to ask a question of Nezaual in Exteca. Albohar finally brought the conversation back to more immediate concerns: ailing horses, fodder supplies, getting through the early spring without anyone starving. Calindor seemed unworried: greenmagic would ensure early grass and a good wheat crop.

"If you will all excuse me," Pervidhu said, "I am more weary than I thought. With your permission, I will retire for the night and wait on you in the morning, electman."

Albohar, looking sour, waved him out of the hall. Pervidhu walked slowly into the main corridor, but instead of going back to his quarters, he hastened up a flight of stairs to Callishandal's room. Outside the door he paused and heard women's voices within. Gently he tapped and announced himself.

"Welcome back!" Ghelasha pulled the door open and stepped aside to admit him. "We hoped you'd visit us."

She, Callishandal, and Deir had been dining at a small table by the window, illuminated by two candles. Though a small fire burned on the hearth, the room was cold. Pervidhu declined their offer of mead and a chair.

"I cannot impose on your privacy," he said. "Tomorrow I will be glad to tell you of our journey, but I am weary tonight. I ask only for a word with Deir in the hallway before I retire."

"If you wish," Deir said. She was wearing a beautifully embroidered sheepskin jacket and skirt—surely a gift from Ghelasha—and her red hair gleamed as brightly as the candles. Pervidhu felt his spirits rise as she stood and came smiling toward him.

He led her a few steps down the hallway and paused. "I missed you."

"I missed you too. It was dull here without you. Except for the spell."

"Did it affect you?"

"No. No more than it did in Burnbaile. I seem to be immune to Exteca magic. But it worked with Callishandal and Ghelasha. I had to look after them all that night."

"And Calindor didn't come to see how Callishandal was?"

She paused. "He came, late that night, and knocked on the door. She did not open it for him."

"A Badakh husband would have kicked it open," Pervidhu said, surprising himself with his own anger. "Deir—what has happened to Calindor? He doesn't seem like the same man."

"He's not. Redmagic is all he seems to think about."

"And perhaps he's right to, if its spells can turn a whole town mad. But how could he leave his wife alone in fear?" Pervidhu gestured nervously, as if trying to hold a hot stone without burning himself. "He should have demanded to see you, and you shouldn't have sent him away."

Her smile was gone; she said nothing.

"Well, it's done," he sighed. "But it worries me. He's becoming more like his apprentice all the time. What if redmagic makes him more Exteca than Cantarean?"

"Callishandal says he must choose his own life, and if he chooses wisely, she will return to him."

"I pray that he does. He frightens me now without even casting a spell." He paused. "My lady, I must speak with you."

"Speak." In the dark hallway he could not see her face distinctly, but her voice had deepened; he felt love and fear struggling within him.

"My lady, did you save me in Bhadvedor?"

"I did."

"Then I owe you my life as well as my love." He sank to one knee. "I fear you may need to save us all, my lady."

Deir bent to kiss his cheek and then touched his arms to bid him stand. "I'd better get back," she said in her girl's voice. "I'm glad you're safely home, Pervidhu. Perhaps we can talk more tomorrow."

And then she was gone, back down the hallway and into Callishandal's room.

Pervidhu turned and made his way to his own quarters. The room smelled damp and unused, and the cold made him shiver, though servants had started a coal fire in the little fireplace. In its red glow he quickly undressed and slid into the narrow bed.

Something cold and hard lay under the heavy wool blanket. Pervidhu reached for it and felt his fingers curl around the handle of a knife. Sitting up, he found a candle stump and lighted it in the glowing coals. Then he lifted the knife into its light.

The knife was the one Elsman had hurled at him.

Nineteen

Calindor and Nezaual walked down from the castle into the town after nightfall. They wore nondescript cloaks over simple tunics and pants, and a small spell made them seem to be middle-aged Cantareans. Calindor had taught the spell to Nezaual, and was amused at the boy's pleasure in casting it.

"Remember to keep silent," he said. "You look exactly right, but your voice and accent will give you away."

"Yes, honored father."

"And so will that kind of expression, especially coming from a man who looks fifty."

"Yes, honored father."

Calindor laughed and said nothing more.

The air was cold but the ground was no longer frozen. That could change, of course, with the spring equinox still ten days away, but Calindor sensed that the worst of winter was past. The Sidigariba, the powers of air, were stirring, playing with rumors of warmth from the south. Soon the swallows would be darting overhead and building their mud nests under every convenient eave.

Spring was always the hardest season. The meadows sent up their first tentative green, and if the hay had run short in winter, the cattle and horses and sheep would crop the new grass down to nothing. People husbanded their last flour and cabbages, opened the last barrel of salt beef and then went without meat for a month or more.

But somehow the taverns always had beer and mead, and men always had enough to pay for a mug or two.

Calindor and Nezaual went into a tavern just off the main market square. A few smoky lamps hung from the ceiling, and fires burned on hearths at either end of the big room. Two boys—one Cantarean, the other Badakh—hurried back and forth with tankards of beer and cups of mead. Their customers sat companionably enough, but separately: Badakhar clustered near one hearth, Cantareans near the other. Neither group paid the other much attention.

Sitting on the edge of the Cantarean group, Calindor and Nezaual ordered beer and sat in silence until it came. Calindor listened to the conversations nearby: idle chatter, mostly, about the weather or market prices. From their accents, these Cantareans were ex-slaves from the south. Good.

Their beer came, and Calindor hoisted his in salute to the men at the next table. "I drink your health, friends. May this stuff be better than the muck we get up north."

The four men grinned and raised their own drinks. "Where are you from, then?" one asked.

"The other side of Staldhuno. Just a couple of cabins pretending to be a village. We've come looking for work until spring planting."

"Good luck to you. Not much this time of year, unless you want to freeze your ears off riding patrol for Albohar."

"We're no soldiers," Calindor said.

"You soon learn. The secret is, when you run into someone wanting to fight, ride like the wind the other way." The four men laughed, and Calindor saw quick looks from the other side of the room.

"But who wants to fight?" he asked.

"Our strawhead friends, sometimes. Had a good set-to not long ago."

"Not likely to happen again soon," another man muttered.

"Why not?"

"Just as soon not say."

"Now we're interested," Calindor said. "Did Albohar post people, like the old days?"

"Worse. His damned Veik cast a spell that drove the whole town mad."

"No. But everyone looks . . . all right."

"We're being careful," a third man said. "His Veik was breaking up a riot. He used his spell to frighten everyone in Vidhumen. So now we don't riot. Of course, if we get a strawhead alone in the dark—" He smiled.

"Well," said Calindor, "perhaps this isn't the place for us. I don't like all this talk of spells and madness. Maybe we should keep going, head farther south."

"Not much down there either," said the first man. "We're from Bhadvedor—well, I am anyway, these dogs are from outside it— and the only work there is building Elsman's ramparts in the freezing cold."

"We hear strange stories about Elsman these days," said another man. "That a jenji came after him."

"A jenji? Then he can't still be alive," Calindor said.

"Well, we hear he lives, but we hear about the jenji too. All on fire it was, and it burned down his castle."

"Chuno, you'll believe any lie if it's big enough," the first man said with a grin. "All we hear is rumor. Something about a jenji, and Elsman going half mad and probably running away."

"What other news do you hear from the south?" Calindor asked.

"Not much. Albohar sent his man Pervidhu south to warn about the Blood People. You've heard of them, haven't you? Calindor the sorcerer says they're coming from far away. Supposed to be ferocious cannibals, full of evil spells."

"Now who's believing lies?" Chuno demanded.

The men quarreled cheerfully among themselves for a time.

Calindor finally broke in: "And has anyone heard that the cannibals are actually coming?"

"Would we be sitting here getting drunk if we had?" said the first man.

"Then you'd all better sober up," a Badakh called from across the room.

The Cantareans fell dangerously silent. Calindor and Nezaual turned in their chairs to see a short, stocky man grinning through a wiry beard. He had come in just a moment before, but already had a tankard of beer in one hand.

Calindor recognized him instantly: he was Sveit, a former slave trader who had carried Calindor—then a disgraced young princeling—into slavery in the kingdom of Ner Kes. Later Calindor had met Sveit again, cured him of a stomach cancer, and taken in exchange six young Cantarean slaves who had helped Calindor and Callishandal to escape to refuge in the mountains.

Sveit does not come by chance into my life, Calindor thought. He almost greeted him by name, but remembered that Sveit would not know him under Nezaual's little spell.

"You think cannibals would be hungry enough to eat old scarecrows like us?" he asked with a smile.

"We'd all do for soup stock," Sveit said with a laugh, and everyone laughed with him.

"Come and join us, friend, and tell us what news you have," Calindor said. Though some of the Badakhar looked mistrustful, Sveit strolled across the room without hesitation. He settled himself at the table with Calindor and Nezaual, within arm's length of the other Cantareans. A moment ago they had looked ready to brawl with him; now they leaned forward to hear his words.

"Not so much news as rumors," Sveit said. "I've been trading down south, farther than I've ever been before. Did you know there are other people down there, neither Badakhar nor Cantareans? Simple people they are, and ready to trade fine furs for a bit of iron or steel. Couldn't understand their talk, sounded like chickens running from a fox, but they told me about people coming up from the south on horses like ours, and some bigger than anything I've ever heard of—if they're horses at all."

Calindor felt his skin prickle. *Too soon! I need more time!*

"How far away were these people?"

"That I couldn't tell. But we must have been ten days' hard ride south of Bhadvedor, and the Blood People were somewhere off still farther south."

"Have you told the electman?" asked Chuno; he looked anxious.

"My friend, we just got into town this evening. I've been riding in all weathers for most of the winter, and my throat's been so dry I couldn't tell Albohar my own name without a beer or two first."

"I expect he'd give you a keg," said Calindor.

Sveit looked thoughtful. "I believe he would at that. Well, perhaps I should finish up here and take myself in search of him."

"And we," said Chuno, "will run like rabbits to the north."

Everyone laughed, but Calindor saw that men were slipping out of the tavern with anxious looks. The news would be all over Vidhumen in an hour, and by dawn the people would be demanding more news from Albohar—and promises of protection.

And what promises can he make that he can also keep?

Running like rabbits to the north did not seem a wholly foolish idea.

A little drunk, he and Nezaual walked the streets of Vidhumen. They needed no light; their focus showed them the mud puddles and uneven cobbles. Others hurried past them, carrying torches or candle lamps. Through the shuttered windows came anxious questions, laughter, argument, the wails of children.

"Word travels fast."

"Yes, honored father."

"Are you happy to learn that your people are coming, beloved son?"

"Of course. We are two great—no, three great peoples. We have much to teach one another. Just as you and I have done, honored father."

Calindor said nothing for a time. Horses whinnied in a nearby stable.

"Yes, you have taught me much, Nezaual. I admire and respect much of what I learned about the Exteca. But I will not let them conquer us as they conquered the Airn."

"The Airn are a lesser people, honored father. Between us and the Cantareans I hope for friendship and alliance."

Calindor stopped and focused on Nezaual, hard enough to make the boy stagger.

"A lesser people? Cantareans were slaves for centuries, while the Airn lived free, at peace with themselves and their neighbors. The Badakhar were our masters, but they never knew a moment's rest, never felt safe even in their own castles. They ruined the land they took from us, but the Airn lived easily with Callia. They were a greater people than we, or the Badakhar, or the Exteca. But your master Yetecuan robbed them of their greatness. Why should he hesitate to rob us of what little freedom we have gained? Why should he think us superior to the Airn?"

Nezaual was shuddering under Calindor's cold anger. "Honored father, forgive my foolish words. I did not mean the Airn are less than we, only that they did not have the True Gods until we came."

Calindor laughed without amusement. "And thanks to you, I at least have the True Gods."

"Yes, and soon all this land will have them too. Not because of our spells of love and terror, honored father—because of the gifts we will bring. Remember how you destroyed the blighted grain and saved the people of Hanashar. So will we save the people of Cantarea, and make them our friends and brothers."

Calindor remembered that night in Hanashar when the blighted grain had vanished in a whirl of sparks. And he remembered the people talking of the spell, and of how little use the Siragi Aibela had been. *Yes, Nezaual is right. All these hungry towns will welcome them as rescuers, not flee them as cannibals. We sent Pervidhu to warn the south of powerful enemies, but we forgot that strong means good to most of us. Cantareans and Badakhar alike are looking for someone strong, someone to take care of them. If the Exteca ask for a few sacrifices, a few hearts, that will be a small price to pay.*

He spun around and started walking toward the castle. After a hesitant moment Nezaual hastened after him.

Callishandal's apartment had become a warm and welcoming place for the women of the castle. Ghelasha was often there, gossiping with the housekeepers and market women. Deir listened to all they said, and was rapidly learning Badakhi as well as improving her Cantarean.

Tonight the talk was all of a trader who had just returned from the south with news of the Exteca. A market woman had overheard him talking with stableboys as he unloaded his horses, and she had hurried to the castle with her news. As the women drank peppermint tea and discussed the report, Deir watched Ghelasha: thanks to her network of women spies and observers, the former queen was probably better informed than her husband.

"Ten days' hard ride south of Bhadvedor," Ghelasha repeated, "and the Exteca still farther south. How much time would that give us?"

"Not much," said Callishandal. "He must have turned homeward at least three weeks ago. The Exteca will have been marching steadily north. Their scouts, at least, will be close to Bhadvedor by now."

Ghelasha turned to the market woman, a Cantarean named

Mimantun. She addressed her not by her name, but with the Cantarean word for clanswoman:

"Thirichana, what about these horses? Did he say how many?"

"No, thirichana. The southerners just told him the Exteca had many horses, and some so big an ordinary horse could walk under their bellies."

"That's impossible," Ghelasha said. "The trader didn't understand what they were trying to tell him."

"My lady, perhaps he did," Deir said. The six other women in the room turned to look at her. "When the Exteca came to my town, they brought a great beast. It had four legs, and long brown hair all over it. It had a nose like a big snake, and great curving teeth like the toes of your slippers."

The women all looked at Ghelasha's slippers, but no one laughed.

"Yes," said Callishandal, who sat on her bed beside Ghelasha. "You've told me about the beast before. The Exteca ride upon its back?"

"It is so big . . . you will not believe me, but it could hold a hut on its back."

Callishandal looked grim. "So the trader's news is true. The Exteca are coming, and they are bringing some of their gigantic beasts with them."

"An army is an expensive thing to move around," Ghelasha said. "If these southerners can send men and horses and giant beasts far into the north, they must be very rich."

"And very worried," said Callishandal. "They had never met anyone like us before—people with steel and strong magic. Calindor knew we frightened them just as they frightened us. If they have sent an army north, it shows that we frighten them even more than we thought."

Ghelasha poured herself some more peppermint tea. "Deir, you've told us that these people came to your town first as traders."

"Yes, my lady. They had many beautiful things and useful tools."

"So they are likely to offer the same things to us."

"Perhaps. Or maybe they will simply offer their magic to the magicians here."

The other women looked as if Deir had slapped them.

"Have I said something wrong, my lady?"

"No, not at all," Ghelasha said. "But I hadn't thought of that—of course our magicians would flock to them in search of new spells. Magicians believe in nothing but gaining new magic. Even your husband, Callishandal."

"So it seems, Ghelasha." Her face was expressionless.

"We can't do anything about the magicians," said a market woman. "Can we?"

"I don't know," Callishandal answered. "Redmagic makes other Cantarean magicians fall ill. Perhaps there is some way we could make Exteca magicians fall ill in the same way."

"Poison would have the same effect," Ghelasha said. "But we would have to give it to all the Exteca magicians at the same time."

Deir felt shock and then interest: the ex-queen was quite serious. Strange to hear a woman discuss killing people not as an empty dream of vengeance but as a housekeeping problem—as if they were rats in a granary. She felt ashamed of her own hatred of the Exteca, because it had never moved from emotion to action.

"We could invite their magicians into our beds and hide knives under the blankets," the market woman Mimantun said with a wheezing laugh. The other women laughed too, until Callishandal said:

"If you cut them, they would think you were simply being religious. Besides, their magicians are all celibates. And they stink like rotting meat."

The women looked more shocked than they had at Ghelasha's discussion of poison.

"Not that pretty boy Nezaual," said one of the women.

"You should have seen him when we took him aboard our boat, with his hair stiff with dried blood and his clothes—" Callishandal said no more.

"Whatever their magic, whatever their stink, they are men like any others," Ghelasha snapped. "We can find their weaknesses."

"Not if they cast their spells first," said Deir. "After that, only we will be weak."

"But you escaped Yetecuan's spell," Callishandal said. "How did that happen?"

Deir paused. "I don't know," she said at last. "I hardly remember what happened that night in Burnbaile, and out on the bay. Some people think I'm a magician, but I'm not. I don't see any Powers, I can't cast any spells."

No one spoke for a while. Then Ghelasha put down her empty cup. "Let us all think for a day about this, and perhaps tomorrow we will know what to do. Sisters, I thank you for your wisdom."

The women made their farewells and departed, but Ghelasha remained.

"I must ask you something, Deir," she said, moving to a chair beside her. Deir glanced at Callishandal, who clearly had no idea what was coming.

"Calindor said you are a magician, though you claim no knowledge of magic."

"Yes, my lady."

"And he brought you from your home in part to keep you from the Exteca, and to teach you."

"Yes."

"Yet he shows no interest in you now, does he?"

"I have not spoken often with him since Callishandal left him."

"Doesn't that seem strange to you? You are supposedly immune to redmagic, and you called some kind of creature out of the sea to rescue you, and Callishandal tells me the dragons fled at the sight of you—yet now Calindor ignores you."

"I am just as glad that he does, my lady. He's become like an Exteca himself."

"Could that be the effect of redmagic?"

"I don't know. Maybe it is."

"But Nezaual doesn't know about your supposed abilities because Calindor told you and Callishandal to say nothing."

"Yes, my lady. Sometimes he wonders why Calindor brought me here."

"And if he knew, do you think he would ignore you as Calindor does?"

". . . I don't know."

Deir saw something strange in Ghelasha's eyes: fear and determination. An instant later Ghelasha's hand lashed out and struck Deir full in the face.

The sound of the blow was strangely loud. Deir reeled back in her chair and nearly fell to the floor.

"You ugly little bitch—I think you're a greater magician than even Calindor knows. If you can summon monsters and frighten dragons, you can deceive a boy like him. You've cast a spell to make him forget you, make him forget Callishandal, make him forget everything but redmagic."

Callishandal raised a hand as if to defend Deir, but Ghelasha's rage made her shrink back again. Deir sat clutching the arms of her chair, breathing hard; her right cheek bore the red imprint of Ghelasha's hand. Her eyes looked straight ahead, seeing nothing.

"And maybe," Ghelasha said softly, "you can strike me dead

this instant. But sooner that, sooner death, than watch us fall under the rule of cannibals."

Deir began to shiver, and then wailed one long, high cry. Callishandal moved at last, stood and drew Deir up into a tight embrace. The girl wept while Callishandal rocked her gently in her arms.

"I don't, I don't, I don't!"

Snarling, Ghelasha ripped her from Callishandal's arms. "Calindor has said the magician is hiding inside you! *You* don't know what I'm talking about, but the magician does. I'd cut your throat if I thought it would bring Calindor back to his senses." She glared into Deir's eyes. "Do you hear me, magician? Do you hear me?"

Ghelasha shoved Deir back at Callishandal. "If I knew a gentler way to deal with the magician, I'd do it. But gentle people don't win wars, do they?"

She left the room, her yellow hair glinting in the firelight. Callishandal led Deir, still weeping, to her bed and sat her down on it.

"You'll be all right. Only catch your breath. And drink this." She took a jug from a cabinet and poured a full mug of mead. Deir drank, remembering that last afternoon in Burnbaile, and gradually her sobs faded.

"Are you feeling better?"

Deir nodded and blew her nose into a kerchief. "I'm not a magician. I'm *not*."

Callishandal sat beside her and put her arm around her. "Oh, but you are."

Albohar summoned Calindor to his office. Sveit sat there, drinking beer but not seeming to enjoy it as much as he had expected. The trader greeted Calindor with a smile; the spell of illusion was gone.

"You remember Sveit," Albohar said.

"Very well. Good to see you again. You've come to report news of the Exteca."

The two other men blinked in surprise. "I should have realized you'd have means of knowing," Albohar grunted.

"I learned only this evening, electman. But I'm sure Sveit can tell me more."

Obediently Sveit told them of his journey to the south and the news he had heard from the foreigners there.

"... Then we got back to civilization, rode into Bhadvedor and tried to tell the electman there. But he was gone, and one of his servants told me he'd ridden south in search of something."

"What of the other towns in the south?" Albohar asked.

"Your man Pervidhu scared them silly. They all asked if the Blood People were coming, and I said they were indeed. Scared them worse than ever, of course, but at least they knew your warnings were right, electman."

Albohar chewed his lower lip. "This is happening too fast. We didn't expect them until when, Calindor? Late summer?"

"We didn't know when they'd come. Only that they would. But I was sure we would have more time than this. Who would have believed they could come so quickly?"

"It's good strategy," Albohar said. "A surprised enemy is always easier to handle. Well, perhaps they'll be surprised themselves, when all the towns close their gates against them."

"Not Bhadvedor," Calindor answered. "If Elsman went south after Pervidhu told him about the Exteca, it was to find them. And if he found them, he sought an alliance with them."

The electman and the trader listened somberly. "Just what you'd expect of a bloody arekakh," Sveit said. "If he'd terrorize his own people, he'd betray them just as easily."

Calindor nodded, staring into the glowing coals. "I should have realized, electman. After all the wars among the Five Kingdoms, I should have realized that not everyone in Cantarea would stand united against the Exteca."

"Not everyone, but most will. Don't blame yourself. I'll send couriers out tomorrow, promising aid to every town that refuses the Exteca."

"Can you afford such aid?"

"Of course not. The granaries are almost empty, the horses are showing their ribs, and my own soldiers don't always trust each other. But what choice do I have? Do we sit here and watch the Exteca take us over, town by town?"

"That's what they'll do in any case. I think we need a Mod."

"A Mod?" Albohar frowned. "A meeting of whom?"

"Everyone. All the towns and villages of Cantarea, and the mountains as well. If we're going to make promises of aid to one another, we should make them face-to-face."

Albohar nodded. "It makes sense. But I wouldn't call it by a Badakhi word if I were you." He drummed his fingers on the table. "Time . . . to send out word and prepare for such a meeting would take weeks. And weeks more for the electmen and speakers to gather here, assuming they're willing to come at all."

"And why shouldn't they, if they're afraid of the Exteca?" Calindor asked.

"Because they're more afraid of their own damned people. Afraid of riots and murders the moment they leave. D'you think Vidhumen's the only place where Badakhar and Cantareans are at each other's throats?"

Sveit cleared his throat. "Perhaps it's not for me to say, but would they not be likelier to come if we were to offer them some hope of resisting the Exteca?"

Albohar's blue eyes locked on the trader's face. "For example?"

"Well—if I understand what these Blood People can do, even the biggest army would fall before their spells. If that's the case, why form an army at all? It'd just make the Exteca's work easier."

Albohar laughed without humor. "That's why my s—why Calindor has been carving himself up, learning redmagic. Well? Can we offer a defense against it?"

"I have hopes that we may, electman," Calindor said. "I think I see how to resist the spell of terror—"

"Pity you didn't show us how before you broke up the riot," Albohar interrupted.

"—but I still don't understand the spell of love. Nezaual knows much less about that one, and it's more dangerous. When people fall under the spell of terror, they can still flee; under the spell of love, they run to their enemies and surrender."

"As longchanters have often observed," Albohar said dryly. "But you're not giving us a very persuasive reason to come to a council."

"I see one strategy, electman. I will not describe it now, and I would not tell it until our army was in the field. Otherwise the Exteca might learn of it and take precautions."

"But you do have a serious strategy?"

"Yes."

Albohar's big hand slapped the table. "Then we'll call the meeting, and promise your counterspell and strategy. Thirty days from today?"

"I'd prefer fifteen," said Calindor. "Twenty-five?"

"Agreed. I'll start sending out couriers tomorrow."

"I think I should be one of them," Calindor said.

"Not a courier. My ambassador, with full powers to act in my name."

"You're not an Aryo anymore," Calindor said gently.

"We can have a nice debate on that, and then a vote, once the Exteca are running for home." Albohar stood up and paced the little office. "You go as my ambassador. We have no time to waste. See how the southerners are behaving, and get them to come to the council. Promise them gold and horses, or blast them with dragonfire, just so long as they turn up. How many people will you need?"

"Not many. Five or six perhaps."

"Perhaps you'll want more," Sveit suggested. "We had fifteen going into the southern lands, and came back with eleven. The roads are dangerous."

"You forget who he is," Albohar grunted, and Sveit grinned in embarrassment.

"I'm not going to get into any fights," Calindor said. "We only need to stiffen the southerners' willingness to resist the Exteca. That will be the key."

Albohar stood up, ending the discussion. "Get some sleep. We're all going to have a busy day tomorrow."

"Of course, electman."

"Sveit, you're my guest tonight. Take the little room just off the dining hall. We'll meet for breakfast so I can learn more about these southern tribes you found."

"I'll be glad to wait on you, electman."

Calindor and Sveit walked down the corridor from Albohar's apartment. "Would you be willing to come south with me?" Calindor asked.

"What, when I've just returned? And the Blood People likely to pop up behind any bush?"

"I need sensible people with me. I'll bring Pervidhu, and perhaps one or two more Badakhar warriors, but I want advice from people who don't like fighting."

"I'm glad to advise you not to fight. Now you have my advice, you don't need me."

Calindor chuckled. "I want Svordo too. You'll remember him."

"Of course I remember him—I bought and sold him, didn't I? Lazy young oaf, always talking about sleeping in a proper bed. He won't see many beds where you're going."

"You and he can talk about old times."

Sveit paused as they were about to enter the dining hall. A sleepy servant, pushing a broom across the floor, looked up incuriously at them. "You really mean it, don't you? You're going to face these cannibals and their monsters with five or six men— including an ex-slave and an ex-slave trader."

"And Pervidhu. A warrior not fond of war."

"We'll need the fastest horses in Albohar's stables."

Calindor patted the old man's shoulder. "We'll get them. Good night, Sveit."

Twenty

"Of course it's snowing; it's almost spring." Callishandal turned from the window and saw Deir's uncomprehending stare. The town below was lost in the whirl of white.

"Just because the new year is coming doesn't mean all will be warm and bright," Callishandal went on. "We can get snow for another two months."

Deir looked wretched, a sheepskin robe pulled around her, and her nose red and running. Her left cheekbone showed a bruise from Ghelasha's blow.

"But that's very rare," Callishandal went on. "Don't worry—soon it will be real spring."

Deir huddled next to the hearth, trying to warm herself at the small coal fire. "Soon the Exteca will be here," she whispered. "And soon they will find out that I'm supposed to be a magician. What will happen to me then?"

"Perhaps they'll find out in defeat," Callishandal said.

"More likely they'll take me south and treat me as they did my mother—drug me and dress me in fine clothes, and then . . ."

Callishandal smiled and would have answered with a joke; then she saw how serious Deir was. She felt a pang of worry about Deir's despondency; it was unlike the girl.

"Listen to me. That will never happen. The Exteca will never rule you. Never." She looked out at the falling snow and then turned back to look into Deir's blue eyes: "They will regret the day they first saw Burnbaile, and they will curse the day they conquered it."

Deir looked unconsoled. "Come with me," Callishandal said.

"Where?"

"We both need a sweat bath."

The two women left the castle by a back gate and walked along the ridge of the hill. Soon the castle vanished in the swirling whiteness. The path was easy enough to follow despite the snow;

it led to one of the horse paddocks, and constant traffic had made it smooth and broad. But today no grooms had gone to see the horses since early morning, and the snow was smooth and untracked.

A smaller path led off into a stand of lodgepole pine. Callishandal and Deir struggled between the trees, laughing as snow spilled onto their hair and down their necks.

"The Badakhar just scrub themselves with a wet cloth," said Callishandal as they came into a little clearing with a snow-covered shed at its far end. "When they remember. The Cantareans in the castle are starting to do the same thing, and not often enough. But some of them still keep clean this way."

"I remember the sweat bath I had with Tilcalli. It was a wonderful night. That was the first time I ever saw snow."

"And now you wish it'd been the last." Callishandal pulled some kindling from the wood stacked under the shed's roof and put it in the sweat bath's fireplace. Taking a flint and steel from under her cloak, she soon had a fire burning. Deir brought bigger sticks as the fire grew, and soon it was roaring. Gray smoke rose from the stone chimney and vanished in the falling snow.

Deir's mood had already lightened, and the cold no longer seemed to trouble her. "Well, let's shiver a bit before we sweat," she said, and pulled her clothes off. She tossed them into the interior of the sweat bath, and walked naked around the clearing with her arms outstretched. Callishandal marveled at the girl's strangeness. White flakes clung to her flame-red hair and gleamed as they melted on her blue-white skin. The freckles on her face and arms seemed very dark.

Callishandal undressed quickly also, then scooped up snow and flung it at Deir. She laughed, ducked, and threw another snowball back. Callishandal screamed in happy outrage as it struck her shoulder, and threw again. After a quick exchange they called a truce and hurried into the sweat bath.

Its heat welcomed them. Shivering together, they sat on the rough bench before the hearth while the flames warmed and dried them. Snow on the roof melted and dripped through, hissing as it touched the hot stone of the chimney.

"Ghelasha thinks I'm a magician, and so do you. What if it's true?"

"I don't know. I've never known anyone like you, not even Calindor before he came to understand his own power. Sometimes I think that gods . . . that gods use you, as Callia used Calindor so she could come back into the world." She paused. "Or as Callia used me to be her voice."

"I don't understand." Deir's body gleamed like copper and ivory in the glow of the fire.

"Calindor has tried to explain it, but I don't know if I understand either. When he faced Mekhpur the Firelord, Calindor had gained so much knowledge that he could open a gateway—in the world, in his own soul, I'm not sure—so that Callia could come back from wherever gods live. But she didn't speak through him. For some reason she chose me, though I have no magic at all. And then she brought her wrath down on Cantarea and in one night she destroyed the Five Kingdoms of the Badakhar."

"So you think some god is using me?"

"Perhaps. Perhaps it is Callia again, preparing us for the next struggle."

"Did you feel Callia when she spoke through you?"

Callishandal was silent for a long time. "No. I have trouble remembering it clearly."

"Well, I don't feel anything or remember anything much. The sea dragon, I remember that, and the land dragons running away." She put a handful of snow on the hot stones of the chimney, and steam puffed back at her. "But I also remember ... forgetting. Sometimes I think of a day and I remember parts of it but not others. Usually it was a day when Pervidhu was around."

Callishandal chuckled. "He's around you a great deal. He likes you."

"I like him. He doesn't look at me as if I were some kind of freak just because I don't look like a Badakh or a Cantarean."

"What is it that you think you're forgetting?" Callishandal asked quickly, embarrassed and wanting to change the subject.

"How would I know?" Deir snapped. "I remember, oh, talking to Pervidhu in a hallway, and then the next thing I know he's gone and I can't remember him leaving. And sometimes I dream about him. Strange dreams, as if I'm with him somewhere far away."

"Perhaps it is a god," Callishandal murmured. "If Ghelasha is right, and you—if someone has put a spell on Calindor to make him stop thinking of you, surely it must be a god. Who else would have the power to enchant such a sorcerer?"

Deir put two more sticks into the fire. "One thing I will always remember, when I was on the Siar Bagh with the candleboat sinking under me. I learned that there aren't any gods."

Callishandal put a hand on Deir's arm. "So it must have seemed. Yet we came to you, and the sea dragon."

Deir said nothing as she stared into the coals. Sweat poured down her face; she wiped her eyes and drew a deep breath.

"I wish I could believe you. Do you know what truly frightens me, Callishandal? It's not the Exteca. They're just stupid men in feathers. But what if I really have a magician inside me? Maybe she's just waiting for the Exteca so she can come out and destroy them." She turned to look at Callishandal. "Maybe she'll come out and never go back in. And then what will happen to me?"

"Take Nezaual? Are you mad?" Albohar tilted back in his chair, looking skeptically at Calindor. "The boy will run for his people the first time he sees them. Or he'll cut your throat before he runs. Better to keep him here as a hostage."

Calindor smiled. "His people think of killing as doing a favor; how could he serve us as a hostage? No, I want him with me. He can explain the thinking of the Exteca. Besides, I don't want him on his own here in Vidhumen, getting into trouble."

"So you want to go up against these damned Exteca with Pervidhu, that scoundrel Sveit, your friend Svordo—at least he's got some sense, that one—and a boy who'll betray you the moment he sees his own people."

"I'm not 'going up' against them; I'm scouting them and reminding the southern towns that we'll back them up. We probably won't even come in sight of the Exteca."

"Ah, indeed. You must think me very young or very old to believe that promise."

Calindor smiled but his voice was calmly serious: "I hope you understand that I have gone to some trouble to prepare for the Exteca. I don't intend to bring my friends into needless danger."

"Well, you're asking for my advice, not my permission. When will you leave?"

"This afternoon."

"In this snow? I forget—weather doesn't trouble you much."

"It will be a nuisance until tomorrow. Then we'll get a dragon's wind and easier riding."

"Good. Take what horses you need. Svordo can talk to the stewards about supplies. How long will you be gone?"

"A month, perhaps. Perhaps less."

Albohar leaned forward and put his elbows on his knees. "Do you think you can drive the Exteca back?"

"No. I can slow them, perhaps. Maybe by a counterspell to their spells of love and terror, but more likely by simple magic that brings them bad weather. But this is like any war in the old days—magicians are just another kind of weapon for warriors, and warriors win wars. If the southern towns resist, it will be easier. If they don't, the Exteca will be very strong."

"You're saying we'll have to fight them? But how can we fight sorcerers who can drive us mad with fear?"

"I am learning the answer to your question, electman."

"Well, go with luck and return with strength."

Calindor left Albohar's office and gathered his companions. While they set about preparing for a quick departure, he went up to Callishandal's apartment. A little to his surprise, Deir admitted him and Callishandal greeted him with a smile. Her black hair hung in damp ringlets over her shoulders.

"We've just come back from the sweat bath. It was wonderful."

"I can tell; you look radiant. I am going into the south."

"So we understand," Callishandal said. "I hope you have a good journey and a happy return."

"It won't be a good journey if I leave without your blessing, nor a happy return without your welcome."

Her smile faded. "I wish Callia's blessings on you every day, Calindor, and I will gladly welcome you back. But I cannot share my life with you while you share yours with the gods of the Exteca."

For a time he said nothing. "They are as real as Callia, and their blessings are as real as hers. They are as much a part of this world as the snow and the wind. If we are to live with them we must know their ways."

Anger burned in Callishandal's eyes. "Their ways are blood and death, and you are a fool if you think you can live with gods that feed on life itself."

"I can bear them better than I can bear your anger. But I do not love them more than I love you, Callishandal." He turned and walked quickly from the room.

Ghelasha and her son Eskel were coming down the corridor. Calindor bowed to them, and they bowed in reply. He saw something in Ghelasha's eyes. Scorn? Contempt? Or merely a reflection of what he felt for himself?

"Go with luck," Eskel said, "and return in strength."

Nezaual understood only that they were to carry an important message for other electmen. He might well suspect what it was, but he asked no questions. Calindor told the others to say little about their mission when the Exteca was in earshot, though he seemed in any case to understand little Badakhi. If Calindor trusted Nezaual more than Albohar did, he did not want the boy to think himself helping his people's enemies.

They rode south with the wind at their backs, and by dusk the snow had stopped. The sky cleared; great curtains of glowing green and yellow and red swept across it, shimmering. By the northern lights the riders made their way without pause until far into the night; at last Calindor called a halt at an abandoned farmstead. The barn was better shelter than the house, and after they had seen to their horses, the men settled in beside them.

Calindor lighted and warmed the barn with dragonfire, and Nezaual cooked a kettle of porridge. The four men ate silently, hungrily, and then talked for a time of the next day's journey. Soon they were in their blankets; Sveit and Svordo were asleep at once.

Pervidhu waited until Nezaual too was snoring, and then spoke softly to Calindor:

"Did you say farewell to Deir before we left?"

". . . Now that I think of it, no. I think she was in the room when I said good-bye to Callishandal, but I don't remember speaking with her." He thought for a moment. "It was rude of me, but I was unhappy to be leaving Callishandal."

"I have something I must show you." He passed Elsman's knife, wrapped in a cloth, into Calindor's hand. "Does it tell you anything?"

Calindor had dimmed the dragonfire ring to a dull red, but Pervidhu knew he would not need light. "A knife of good steel, well balanced. Probably Halamori."

"It carries no magic aura, no Powers?"

"Only the Powers some stalmagh invoked in its making. Why?"

"It's the knife Elsman threw at me, just before something saved me. I found it in my bed when we returned to Vidhumen."

"And how did it come to be there?"

"I don't entirely know, but I think Deir had much to do with it."

"That spell she cast when I was in the marketplace during the riot. Yes, that would make sense."

Pervidhu laughed almost soundlessly. "I'm glad it makes sense to *you*, hemamagh. How could a strange-looking girl know what was happening so far away from Vidhumen, and stop it from happening? How could she seize a knife from the air and carry it back to the castle?"

"If that is what happened, it's a magic beyond me. She's a great magician."

"Yet you've largely ignored her in favor of learning redmagic."

"Redmagic is the more urgent problem. When we have dealt with the Exteca, we'll have time to learn what Deir knows."

"You know best, Calindor, but I wonder—if she could transport herself in a twinkling from Vidhumen to Bhadvedor to save me, could she not also transport herself to kill someone?"

Calindor chuckled and handed back the knife. "If you knew any magic, Pervidhu, you'd know how fanciful that is. Enough—get some sleep. We have a long ride ahead of us tomorrow."

Soon he too was asleep. But Pervidhu lay awake for a long time, watching the northern lights blazing through the gaps in the roof.

Calihalingol and Tilcalli sat beside the river in the Open Dream, watching slow ripples move across its dark green surface. An aspen shaded them.

Here was where we sat when we first planned your journey to Aishadan, Calihalingol said.

I wish we had chosen not to. I wish we had killed those boys when they came to take me.

We would have lost everything. Everything.

And what have we gained? The Cantareans on the prairie are bitter and resentful. The mountaineers mutter about the newcomers in their villages. Now they even complain about the Siragi Aibela. They say the Exteca boy is a greater magician.

Calihalingol smiled, but only briefly. *We have heard about his cleansing of the grain. And about how his magic sickens the Siragi Aibela. But you are unhappy for other reasons, great-great-granddaughter. You feel you have lost your husband and your son.*

I fled from one, and the other fled from me. Yes, I have lost them. And she leaned against the old woman's shoulder.

The green water foamed a little as a woman's head broke its surface. Red hair streamed over her shoulders and breasts as she climbed from the water and walked lightly over the rounded stones of the river's edge.

Again you come to us, Calihalingol said, and Tilcalli saw fear leap in the old woman's eyes. Deir said nothing, but sat cross-legged beside Tilcalli. In the heat of the unmoving noon sun, her simple white dress was suddenly dry.

What do you want of us? Tilcalli demanded. *If you want to show your power, you succeed. If you would speak with us, then speak.*

But Deir said nothing; she looked at the slow-flowing river and the aspen leaves fluttering in the light breeze, and then at the two women.

Why do you come, and not Calindor? Tilcalli asked. Deir smiled a little as she drew one hand across her upper arm; blood flowed as if from the slashes of a knife, or seemed to flow. It was answer enough for Tilcalli.

So he is deep in redmagic. It conquers him as he seeks to conquer it.

Deir's faint smile did not change; she neither agreed nor disagreed with Tilcalli's words. The blood vanished from her arm.

I ask you to save him as he saved you, Tilcalli said. Deir made no reply, seemed not to have heard.

Perhaps he did not save you as you needed to be saved, said Calihalingol. *I ask if we may help you.*

Deir turned to look at her and her mouth opened. In the Open Dream there was no sound, but all the Siragi Aibela, as they danced the past and future, heard the scream until Deir leaped up, ran to the river, and disappeared beneath it.

The first day of spring: in Tola the dancers would be filling every plaza with more color than a field of wildflowers. Music would rise from every street, and the special aroma of stewing flesh with chili would fill every kitchen.

How many years since I greeted this day in Tola?

Yetecuan looked from his tent across the camp of the expedition: endless rows of conical skin tents, each with its plume of smoke rising against the brightening eastern sky. Corrals where horses snuffled and whinnied, and open spaces where the mammoths drowsed. Now the priests' songs rose into the predawn sky, giving thanks to the True Gods for their goodness. The special sacrifices for this morning were all Chontalteca, foreigners, with no idea of how significant today was and of course no knowledge of the songs they should be offering to win the favor of the Gods they would soon be serving.

Well, it could not be helped. Every Exteca in the expedition was precious now; if any were to go to the Gods, it would be on the battlefield. And no doubt the Gods would be amused by their new Chontalteca servants.

Yetecuan walked slowly to the portable temple not far from his tent. Other priests, chanting, came out of the darkness and accompanied him. Beside the altar, a fire was already crackling.

The songs of thanksgiving did not take long; no one wanted to make the Gods wait. With the efficient help of the other priests, Yetecuan took ten hearts in less time than it took the sun to clear the horizon. Golden light blazed in his eyes as he rinsed his hands and poured the water reverently into the soil.

Magician's Land, you are sacred now, a gift to the True Gods. May you be worthy of their kindness.

He looked north. Beyond the camp the land fell away into a broad, shallow valley still streaked with snow. A stream twisted through the valley, and beyond it stood the first real town they had seen since leaving the lands of the Airn: Bhadvedor, on the marches of the land they called Cantarea. It was a sorry collection of stone huts, a slum that any provincial governor would be ashamed of; but its castle was a respectable size and would have posed problems if a siege had been necessary.

Yaocatl and Colotic had appeared near the altar as Yetecuan made the last of the sacrifices. Now they approached him.

"I wish you the blessings of the True Gods, honored father," said Yaocatl. The general was a barrel-chested man who wore furs as easily as feathers and walked on foreign soil as easily as on his own tiled floor in Tola. Colotic stood two steps behind him, his eyes fixed on Yaocatl. Yetecuan felt a sudden nostalgia for Nezaual.

"May they bless you also, beloved sons. And may they bless all those whom we bring under them. When do we enter the barbarians' town?"

"Just before noon. Most of the expedition will remain here for now, but about a thousand of us will occupy the town."

"As you wish it." He smiled at Colotic. "It will be an easier occupation even than Burnbaile."

The young warrior nodded, but did not smile. "We have a favor to ask of you, honored father."

"Of course, beloved son."

"We ask for a spell of love on this town."

Yetecuan looked at him in surprise. "Why would you need such a spell? Their chieftain has given us the town. We have only to walk in and accept their surrender."

Yaocatl nodded, making his tall red plumes nod in the golden light of dawn. "We are thinking not of this town, honored father, but of the others. Many of these northerners have heard of us, and have come into this town to see us. I want them to yield in love to us, and then return to their homes and praise us so that all will welcome us."

"Beloved son, of course I accept your judgment as a warrior. I only wonder why you would chop down the tree when the fruit will fall into your hands anyway."

"I am not chopping the tree, honored father," Yaocatl answered. "I am giving it a good shake, so that the fruit falls more quickly. Elsman's people are only one town among many. The next towns will not surrender easily unless their own people bring them good reports of us. If they resist us, we will have great need of your magic. One small spell now will spare you from casting many spells later on."

"I understand." He shook his head. "A strange business. Elsman's greatest enemy is Calindor, who will become our greatest friend. Yet to make him such, we must conquer and overwhelm his people."

"Everything here in the north is strange," said Yaocatl with a shrug. "But as the True Gods come to know this land, it will become more like home."

"You speak wisely, beloved son Yaocatl. And being in their hands, we can go ahead in confidence. I shall prepare for the spell."

Matari Kleir was another of the new towns risen on the ruins of some Badakh manor: a couple of hundred shacks huddling close to the wall around the castle, which stood on a bluff above a winding river valley.

"The old upermannar knew what they were doing," Pervidhu said as they squinted south into the sun at the castle on the horizon. "Always pick a spot with good water and high ground, and room for the livestock."

"None of which will do much good against the Exteca," said Calindor. He glanced around: the other riders were some distance back, riding slowly and enjoying the new warmth of the sunshine. In the muddy fields, magpies flashed their black-and-white wings and a few horses looked for something to eat. Their herders, two boys on horseback, watched the newcomers from a safe distance.

"Are we fools to promise them help, or are they fools to believe us?" Pervidhu asked. "Can we really defeat them?"

"Their spells have direction and focus," Calindor said. "Otherwise the sorcerer's own people would feel them too. And they do not carry far. Whoever casts it must be close. When I cast the spell of terror, I could not control it properly, but it didn't reach much beyond the edge of Vidhumen."

"This is not encouraging me, Calindor."

"Well, the Exteca are like most magicians—casting a spell wearies them, and the greater the spell, the longer they must wait until they can cast another. If we can tempt them into casting a very great spell, and then strike at them from an unexpected direction, they will be easy to fight."

"So the trick will be to hide an army somewhere close to them, yet not so close that it feels the spell. This is your secret strategy?"

"Exactly."

"I don't like the sound of it at all."

* * *

Almost everyone in Matari Kleir was Badakh; the exceptions were a few old men and women, clearly longtime slaves of the manor who had preferred to stay on rather than adjust to life in some new place. Looking at them, Calindor could admire their common sense. *I've traveled to many places, and my only real home is a ruined castle under a mountain of ice.*

They rode into the outskirts of the town, past steep-roofed huts and well-fenced corrals. Dried flowers hung in bunches over every doorway, welcoming the new year that would begin next morning with the first day of spring. The people stared at them, only rarely nodding in answer to a greeting. The Badakhar men wore their hair in tidy braids wound with red and green ribbons; the women and children looked thin but not malnourished. They did not seem in a festive mood.

The three patrolmen who rode to greet the visitors carried lances with polished, well-honed spearheads that gleamed against the blue sky.

"Homemade steel," Pervidhu murmured to Calindor as the patrol approached. "Looks good. We didn't visit this place, but I wish we had—could've done some trading. They must have recruited a couple of good stalmaghar."

"And found a decent coal deposit," Sveit added. "This was just cattle country in the old days. You had to burn cow shit to cook your supper."

The patrolmen halted and their leader challenged them.

"My name is Calindor. I'm here as a courier for the electman Albohar of Vidhumen. I'd like to talk to your electman—Tenarakh, isn't it?"

"It is," said the patrolman. He was a flat-faced boy with cold eyes that showed nothing but suspicion. "You'll hand us your weapons if you want to see him."

"As you wish." Calindor carried no weapons; the others handed over an assortment of knives, swords, and clubs. The patrolmen stored them in their saddlebags and then, without a word, led them to the little castle.

It was really no more than a fortified farmhouse, Calindor thought; it relied for defense on its terrain more than its own walls. Still, even a determined and well-armed attacker would have an ugly time taking it—and he would have to take it, or Matari Kleir would menace his flank or rear as he moved north.

Tenarakh was in the corral just inside the main wall, riding a black horse that still carried much of its winter coat but was losing it in patches. He was a young man with long braids and not much beard for a Badakh, but he rode with the confidence of one of the old upermannar. While the visitors waited, the electman made two more circuits of the corral and then rode out into the larger yard.

"Welcome!" he called in a surprisingly deep voice, and extended a hand to Calindor. "And happy new year. I remember you. I was at the Mod at Aishadan when the old Veik put his spell on you and stole your voice."

"I got it back," Calindor said, and the Badakh laughed.

"Seems like a long time ago now. Well, come in and we'll see if there's something to eat."

Calindor set Nezaual and Sveit to looking after the horses, with a murmured request to Sveit that he keep them both in the stable for a good long time. Tenarakh started to protest that his own stableboys could do that task, but a glance from Calindor silenced him. He led them into the castle.

The dining hall was little more than a big kitchen with a table that would hold no more than twenty. This afternoon it held only the visitors, Tenarakh, and his mother—a gaunt woman, surely an upermanna's widow, who said nothing, but knitted and listened while the men talked. Around them servants clattered about the kitchen preparing the new year's feast; Calindor saw that it would not be sumptuous.

Matari Kleir had received Albohar's warning, though not directly from Pervidhu's last journey, and had taken it seriously.

"Most of our neighbors are Cantareans," he said, "and they're not too fond of us strawheads, so we've kept up our defenses on general principles. When we heard about these Blood People, we decided we'd have to do a bit more."

"You know about their spells of love and terror?" Calindor asked.

"We know a bit about terror ourselves." Tenarakh's smile was broad, but his eyes were cold. His mother kept knitting; when she looked up for a moment, Calindor saw that her eyes were even colder than her son's.

"And have you heard any news about them from the south?" asked Sveit.

"Just in the last day or two, and nothing much. Some trappers came through with news about strangers coming north."

"Had they seen the Exteca?" Calindor asked.

"Said they had, but I doubt it. They told a lot of lies about some huge creature with a house on its back." He grinned at his guests, but the grin faded as he saw their expressions.

"So they're close," Pervidhu muttered. "We should have called the meeting for earlier."

"What meeting is this?"

Calindor explained the planned council of all the towns of Cantarea, where those who wished could form an alliance and aid one another.

"What aid would help against the Exteca's spells?" Tenarakh asked.

"I am working on counterspells. And I have a strategy which will use their own magic against them."

"Good, but I hope it's gentler than the storm that killed the Firelord. When is the meeting?"

"The twenty-fifth of Firstmonth, in Vidhumen."

Tenarakh rubbed his sparse beard. "Another Mod, after all this time. Let's hope this time you don't lose your voice."

"I won't."

"Damned bad time to leave, a hundred jobs to do, but I'll be there. Now let's have some beer and bread and hear all the news."

Calindor, pretending annoyance at their slowness, called in Sveit and Nezaual to share the meal. The conversation turned to the weather, the state of the herds, the slowness of the soil's recovery from Callia's great storm. As the afternoon turned into evening, townspeople came calling to wish Tenarakh and the visitors a happy new year; they sang old songs and drank mead, and none left without a loaf of bread and a cup of salt. If they wondered why a famous sorcerer chose to spend new year's eve in a small town among strangers, they kept their thoughts to themselves.

At midnight all greeted the new year and departed without ceremony for their homes. "Typical Badakhar," Svordo muttered in Cantarean to Calindor as Tenarakh led them to their quarters. "End the party just when it's getting good. Last year in Tanshadabela we were up all night celebrating."

"And then you slept all day in a proper bed."

"More than I'll likely get here."

And indeed the beds were not good. But after a long day's ride and so much food and drink, all slept well. When Calindor woke next morning, sunlight was already spilling into his window.

He rose and dressed, and went lightly down the hall to the deserted dining hall. The dogs slept by the smoking hearth and scarcely lifted their heads as he passed.

Outside, the morning was still and clear. Calindor went to the edge of the bluff overlooking the river and the valley beyond it. For all the damage done by Callia's wrath, Cantarea was still beautiful, and he rejoiced to see the Gariba reveling in the water, the air—even the Powers trapped in the castle's stone walls stirred and basked in the heat of the rising sun.

Something passed over him, as if the shadow of a cloud had slipped quickly across the face of the sun. He drew in a shuddering breath and turned to the southeast. Yes, it had come from there, a long distance. He had felt the casting of the spell, and not the spell itself: a spell of love. Now he almost heard the dry shuffle of Lady Serpent and the other True Gods here in this silent barnyard.

You are the True Gods, and I honor you. But I must fight you. I must.

Twenty-one

Yetecuan's spell had gone well but left him wearier than usual. Even his protests lacked strength as Colotic summoned a litter and six husky bearers.

"I've always walked into the towns we've taken," he said to Colotic's smiling face. "Always."

"This time, beloved father, they are too impatient to greet you. And they will be able to see you better." He bent, took Yetecuan from his stool, and carried him easily to the waiting bearers. Shivering a little, Yetecuan allowed them to prop him up in his seat and to wrap him in furs. *How warm it must be in Tola today . . .*

Something else was troubling him besides weariness, but he could not identify it: a fear, as if an awareness of evil had crept into his mind. He turned his mind from it, rejected it as the groundless worry of an old man. And what did he have to fear, with Yaocatl's thousands around him and the True Gods looking over them all?

Many warriors had entered Bhadvedor ahead of Yetecuan and his retinue; some silently clubbed the people aside when they pressed too close. Now the muddy streets were clear, while Tola's newest subjects knelt in the gutters, calling out welcome in their strange northern tongue.

Yetecuan waved wearily to them, forcing himself to smile a response to their adoration. After all these months in the wilderness, it felt strange to enter a town again—though it was only a filthy barbarian settlement like this one. The brown faces and black hair of the Cantareans seemed natural even if their clothing and language did not. But it was strange seeing them shoulder to shoulder with the hairy white-skins, the Badakhar. The True Gods needed to know about the Badakhar; all the first sacrifices would be from them. He suspected that Elsman would not have minded even if he had been exempted from the spell of love.

And of course he had had no exemption. The bearers approached the town's crude castle, and Elsman was at its gate, on his knees and arms spread wide. He was sobbing uncontrollably, his tattooed face twisted in an agony of love.

Such is the power of the True Gods, that they can redeem even a monster like him. Yetecuan smiled upon the former lord of the town as the bearers gently lowered the litter onto the paving stones outside the castle gate.

"Honored father," said Colotic, who had walked alongside, "shall we bring you sacrifices?"

"Please do, beloved son. Make all of them white-skinned. The brown-skins can join the True Gods soon enough."

"As you ask."

"And would you please ask the warriors to survey the town and tally its resources? The people here look better fed than our own. We should take whatever they will not need."

"Of course, honored father."

"And collect all weapons of metal. These people are skilled in metallurgy."

Yetecuan leaned back in his seat, silently grateful that Colotic had kept him from walking. He watched the warriors moving quickly and efficiently around the streets. Even after all these months in the wilderness, they were disciplined soldiers who knew how to behave in a newly conquered town. Yet something seemed wrong, something he was sure he would have recognized if he were not so tired.

Anyone under the spell of love behaved in a kind of daze, but these northerners seemed more than usually confused. The warriors shoved them, clubbed them, shouted—but the people did not obey as they should have. When a simple order should have caused them to move or stand still, open a door or follow a warrior, these people responded in grinning bafflement.

. . . Of course. Casting a spell over a little encampment of the Chontalteca was different from doing so over a town of many hundreds. Here, one warrior had to take charge of many captives—and here the pochteca had never come, learning the northerner's language and behavior.

Sobbing in perplexity, a Cantarean captive staggered behind the Exteca who pulled him by the hair. When the Exteca paused at a closed door and demanded it be opened, the Cantarean fell to his knees and spoke rapidly—but what he might mean was impossible to tell.

We are fools and the True Gods must be laughing at us.

All this distance, and they had no one who could speak the language. He would have to assign a half dozen of his priests, and twice as many warriors, to learning the rudiments as quickly as possible. *Perhaps it's my fault. I should not have counseled such haste; we could have sent pochteca and followed them by half a year. But Calindor would have heard about them; he would have had them imprisoned or killed before they could learn a word.*

Despite the confusion, the warriors were quickly gaining power over the whole town. Physical control of one settlement was the least of their problems; by tomorrow morning the expedition must begin learning all it could about this unknown foreign land. The people of Bhadvedor would want to help, but they would be unable to; and while the expedition slowly learned the basic words, Calindor and his unknown forces would be marshaling for an attack.

That odd fear was troubling him again, on so subtle a level that he did not recognize it for some time. At last he gathered his energy for a focus, and instantly got to his feet. Swaying dangerously, he looked around for help. One of the bearers leaped up and offered an arm for him to lean on.

"Beloved son . . . please carry me away from this gate."

"Of course, honored father. We shall be glad to take you wherever you like."

"To the northern edge of the town. Away from the gate, from the castle." Yetecuan sagged back into his chair as the bearers lifted it to their shoulders. After they had taken him some distance through the town, he began to feel more at ease.

What spell had struck this castle, and Elsman, that could leave such a subtle, dangerous residue? Whatever it was, Yetecuan wanted no part of it. *If it was Calindor, we will have to teach him that some kinds of magic are evil. Like this one.*

At his request, his priests set up camp in a meadow on the edge of town, one that evidently often served visitors. If they were disappointed not to be inside solid walls, they did not show it; but after all, Yetecuan reflected, all were priests accustomed to hardship.

A little after noon he ate some cornmeal mush—it must be almost the last of the cornmeal, he thought, and he would miss it. Then he slept for a time. When he woke, a middle-aged priest named Tlacalel was squatting at the entrance of the tent.

"We have examined much of the town, honored father," he said after Yetecuan invited him in. "These people are poor builders, but they have many strange arts. I have brought you a knife made of one of their metals."

"Ah." He held it on the palm of his hand. Details were different, but it was a knife like the one Calindor had given him. "Is this the only one you found, beloved son?"

"Oh no, honored father. We found hundreds of them. Some of them are as long as my arm. They're something like our obsidian swords."

"Indeed." The knife reminded him that he had not recently used the first one to locate Calindor. He would have to do so soon. "Have you found the makers of these weapons?"

"Some. Of course we cannot understand them, though they offer us everything in their smithies."

"Put two priests to work learning the smiths' language. As soon as we can talk to them, we will send some of them south to Tola."

"As you wish, honored father. I must tell you of something else. We have found several granaries, and they are all infested with rats. It seems Elsman was about to run out of food within a month or so. Should we cast a spell to destroy the pests?"

"By all means, and at once. It will give the people something to thank us for once the present spell wears off."

Yes, it would help. The Exteca needed all the allies they could bind to them. But hungry allies who could not fight would be of no use. And soon, soon a fight was coming.

Matari Kleir was well behind them, and so were two other settlements; Calindor set a hard pace southeast across the prairie. As they approached another village, Svordo caught up with him.

"We'll start losing the horses at this rate, and it's a long walk home from here."

Calindor seemed not to hear at first; then he said: "We'll rest in this place for a time and then go on more slowly. I'll heal the horses' weariness."

"Save some for me as well. This is no way to spend new year's day, with a headache. And what's troubling you today? A headache too?"

"You're not far wrong. I felt them cast a spell of love in Bhadvedor. It is strange to know they are here in Cantarea. To *feel* them here." He slowed his horse to a walk and beckoned to the others, who were riding some distance behind. When they had caught up, Calindor looked at Sveit: "How far from here to Bhadvedor?"

"Less than a day's ride to the southeast. When we come to that ridge we may even be able to see it."

The ridge was not high, but it served to shelter the village of Cadorsanbea from the north wind. Calindor glanced down at the cluster of houses on the edge of a pond, and then looked beyond, over the vast plain. Yes, that must be Bhadvedor on the horizon. He was about to focus, the better to see, when a different kind of focus brushed over him. He heard Nezaual grunt; the boy felt it too.

"What was that, beloved son?"

"A priest, honored father."

"A priest searching. For what?"

Nezaual looked uncomfortable. "For you, honored father. It is a searching spell."

"From what you've told me of such spells, they need an object to link the searcher and the sought. What object would I have that Exteca priests could search for?"

"It's a gold lip plug, honored father. Yetecuan gave it to you in Burnbaile. He no doubt uses it to tell where you are, but you would not normally feel it. This time we're close and in direct line of sight."

Calindor opened a saddlebag and plunged his hand into the spare clothing and boots. A small packet came into his fingers: needles, thread, bone buttons, and the lip plug. He recalled putting it there as they packed for this journey; he hadn't wanted to leave a gold object around the castle, least of all a keepsake of his one meeting with Yetecuan. And with it the Exteca had traced his travels since last summer. They might not have iron and steel, or know as many spells as Renjosudaldor, but they knew enough.

Well, for now he would do nothing. The magician searching for him would have realized how close he was; it was pointless to cast it into a stream or gully. Let them trace his movements; it would not save them to do so.

The villagers had seen them—had probably known they were coming for some time, Calindor suspected. As they rode down the lee side of the ridge, men and women turned from their work in the fields and gardens. Without haste or hesitation the men walked to meet the riders. Calindor saw men—and some women—appear in doorways and windows with arrows nocked on bowstrings.

A Cantarean, unusually short but tough and wiry, approached

with a pitchfork on his shoulder. Calindor saw alertness in the man's eyes, and caution, but no fear.

"We've come from Vidhumen with news. My name is Calindor."

"Welcome. I'm Michuna, the electman here. We've got news as well. Those southerners have turned up in Bhadvedor."

"We know."

"And you're not happy about it, I'd guess. Well, come to the hall and give us your news. Then we'll give you supper and a bed for the night."

"We'll be grateful for a little food, but we still have far to go before we camp for the night."

"As you like." Michuna led them through the village while children clustered giggling around them. They were Cantarean and Badakhar, and seemed at ease with one another; they spoke both languages, with no special preference for either. Good signs. So were the adults, who followed at a more respectful distance. Calindor saw a pregnant Badakh woman with her arm around a Cantarean man—an act that would have earned them death not long ago. Their neighbors paid no attention.

The village hall stood between the pond and a square that was really just a barnyard. Michuna hurried ahead to open the door, while others went to nearby houses; they came out bearing fresh loaves and pots of preserved meat.

"I feel bad taking these people's food so early in the spring," Svordo murmured to his companions.

"They're better off than most," Pervidhu said. "Good soil, water and sun, and still plenty of grain and hay. Look at their horses."

They dismounted and eager hands reached for the horses' reins.

"Honored father, I will look after the horses."

"I don't think you need to, beloved son. These people will care for them well."

"Even so, let me make sure."

"As you wish. Then come and join us in the hall."

It was a large room of white-painted log walls with a low ceiling and a single hearth at one end. But it was soon warm with the sheer numbers who crowded in. When everyone in the village seemed packed inside, Michuna thumped a staff on the floor and demanded quiet.

Calindor spoke briefly, explaining the significance of the Exteca's arrival and the urgent need for a council of all electmen and speakers. When he was through, a young woman spoke from the crowd:

"What good will a council do us if the Exteca can be here by this time tomorrow?"

Anxious murmurs answered her.

"They will stay in Bhadvedor for a time," Calindor said. "Now that they're here, they must learn about us. I doubt if they even have anyone who speaks our languages." He paused. *I don't know this country, the distances. I didn't realize we were so close to Bhadvedor.* "But you are right—they will not take long to search the countryside. You may have to abandon your village."

"Give all we've built to those magicians and cannibals?" an older Badakhar cried out hoarsely. "After all we've suffered to make this a decent place to live?"

"And where would we go?" demanded a woman. "Do you have empty houses in Vidhumen? Fields for our livestock?"

Calindor hesitated. He could see the Gariba flowing around the room, springing from the flames on the hearth, playing in the air above the people's heads, locked with one another in the log walls and roof. They were easy to read and control; but the people among whom they played were mysterious and unpredictable. He could cast a spell of terror on them, but he could not understand them. *I have given up one knowledge for the sake of another.*

"You would not need to go that far. But I know it would be hard wherever you went."

"You're supposed to be a magician," said the old Badakhar. "Why don't you put a spell on them?"

Calindor felt a little more confident. "I plan to put many spells on them. And spells on us that will protect us from their magic. I can bring a storm upon them that will keep them under the roofs of Bhadvedor, for a few days anyway. That will give you time to plan an escape."

"Do it," the old man said. Others echoed him.

"We should vote upon it," said Michuna. "First, though, we should decide whether we are willing to leave for the north."

Reluctantly, most hands went up.

"And whether we should ask Calindor to call up a storm upon the Exteca."

Again most agreed.

"Very well," Calindor said. "I shall cast it tonight, before we leave. I thank you all for your welcome, and for your courage. I wish we had more people like you in the north."

"You soon will," said Michuna with a smile. "Very well. Let us share a meal together before you go."

It was simple food, fresh bread and salt meat and pungent pickled onions that made Pervidhu's eyes water while his companions laughed at his tears. The hall heard little other laughter; conversations were low and subdued. Everyone was discussing what to leave and what to take.

"When this is over I will restore your village completely," Calindor promised Michuna. "And may you and your people teach us how you have made such a place of peace together."

The electman looked at him in some surprise. "What choice have we had? We love our children more than we hate our enemies, and all our children . . . are all our children."

Calindor smiled; for some reason the sentiment reminded him of Nezaual, and he looked around to find him. He was nowhere in sight; the rest of the party were at nearby tables, happily eating everything put before them.

"Sveit," he called. "Where's Nezaual?"

"Haven't seen him since—" Sveit's eyes widened. "Since he said he'd look after the horses."

Calindor excused himself, stood and left the hall. It was growing dark outside, though the western sky still glowed with red and orange clouds. Across the square was the barn, its interior dark. He did not need a light to see that it was empty. The villagers' horses were gone as well as his own.

His focus swept out into the twilight; a child, doubtless one with potential for magic, screamed somewhere inside the hall. And far out on the prairie to the southeast, Calindor sensed Nezaual flinching from the focus as he rode steadily toward Bhadvedor with a string of horses behind him.

Before he had returned to Bayodar, Renjosudaldor had bought a house in Vidhumen's old quarter. It had belonged to some upermanna family, and contained stables and storerooms within its walls. Now, at the end of the winter, the first traders had moved into it.

Silisihan, their head, seemed unsurprised by the arrival of Ghelasha and Callishandal in his house. The two women had simply arrived early one morning, pounded on the outer door, and gained admittance. He had greeted them, escorted them into the dining hall, and served them tea and cakes by the fire. Smiling, he drank his own tea and asked them nothing about their reasons for coming.

Callishandal began to feel uneasy. She had come to know and like the Gulyaji after Callia's storm, when they had saved so many from death. She knew Silisihan personally, and knew he had rescued Calindor and Svordo from capture after the fall of Ner Kes.

But the stories she had heard in childhood still lived, making her wish herself elsewhere. They might be Cantareans, but the Badakhar had made them terrifying even to other Cantareans: Burrowers, deceivers, masters of strange magic, dwellers in darkness who would snatch any unwary person who ventured too far into a cave or mine shaft.

Callishandal glanced at Ghelasha. If the former queen felt a similar anxiety, she did not show it. Her beautiful face was composed in a smile; her hand did not tremble as she lifted the tea bowl to her lips.

"How far is it to Bayodar?" she asked after a long exchange of pleasantries about weather and architecture.

"A little over four days' hard ride, my lady. With our trade goods, we will be lucky to make it in seven or eight."

"Too long."

"My lady?"

"Seven or eight days would be too long for us. We need to talk to your master, Renjosudaldor. The matter is urgent."

"Then I owe it to you, my lady, to ask whether I or my companions may not help you also. If we can, perhaps you can resolve this matter even more swiftly."

"Are you a great magician, Silisihan?"

"Not a great one, my lady. I can weave a few spells of deception."

"We need your best magician."

"Then you do indeed need Renjosudaldor, the Protector." He studied the bare wooden floor. "I recognize your urgency, my lady, and I will not inquire into it—no, you do not need to explain anything. I am only considering which of my people I can spare as your guide to Bayodar. Well, it had better be me. My people can get along without me better than I can without them. When would you depart?"

"This afternoon."

Silisihan smiled very slightly. "And how many in the party?"

"Four: you, me, Callishandal, and the foreign girl Deir."

The Gulyaji trader looked surprised at last. "I should advise you, my lady, that the countryside is not safe for women these days."

"It never was. But you Burrowers know some spells of deception, and I've never heard of any of you being waylaid."

His smile broadened into a soft laugh. "Very true. Well, may I ask that you supply your own horses and their feed? I shall provide our food and shelter."

Ghelasha put down her tea and stood up. "I like a man who decides and acts. We'll be back in three hours."

Silisihan rose. Tall though Ghelasha was, she had to look up to meet his gaze. "I assume the electman is fully aware of your intentions, my lady, and has no objection."

"He is and he hasn't, not that it would make any difference if he did. He's not the Aryo of Aishadan anymore."

"I ask only because the Protector will want to know the political implications of your visit."

"He'll know them. Thank you, Silisihan." She shook his hand, a ceremony he seemed not quite comfortable with. Callishandal bowed slightly to him and then followed Ghelasha out of the house.

"Three hours!" Callishandal exclaimed as they walked up the street toward the castle. "Can we persuade Deir to come with us at such short notice?"

"We'll tie her up and sling her over a saddle if we have to."

"But if you anger the magician inside her—"

"Hitting her didn't seem to matter. Sometimes I think these damned magicians are too scared of one another. No wonder they're our servants and not our masters."

Callishandal saw the truth in that. In the old days, magicians had served the upermannar and Aryos of the Five Kingdoms in exchange for little more than food and shelter. They were too interested in learning about the Powers to exercise mere power. The Veikar, greatest of the Badakhar sorcerers, had watched each other jealously, never allowing one to gain too much strength over his colleagues. Even Cantarean magicians were often bemused and distracted in their contemplation of the Gariba . . . including Calindor.

Yet somehow Calindor would have to pull himself out of his rapt attachment to the Exteca True Gods and devise a way to push them away; so far he seemed only to have drawn them closer.

Preparation took nearer five hours than three. Still, they were away while the sun stood high in the west. The smoke of Vidhumen's chimneys was visible long after even the castle had sunk behind the hills.

Silisihan led, with the packhorses following. Then came Deir and Callishandal; Ghelasha was at the rear with the spare mounts. The last snowfall still clung on every north-facing slope, but the afternoon sun was warm.

"He doesn't ride very well, does he?" Deir said of Silisihan.

"None of us do except Ghelasha. She's the only one who grew

up riding. The Gulyaji didn't have much chance to, down in their caves, and I never sat a horse until a couple of years ago. At least he's not galloping the way the Badakhar do."

Yet Silisihan's easy pace soon carried them out of the settled regions around Vidhumen. The plateau on which it stood sloped down to the east into scablands where Callia's floods had raged. Little grew. The great storm had stripped the land of most of its soil down to bedrock. Yet here and there a clump of sagebrush still held a handful of earth within its roots.

"Where will we stop for the night?" Callishandal called out.

Silisihan looked over his shoulder. "We'll stop at midnight."

"How will we see?"

"Moonlight. And coldfire."

Just before sunset they paused for a cold meal of bread and cheese, and to rest the horses. The sky was a burning banner overhead, and a chill wind sprang up out of the south. Deir and Callishandal walked about to ease their aches.

"If they liked living underground so much," Deir said, "why did they bother coming back from their caves?"

"Their magic wasn't working well. They couldn't keep their animals healthy, and their crops were failing. And I think they had dreamed for a long time about being out under the sky."

"Strange, to live always in caves. Always hiding."

"Yet they survived, and now they're in their own city. I wonder what it's like."

"What is it that Ghelasha wants to talk to Renjosudaldor about? And why didn't she ask him before he left Vidhumen?"

"Good questions. You should ask her."

"I tried, before we left. She only said it was an urgent problem that needed a Gulyaji magician. Don't see why it needs us, though."

"Well, it's an adventure, isn't it? I like it better than moping about in the castle, waiting for news."

"Yes. But I hope the news will be good when we get back."

Silisihan mounted and rode eastward again; the women hurried to follow. As twilight deepened to darkness, the full moon rose above the horizon. Then a blue glow brightened around each horse's hooves, so that each seemed to move in a pool of light.

All around stretched the prairie, immense, silent, and alive. Callishandal looked at it with awe. No matter the scourging it had endured, it was not dead. The coldfire around the horses' hooves reflected from the eyes of rabbits and foxes and threw brief light over the new buds of wildflowers not yet blooming. The steady clop-clop of the hoofbeats was almost unheard under the hum and murmur of the wind.

When they stopped at last, in the midst of the empty plain, everyone helped pitch a simple tent and then burrowed into a sleeping bag. Silisihan slept outside, beside the horses.

Callishandal, half asleep, called to him: "Thank you for bringing us through so much beauty."

She saw him looking up at the moon. "More beauty than we ever dreamed of," he said.

They put Yetecuan in the best room in the castle, though it was little better than a priest's cell in a pyramid. A narrow window overlooked the town of Bhadvedor, and the westering sun blazed through the rippled glass.

He is so close, so close!

He shivered on the bed where Elsman normally slept, while priests clucked and murmured around him. Those with real talent shivered also, for they too had felt Calindor's focus sweep over the castle like a bolt of lightning.

He had been a fool to use the lip plug, and a worse fool to locate it now that they were in Cantarea. Calindor had probably seen it at once for what it was. Perhaps Calindor had planted his own means of following him; surely it was no coincidence that Calindor should be almost within the first town the expedition had taken.

Has he drawn us into a trap? Is this miserable town the bait he set out for us?

Someone tried to draw a blanket over Yetecuan, and he pushed it away. Better to shiver wide-awake than sweat and drowse. He looked up at the anxious faces around him, each framed by a mass of matted hair. Most of the priests of the expedition were here, and he loved them all like sons and brothers, but now they looked like toddling children unaware of the cougar crouched close by. Most of them were good only for small spells of love or terror, and for simple housekeeping like driving pests away. They could honor the True Gods and open a rib cage as well as anyone, but against a sorcerer like Calindor they would be helpless.

And I am helpless too, now that I have cast this spell. It will be days until I am fit again. We must win more of these people, and do it without much magic.

His spirits began to rise: after all, they now had one town and all its people, including Elsman's warriors with their beautiful weapons. If Yaocatl and Colotic moved quickly, they could bring much of the surrounding country into their hands. A day of many sacrifices would not only please the Gods, Yetecuan thought, but restore his strength more quickly. Success would lead to success; Yaocatl's strategy had been wise. The barbarians from other towns would now return to their homes with news of the beloved invaders. Many would join them without need of a spell. And each one who came to the Exteca would be one less for Calindor.

He's an intelligent young man. When he sees that his own people prefer us, he'll come around. He must.

The sun was down now, and candles glowed in the room. Someone offered him a sip of milk and a morsel of bread, but he turned them aside. Something was happening out there in the northern darkness, something that made his skin prickle. He saw that some of the priests sensed it also; it made them sway and grunt and giggle.

"Take me outside, beloved sons. I would like some fresh air."

Strong hands lifted him from the bed, carrying him from the room and down a corridor to a door that opened onto a terrace. Beyond a half-built parapet he could see the lights of the town and the roofs gleaming in the blue glow of the new-risen moon. The voices of Exteca warriors rose in familiar songs as they patrolled the streets of their newest conquest.

But to the northwest something else caught the moonlight: a mass of cloud. Was it rising, or merely coming nearer? Or both?

The power within it was growing, even more visible to Yetecuan than the cloud itself. *He has called the Powers of air and water, summoned rain and thunder. And he is sending them against us.*

He knew he should warn everyone, urge them to return to shelter. But the sight of a thunderhead, hurled like a pebble from a sling, was too beautiful. That a human being could wield such power seemed beyond belief; that he would soon wield it for Tola, the Exteca, and the True Gods, was a joy almost too great to comprehend.

"Honored father, we should get you back inside," one of the priests said. "It's going to rain."

Poor foolish, insensitive boy! He could not even see the spells at work before his eyes. "In good time, beloved son. Our host is entertaining us. We would be rude to turn away."

Lightning flared within the cloud, flared again. The first thunder muttered in the distance. Something echoed it in the streets below, a rumble along the ground. Warriors broke off their song and shouted a challenge. Yetecuan shuffled closer to the parapet, the wind tugging at his hair and robe, and looked down.

Horses? Almost a herd of them, running through the street.

Warriors were trying to halt them, rope them—no, most were already roped together. A man was astride one of them, calling out in Exteca that he was hungry, hungry—

"Nezaual! It's Nezaual. Beloved sons, go and welcome him at once. Bring him here, quickly, quickly. The storm is almost upon us."

The night sky exploded in light, making every man and horse in the street as visible as if it were noon. There was the rider, dressed in strange garments like the northerners, his hair scarcely reaching his shoulders; but when he looked up, a second lightning bolt showed that it was Nezaual—gathered safely in by the True Gods just as the storm was about to break.

Twenty-two

Calindor walked back up to the ridge above the village. To the north and west the sky was clear, and a bright full moon loomed enormous above the eastern horizon. But to the south it shone on a thunderhead that flared with its own internal light.

He saw the Sidigariba, the Powers of air, shooting exuberantly to the top of the thunderhead, carrying with them the Belagariba of water, then falling and rising yet again. The Powers of fire, Fusigariba, quarreled with them in bolts of lightning; the Powers of air answered in whirling tornadoes that reminded Calindor of Callia's fury.

Yet this is a single raindrop compared to her torrent. He considered giving blood to Cihuacoatl the Lady Serpent, so that she might add to the storm. No—the Exteca would sense what he was doing, and perhaps gain confidence that he was coming over to their side even as he seemed to resist them. Nezaual would tell them enough about his interest in redmagic, his experiences with the True Gods.

Albohar had been right, and he himself had been a trusting fool. When would he learn that knowledge of magic was not knowledge of people? *Now I have to lead these good people north to safety behind the shield of this storm. But I cannot hold this shield against the Exteca forever.*

Thunder rolled across the dark prairie as he paced back and forth, hands clasped behind his back. Lightning turned the darkness into blue-white glare every few seconds, but he scarcely noticed.

Then Svordo paced alongside, his posture mocking Calindor's. But in the flash of lightning Svordo's face was grim.

"This reminds me too much of Aishadan when Callia came. How long are you going to keep this storm going?"

"Another day and night. By then it'll have dropped enough water to keep Bhadvedor flooded for ten days. That should be enough time for these people to get safely north."

"Why not just throw another storm in ten days, then? It's a very pretty storm, and I'd look forward to seeing another one."

Calindor smiled. "Magic doesn't make something out of nothing. I had to summon Gariba of air and water from here to Vidhumen, just to make this storm. Cantarea won't see much rain now for weeks." He looked at the lightning as it marched south. "And the floods will ruin much of the land around Bhadvedor for months to come—maybe years. Even if I could send more storms, I wouldn't. I would harm Callia more than I'd harm the Exteca."

"I always thought magic was a doubtful talent, and now I'm sure of it. This is why you don't just smash them all with dragonfire and be done with it."

"You're right. Plenty of Badakh magic would serve to kill the Exteca, but . . ." He paused and looked at Svordo. "You know I can see the Gariba, the powers that give life to the world. And I can sense Callia working within that life, seeking to balance life and death. If I kill what still wishes to live, I harm her and I harm myself."

"Because you tip the balance against her."

"Yes. And the dead . . . don't go away."

Thunder banged suddenly and echoed from some nearby hill.

"Ghosts? You see ghosts?"

"Memories of the dead. In places where many have died, especially before Callia was ready for them, I can sense their presence. When Mekhpur came to face Callishandal and me in the castle in Aishadan, we were in the Hearing Hall. The Veikar had sacrificed hundreds there to please Mekhpur, and I felt their presence more than I can feel yours this moment."

"Am I being foolish to ask you, then, why you've been learning redmagic from that boy? He does seem fond of cutting people's hearts out."

"Perhaps I can explain it better to you than I could to Callishandal. Their killing is wrong, and hurts Callia. But they have found something in blood, something deep and strong. Giving it to the True Gods allows a magician to do great things—"

"Like make his relatives too sick to do magic."

Calindor laughed with little pleasure. "You're a good friend because you don't take me seriously. Yes, it's harmful to the Siragi Aibela, and if you let it go too far, it turns you into a stinking madman like Nezaual's master, Yetecuan. But if you can find the balance, use the power wisely, the pain and the blood are worth it."

"So." Svordo looked at the thunderhead gleaming in moonlight. "You can't wave a magic staff and make them go away. You can't kill them. Maybe you can find a counterspell to their magic, but if you're not careful, you'll go mad and start cutting people's hearts out. It must be wonderful to be a great sorcerer."

Calindor laughed again, more happily. "Let's get back to the village. I need to talk to Michuna about moving his people north."

The sky was brightening in the east as Silisihan woke and built up the fire. A pot of oatmeal was soon steaming, and the women in the tent began to stir. He murmured his greetings and went to see to the horses while the women dressed. By the time he returned, the cloudless sky was turning blue and Deir was ladling out porridge. She handed him a bowl; he thanked her and settled cross-legged by the fire.

"I think Calindor cast a great spell last night," he said. "It will give us fair weather."

"A spell? What is he doing, and how can you tell it is Calindor?"

"A weather spell, some kind of Badakh magic. It felt as if it would create heavy rain. Perhaps someone else cast it, but I remember the spells he cast in Bayo Bealar, the caves where we lived before Callia's wrath. This one felt very much like it. And I don't know of any Badakh who could cast so great a spell. He is far from here, but he has drawn the moisture from the air around us."

Smiling, Silisihan drew his hand over his graying black hair; it rose in a fluffy mane. The women laughed, then looked at one another's hair and laughed again.

Ghelasha was soon over her merriment. "He must have met the Exteca. He wouldn't cast a spell like that just to fill some farmer's pond. But he might do that to impress the Exteca."

Silisihan nodded. "I think you are right, my lady. That means the Exteca are only a few days' ride from Vidhumen."

Ghelasha spooned up the last of her oatmeal. "Then let's clean up and waste no more time."

The Gulyaji led them east across the scablands, where none could live, and up into higher ground. In the shallow river valleys grass was greening and Badakhar herders tended their undersized sheep and scrawny cattle. The herders' camps were simple clusters of tents and carts, arrayed to keep the livestock safe at night and the herders safe by day. Horsemen bearing crude lances and battered swords watched suspiciously as the strangers rode through. But they offered no threat and made no demands; Silisihan in his black cloak was clearly a Gulyaji and therefore no one to trifle with.

That night, exhausted by the long ride and parched by the dry air, they stopped at last by a stream in a canyon. The water might be sour with minerals, but it tasted wonderful all the same. As they sank into their sleeping bags under the simple tent, Deir turned to Ghelasha:

"Why are we going all this way to see Renjosudaldor? Is it something to do with Calindor?"

Ghelasha glanced at Callishandal, who was already asleep. "A great deal to do with Calindor. Now go to sleep. We've two more days of this."

She said no more and was soon asleep. But Silisihan, lying nearby outside the tent, sang softly in the bright moonlight. Deir could not understand most of the words, but she recognized a lullaby and joined in, singing without words. Their two voices blended, making a murmur in the windless silence.

Then Deir sang a lullaby of the Airn, while Silisihan hummed an accompaniment. Something tugged at Deir's memory but she could not place it: something about a man's deep voice, humming that ancient tune, made her feel like a little girl again.

Wrapped in her sleeping bag, she shivered without feeling cold.

Sveit looked over his shoulder. The thunderhead in the southeast was growing again, strengthened not by Calindor's magic but by the heat of the early afternoon sun. Elsewhere the sky was cloudless and intensely blue down to a far, sharp-edged horizon.

Down the hill, the village looked oddly still; no smoke rose from the chimneys, and ducks on the pond were the only creatures moving. The path up the hill was wider and dustier than yesterday; the last of the village herds had passed by just a little earlier.

Turning back, Sveit looked north. The villagers were walking in an orderly column, with a few herders and their dogs moving the livestock down the hill and across the greening prairie.

"Never saw Cantareans work so fast in the old days," he said to Calindor. "And never thought I'd be looking after so many of them without selling even one at the end of the trip."

Calindor snorted. "If I knew a spell to turn a man into a donkey, you'd be carrying your share of their goods."

Sveit glanced back again as thunder rumbled by. "You can always strike me with lightning."

"Not today." He pointed north, beyond the column of villagers. "Svordo and Pervidhu will be far ahead of us by now, and we'll have to walk fast to catch up."

Calindor smiled as he lengthened his stride. Sveit was incorrigible, but useful: he was accustomed to moving people long distances in a hurry, and delivering them in salable condition. He had sketched out a plan for moving the whole village and most of its remaining livestock, and it had gone off smoothly. By the time the storm dissolved over Bhadvedor, the villagers would be well north—even though all were walking.

So would many others. If he could persuade more to evacuate also, the Exteca would have fewer to recruit through either magic or arms. Then, as they ventured north in pursuit, he would somehow have to lure them into wasting their strength in vain spells so that Cantareans and Badakhar could trap them.

That would be real magic, he thought: to deceive the Exteca into surrendering without a fight, so that he could send them south without bloodshed that would harm Callia. And to keep his own Cantareans and Badakhar from slaughtering the Exteca anyway.

The paradox had been taunting him for weeks now. He was a magician whose magic must not kill, fighting a magic based on killing. The warriors on both sides would rejoice in slaughtering one another, but he must not give them the opportunity.

. . . It will have to be a spell of love or terror—and I don't know the spell of love.

Lightning crashed again and again, shattering trees and blasting away a wall of Elsman's castle. The rain was a collapsing wall of another kind, roaring out of the storm and pounding the Exteca tents into the deepening water. The stream that bordered the field rose above its banks around midnight, while Yetecuan's priests and Colotic's warriors struggled to get him to safety and warmth. Staggering through the mire, they carried him in his litter to a stone building up the road. It was a hut, no more, whose crude wooden shutters had blown off in the storm's first gusts. But its roof was sound, and its floor only a little wet.

And magic has not poisoned it like the castle, Yetecuan thought.

The natives who lived in the hut—three generations of the white-skins, including an old grandmother and two squalling babies—pressed forward affectionately until Colotic's men shoved them against the walls. One of the warriors managed to light a lamp from the smoking embers in the fireplace; the wind soon blew it out, but in that time his companions carried Yetecuan to the bed the grandmother had left. He let the warriors try to dry him with half-soaked rags, but it made little difference.

He did not much care. The sheer quantity of rain, drumming on the roof and hissing in the floodwater, delighted him.

O True Gods, let us take him in your names to Tola, and let him there call down such a storm as this, so that the hills will turn green and streams turn into rivers too deep for mammoths!

Yes, Calindor might now be defiant of the True Gods, but he would learn; he would change. And he would make the brown lands rich and green in their honor, with their blessings.

Lightning flared again as the door swung open and Nezaual stepped into the hut. He looked dazzled by the light—everyone was—but he walked without hesitation to the bed and knelt beside it.

"Honored father, I have spoken with General Yaocatl, and he has sent me back to attend you."

Yetecuan did not trust himself to speak for a moment. He reached out to touch the boy's shoulders, sensing through his fingers much of what had happened to Nezaual in half a year.

"My very beloved son. What adventures you have had! How often I feared for you."

"I was safe in the service of the True Gods." Nezaual submitted with a smile to the old priest's focus.

"You hold the residue of some strong spells, and you did not cast all of them."

"I taught some to Calindor, and he taught some to me."

Yetecuan would not let fear show in his voice. "So he knows redmagic."

"A little, honored father. The only important magic he knows is the spell of terror. He is strong, but not yet controlled."

"The control will come. But I hope it comes late, after he has joined us in serving the True Gods."

Thunder deafened him. When it had passed, he went on: "He has met some of the Gods, or he could not do redmagic. Yet he still opposes us. Can you explain this, beloved son?"

"It is hard to explain, honored father. Until a few years ago, Calindor and his people were the slaves of the Badakhar, the white-skinned people. He did some great magic, the spell that many of us felt even in Tola."

"Yes, yes, I remember."

"The spell unleashed a storm far greater than this one, that swept all Cantarea and overthrew the Badakhar. Now the people are all poor, and they quarrel shamelessly with one another, but neither the Cantareans nor the Badakhar wish to give up their freedom."

"Freedom? To live in this squalor is freedom?"

"So they think, honored father, and Calindor thinks so too. He sees us as conquerors who will make them all slaves again, so he has tried to rally the people against us."

"He knew we were coming."

"Oh yes, honored father. I think he knew from the day we first met him that we would seek him out. But he did not expect you so soon. He learned of your arrival a few days ago. We came south to renew his warnings and to learn of your progress."

"Is this storm an attempt to frighten us away?"

"Oh no, honored father. He is simply trying to keep us here while he warns the other towns nearby to flee us."

"How can they flee in such a storm?"

"Honored father—the storm is only here. A short ride away the sky is clear and the ground is dry."

"What a clever young man he is! Then if we march out of this miserable town, we shall soon be out of the storm."

Nezaual shook his head. "I don't think that would be wise, honored father. The streams are over their banks, and the roads are thick mud. I had to leave behind three of the horses I stole—they sank into the mud and could not escape."

"Poor beasts. Well, this storm cannot go on forever."

"Perhaps another day, honored father, and then a day or two more before the land is dry enough to support horses and mammoths."

"That is no inconvenience. We will rest, and enjoy the spectacle that Calindor has sent us." Yetecuan leaned back against the pillows that Colotic's men had placed behind him. Someone drew a blanket up to his chest. "You have served the True Gods well, beloved Nezaual. With you beside us, we do not enter an unknown land. Please forgive an old man who must rest now and regain his strength."

"I will sit beside you, honored father, and wait until you wake. May the True Gods grant you good sleep."

"Sing me a song, Nezaual. A lullaby."

His voice almost lost in the roar of rain and the boom of thunder, Nezaual sat beside the bed, holding the old man's hand and singing until the hand relaxed and Yetecuan's eyes closed.

The storm ended at dawn after two nights and a day. With its shutters blown away, the hut had gradually flooded and the hard dirt floor had turned to mud. Yetecuan had not much minded; he had stayed in the bed, joking with the warriors as they came in and out to look after him, and admiring the sheer quantity of rain.

Nezaual went to the window, his bare feet squelching. *If he sends a spell of freezing, he will trap us here.* But the air outside was warm, almost muggy. The clouds were tearing apart, turning crimson along their eastern edges; pools of water everywhere reflected the colors back to the sky.

Nezaual decided to walk—or wade—around the town so that he could report to Yetecuan on its condition.

Others were doing the same. In a field on the east of the town, warriors were looking after the horses and mammoths, who had endured the downpour with no shelter and were now loudly hungry. For a time Nezaual helped carry hay from a barn to the mammoths, and then went on to see the rest of the town.

Many of the houses were deserted and destroyed. Scores of people had left their homes for the higher ground of the castle, though the lightning strikes had opened much of it to the storm. The town's little river was now a broad brown lake, engulfing the market square and the houses around it. The people wandered aimlessly through the flooded streets, looking for food or salvageable goods. When they saw an Exteca, they hurried to him and sought to embrace him; Nezaual had to shove several away.

This was the nuisance part of the spell of love: the blind affection that made its victims like children. After a few weeks the spell would wear off into a dull dependency mixed with fear—and by then they would have learned to fear the invaders they loved.

The chilly water, often as high as his hips, did not improve his temper. More than once he stepped into a mudhole and had to struggle to free himself. Exteca warriors seemed even angrier: they were trying to find dry fodder for the animals and food for themselves, while Badakhar and Cantareans pestered them with caresses and smiles.

At length he returned to Yetecuan's hut. "Honored father, Calindor has trapped us here. It will be days before we can move on. The ground is more water than soil."

"Imagine such rain in Tola." Yetecuan chuckled. "Imagine the crops it would grow."

"I would sooner be in Tola as it is, honored father, with dry clothes and the sun hot on my back." Then he paused. "Once Calindor taught me a spell to drive water away. Perhaps—"

He murmured the four-word spell he had learned in the cabin on the way to the great valley of Burdan Atana, where Calindor in turn had learned his first redmagic. He focused. Steam puffed and swirled out of his sodden clothes and hair; only his feet, on the muddy floor, were still wet.

Yetecuan laughed aloud.

"If you were strong enough, beloved son, you could drive all the water from this place and we would walk north cursing the dust. What a clever spell! Have you tired yourself?"

"Only a little, honored father. It doesn't demand much effort. I wish I had remembered it sooner, and used it to keep you dry."

"No matter, no matter. Well, you have certainly benefited as the sorcerer's apprentice. Calindor did us a great service when he took you with him on that strange craft of his."

"I do not think he meant to do us a service, honored father."

"What we mean to do, and what the True Gods mean us to do, are not always the same thing. And the True Gods were watching over us that night in Burnbaile."

"Of course, honored father." Nezaual smiled. The floodwaters, the ruined houses of this strange and squalid town, the enchanted barbarians who lived in it—none of that mattered. For the first time in over half a year, he felt himself at home.

Twenty-three

Yaocatl did not trouble with the litter to bear him through the flooded streets to the hut where Yetecuan had sheltered; he stripped off his feathers, ruined in any case, and waded impassively to his appointment with the priest.

Behind his blank face he seethed with anger that almost masked the fear beneath it. Perhaps he had misjudged the situation when he had asked for the spell of love; now the strongest magician in the expedition was incapable of magic for days to come, while this mysterious northern sorcerer had almost casually flung a storm like a net over the whole army. Yetecuan had even refused to enter the castle, and rumors were that the sorcerer Calindor had placed some other spell on it—which did not help the mood of the warriors who must occupy the castle as the local strongpoint.

Yetecuan's insistence on staying away had created another problem. Only the most insensitive priests seemed able to enter the castle, and in this flood it was the only place for conducting proper sacrifices. This morning's six men and six women had been a noisy, messy business: the spell of love made them willing, but the priests had shown almost comical incompetence in extracting their hearts. If practice did not bring quick improvement, the priests would irritate the True Gods; they did not like messy corpses.

The Chontalteca allies looked miserable and alarmed as they carried sacks of grain to the few places high and dry enough to support cooking fires. Horses whinnied in protest and kicked out at their shivering grooms. Exteca warriors showed no concern, but Yaocatl knew they felt as angry as he. Only the mammoths seemed not to care whether they stood in deep mud or on dry ground; they even amused themselves by squirting water from their trunks onto anyone who ventured too close to them.

The northern steel sword in its scabbard was strangely heavy in Yaocatl's left hand. A terrifying weapon; if a few hundred determined northerners had attacked just after the storm, with swords like these, the expedition would have come to a disastrous end. Even as it was, many of his men would surely fall ill of contaminated water and food, of sleeping cold and wet. If disease spread, it would take endless sacrifices to induce the True Gods to relent.

We are too far from home.

This was a large and populous land; if he did not strike hard and soon at its strongest towns, the northerners would eventually drive him south into the desert again. He would do the same in their place. Yetecuan had a wonderful optimism and faith in the providence of the Gods, but of course a priest should feel like that. A soldier had to worry where his next meal, his next arrow, were coming from.

Without ceremony he walked into the hut. Yetecuan and his priests extended their hands in welcome, while the original inhabitants bowed and smirked from the corners.

Yetecuan half giggled at the general's appearance. "Beloved son, you look as if you have been battling the Water Demons."

"Perhaps I have, honored father. You asked for an urgent meeting?"

"Look at our beautiful Nezaual, beloved son."

The boy looked odd with his short, clean hair and his foreign clothes. Almost like one of the Cantareans. Then Yaocatl looked again.

"Those are the clothes you wore when you arrived. How did you get them dry?"

"A barbarian spell that the boy had learned here," Yetecuan whispered hoarsely, and then he burst out laughing. "A spell to drive water *away*. Isn't that amazing, beloved Yaocatl?"

"Indeed, honored father." Yaocatl wondered how the boy had done it. Could one pour blood *into* oneself, and thereby drive away water?

"And here is the best part. It's a very simple spell, and not very tiring at all. Nezaual is going to teach it to his brother priests."

"Excellent," Yaocatl said tonelessly. After what he had seen at this morning's sacrifices, the brother priests might be hard to teach. In any case, what did this magicians' amusement have to do with him?

"And then," Yetecuan went on, "they are going to cast the spell together, and drive away all this water."

Only years of discipline kept Yaocatl from laughing in the priest's face. Then he thought through the implications. *If the old man is right—*

"When do your priests plan to do this, honored father?"

"Whenever you are ready, beloved Yaocatl. I think we will be wise to move quickly once the ground dries out."

"It seems impossible to believe such a thing could happen."

"Half a year ago would you have believed yourself the conqueror of half the world?"

Yaocatl turned to Nezaual. "Are you going to make all the water disappear?"

"Not all. But I'll dry out the northern side of the town. If you move the men and animals into this neighborhood, we should be able to move quickly."

Most of the army was south of the town, encamped in a vast new lake. Yaocatl tried to estimate how soon they could break camp and march through Bhadvedor.

"We will be ready before sundown."

"Very good. So shall we." Nezaual glanced at his fellow magicians and giggled. They giggled back.

With no time to waste, Yaocatl struggled back through the flood to the castle. Orders went out to strike and pack their tents and to march through the town. *If this doesn't work, we will be worse off than ever . . . mammoths trapped in mud holes, men drowning—*

But that was the professional warrior in him, always worrying about what might go wrong. The Exteca in him relaxed, confident that once again the True Gods were serving their people as their people served them.

The column of refugees from Cadorsanbea had made surprising progress. They walked steadily north, in good order, and seemed even to be enjoying themselves. The sun was warm, the ground dry, the air full of songs and laughter. Only a few paused to rest, and soon hurried to regain their places.

Around noon they had passed another village, and Michuna stopped to talk with its electwoman. She was a middle-aged Badakh; Calindor saw her watching the passing column as if it were so many brigands.

"You can run if you like," she said when Michuna fell silent. "We'll stay and take our chances."

Michuna looked at Calindor, who only shrugged. If these people chose to become slaves of the Exteca, he could not force them to do otherwise. He could drive them off in all directions with a spell of terror, but what would be the point? Respecting people's freedom also meant respecting their stupidity.

The electwoman would not sell any horses, and that decision demanded respect also. When the Exteca came, Calindor reflected, they would simply take the horses—or the electwoman, lost in the spell of love, would give them away.

The afternoon wore on. The cattle and sheep grew louder as their thirst grew; the people grew quieter. Calindor walked near the end of the column, keeping the wind from the west so that the dust of the herds would blow away from the people.

"The first trick I taught myself was moving dust motes," he said to Pervidhu. "I never even considered it magic, just a game. Now I'm moving dust motes again."

"Pity you can't move something useful, like people," Pervidhu answered. "My feet are sore already."

"If we had boats, and deep enough water in the rivers, I could have us all in Vidhumen by this time tomorrow ... well, two days, anyway."

"But we have no boats, and the rivers are mostly rocks at this time of year. Why can't you summon some great bird from the Black World to carry us through the air?"

"Perhaps I should," Calindor said, smiling, "but you wouldn't like where it took you."

"At this rate we won't be back in time for the Mod."

"Once the people have found a place to stay, we'll go on more quickly—and on horseback." Calindor was about to say more, but paused and gripped Pervidhu's shoulder as if to steady himself.

"What's the matter?"

"Magic. Behind us." He stood still for a time, while a few villagers passed by. Then he laughed softly. "Nezaual is a good pupil. He doesn't forget anything, and he thinks."

"I don't understand what you're talking about. What's he done?"

"Taken a little spell I taught him for driving away water, and turned it into a big spell. He must have used several other magicians to help him." He glanced over his shoulder, though Bhadvedor had long been out of sight. The hazy blue sky to the south was unchanged. "They've dried up most of the flood I sent them, so they'll be out of Bhadvedor by tonight."

"And on our heels by tomorrow." Pervidhu looked worried.

Calindor turned and began walking again. "Maybe, but I don't think so. We're just a couple of hundred people, and more trouble to look after than if we'd stayed in Cadorsanbea. They'll take their advice from Nezaual, and he'll tell them about Matari Kleir and their steel."

"Didn't you tell me they want you to join them? Aren't you a little more important than a few steel spearheads?"

"They can't capture me, least of all if their best magicians are exhausted. They have to spread out and take as much land as they can, as many people as they can." He looked at Pervidhu. "Do you see? I can't cover all of Cantarea with storms. I can't walk up and down the land throwing dragonfire at everyone. All I can do is help to draw them into a trap and use a spell of terror on them."

"And if they can protect themselves from such a spell?"

"They won't. Nothing can protect against a spell of terror."

Pervidhu did not answer.

All day they had been riding under an enormous sky across a gently rolling prairie. Abruptly it fell away into a river valley whose steep walls had eroded into strange pillars and whose floor was a patchwork of new-plowed fields gleaming in the late afternoon. Yet no houses were visible.

"This was desert land before, wasn't it?" Ghelasha said as they rode along the rim of the valley.

"Yes, my lady," Silisihan said. "None wanted it, so we took it for ourselves. It is open to the sky, yet sheltered."

"Where is everybody?" Deir asked. "No houses, no one in the fields."

"Over there." Silisihan pointed north to the far wall of the valley. Among the irregular pillars carved by erosion were others of dressed stone. Dark plumes of smoke rose from higher up in the cliffs, as if from chimneys. "We found we missed the safety of being underground, so we are cutting new caves. That is the gate of Bayodar."

Ghelasha smiled without much humor; they were, after all this, about to go underground into the realm of the Burrowers. "Not the only gate, I'm sure."

Silisihan smiled back and nodded.

Their path led them down a gully onto the valley floor, and across it to the pillared cliffs. The path was now a road, smooth and level, but it soon climbed again across the face of a scree slope and then onto a broad terrace.

Ghelasha and Callishandal said nothing as they stared up at the great colonnade. Deir, oblivious to the other women's anxiety, chattered in amazement at the images carved into the pillars, each four times the height of a man: birds, trees, dancers, twining vines. Beyond the pillars they glimpsed an open space, a cave with a high ceiling, where people sat at benches or walked to and fro.

Three young men in black, bearing bows and quivers of long arrows, approached. They spoke with Silisihan in a Cantarean dialect that even Callishandal had trouble following, and then gestured to dismount.

"They will care for the horses," Silisihan explained. "We will go in and join the Protector for the evening meal."

Though she was out of the saddle, Ghelasha seemed reluctant to let go of her horse's reins. "You know my people don't like to go underground," she muttered.

"Yet you came into the shelter of the mines at Aishadan when Callia scourged the land," Silisihan answered. "This is a far safer place, and it is becoming almost as lovely as our old home in the Bayo Bealar. Come, my lady; you are welcome among us."

Callishandal saw Ghelasha take control of herself; she handed the reins to one of the young men, ran her fingers through her thick yellow hair, and stepped forward. Nervously, feeling much less confident, Callishandal followed. Deir hurried ahead, then seemed to remember her manners and fell in beside Callishandal.

Within the colonnade stood a kind of open marketplace, filling much of the front of the great cave. Sunlight fell in great streams between the pillars, bathing the air with a yellow glow. Benches and tables stood in casual disorder, each with piles of cakes or pots of preserved vegetables or tools of wood and metal. The people selling their wares were tall, dark-haired, yet pale, and they dressed far more colorfully than did Gulyaji who went abroad. They stared at the women in some surprise, but with no hostility; Ghelasha's blondness first caught their attention, but Deir's hair and skin seemed the greater wonder. Some spoke to Silisihan in their quick dialect, and he answered then with smiles and waves. Then, without seeming to hurry them, he led the women deeper into the cave.

At its rear, perhaps a hundred strides from the colonnade, four doorways led into the rock. Each was half again the height of a tall man, and wide enough for four to walk abreast. The corridors beyond seemed recent; their walls were faced with rough-finished sheets of stone. In the arched ceiling of each corridor a thin line of blue light glowed: coldfire, one of the great magics of the Gulyaji.

"We are still a new community," Silisihan said almost apologetically as he led them into the easternmost corridor. "We have not had time to adorn the stone as it deserves, but every day we do a little more."

"The pillars are very beautiful," Callishandal said, trying to ignore her fear. "You must have some fine artists among you."

"We all take our turns at the carving. It is part of life, like carrying out the ashes or emptying the dung pits."

The corridor ran straight and then began to branch—sometimes into another hallway, sometimes into a single room where people baked bread or wove wool. Voices echoed off the stone walls, yet carpets of sand absorbed much of the sound. Coldfire gleamed everywhere, and many rooms had fires as well.

"Why isn't it smoky?" Deir asked.

"We cut our air shafts carefully. The fires carry smoke out into the open air, and fresh air replaces it. It was much worse in Bayo Bealar because the caves were so large and had so few outlets."

They were deep in the valley wall now, and Silisihan had led them through a bewildering series of turns. This corridor must be very new, for it lacked even plain stone sheets; the walls were coarse sandstone with belts of yellow clay, still showing the scars of Gulyaji chisels. At its end was a doorway screened by a curtain of undyed wool; it parted as Renjosudaldor came out to welcome them.

A wry smile was on the old man's lips as he extended his hands to the women. "The brave can always overtake the coward, and you have overtaken me. This may be the most terrible night any of us will ever know. Come in, and let us begin it."

Yetecuan had wanted Nezaual to ride the mammoth with him, but Yaocatl's and Colotic's arguments overwhelmed an old man's affectionate whim: the boy spoke Cantarean well, and Badakhi well enough, and the army was in desperate need of a translator.

Marching with the expedition now were over a hundred of Elsman's warriors, half of them on horseback. They were forever pestering the Exteca with gestured appeals to go this way, no that way, to pause or to hurry—no one knew what the northerners really meant.

So Nezaual rode in the vanguard with Yaocatl, talking with a succession of foreigners and explaining to the general what the issues were. Yetecuan, perched in his little hut, could see the boy clearly: he still wore his foreign clothes, and his short hair set him off from the feathered warriors around him.

What a brilliant youth! What a splendid future the True Gods must hold for him, after this beginning. A strong and growing talent for magic; courage to face the unknown, and intelligence to learn from it. When Calindor finally took his proper place as a servant of the True Gods, Nezaual would be beside him. *And I am like a father to them both. If the True Gods send me such joy, I must have served them well.*

After starting out so late in the day, the army did not travel far; it hardly mattered, with all of Cantarea before them. The marchers were dispersed over the prairie, spreading northeast and northwest behind a screen of scouts, and camped where darkness found them. Tomorrow, or the next day, the scouts would be looking for food as much as for threats. Tonight they could sit around their campfires, laughing about the flood they had just escaped.

At last Nezaual came to Yetecuan's tent and joined him for the evening meal. They talked happily about the spell, and about the army's progress.

"We may overtake Calindor at this rate," Yetecuan said with a chuckle.

"I hope not, honored father. You are still weary, and his power is always there. I argued to Yaocatl that we should let him get away back to Vidhumen while we win the rest of the country to our side."

"What is worth more than Calindor himself?"

"To him, his people are worth far more, honored father. If they are with us, he will abandon his resistance. If they oppose us, he will support them."

"You speak very wisely, beloved son. Still, I worry. We have no strong magician with us at the moment except for yourself, and you must reserve your power at least until I recover. The others are competent at small spells, but they cannot defend us against Calindor or the swords of the northerners. If we approach a large town that does not accept us freely, we will have to fight—and I do not know if we would win."

Nezaual looked up from his bowl of beans and chilies. "They will not fight, honored father, not unless Vidhumen sends help. And by the time Vidhumen can send help, everyone will have joined us."

And so it seemed for the next few days. Scouts would enter a village or town to a fearful but generous welcome: loaves of unfamiliar bread, salted meats, pickled vegetables. The people made no resistance, and among them were many who had been in Bhadvedor. Still held by the spell of love, they had returned to their homes and prepared the way as Yaocatl had foreseen.

Yetecuan scarcely saw his priests; they were scattered everywhere, consecrating each new town with a batch of sacrifices. He could sense the True Gods moving farther north with every new gift, inhabiting this new land the Exteca had won for them. The conquest was a peaceful one, and for that Yetecuan rejoiced.

Yet he thought always of the younger sorcerer somewhere in the north. He had not dared to seek Calindor through the lip plug, but the scouts soon brought useful news: the village where Nezaual had stolen the horses was abandoned now, and the tracks led straight north. Other villages reported the passage of many people with their herds; when Nezaual spoke with the natives, they described "foreigners" who must be Calindor's company.

The generals, if they thought of Calindor, had other worries: the army was growing so rapidly that simply feeding it was a major achievement. Scores of sacrifices provided food for the Exteca, but their barbarian allies would not touch human flesh. The land was still winter-poor, yet the scouts soon found the herds of cattle and sheep, while the priests opened every village's granary and sent some of its stores to feed the army.

"Still it is not enough," said Yaocatl.

The army's leaders had met late into the night in the castle of Matari Kleir. Its master, and many of the people, had disappeared. So had most of their food. Worse yet, the steel weapons that Nezaual had seen were gone.

"We cannot long continue like this," Colotic agreed. "A marching army eats everything in its path. We have consumed all the supplies we brought with us from the south, and now these northerners join us—hundreds every day. They expect food, but they bring almost none with them."

"Can we not send the barbarians home again?" Yetecuan asked. "We don't need them for fighting."

"We may," Yaocatl said quietly. "If the magician's people attack us, I want a shield of northerners between us and them. And we must feed the True Gods as well, honored father."

"You are wise, beloved son. Should we not then stop, and wait until the new crops are ready for harvest?"

"We have done so before," Yaocatl said, nodding until his plumes waved and bobbed. "But never when we faced so strong and dangerous an enemy. As long as we move, we keep the advantage. If we stop, they will test us and then attack us."

"Then we must move quickly," Nezaual said. "Straight to Vidhumen."

"It would be difficult," Yaocatl muttered, "but if we seize the heart, it does not matter if the limbs twitch."

Yetecuan saw a light glow in Nezaual's dark eyes. "You are right, honored Yaocatl," the boy said. "The heart—the heart is all-important."

Twenty-four

Holding coldfire in his hand, Renjosudaldor led Deir into a natural cavern beyond the tunnels the Gulyaji had dug. The floor of the cave was uneven, the walls close and wet and dark.

"We were dying in our old caves," he said, and his voice echoed from the stone. "But we loved them. These caves are too small to live in, but they bring us close to the Powers of earth."

They stepped up over a pile of stones crusted with white crystals, into a slightly wider passage, and then into a shaft whose floor held a small pool and whose gray walls rose steeply into darkness. Renjosudaldor pointed to a stone beside the pool; Deir sat, shivering a little in the chill.

The old man sat across the pool, close enough that he might have reached out and touched her. The coldfire glowed on his palm, pale blue and without a flicker.

"My lady, I speak to you both, to the girl and the magician. I know I have your permission to do so, or you would not have allowed yourself to go on this journey." He smiled faintly. "You would not have allowed Ghelasha and Callishandal to go on this journey either."

"If you say so," Deir whispered. "I'm frightened."

"Of course. You are afraid that the magician will come out and you will disappear. But it will not happen, Deir. You and the magician are the two parts of one woman, and neither of you is complete without the other. And my lady, I am frightened also. You have hidden for a long time, and we Gulyaji know how easy it is to love a hiding place even when it is a prison. If I can summon you out into the world, you may change your mind and decide to hide again. If you do, you may kill me. Perhaps that is no matter, but you will also harm Deir. At the very least she will go mad, and she may break from you and kill herself."

Deir's eyes widened in terror. "I don't—I don't want you to die, Renjosudaldor."

"I don't think I will, and I don't think you will go mad. But the magician must understand that strength in the service of fear is very dangerous. The Badakhar are just beginning to learn that lesson. I know you are a brave young woman, and I must hope that the magician is equally brave."

He looked into her eyes: "If you are willing, my lady?"

The coldfire died slowly and the darkness was absolute. Water dripped from a height into the pool, striking the surface with oddly musical sounds. A hum, a chant filled the air: Renjosudaldor was calling on the Gariba to shelter this place from all harm. Then, in a calm voice, he spoke in the language of ancient Cantarea, the tongue spoken by the firstcomers whom the Great God Bha had placed on the prairies of Sotalar.

"I call on the Powers of air to fill your mouth, your throat, your lungs. I call on the Powers of water to drive your blood. I call on the Powers of earth to strengthen your bones, your flesh. I call on the Powers of fire to illuminate your mind."

A new light appeared and grew slowly brighter. It was in the pool, far down, a spark of white that shimmered and rippled as it rose. Renjosudaldor saw its reflections in Deir's eyes as she looked down.

"I call you, magician, from your darkness. I call you, magician, from your sorrow. I call you, magician, from your fear."

The light was brighter still, rising from an unimaginable depth; something seemed to be following it, a shape the light could not illuminate.

The old man leaned forward, cupped his hand in the water, and then raised it. He let the water trickle between his fingers onto Deir's red hair, now visible again in the growing light.

"I call you, magician, I welcome you as sister and daughter, I cherish you."

He hummed a melody that brought an old memory back to Deir, and she too hummed in counterpoint to the Protector's song. Then he fell silent and Deir smelled saltwater and smoking candles. She drew a breath and sang a song:

> "We summon you back, summon you back
> From dark and silent earth;
> We summon you back, summon you back
> To sail the sea and sky
> Our love will abide, our love will abide
> When sun and stars are gone . . ."

Deir looked down into the pool, and the glow beneath the surface threw ripples of light over her face and hair. Now she saw the shape beneath the light more clearly. The light rose almost to her feet at the edge of the pool.

Below it, rising through the water, was a human figure curled upon itself like a sleeping baby. Slowly the figure straightened, the hands reaching up toward the light and air. It looked up and the eyes met hers.

Deir's cry rang on the stone like breaking steel, and echoed for a long time. The light went out.

After a time, Renjosudaldor called forth coldfire again. The pool was dark; Deir's eyes were wide and blank.

"Deir. What did you see?"

"I saw myself. She was myself."

"Good. The process has begun. The magician is coming to join you, to become one with you. It will be a long time, weeks or months, but it has begun."

"You don't understand," she whispered.

"What is it?"

"Someone else was coming close behind her."

For five days the army camped around Matari Kleir, while scouts rode deeper and deeper into Cantarea. Each day they returned escorting yet more northerners seeking alliance with the Exteca.

"I know you are tired, Nezaual," Colotic said one evening. "But without your help we could not understand the barbarians. We would be fighting for every stride of land."

They were walking around the corral where Tenarakh the electman had been riding his black horse. Nezaual wondered vaguely what had become of Tenarakh; that had been a long time ago.

"I am glad to be of service, brother Colotic. It reminds me of Burnbaile last year."

"That was easy. Here we are walking in the dark. We can hardly feed ourselves, and all these northerners come to join us. If you did not explain that they must go back to their homes, they would stay with us until the last bean."

Nezaual leaned against one of the poles forming the wall of the corral. "I tell them to bring more food, and they will, but they have very little. They are very poor people."

"Not as poor as we will be if we do not gain a victory soon. Without plunder we could starve."

"I have told you about the hatred between the Cantareans and the Badakhar. You should encourage it."

"What do you mean?"

"Tell the Cantareans to bring us food from the Badakhar."

Colotic looked baffled. "But many Badakhar have become our allies. They have accepted the True Gods, just as the Cantareans have. How can we ask subjects to turn upon one another?"

Nezaual smiled wearily. "They all come to us out of fear. Calindor warned them of our magic, and then beloved Yetecuan cast his spell of love. Many caught in the spell went home to tell their people Calindor had been right. They come to us because they do not think Calindor can protect them, and they fear each other as well as us. They are already fighting one another; each side thinks we will protect it against the other."

"So we have heard, especially from Elsman." Colotic turned and watched other warriors hurrying in and out of the little castle. "Well, brother, it makes sense. I will suggest it to Yaocatl. And what of the Badakhar who are marching with us?"

"Leave them alone for now. But tell the Cantareans who come to us that they must bring us food and weapons from their Badakhar neighbors."

"It does seem hard," Colotic muttered. "The Badakhar are strange, but they seem to know something of fighting. Perhaps we should ask them to plunder the Cantareans instead."

"Brother, listen to me. Albohar is Badakh, and many of his warriors, and they will never be our allies except under a spell of love or terror. But most of his people are Cantarean. When he learns that Cantareans are plundering and killing his own people, he will lose his trust in all Cantareans. Perhaps he will even fight them while we wait for the outcome. In any case he will have a far smaller army, and thousands of unhappy people in his towns."

"The True Gods foresee all things. Yes, I see how it will work. I will speak to Yaocatl about it tonight. You have given us good advice, brother Nezaual."

"We all serve as we can, brother Colotic."

Tilcalli walked along the silent river under the unchanging noon sun. Her ancestors, dancing the past and future, smiled in welcome. Calihalingol, laughing, left the dance to take her in an embrace.

You have not come to the Open Dream for a long time.

I thought time here is never long or short, great-great-grandmother.

The old woman laughed. *You are right, yet we can tell when time has passed in Sotalar. Come and sit with me by the river. Perhaps Deir will rise from the river again.*

We were frightened then. Now you smile about it?

I have thought about it as we danced. She came into the Open Dream, which even the Gulyaji cannot do. So she came with Callia's welcome, and I think she will come again.

Why should she? What can she find here that would serve her? She didn't even speak, only scream.

The old woman sat cross-legged in the shaded grass beneath her favorite tree. Tilcalli sat beside her, leaning against her, and took comfort from her great-great-grandmother's solidity.

I would scream too, Calihalingol said, *if I found myself in a place as strange as this. And if I carried a burden as great as Deir's. But she will be all right. She will come out of hiding as you and she came out of the sweat bath that night last fall. I think she will come back.*

I still don't understand why she would.

This is the mind of Callia, Calihalingol said, with a gesture that included the river and the trees beyond it. *We are her thoughts. And Callia's is the greatest mind of all the gods, except I suppose for Burvala.* She used the Cantarean name for the being whom the Badakhar called Bha; in both languages it meant brightness. *If other gods live in Callia's mind as we do, then perhaps we can find them.*

Even the True Gods of the Exteca? Tilcalli felt oddly dizzy.

They are the ones we must find. Only Calindor knows anything about them. Perhaps if we learn about them, we can help him.

Tilcalli looked around at the familiar landscape: the river, the village, the forests that surrounded both and the mountains that loomed in the distance into a cloudless sky at noon. If the True

Gods of the Exteca also dwelt within the Open Dream, then the Open Dream was a dangerous place. Worse than dangerous.

Calihalingol stood up, brushing grass stems from her buckskin skirt. She took her great-great-granddaughter's hand.

Come, Tilcalli. Let us go and seek the True Gods.

But the ancestors who leave here never come back.

They have never left in the company of a living descendant. And if we do not come back, what of it? If the Exteca conquer Cantarea, and redmagic destroys the Siragi Aibela, we will no longer dance the future. We will have no future. She leaned closer to Tilcalli. *And I am tired of dancing the past.*

In a nameless village boys threw stones at Sveit and Pervidhu and any other Badakh they saw as the Cadorsanbeans marched past. The boys were young, not more than twelve or so, and their aim was poor. But their insults were as sharp-edged as their shrill voices: *"Parpudusu! Tahalalindora rastijisuma! Jenarazi!"*

"They're calling you—" Calindor began.

"I know what they're calling us," Sveit said. "Assholes, pig lovers, and enemies. My slaves used to call me worse." He ducked a pebble and blew a kiss to the boy who had thrown it. In the doorways of the hovels behind the stone-throwers, adults glared.

"All Cantareans," Pervidhu said, "with long memories."

"Not long enough," Calindor snapped. "They should remember that vengeance is a Badakh idea. You and Sveit haven't done them any harm. I have a better right to throw stones at Sveit than anyone else—"

"Except me," Svordo called from close behind. He turned and left the muddy trail, approaching the boys and the adults behind them. The children held their ground; the adults stepped out of their doorways, some carrying truncheons or axes. One man had the swastika tattoo of an arekakh on his forehead, and a short sword in his hand.

Svordo spoke briefly, too quietly for the others to hear. The boys dropped their stones and sidled back into the protection of the adults. By the time Svordo caught up with the others, they were past the village and walking through badly plowed fields.

"What did you tell them?" Calindor asked.

Svordo grinned. "I said we were taking the Badakhar to have their hearts cut out by the Exteca, and if they harmed a sacrifice, the Exteca would come and cut *their* hearts out."

Pervidhu burst into laughter. "I wish I'd thought to say that to Elsman when he was about to shove me into his fire!"

Calindor looked ahead at the Cadorsanbeans trudging steadily northward. "News of the Exteca travels faster than we do. But have you noticed how hardly anyone is trying to escape them? People hear about their magic, about their sacrifices, but few try to escape."

Sveit smiled. "They've had too much change in their lives. No more Five Kingdoms, no more upermannar telling everyone what to do. People have to grow their own food and do their own thinking and take their own revenge. Now these strangers turn up with new magic, offering to be their friends and caretakers. That ought to be worth a few sacrifices now and then."

"Surely not!" Calindor said almost angrily. "Surely people who were slaves would prize their freedom more than that."

"Slaves are people who sacrifice their own lives one day at a time, sooner than risk death. Remember, I was a dealer in slaves. I knew my commodity."

Calindor said nothing, but Sveit was not finished: "And I'll tell you something else about slaves. Slavery doesn't do them much good. It makes them lazy, fearful, and stupid."

"Just like their masters," said Pervidhu.

"Exactly. And maybe Callia overthrew the Five Kingdoms, but she didn't overthrow stupidity. Even gods have their limits . . . unless stupidity itself is a god," he added, laughing.

"Then why are we poor humans trying to save all these stupid people?" Calindor asked.

Svordo joined in Sveit's laughter. "We're stupid too."

They left Bayodar in a frosty dawn, under a sky still cloudless. Again Silisihan rode with them, but now Renjosudaldor and three young Gulyaji, all armed, joined the party. They were bound for the Mod in Vidhumen, but Callishandal suspected the Protector had other goals as well. He stayed close to Deir, though he rarely spoke to her or the others.

They crossed the valley, ascended the trail to the high prairie, and felt the sun's brightness and warmth. Silisihan set a steady pace as they turned to the west.

"Was the journey worth it?" Callishandal asked Ghelasha.

The older woman looked up at the bright blue sky. "Deir will tell us that, someday."

Twenty-five

Vidhumen reminded Calindor of Aishadan in the old days of the Five Kingdoms: crowded with workers, smoky, full of the spells of stalmaghar and small sorcerers. Tents and lean-tos filled the fields around the town, and the streets were full of strangers. Badakhar swaggered into the taverns, elbows out and hoping for a fight; Cantareans stepped silently aside. Hammers rang on glowing iron, blood ran in the marketplaces from slaughtered pigs and sheep, and rumors ran from door to door on children's bare feet.

The Cadorsanbeans had finally found a cluster of farmsteads willing to take them, two days south of Vidhumen, and Calindor had bought horses for his own party and Michuna. Now they rode up to the castle to find a squad of guards at the gate, fending off a small mob of refugees.

"Calindor!" cried a Cantarean in the crowd. "Tell Albohar we left our homes on his account; now he owes us at least a roof over our heads."

"And food for our families!" shouted another. "Let him throw some of his kinsmen out of their fine houses, and feed them as they fed us all those years."

Calindor said nothing as he and his companions rode through into the castle courtyard. Carpenters were busy building crude stables along the inner walls, and the place stank of horse dung. Men and boys hurried past on errands, while in one corner of the courtyard women tended huge soup pots in an open-air kitchen.

"The stableboys are busy enough," Calindor said. "We'll look after our own horses before we see Albohar."

It took longer than they expected, but at last their horses were sheltered, fed, and watered. Calindor led the way into the castle, occasionally trading a smile with Pervidhu or Svordo about the crowds pushing their way down the corridors. Michuna seemed taken aback by the noise and bustle, but smiled also.

Albohar was not in his office, where four harried clerks were compiling lists.

"You can usually find the electman in the dining hall these days," one of them said. "It's the only space big enough to hold all the people who want to talk to him. And the Mod starts tomorrow—I don't know what we'll do then."

The dining hall was indeed jammed with people, all talking at the same time. In his usual chair at the long table, Albohar was listening intently to one of his cavalry commanders; Calindor found himself marveling that the warrior should be a Cantarean, when everything else in the castle reminded him of preparations for war in the old days.

The gleam in Albohar's eyes was much like the old days also. He welcomed them, fended off the next delegation with a raised hand, and then gripped Calindor's hand.

"I don't think you'll surprise me much," he said, "but tell me what you learned."

Calindor sketched the events of the journey and the attitude of the people toward the Exteca. Occasionally Sveit or Pervidhu or Michuna added some detail or explanation. Albohar listened, fingers in his beard, and nodded.

"Wouldn't have been any different in the old days," he said. "Those bastards down south in Kormannalendh and Halamor would have gone over to the Exteca without any spells, just for the joy of conquering Aishadan and Ner Kes and Ghrirei. Their Veikar would have cut their own balls off to learn redmagic."

"Our warnings weren't entirely wasted," Calindor said. "Many people have come north, and they'll be of some help."

"They're certainly helping us eat every loaf we can bake. Well, we'll count the cost when we've beaten the Exteca." He stood up, stretching. "Come and walk with me, Calindor. It's too noisy and smoky in here."

Albohar moved through the corridors as if no one stood in his way, and despite the crowds, no one did. He and Calindor went out the north gate, up onto the ridge of the hill, and along the path that led to a paddock. Here the only people were a few stableboys and a couple of riders exercising their mounts. They greeted the two men and then went on with their tasks.

Albohar rested his arms on one of the cross poles that fenced the paddock. "Good to be outside smelling horses and dust. Those boys have the best jobs in Vidhumen."

Calindor remembered his own cavalry training less fondly, but said nothing. Albohar watched the riders for a moment and then asked: "All right, what now? What do we say tomorrow at the Mod?"

"The Badakhar will want a fight, won't they?"

"Of course. Sabers out, ribbons in their beards, screaming their family names."

"And the Exteca would destroy them. Redmagic would throw them to the winds like so many dandelion seeds. But redmagic can also work against the Exteca."

"Explain."

Calindor set out the plan that Pervidhu had not liked the sound of: a feint against the Exteca, then a seeming retreat. The defenders would lure them into a narrow place where the Exteca would use a spell of love or terror—but the defenders would be gone through an unexpected route, and while the exhausted Exteca sorcerer watched helplessly, the defenders would turn a spell of terror on the invaders themselves. Few would die; Callia would suffer, but not greatly. The Exteca would retreat south, herded by Albohar's warriors, until they were well out of Cantarea.

"Callia, Callia," Albohar muttered. "If I hadn't been half dead when she brought the storm on us, perhaps I'd take her more seriously. Why can't we just butcher these Exteca and leave them for the crows?"

"I won't argue with you about it," Calindor said quietly. "You know what a spell of terror can do, and only such a spell can stop the Exteca. Once I cast it, killing them will be a waste of effort. And when the survivors finally get back home, they'll tell their masters not to invade the north again."

"All right. Say we do this. We have to keep the plan secret from everyone, or someone will betray us."

"I agree. The Exteca have surely sent some of their allies north to spy on us. So we must give the Mod a story and swear them to secrecy. It must sound believable, to our people as well as the Exteca."

Albohar turned and lifted his face to the sun. "The Mod will argue a hundred different strategies. The Badakhar will want to fight. The Cantareans will weep over poor Callia's suffering and call for raids and guerrilla war. We'll let them thrash it out and then offer a compromise: no frontal assault, but the appearance of one and then a quick sweep that cuts off their supply lines. We'll say the army has to stay out of range of the spells, and you've devised a counterspell to help protect them."

"If only I had. Go on."

"We'll argue that the enemy will starve without being able to break through. If they try, we'll retreat and draw them back south. The Mod will like that idea."

"What if the Exteca try to break out to the north?"

"We'll burn every field south of Vidhumen. Don't look at me

like that—this is a war, isn't it? If they go east they hit the scablands and eat sagebrush. If they go west they find a few farms and then that endless forest up into the mountains." He put his hand gently on Calindor's throat. "This is how I'll show the Mod our strategy. Start to strangle a man and he'll pull back. Keep pressing and he'll back up as far as you like."

Calindor nodded. "I think they'll accept it."

"But will the Exteca?"

"It depends on Nezaual. He doesn't know how much redmagic I've mastered. When he hears of a counterspell, he'll know that's a lie, something to encourage our side. But I don't know if he'll guess the truth behind it."

"Will they listen to him? He's just a boy."

"He's only a year or so younger than I."

Albohar chuckled. "I don't even have to close my eyes, and I can see you running about the old castle, waving your little toy sword and chasing the slaves."

"I remember riding on your shoulders."

"But for you it's long ago, and for your mother and me it's yesterday."

Calindor blinked, as if suddenly remembering something. "You sent couriers to Tanshadabela. Has Dragasa come to the Mod?"

"He said he would, but he's not here yet. I hope he brings your mother as well. I'd like to see her again."

"Would Ghelasha approve?" Calindor asked, half joking, remembering the fear and hatred Ghelasha had felt for Tilcalli.

"Who knows what Ghelasha would like or dislike these days. She went off with Callishandal and Deir to Bayodar, and they're not back yet."

"To Bayodar? What for?"

Albohar looked him in the eye. "I was hoping somehow you'd tell me, Calindor. In my old age I'm learning I don't know the first thing about the way women think."

"Surprising." Calindor was silent for a moment and then shrugged. "Well, we'll find out when they're back." He paused again. "I would like to see Callishandal. I miss her."

"So do I. She reminds me of your mother. Come on, let's get back before they come hunting us."

Sitting behind the mammoth's head, Mixnal sang his beast a simple song while he scratched its ears. Close behind him Yetecuan dozed in the little hut on the mammoth's back, half listening to the song and half listening to the conversation of the men riding alongside.

The song at least was understandable. Much of what the riders said was in one northern tongue or another, with Nezaual translating for Colotic and the other soldiers. Sometimes he reported another town giving itself to the Exteca and their distant emperor; sometimes it was a northern scout's account of the terrain ahead.

Yes, it was all going well. The wretched little towns either surrendered or stood open and abandoned, convenient shelter for an army that grew by the day. But those who surrendered had little food; those who fled had taken every crumb with them. The army was not hungry yet, but Yaocatl feared that it soon would be.

Yetecuan's recovery was going well, but slowly. He considered the other priests: many were good, especially at minor magics like driving out pests, and some could cast a spell of terror or love. But even the best of them could cover only a small area with such a spell, and the army would soon face an enemy covering a very large area indeed.

Calindor knew redmagic, as much as Nezaual did and probably a bit more. He would know enough to keep his army scattered, to probe, and to kill priests at every opportunity. Even if he failed to kill them, he could provoke them into casting strong spells that would render them helpless.

As I am helpless now. The Exteca army would become an empty quiver, an unstrung bow, and then Calindor would strike.

Yaocatl understood that also, and so he kept the army pushing north, north, toward a town Nezaual called Vidhumen—Forest Mountain. A strange name in this flat and treeless land. But there, or close to there, the army must meet Calindor. And there it must conquer him, or accept his surrender, or fall before his might.

But the True Gods will not permit that. He is a gift from them, a gift to them. He will bring rain to Tola, and he will feed the True Gods on the hearts of all these northern barbarians.

He leaned from the hut and called to Nezaual.

"Yes, honored father?"

"Would you ask all the priests to meet with me after the sunset gifts?"

"Gladly!"

The army soon halted for the night, and Yetecuan allowed Nezaual to help him down. Several priests were already there, erecting Yetecuan's tent not far from a clear stream running over round stones. Others arrived soon after, and the last of them came with blood steaming on their hands.

"My beloved sons," Yetecuan began. "Soon we will be facing the great sorcerer Calindor, who does not yet know he must serve the True Gods who give him his power. Our own powers are small defense against one who can fling thunderstorms. So we must be cautious and prudent. I have not yet recovered from the spell I cast at Bhadvedor, yet I sense you will have need of me."

"What should we do to help you, honored father?" asked Nezaual.

"Did you not feel your own strength grow a little just now? Just looking at the blood on the hands of your brothers should tell you the answer. Sacrifices feed us as well as the True Gods. A great sacrifice will restore me quickly, and give strength to all of you as well."

"How great a sacrifice, honored father?" asked another priest.

"A thousand. Two thousand."

They laughed and smiled, their lip plugs bobbing.

Nezaual, though, did not laugh. "I will gladly do my part to give such a gift to the gods and to Yetecuan. But it will take a long day's work, and first we will need to prepare a proper altar. I do not know if Yaocatl will agree to stop the army when we are so close to facing Calindor."

"I'm sure he will agree, beloved son. Two days, even three, will not be too long a delay. We will be much stronger for it." He giggled. "Our own warriors will eat well, and we will have far fewer mouths to feed."

"But these Chontalteca, these foreigners," said another priest, an older man. "Many are under the spell of love, but many are not. And they are still not used to sacrifices. Many of them weep when they see the sunrise and sunset gifts."

"We should not deny the True Gods because savages weep. If Yaocatl agrees, then we will conduct a great sacrifice." Yetecuan smiled wearily. "I wonder what Calindor will do when he senses it."

Pervidhu found pretexts to stay in the courtyard, stepping out of the carpenters' way and lending a hand with the horses. All afternoon the delegates had come, some alone and some with retinues. None looked rich. A few had troubled to wear old finery, doubtless salvaged from the ruins of some upermanna's manor, but such gaudy clothes looked even shabbier than the homespun that most people wore these days.

Albohar's servants met them all with the same harried courtesy and escorted them into the castle. Many would end up sleeping on the roof or back here in the courtyard, Pervidhu suspected. He had seen the rooms where the delegates would sleep, and they had not been pleasant.

The late afternoon was growing cold, and a thin overcast was drifting in from the west: the first clouds in many days, after Calindor's storm. Maybe they would get some rain, and the grass would grow faster ... though not fast enough for most of the herders.

The outer door, never shut completely, swung open yet again and another party rode in: five tired-looking Cantarean men and three women. Pervidhu looked again and recognized Deir, Ghelasha, Callishandal, Silisihan, and Renjosudaldor—and recognized three young strangers as a warrior escort.

He reached the Protector before anyone else could and took his horse's reins. "Welcome back, sir. We are glad to see you again. And your friend Silisihan. May I help you dismount?"

"Thank you, Pervidhu, but I can manage. Perhaps you might look to the women."

He needed no further argument. Quickly he hurried to Ghelasha, helped her down, and turned to Deir. But she and Callishandal were already out of their saddles and handing their horses' reins to a stableboy.

"Everyone will rejoice at your return, my ladies," he said. "You have ridden long and hard. Please come in and rest. I will advise the electman and, ah ..."

"You may advise Calindor as well," Callishandal said with a slight smile. "But I will be in no condition to talk with anyone until I've had a hot bath and a meal."

"That would be wonderful," Deir groaned. "Hello, Pervidhu. I'm glad to see you."

"And I you. My lady," he added softly. She looked at him, surprised.

"Your lady? I'm a little young for such courtesy, aren't I?"

"Ah, well, perhaps so. In any case, come in and refresh yourself. I hope to hear all about your adventures."

"No adventures—just riding and riding. But it was interesting to go into Bayodar."

Pervidhu could not entirely suppress a shudder as he escorted her from the courtyard, while the others went on a few steps ahead. "You went into the city of the Burrowers? You're very brave."

"Or you're very cowardly," she said teasingly. "And you must tell us what's happened here."

"What's happened is less important than what's going to happen. Tomorrow the Mod begins."

A commotion at the gate made him turn and glance over his shoulder; at once he stopped.

A small party of riders had entered, with two of the horses tethered close together. A blanket was tied between them, clearly holding someone too ill to ride. The riders were Cantareans, mountaineers by the look of their buckskin tunics, and Pervidhu finally recognized Dragasa. His face was hard and grim.

"Excuse me. I think there's trouble here." Pervidhu strode back across the courtyard, while Deir followed close behind. Dragasa saw them at once, but did not smile.

"I'm glad to see you again," he said tonelessly.

"What's the matter?" Pervidhu asked.

Dragasa went to the tethered horses and untied one corner of the blanket.

"Tilcalli!" Deir cried, and went to help as Dragasa took his unconscious wife in his arms. Servants came to help, but he shook his head; they retreated.

"She has been like this for four days. I hope our son can bring her back."

"Bring her back? Where has she gone?" Deir asked.

"Out of the Open Dream."

Dragasa, carrying Tilcalli, walked past the milling horses and workmen and soldiers, into the castle of Albohar.

Twenty-six

Pervidhu remembered the Mods of the old days. They had been out in the open air, in a field purified by a Veik. Only the Aryo and his upermannar could debate, though their retinues could cheer and bang swords together. Pervidhu had memories of shouting in support of his uncle Aghwesi, the murderous old fool who had once owned Vidhumen; now he almost wished his uncle were still alive, so he might die of apoplexy to see his own castle the venue of this strange new Mod.

This morning the delegates had gathered in the dining hall; it held almost two hundred men and women, who could crowd in only because most of the tables were gone. People sat on benches or stood wherever they could find room; some, like Pervidhu, perched on the windowsills. A thin drizzle was falling, and it was cold at the windows, but at least the air was breathable. Most of the dining hall reeked of smoke and unwashed bodies.

Well, the upermannar didn't wash often either, he reminded himself. *My uncle least of all.* And now that he looked more carefully, he saw that some of the electmen and speakers were indeed upermannar; Albohar had not been the only aristocrat to win votes.

But in the old days the upermannar had flaunted their wealth at such gatherings, competing to see who could pitch the most gorgeous tent and strut in the most splendid clothes. Now they, like the others, seemed very ordinary people: tired, gaunt, dressed in patched and threadbare clothing. Most of the delegates were Cantareans; they tended to cluster near the front of the dining hall, close to Albohar's table, while the Badakhar sat or stood at the back.

The electman was standing behind his table, waiting for the last delegates to push their way in. Sitting at the table also were Calindor, Ghelasha, and two clerks with piles of blank paper and a large inkwell.

Pervidhu scanned the hall. Renjosudaldor was near the front, surrounded by other Gulyaji; they alone enjoyed some elbow room. Callishandal was standing not far behind him, at Dragasa's side. Michuna, across the hall, was speaking with other Cantarean electmen. Deir was absent, as were Svordo and Sveit.

He wished she were there, if only so he could watch her discreetly and wonder what had happened in Bayodar. Neither the women nor the Gulyaji seemed willing to talk about it, and of course Tilcalli's strange trance had distracted everyone else. Deir was no doubt with her . . . or at least with her body. Calindor had worked most of the night, trying to bring Tilcalli back. But he could no longer enter something he called the Open Dream, where mountaineer magicians could consult their ancestors—in the damp gray light of morning the idea seemed absurd, but last night Calindor's explanation had made Pervidhu's skin prickle with fear.

So Tilcalli was lost, and not even a sorcerer like Calindor could find her. That boded ill for the future, and explained the look of blank weariness on Calindor's face.

At last Albohar thumped his fist on the table and the crowd began to quiet.

"To all of you who have answered my call, I give you thanks." He spoke in Cantarean, which everyone understood, though few Badakhar spoke it as well as he. "You know something of my reasons for convening this Mod, but before we turn to debate and decision, I should tell you what we know so far about the southerners who have invaded Cantarea."

Tersely and without emotion Albohar summarized the discovery of the Exteca by Calindor and Callishandal, and the threat of the southerners' magic.

"And now they have taken some towns and farms," he finished. "Their spells have deceived many into joining them. Yet they are still few, and ignorant of this land. If we can devise a plan, we can stop them and drive them back to wherever they came from. I ask for your wisdom. Who would speak first?"

In an old Mod, Pervidhu thought, that question would launch endless boasts and complaints from braying upermannar; here, it produced first silence and then tentative questions from the Cantareans. Albohar did his best to answer them, with occasional help from Calindor. After a time the Badakhar asked their own questions, usually after long speeches in Badakhi that required translation. Again Albohar answered.

He's still an Aryo, Pervidhu thought. *Still the king, letting his subjects express themselves. Even the Cantareans recognize his authority. But how can he seem so confident and at ease when he knows the Exteca are coming?*

The morning wore on until one of the Badakhar proposed a direct attack on the Exteca. Another Badakh electman jeered at the idea, the first snarled back, and Albohar had to pound the table with his fist to regain order.

"I ask the pardon of the Cantareans," he bellowed, "while I speak to my brother Badakhar." His blue eyes glared danger at them as he switched to Badakhi: "*Skeiar!* Stupid shits! We're on a battlefield already, and on the battlefield we don't settle our personal scores until the battle's won. Argue your points like men, not like snot-nosed boys."

The Badakhar glowered sullenly but held their peace. The Cantareans pretended not to have understood, and the debate resumed.

By noon the delegates were tired and hungry and seemed no further ahead. Albohar turned to Calindor.

"I ask the Mekhmagh Calindor for his advice, since he knows the Exteca better than anyone else here."

Though not well enough, or he'd never have let Nezaual come with us, Pervidhu thought. *But here comes the plan.*

"I have considered ways to fight the Exteca," Calindor said slowly. "Their magic makes it very dangerous to confront them. But I think I have found a way to drive them out of Cantarea without giving them a chance to use their spells of love and terror—and without the mass killing that would provoke the rage of Callia."

If the prospect of scant killing disappointed the Badakhar, Pervidhu thought, mentioning the rage of Callia would calm them; and when he looked around, he saw concern in their faces but not the contempt he expected.

"Before I tell you my thoughts," Calindor went on, "I must swear every person in this room to secrecy. If you accept my plan, no word of it must reach the Exteca and their allies or we are doomed."

The hall was utterly silent. "Will you give me your promise by all you hold most holy?"

"By Callia," a Cantarean woman cried out, raising her hand.

"By the Great God Bha," said a Badakh, extending both hands before him. The hall rumbled with oaths until every hand was visible.

"Very well," said Calindor. "I thank you for your trust."

It was not the perilous strategy Calindor had mentioned on their way south, but dangerous enough: a feint to draw the Exteca quickly north, encouraging them to outrun their supply lines from the towns they had already taken; then a sweep from the northwest that would cut those lines, while the Exteca found nothing before them but scorched fields and abandoned farms, and an army that stayed out of contact.

"They dare not waste a spell on a squadron of skirmishers," Calindor said. "For that they need many people in one place. So we will put pressure on them to retreat, to restore their supply lines. But they will find their supplies gone, their conquered towns burned to ashes."

Growls of pleasure rose from the Badakhar, while the Cantareans looked thoughtful.

"What if they decide to strike right through us?" asked the woman who had sworn the first oath. "Should we burn all our fields, all the way to Ner Kes and Tanshadabela?"

"I have a counterspell." Calindor waited for the noise to die down. "If they try to break through us, they will have to use one of their great spells, but it will fail. Their magicians will be helpless, and the Exteca warriors will be no match for ours. Again, we will not slaughter them—but we will drive them south, always south."

"And how can we do this if they choose to stand and fight without magic?" demanded another Cantarean, a man with a slave's scarred face. "Then we'd have to slaughter them."

"I know their spell of terror," Calindor said. "If I cast it on them, they will flee like sheep before wolves."

Albohar stood up beside Calindor. "So your plan is something like this." He put his hand around Calindor's throat; someone gasped, but Calindor's smile belied the threat. "If I clamp your throat, you pull back. If I keep pushing, you pull back farther." And Calindor was indeed retreating, step by step toward the wall behind him. At last he broke free and pretended to flee, while the watchers laughed—nervously at first, then in genuine relief as Calindor returned to Albohar's side and they put their arms around each other.

"I like this strategy," Albohar said. "But what do you say, you who must bring your people into war and fight alongside them?"

"I vote for Calindor's plan," said Michuna.

"As do I," said Renjosudaldor, in a soft voice that still carried to the far corners of the hall.

"A show of hands," Albohar said. "All for?" Hands and fists rose everywhere. "All against?" No hands rose, though a few looked unhappy. "Then we have accepted Calindor's strategy and sworn ourselves to secrecy. May the gods save this land and all who dwell within it. I declare this meeting adjourned until mid-afternoon. Let us eat!"

Driving thousands of warriors across the prairie, Pervidhu thought, *is going to be harder than the biggest herd my uncle ever tried to move.*

While the cooks came into the hall with great pots of soup and baskets of bread, Pervidhu left to seek Deir. After the crowded hall, the corridors were pleasantly quiet and empty. Coming to the door of Tilcalli's room, he looked inside and saw Ghelasha and Callishandal already there.

"May I enter?" he asked. Ghelasha nodded.

The room was scarcely large enough to hold them all. Crowded around the bed were Deir and Dragasa as well as Ghelasha and Callishandal.

"Excuse my intrusion," Pervdihu murmured. "I had to see if her condition had changed."

"The same," Dragasa said. He seemed tired, almost numb. "I have gone into the Open Dream three times in the last two days, but the ancestors have not seen her. Or Calihalingol." The name meant little to Pervidhu, though he knew she was supposed to be a kind of ancestral ghost.

Tilcalli seemed to sleep; from time to time her eyes moved behind their lids, or her limbs twitched. When Deir held a damp cloth to Tilcalli's lips, she seemed to welcome the moisture.

Calindor arrived next, looking worried, and Pervidhu excused himself. "Will you speak with me for a moment outside?" he murmured to Deir. She nodded and followed him into the corridor.

"How are you? I've missed you," he whispered as he took her hand.

"And I've missed you. I wish you could have come with us to Bayodar."

"Someday you will take me back there," he said without enthusiasm. The thought of being underground with the Gulyaji was not one to dwell upon. "And—are you well also, my lady?"

Deir did not change; she took her hand from his. "You call me 'my lady'? As if I were someone else?"

"I'm sorry."

"Sometimes the magician comes out and talks to you, doesn't she? You call *her* 'my lady.' And later I wonder why I can't remember leaving you, or what we said."

"It—It's true. Sometimes she does talk to me. But—how do I say this? You are both my lady. No, that sounds stupid. I love you. I love you both."

"Do not say such a thing unless you mean it."

"My lady, I mean it. You know I am in your service always."

Her smile lifted his heart. "And I love you! But does she? Does the magician?"

The thought had not occurred to him, and he knew his surprise must show. "It doesn't matter. She speaks to me, and lets me serve her, and that's enough."

"What is she like, Pervidhu?"

"I must stop saying 'she' when she's still a part of you. *You* are lonely, and very wise, and your voice is a little deeper and you are very gracious to me."

"Gracious?" She laughed. "You make me sound like Ghelasha in a good mood."

"I mean them no disrespect, but you are the greatest of the great ladies in that room." He yearned to take her hand again but did not dare somehow. "I must ask you what happened in Bayodar. Why did you all go there?"

"Ghelasha wished me to see the Protector, to bring the magician out of hiding."

He felt a little dizzy. "And?"

Deir's face was troubled. "She is coming. He said it would take weeks or months, but she will become part of me—or I part of her, or the two of us something different." Unexpectedly she was in his arms, embracing him with startling strength. The scent of her hair made him drunk. "Pervidhu—someone else is coming too! Someone else is buried in my soul and I don't know who it is."

He felt her shudder, and reached up to stroke her hair. "It's all right. It's all right." But he shared her terror.

In Tola, or even in a good-sized provincial town, two thousand gifts to the True Gods would be little effort; the whole community, after all, existed for no other real purpose. Here in the barbarous north, the preparations involved most of the army.

Hundreds scoured the countryside for fuel. Hundreds more built a simple altar, an earth mound only about twice a man's height and faced with loose stone. Morter would have to wait until later; the altar would be a historic site worth preserving. Still more built a rough holding pen for the gifts, walling it with bricks from a nearby abandoned village.

The allies knew little of what was going on and took no part in the preparations; Yaocatl kept them busy on patrols, and on finding food in the deserted countryside. More Cantareans came to join the Exteca; Nezaual sent them back out to capture Badakhar, but he did not say why he wanted them.

Yetecuan spent most of his time in his tent, sleeping or talking with his priests. All were weary and looking forward to the new strength that the sacrifices would bring. Sometimes, when he had time, Nezaual visited briefly. He too was tired, yet he moved with a calm serenity and laughed readily at Yetecuan's jokes.

"Now I know what it feels like to lie with a woman and sire a great son," Yetecuan said to his priests when Nezaual had gone. "He is already the greatest among us, even if his magical powers are not yet mature. Who else has achieved so much since Patlikimili himself first learned redmagic and restored water to Tola?"

"You are right, honored father," the priests answered, and smiled to think that they were in the same army. "And what he will teach us!" one exclaimed.

The others laughed, and Yetecuan joined in. They might be priests of the True Gods, but they were magicians too, eager for new lore. Once this land was part of the empire, it would be agreeable to master the spells of their new subjects—especially, thought Yetecuan, the spells of the stalmaghar who forged such astonishing weapons. That would create a new bond between the priesthood and the warriors.

Three days passed before all was ready. During that time

Cantareans brought in hundreds of Badakhar captives, who went into the holding pen. On the morning that the sacrifices were to begin, one of Yetecuan's priests counted the gifts and reported seven hundred and eight in the pen.

"Very well, beloved son. If you would, please advise Yaocatl and Colotic and Nezaual that we will need twelve hundred and ninety-two of the Badakh allies to complete the number."

"And if we do not have that many, honored father?"

"Oh, I'm sure we do. But if not, we will make up the difference with the Chontalteca from the south. The Cantareans for now will not be sacrifices."

In a proper gift of this size, the sacrifices would all have been well-fed and heavily drugged, but no one was eating well and the supply of drugs was short as well. Uetzcayotl, a moderately talented priest, would prepare the gifts with a mild spell of love.

Through the morning, Yaocatl's warriors went among the Badakhar warriors and their camp followers, inviting some to prepare for an important ceremony. Most went willingly enough; the warriors did not force those who refused, but marked them for later.

By late morning the holding pen contained a little over two thousand men, women, and children. They were uncomfortable in the chilly air, with the sky overcast and threatening rain, but they made little complaint. By now, Yetecuan knew, they were resigned to uncertainty. Only Nezaual could translate reliably, so much happened without explanation.

Uetzcayotl had spent the night and morning in preparation. Now he came to the edge of the holding pen, borne on a simple litter by four younger priests. Yetecuan smiled a welcome to him, but inwardly he felt a vague frustration: Uetzcayotl was a fine man and a pious priest, but he had to be in actual sight of his subjects if he was to cast a spell of love. Nor could he cover an area much larger than this holding pen. How could the priesthood fulfill its obligation to the empire if this was the best it could do?

Well, give thanks for whatever the Gods send . . . and soon they will send us Calindor. The thought cheered him. In moderate focus, he felt the sting of Uetzcayotl's self-inflicted wounds. Divinity was abruptly present, as unmistakable yet intangible as a fog. The spell enveloped the thousands in the pen; they cried out in joy and surprise.

Another priest blew on a conch shell, signaling to those on the altar that the first gifts would soon arrive. A detachment of warriors, splendid in red and green plumes, ran into the pen and began marching the dazed Badakhar out of the pen and across the camp to the altar.

Yetecuan sniffed the cold northern air. Soon it would be rich and heavy with the smoke of burning hearts, and the True Gods would share their renewed strength. He turned and walked slowly toward the altar. For the rest of this day, and long into the night, he and the other priests would work as hard as any toiler in the fields, and for the same reason: to create and sustain the life of the Gods and their people the Exteca.

I humbly ask for some of your strength, Gods, so that I may better serve you.

It was a prayer they had often answered.

He could not get away from the smiling faces of his fellow electmen; he must smile back, and speak seriously of their petty complaints, and offer them honey cakes. Yet Albohar would have preferred to plant his fist in each man's nose and leave the hall.

He had won support for Calindor's deceptive plan, and in half the time he had expected, yet he would have gladly left the Mod to fend for itself, even if the outcome were chaos. And yet, and yet . . .

She is not my wife. She never was, nor ever was the mother of my child. Her son is not half the master of deceit that she was; he fooled only these simple oafs, but she outwitted a whole kingdom, misled a great Veik and all his lesser magicians . . . and of course me.

When he had heard of her trance last night, he had forced himself not to run to her. Then he had felt an awful, humiliating dread of seeing her so, her body empty of its soul and perhaps close to death. He dreaded revealing his love for her, though Ghelasha knew it, Dragasa and Calindor knew it, Callishandal must know it, and perhaps every Cantarean who ever passed through Tanshadabela.

Now he contented himself with hourly reports, whispered in his ear by one of the clerks, on Tilcalli's condition. And it was always the same. Dragasa, the clerk reported, was exhausted to the point of incoherence; he had tried too many spells to try to bring her back, or at least find her. Now Calindor was studying his mother again, yet seemed thwarted.

The clerk departed; Albohar went on smiling and drinking with the delegates; and then the clerk was back again, his face gray with shock.

"My lord—I mean, electman—may I speak with you in private?"

"You'll excuse me, I hope," Albohar said cheerfully to the four men he had been chatting with. He bowed and led the clerk out of the hall into the noisy kitchen. While servants crowded past with platters of stew and bread, the clerk spoke almost inaudibly in a breathy, fluttering murmur:

"The Mekhmagh Ca-Calindor ... he seemed to turn from his study of his mother, my lord. He looked up, as if seeing more than the four walls of the room, and began to shake his head. Then—Then he covered his eyes and cried out, 'No, no!' And then he cried out again, 'Stop it! Stop it!' And then he said to his father: 'They are killing and killing, but only Badakhar!' "

"*Who?* Who, damn you?"

"The Exteca, my lord. Calindor said they are not far from the town of Tilortulucu, and they are slaughtering great numbers of people ... but only Badakhar."

"And he can feel it?"

"So it would s-seem, my lord. And now he has gone to his bed. He seems very ill."

Albohar felt as if five or six men, each of them clamoring about a different problem and insisting on his attention, were yelling inside his head. Tilortulucu was only five days' ride away. Calindor was ill just when everyone most needed him. Tilcalli was lost in some unknown horror. The electmen were here, but not their warriors. And the Exteca had singled out Badakhar for some reason.

"You were in the room when you heard all this?"

"Just outside, my lord."

"Anyone else hear it?"

"Yes, my lo—yes, electman. Four or five servants, as well as Pervidhu and several other warriors. And your own lady, Ghelasha, was in the room."

He had clung for a moment to the sad hope of concealing the news, at least until the morning, and thus buying himself some time. Now the whole Mod would soon know it.

"Find Pervidhu and Ghelasha and ask them to meet me in my office at once."

"At once, my lord."

He went back into the dining hall, smiling. *It's all coming apart. The Exteca are striking straight for us, and we have only a few hundred fighting men to stop them. Tilcalli is dying, admit it, dying, and now Calindor is ill and all these people will be at one another's throats by sundown.*

He laughed at someone's joke. *May the Great God Bha at least grant us a decent death in battle, and not on some stone altar.*

Twenty-seven

While the delegates noisily resumed their places, Albohar summoned Pervidhu to his office. The younger man looked pale and tense, his yellow-brown hair tousled and falling in his face.

"I've heard about Calindor."

"It looks bad, electman."

"He's no better?"

"They've moved him into another room. His father is trying to calm him, but he himself seems ill as well. I gather that the practice of redmagic makes Cantarean magicians unwell."

"And at a considerable distance."

"The Mekhmagh wasn't very clear, but it sounded as if the Exteca are murdering hundreds of people all at once."

"Hundreds of Badakhar."

"So he says."

Albohar glanced at the door. "People here will know about it before long. It'll cause doubt and fear, just when we need to trust each other."

"If the Exteca are already at Tilortulucu, we won't need trust. We'll need fast horses to get us out of here."

Albohar teetered between fury and laughter; laughter won. "What horse could run faster than you in your bare feet? Now counsel me, Pervidhu. Calindor chose you to go south with him because he knows you don't like fighting. How do we prevent fighting among ourselves?"

"Tell them everything, electman. Everything. And give them a choice: to run for their lives or fight for their lives."

"To abandon us?"

"No one wants an enemy at his side in a battle—as you yourself said to those fools this morning. A coward is the worst enemy of all. If they're not with us, let them go and good luck to them."

"We may have only the Badakhar sticking with us, and even if we win, we'll have more hatred between us and the Cantareans."

"I think the Cantareans will stick with us, especially if Calindor recovers. But we'll have to move fast. Tilortulucu's not that far away."

The noise from the dining hall was getting louder. "Only the closest towns can send us more people in the little time left. We'll have to fight with the men we have now."

Pervidhu glanced at the ceiling, estimating. "Perhaps a thousand? Against five or ten times that many?"

"With Mekhpur behind them, my ancestors won against such odds. Now Calindor's behind me, and he defeated Mekhpur."

"Very well, electman. I think you had better break the news."

His arrival in the dining hall stirred more noise, especially when he leaped to the tabletop. But when Albohar's hand rose, they fell silent.

Oddly, Albohar remembered something his father had said when he was a boy, planning the raid that would bring Tilcalli home as his slave and mistress: "When your life is most in danger, let your soul act and your mind only watch."

Then let my soul speak.

"Brothers! Brothers and sisters, Cantareans and Badakhar alike, I bring you grim news. The Exteca are at Tilortulucu, that once we called Beinizdush, the Beehives. That is only five days' easy ride from here. They have stopped to sacrifice hundreds, perhaps thousands, to their gods."

They made no sound.

"Calindor the Mekhmagh has sensed this, and the redmagic that this slaughter has stirred. It has driven him half mad with anguish. I do not know if he will recover."

They made no sound, but two electwomen covered their mouths with their wrinkled hands.

"And the Exteca are killing only Badakhar. *Only Badakhar.* Do you know why? They do it to drive a wedge between our peoples. They wish the Cantareans to think they will escape death if the Exteca win, and they want us Badkhar to mistrust our Cantarean allies. They know we are dangerous if we stand together, and doomed if we turn against one another."

They moved restlessly, like warriors in the moments before a charge.

"These people are not fools. They know how we enslaved the Cantareans for centuries, and what a price we paid. They know we Badakhar fought one another right up to the moment that Mekhpur fell and Callia scourged the Five Kingdoms. They know about our riots, about the killings in alleys, about the quarrels between Badakh villages and Cantarean villages. Now they kill a few hundred unarmed Badakhar, in hopes that we will oblige them by killing one another.

"Well, if any man here bears a grudge against me because I was once his master, let him step forward and settle old scores now. I will not defend myself, and I forbid any other man here to defend me. Kill me and you will leave this castle in peace. Then you may do as you like—join the Exteca, run to the mountains, or drown yourself."

Now, like a line of foot soldiers seeing the enemy charge, they took on a perfect stillness. Albohar did not let himself relax.

"I ask you again. Kill me and go. But if you choose to stay, you will almost surely die somewhere between here and Tilortulucu. And that will be the end of your freedom, just a couple of years of struggle and hunger and then a bitter death. I will tell you this, though. I will die at your side, defending you as I would defend my own family."

His son Eskel, standing in a far corner, spoke out: "And I will be at your side also, to the last breath."

"And I!" shouted Pervidhu, and then a score of Badakhar echoed the promise.

Renjosudaldor rose. "We Gulyaji are few, but we still stand by our brother Albohar."

Michuna, the electman from Cadorsanbea, clambered onto a table. "We will stand too. Let them leave who live in the past. We will fight to go back to our village and make a new life for our children—Cantarean and Badakhar alike."

Over the roar of voices, Albohar's shout carried as on a battlefield: "Who is with us?" And every hand went up, many gripping a sword or knife.

Calindor's stomach was empty; his throat burned with sour vomit. Vaguely he sensed his father's arms around him, and his father's own pain.

"Was it like this when Nezaual killed the rats in the field?"

"That was worse," Dragasa said. "It was close. This is just an ache, a grief that keeps coming back."

"Ahh . . ." He felt another death. "No, this is mad. They're too far, yet I feel them all. Yetecuan. Yetecuan and Nezaual. They're doing something, focusing on us, sending this to us."

His father rocked him like a fretful little boy. "No. But you are finally becoming sensitive to their magic. Your strength shielded you, but doing redmagic was like eating poison."

"I have to. I have to. Only redmagic will stop them. Only redmagic. Only—" He slumped against his father, falling asleep.

After a time, Deir looked in from the next room. Her face was pale beneath the freckles. "Is he better?" she whispered.

"I hope so. At least he has escaped some of the deaths. How is Tilcalli?"

"No change."

"And you?"

She sank into a chair beside the bed where Dragasa held his son. "After Bayodar, I was frightened. Now I'm not. What will happen will happen."

"No. Listen to me." Though he murmured, his voice was urgent. "I am just an ordinary man. I have not had a very happy life, and I have not done much with my little talent. But this much I know, Deir: what happens is what we *will* to happen. If we act, the world changes. If we don't, the world obeys someone else. You came here seeking some kind of revenge against the Exteca. We don't understand revenge. It seems like trying to heal a wound by stabbing yourself. But if you have grown past revenge, maybe you can act to save the Exteca as well as us."

"I . . ." She paused, looking at the narrow window that threw a patch of afternoon light on the wall above the bed. "I think I have learned from you, Dragasa. I don't think I want revenge as I first did. But I do not know about the magician who is coming to join me, or about the other soul that follows her."

"I think they have been listening too." He fell silent for a moment. "I would like to sit with Calindor for a while. Go and rest."

"I will see if Tilcalli needs anything." She rose and slipped out, closing the door behind her.

Dragasa leaned back against the cold wall, feeling his son's feverish warmth and the distant horror of the sacrifices. "Oh, Tilcalli," he whispered, "if only you had needed me."

A happy ferocity had swept the hall. Albohar recognized it: the joy of men who knew what to do next. Every Badakh in the room had fought in at least one war, and most of the Cantareans, as slaves, had served warriors. A hundred tasks faced them: horses, fodder, fuel, shelter, extra weapons. Albohar remembered the old saying that "Aryo Gveipedi's foes hanged him with the rope he didn't bring."

Old habit broke up the delegates into war teams. He smiled to see men who had fought one another now conferring as cheerful allies. Almost too cheerful—they laughed too much and talked too little, at least at first, but he understood that too. Human sacrifices, spells of love, redmagic: that was for the sorcerers. But a fight was within their understanding, and they had not lost their old taste for violence. *Win or lose, we'll give the Exteca gods enough blood to quench their thirst.*

The logistics teams scattered to the paddocks and granaries and smithies. Recruiting teams raced to every village within a day's ride, though the afternoon was darkening into evening.

The strategy team stayed in the dining hall. Two warriors brought in a blanket loaded with sand and spilled it on the floor; sword points turned it into a map complete with hills and streams and villages.

"If Calindor recovers, well and good," Albohar told the six other strategists. "But we must expect to fight on our own with little magic to help us."

"What about your Veik?" someone asked.

"Sengvakh? We'll take him, of course, and his helper Dvoi and anyone else we can find. Perhaps the Gulyaji will help. But we will win or lose with steel, not spells."

With the point of his own sword, he sketched his plans in the sand map: "Calindor was right about staying in small groups, too small to warrant a spell of love or terror. In a way we're lucky to have so few warriors—we'll be scattered and mobile. Here's Tilortulucu; the Exteca will come north through Silovel, the Quiet Valley. We'll hit them from northeast and northwest, just skirmishing, and try to draw them away from Vidhumen. Then we bring the bulk of our forces right around them, through the Pelsvambo and Ghaidovel, and cut off their supplies. We'll join up and move south, living off the supply trains we intercept and burning everything the Exteca might use. But if that's not enough to slow them down, we leave enough men right at the Exteca rear to tempt them into turning south and giving chase." The sword point cut thin grooves in the sand.

"As they pursue, we harass their flanks. We kill or capture every horse and donkey."

"And every magician," grunted another man.

"And every magician. But they may be hard to find."

"What about these huge beasts they're supposed to have?" someone asked.

"Stay away from them. Dig some traps for them and the horses, but don't try to fight them face-to-face." He smiled unpleasantly. "They've had an easy time of it so far. We'll see how they like actually suffering in this country."

At the end of the night, when the dawn was near, Pervidhu walked swaying to his room for a few moments' sleep. The candle he carried threw uncertain light on the cold stone walls. The castle was still noisy, but he hardly heard the clatter of boots or the hoarse voices of men who still had much to do. He passed the corridor where Callishandal, Ghelasha, and Deir slept, and where Calindor now lay ill. Too drunk with fatigue to care if he stayed up a little longer, he turned and went slowly past the doors.

No light showed beneath any of the doors except Callishandal's; it was half open, and he looked in.

Callishandal was not there; on the bed lay Tilcalli, a blanket drawn up to her shoulders. Sitting beside her was Albohar, who glanced up and nodded.

"Where is Callishandal?" Pervidhu whispered.

"Sleeping in Ghelasha's room. Deir is helping the cooks with breakfast."

"And Calindor?"

"He's with his ... father next door. Asleep, I think."

"As you and I should be."

"Go to bed, Pervidhu."

"Good night, electman. Or good day."

He drew the door almost closed. A voice called from the next room, indistinct but alarmed, and Pervidhu hurried to it. He pushed the door open and saw Dragasa fumbling with a flint and steel as he tried to light a candle.

"What is it?" Pervidhu asked. "Is Calindor worse?"

The magician's face was hard, anger a fragile mask over fear. "He's gone."

No one had seen him, and none found him in the search that Pervidhu organized. Dragasa walked with Pervidhu, saying little until they had looked into every part of the castle and the sky was blue.

"The killing must have stopped," Dragasa said. "I can feel ... something down in the south, but it's not death. I fell asleep sometime after Calindor did. He must have recovered and gone out."

"It doesn't make sense."

They were on the roof of the castle, on a walkway overlooking the town and the prairie beyond it. Vidhumen was already bustling, and the shouts of herders carried easily from the streets below. The markets would run red with blood this morning as the butchers slaughtered sheep and pigs and cattle. Supply caravans would be going out before noon, hastening to stock caches for the army that would follow by tomorrow.

"No," said Dragasa. "It makes sense. He feels responsible for bringing the Exteca here, and for letting redmagic master him. Now he is atoning for his mistakes."

"How? Is he going to harm himself?"

"Perhaps, but not by his own hand." Dragasa rubbed his face and looked south. "Just like his mother, he thinks he must save his people single-handed." He turned to smile wryly at Pervidhu. "I think he has already gone to war with the Exteca."

Twenty-eight

He could feel the presence of the True Gods; they were like the mountains to the west, invisible in the darkness and beyond the horizon, yet an unchangeable part of the world. To challenge the Gods was like seeking to demolish the mountains—not only futile, but an attack on the world itself.

Yet he rode steadily south through the night, with moonlight to guide his horse and his own focus to show him the sleeping land.

Redmagic was at work in the south; he sensed it as he might hear a distant waterfall's roar long before seeing it. The sacrifices had fed the priests as well as the True Gods; Yetecuan and Nezaual and the other Exteca magicians would be strong enough to overthrow Albohar's little army and then to sweep through Cantarea and on into the mountains.

But if I can scatter them, drive them south, then perhaps I have not paid too high a price for what I have learned. And perhaps I will regain something of what I have lost.

If he failed, the Exteca and their allies would come north along this road. Albohar's raiders would need every advantage if they were to survive that thrust, so Calindor paused now and then to cast a spell. The Gulyaji were great masters of illusion, and Renjosudaldor had taught him many useful ways to mislead and confuse.

Here it was a spell that made the road seem to curve down into a bog; there it was a strip of land, extending well beyond the road into the fields, where anyone coming north would lose all sense of direction. In a third place, the footfall of a very large beast would surround it with a sudden wall of illusory dragonfire. If only he could leave a spell of terror the same way . . .

Not long after dawn he stopped in a village for a breakfast of cheese and bread. The shopkeeper was a Cantarean youth with quick eyes and a suspicious mouth.

"They're still talking in Vidhumen? Lot of good they'll do. Those Badakhar will fight the strangers whether they need to or not. I don't believe all those rumors about cutting out hearts and eating human flesh. At least they've got brown skins—not like the strawheads."

"So you'll welcome them when they come here?"

"I'll sell to them, same as I would to anyone with the price. If they want to squabble with Albohar and the strawheads, it's none of my concern."

"If I told you that the Exteca killed hundreds of Badakhar yesterday, would that change your opinion?"

The young man smiled crookedly. "I'd want to see the bodies before I gave thanks," he said, and laughed.

Calindor bought more bread and cheese, and wished the young man luck.

Albohar's patrols were on the road, but they passed Calindor without interest; he looked like a middle-aged Cantarean with gray hair, as he had in the tavern when he and Nezaual had met Sveit. In any case, he was still ahead of the news of his own disappearance.

The road was potholed and rutted after the winter, but carried plenty of traffic: peddlers walking from town to town harnessed to little carts full of trade goods; herders driving sheep or goats from one stony meadow to another; families trudging north with heavy packs.

"We've been seven days walking," the father of one such family told Calindor. They were Badakhar. The man's boots were in tatters, but he carried a saber and looked as if he knew how to use it. His wife and three little girls sat on stones at the side of the road; the mother looked gaunt and exhausted, the girls little better. Bloody rags wrapped their feet.

"Have you seen the Exteca?" Calindor asked him.

"From a distance. Those creatures of theirs, they're the size of a horse barn, with great tusks that curve like the Horn of Kenokhar. You'd need a long lance to stick them and not be trampled flat the next moment. I guess the Exteca are the ones with the big feathers, but they have a lot of ordinary people with them. Even Badakhar," he said with a snarl. "I hear the Exteca have some kind of magic that makes you their slave if you're too near them. I don't intend to find out if it's true."

"You won't get much farther with your feet bleeding."

"I'm better off than my wife and the oldest girl. We carry the two little ones as much as we can."

"Put your feet on my knee," Calindor said. The man gaped at him, but awkwardly obeyed.

A quick focus showed some infection in the blistered, bleeding soles. Calindor called on the Powers of water to flush the infection out; they obeyed with a gush of yellow fluid that quickly cleared. He set a quick-healing spell on the oozing wounds. The man's round-eyed stare grew rounder still.

"Do they still hurt?"

"A little, but only a little."

"Rest until mid-afternoon, and then you'll be able to walk easily again. May I do the same with your lady's feet, and your children's?"

"Hemamagh . . . do what you wish, but we cannot pay you."

Hemamagh: healer, blood magician. The word would never again carry its original meaning for him. "This is a gift. Travelers should look after one another." He healed the woman's feet, and then the children's. The youngest girl, he saw, was also running a fever and showing a rash on her face; he focused deeply, found the disease within her bloodstream, and destroyed it. She looked at him with the bright eyes of a healthy eight-year-old.

"I'm hungry!" she said.

"Of course you are," Calindor said, and gave her a half loaf of flat bread. "I have more for your sisters and your parents. But after you have eaten, take a nap over in the shade of the cottonwoods. You'll want to run around, but your feet need to rest a little more."

"And *then* I can run around," the girl said.

"You can run all the way to Vidhumen."

The parents' thanks were loud and sincere. But when he was riding south again, and saw still more people fleeing north, he wondered whether he should have bothered. Hundreds were in need of food and healing, far more than he could help, and if the Exteca won, they would face only slavery and death anyway.

Late in the afternoon he stopped to rest in the shade of a wooden bridge over a creek. Rummaging in his pack for his last loaf of bread, he found the gold lip plug. Yetecuan and the other Exteca magicians had not tried to locate it since the day at Cadorsanbea, just before Nezaual's escape. But perhaps he might be able to use it to distract them, to draw their attention in the wrong direction as he prepared for the spell of terror.

Sitting by the creek, listening to the creaking of frogs, he smiled and snorted. He had planned on the distraction of a whole army to hold the attention of the invaders; a little gold bauble seemed much less plausible.

Of course, for a seribi, a Badakh small sorcerer, distraction was half of every illusion; and today he felt himself a very small sorcerer indeed.

"We won't find him," Pervidhu said.

"I know," said Renjosudaldor. "In the caves of Bayo Bealar, I gave him his deep name: Calindor, the One Who Goes Away."

They were walking along the ridge of the hill behind the castle, toward the paddock holding the few horses of the Gulyaji—not that the Gulyaji would be any use as cavalry, Pervidhu thought; they were new to horses and indifferent riders. But they would need to be mobile if they were to set the spells of illusion at which they excelled.

Men hurried past them in both directions, carrying sacks on shoulder poles. Even the horses in their stables had caught the excitement in the air, and whinnied impatiently, as if eager to be out on the prairie.

"Can he do anything by himself?"

The Protector shook his head. "Perhaps a great deal, but he is going against a magic he hardly knows. And now he is vulnerable to redmagic, just as his whole clan is."

"Yet you are not vulnerable, you Burrowers."

"No . . . or not yet. Our magic springs from different principles. We see the Powers differently, and respond to them in our own way. The Siragi Aibela have their special sensitivities, as we have ours."

"So it may be that you can withstand redmagic."

Renjosudaldor smiled. "You are trying to cheer yourself up. Perhaps we can withstand them, perhaps not. We will learn in the trying. But think of this if you need cheering: Calindor, alone of all magicians, has mastered the magics of Gulyaji and Siragi Aibela, Badakhar and dragons. Now he has at least some understanding of redmagic. Those are considerable strengths."

"They are." They entered the paddock, where Silisihan and other Gulyaji were inspecting the horses and saddles. "If only he had some understanding of people as well—especially himself."

"Ah. For magicians that is sometimes the greatest secret, the one we do not always learn. Come and tell me if this horse will serve for hard riding."

From a hundred fires the smoke rose to feed the True Gods. Around each fire, warriors clustered to receive sacramental flesh and blood. Their songs rose to the foreign sky, praising the kindness and generosity of the True Gods.

Yetecuan had lost count of the hearts he had offered; then he had fed strips of flesh to scores of men, perhaps hundreds, until his hands were caked with a rich mixture of grease and blood. But he was untired. The great sacrifice had filled this little village with a shimmering mist of divine energy, endowing every priest with a rare strength. Even the warriors, lacking any hint of magic, seemed to stand straighter, to walk more firmly, even before they took the flesh and strength of the sacrifices into their own bodies.

Of all the priests, he thought Nezaual had most benefited. He was back in black robes, now dense with blood, and though his hair was short, it was stiff and matted again. All those months without more than minor gifts of blood! When Yetecuan considered what Nezaual had endured, he half regretted allowing him to go with Calindor. Well, his sufferings had strengthened him in other ways, made him preeminent among young priests.

Ometollin is old, and I have no desire to be Chief Priest. But Nezaual—yes, I can see him on the Great Pyramid at dawn, and giving counsel to the Tecutli and the nobles. When I was young, and knew I had the talent, I wondered how it might serve me. Now I am old, and I seek only to serve the talent . . . in Nezaual, in Calindor.

The sun was going down; the sacrifices had taken a full day and most of the night, and the sacraments had taken yet another day. No doubt Yaocatl and Colotic would be impatient to move; they equated speed with success and were surely wise to do so. But perhaps they would feel a pleasant surprise at how quickly the army traveled tomorrow. Soon they would stand at the gates of the castle of Vidhumen; after Nezaual's detailed descriptions, Yetecuan could visualize every street, every wall.

Only do not let this castle carry the taint that Calindor left in Elsman's fortress! He shivered at the recollection.

—And shivered again as a focus swept over him. Another priest, administering the sacrament at a nearby fire, fell against the warrior he was serving.

Distant, but powerful: it could only be Calindor, and though he was far away, he was not as far as Vidhumen. He was coming to meet them. The focus was a challenge, not a greeting, a warning that he would yield to the True Gods only after one more struggle.

As the True Gods will it.

Deir had slept on the floor beside Tilcalli's bed while Dragasa sat awake on the other side. She had dreamed of Burnbaile, of her mother. They were sitting outside their little house, with the candleboat at their feet. Sivon was singing a lullaby, while Deir shrieked in blind fury at her; yet her mother seemed not to hear, and went on singing.

Then the Exteca were coming down the street, and Deir was running for the river. She had forgotten the candleboat, yet it was there, and on it was her father—not just his bones, but his dead flesh, and he was looking at her.

With a shudder she was awake. The room had the dim blue light of early dawn. Dragasa's deep voice was singing a lullaby, one of the old Cantarean songs she had learned last fall in Tanshadabela. She sat up and saw him leaning over Tilcalli, his hand stroking her long black hair. He smiled sadly at Deir and went on singing.

Through the window came the sound of hoofbeats and jingling harness. Springing to her feet, Deir ran to the window.

Below were the outer wall of the castle and the road down the hill to the town. Horsemen were riding slowly out the castle gate and through the streets: a long column, two abreast and seeming to go on forever. Even at the far end of the town, where the road ran south, she could see them as a dark line against the pale fields. Above them was a huge sky full of pink-edged clouds.

Pervidhu was out there. She thought of him with yearning and anxiety, thought of his grin and easy laugh, thought of his love—

For a moment she thought she was still dreaming, or going mad: she seemed to be thinking two sets of thoughts, seeing Pervidhu as a humorous youth who loved her, and as a dedicated man who saw her as she was and served her without question.

The second set of thoughts faded; she heard again the rumble of horses and wagons, and Dragasa's lullaby.

So, my lady magician: we are growing closer still. And who else is behind you?

Twenty-nine

He did not sleep. When the horse wearied, he stopped for a few hours deep in the night; while it slept, he sat and watched the Powers whirling around him.

Others were on the road all night as well: more refugees trudging north, patrols galloping south, and brigands seeking someone to rob. One gang of four horsemen, seeing him sitting in the moonlight, demanded his horse and pack. Calindor changed his appearance to that of a skeleton clad in coldfire, and that of his horse to a small dragon. The brigands' horses threw their riders and raced away in terror; the brigands themselves, screaming, ran after them.

By dawn he had been riding again for hours when nausea seized him; he dismounted and vomited. More redmagic: not as bad as before, but bad enough. The Exteca sacrificed a few people every morning and again at sunset; he was closer now, and more sensitized to it, so he felt each death.

Lurching from the road to a stream to cleanse his mouth, Calindor realized he was more sensitive to all deaths: he felt the presence of a little girl who had drowned in this stream many years ago, and sensed as well an old man dying in the next village. He at least was willing to return to Callia, and when his dying was done, Calindor felt an ache and then a kind of relief.

How will I manage if they can sicken me each time they tear out a heart? What if they slaughter more hundreds? What if they go into battle?

The thought of experiencing the deaths of thousands in a pitched battle made him shudder. All the more reason to reach the Exteca quickly and drive them out of Cantarea, out of range, at whatever cost to himself. *What will happen when I myself do redmagic? Will I even be able to cast a spell of terror?*

All day he rode through empty countryside, meeting occasional groups of refugees. In the villages, though, many remained; like the Cantarean shopkeeper, they seemed to look forward to the Exteca as allies against their Badakhar neighbors.

Sometime in the afternoon, while he rested his horse again, Calindor felt the pulse of a searching focus. He did not respond; he did not need to. They were tracking him through the gold lip plug, as he had hoped they would, and they had found it coming toward them. Yetecuan and Nezaual would be preparing for a struggle; at the last moment he would draw their attention away and strike with all his strength, whatever redmagic might do to him.

At least they don't know what their killing does to me.

If they did, they could simply sacrifice a few people, at close intervals. The impact would leave him writhing on the road, defenseless against brigands as well as Exteca.

He wondered what might have happened if he had shown this sensitivity early in his experience with redmagic, as his parents had; he would have mastered nothing, but at least Callishandal would not have left him ... and he might have paid more attention to Deir.

He recalled something Pervidhu had said on their journey south, a comment about how he had ignored Deir; but he could not even remember his own answer. It was odd, he thought absently, how he had lost interest in her powers as he explored redmagic. She had been immune to Yetecuan's spell of love, and to the spell of terror he had awkwardly inflicted on the whole town of Vidhumen. But he had not sought the hidden magician after that one experience in Tanshadabela when she had struck out at him.

Was that the influence of redmagic, occupying all his thoughts, or of Deir's hidden self? Could she have cast a spell on him, on his soul, and turned his thoughts away from her? No; it had to be redmagic itself that had sealed him off from her as well as from Callishandal, and his parents, and the whole Open Dream. *I have given up too much, too much ...*

The thought goaded him back into the saddle again, and he urged his horse south.

By the end of the first day on the march, Renjosudaldor was laughing and joking; Albohar found a cheerful Burrower more alarming than a somber one.

"He has done half our work," the Gulyaji said. "The road is full of traps and illusions. You do not see them because you are moving south. But if you were to turn north again, you would think you were going mad. Try it—turn and ride north to the crest of that hill."

"Thank you, but I will take your word for it. Do you sense Calindor himself?"

"No. He's still far ahead of us."

"You know why he's laid these traps."

"To aid us, of course," Renjosudaldor said.

Albohar sucked his teeth and spat. The column of riders straggled behind him. He could hardly bear to look at them, they were so unsoldierly. A damned good thing they weren't going into action as a massed unit. Even as small groups of guerrilla raiders they would be more dangerous to themselves than to the Exteca—at least until they understood their business. The Badakhar had forgotten all they'd ever known about war, and the Cantareans had it all to learn.

"It's to aid us if they kill him. If we have to retreat, we'll scatter and they'll advance on Vidhumen up this road. He hopes his spells will delay and confuse them while we reorganize ourselves. Which means he's not very confident about his chances. Or ours."

Albohar felt an irritable pleasure at Renjosudaldor's new solemnity. Then he despised himself for causing it, when the Gulyaji had supported him in the Mod's critical last moments.

"Forgive me, companion. This is a different kind of war from any I've ever fought. Looking at this sorry excuse for an army puts me in a foul mood."

The Protector of the Gulyaji smiled again. "We haven't fought a war in three hundred years; imagine the mood we're in."

The army recruited a few more fighters—Albohar couldn't bring himself to call them warriors—in the villages they moved through. In the old days he would have taken every male between ten and sixty, even if it meant arming them with sharpened sticks; now he obeyed Pervidhu's advice to fight only with willing companions.

But it rankled to see big, healthy blank-faced boys—Cantareans mostly, but even a few Badakhar—standing in their doorways watching their neighbors go off to war. When the Exteca were gone, these stay-at-homes would live to regret their caution. And the veterans of the Exteca War would return to run their towns and to enjoy the gratitude of their electman.

A few beheadings wouldn't hurt either, he reflected.

The castle was now the domain of women: only a few males, mostly boys and infirm old men, remained. Ghelasha took up her husband's place at the long table in the dining hall, and administered the town as Albohar would have.

Only faster, she decided. By late morning she had dealt with chores that Albohar would have taken until sunset to complete. He was a good man, and a good electman, but he did talk so. Better to give an order and demand a report, and give another order. Albohar would call for a beer, ask for three alternative actions from his advisers, and spend an hour exploring their consequences while the next messenger waited patiently at the far end of the table.

The noon meal was a mutton stew, heavily spiced and accompanied by a bread flavored with herbs. Dragasa and Deir joined her for it, while Callishandal kept watch over Tilcalli.

"No change?"

"None." Dragasa looked exhausted. "If I have the strength, I will go into the Open Dream again tomorrow."

Ghelasha grunted and scooped up a lump of mutton with her spoon. "All these years we thought we knew you mountaineers, and we never heard a whisper about this Open Dream."

"The Siragi Aibela don't talk much about it, even to other Cantareans. If Tilcalli hadn't disappeared within it, I wouldn't talk about it now."

"It's not the afterlife, is it?"

"It's *an* afterlife, I suppose. We don't know when it started. Sometime during the Slave Wars the Siragi Aibela found they could speak with their ancestors. Callia—I suppose she created it for us as a place for us to remember what we had been."

"How strange to think of meeting all one's ancestors," Ghelasha murmured.

"Not everyone who dies goes into the Open Dream. My father's lineage has not appeared there in many generations. Tilcalli's ancestors are not there either, except for her great-great-grandmother Calihalingol. She was the one who planned Tilcalli's abduction by Albohar."

"Indeed. I would very much like to meet that old woman some day, and talk with her about what she did."

Unexpectedly, Dragasa laughed. "I have talked with her often about that, and sometimes I get very angry, but she never apologizes." He turned his tired eyes to Deir. "The only person who ever worried Calihalingol is Deir."

The girl looked up, but she did not seem surprised. "I think I remember her. An old woman with braids, and wearing white buckskin with many beads."

"What?" Ghelasha put down her spoon and pushed her bowl away. "You remember a woman who died almost a hundred years ago?"

Deir looked pensive. "I didn't until Dragasa mentioned her. It's like seeing something that reminds you of a dream you've forgotten. I was sitting there in the sun, and she was talking to me. And then I started crying."

"No," said Dragasa. "You screamed. It was the first sound that anyone ever made in the Open Dream."

"But—that doesn't make sense. She was talking to me. I heard her."

"We hear each other's thoughts, but we don't speak. Only you have ever truly spoken in the Open Dream. And now you remember it. The magician is coming out."

"I know."

"Are you frightened? I hope not."

Her blue eyes met his brown ones. "I used to be. Now I only wait."

Ghelasha stood up. "Deir—I apologize for striking you. I am very sorry I did."

Deir smiled at her. "It's all right. I owe you thanks for taking me to Bayodar. It's time for me to grow up. Dragasa, shall we go back to Tilcalli?"

"Yes. Would you like me to tell you something about our magic?"

She shook her head. "I think the magician knows it already."

Dragasa said nothing, but as they walked out of the dining hall, Ghelasha saw how pale he was.

The servants came to clear the table. Ghelasha sat down again, resting her hands on the table's edge. She would not allow the servants to see her trembling.

"Will you want anything else, my lady?" one of them asked. She shook her head silently. She did not trust her voice any more than her hands.

For the first time in many years, she missed Albohar.

Behind him, to the north, Calindor felt the spells that the Gulyaji were laying like traps; to the south, redmagic rose and fell like a tide with the dawn and sunset sacrifices. He expected them now, and awaited them in whatever sheltered place he could find. But each time he was closer, and each time it was worse.

The focuses came three or four times a day, and sometimes at night. Good. They were tracking him, preparing for him. He would do alone what he had planned to use an army for.

The prairie was oddly unchanged. Herders tended their cattle and sheep; plowmen broke the soil; women washed clothes in the streams while their children splashed and squealed. Yet armed men, often on horseback, guarded the villages. Sometimes they offered to buy his horse. They seemed more worried about thieving refugees than about the Exteca and their allies.

"Seen some of them," one Cantarean told him. "Two of them, with a squadron of Badakhar cavalry. Good riders. Look like us only shorter, with feathers in their hair. They wanted to buy horses, but we need all we've got. They could've just taken what they wanted, but they didn't. The strawheads don't speak their language, but they seem to get along. Never saw a strawhead smile at anyone with a brown skin before."

Good riders indeed, Calindor thought as he rode on. The Exteca were astoundingly quick, able to cover great stretches of country. Their scouts were far out in front, finding the best routes—and making friends with anyone who didn't flee. When the Badakhar fought one another in the old days, they had been capable of sudden bursts of speed. But too often they dragged their heels, looting and foraging even when it gave their enemies time to prepare. If Albohar tolerated that now, a guerrilla war would be impossible; looting hungry farmers and herders would only make enemies of them.

All the more reason to drive the Exteca away before Albohar's army got itself into trouble.

Well before sunset he found a shallow creek running noisily over stones, shaded by cottonwoods on either side. Some had fallen across the stream bed during Callia's rage, partly damming the creek and creating deeper pools. He was well off the road, concealed from anyone who might be passing by—and refugees were still walking north, though they must know the Exteca would surely overtake them by tomorrow.

Stripping off his dark, dusty clothes, Calindor stepped into a waist-deep pool. The Powers of water swirled lazily around him, too slow and cold to take much interest. But he asked them to purify him, to cleanse him and renew him. For a long time he stood singing to the Powers, and then immersed himself. When he stood again, he felt both strong and relaxed.

He walked back up on the grassy bank, picked up his clothes and soaked them in the stream as well. Then, lifting them out, he used the spell he had taught Nezaual and drove the water out.

"A very useful spell," he muttered to himself, thinking of the use Nezaual had made of it. Then he sat down and thought about what he must do next.

As the clouds turned red and the cottonwood grove darkened, he felt the familiar probe of a focus and wondered who it was: Yetecuan? Nezaual? No, it didn't feel like Nezaual. Maybe some other magician, another boy assigned to keep track. Whoever he was, he was close—less than an hour's ride to the south. And the Exteca would know it too.

The timing would be critical. Impatient, he began to wish for the sacrifices to begin, and then felt ashamed of himself.

They began soon enough. He was grateful to the Powers of water; their cleansing had given him strength, and though the deaths were so close, they were little worse than they had been this morning or the night before. His stomach was empty, so the vomiting was less violent.

At last it passed; the True Gods had fed enough to keep them content until sunrise. He wondered if they would be surprised to be invoked by a stranger, at night, against their own people. Probably not. Gods, like Powers, had little self-awareness.

While he lay gasping, Calindor weighed his choices. Knowing him to be so close, the Exteca might send men to talk to him. Or they might wait for him to arrive in their camp. Either way would be perilous for him; he suspected the Exteca knew far more magic than Nezaual had revealed, and might attack him with some unknown spell. If the spell worked, he might succumb to Yetecuan without resistance; if it failed, they might well have something else in reserve.

Well, he himself had little left but one spell of redmagic. If it failed, he could perhaps fight his way free with dragonfire and other spells, but more likely he would be helpless, crawling on the ground under the impact of his own spell or some Exteca's. He had some small consolation: if they thought they could make him a priest of the True Gods, they would find themselves sadly mistaken. He could no more cut out a human heart that he could dive to the dark homes of the sea dragons. His only value then would be as another gift to the Gods.

His head ached, but he forced himself to his feet. His horse looked at him briefly, then went back to cropping grass.

"I wish you luck," Calindor said to the horse, and walked back downstream to the road, leaving his food, his pack, and the gold lip plug within it.

On the way, he changed his appearance. Again he was a middle-aged Cantarean, black hair streaked with white, and lines deepening around the eyes. He carried no weapon but a short-bladed knife; a bark-stripped branch made a passable staff.

He needed no dragonfire, no coldfire to light his way; he simply strode along in the dark, while the stars brightened in the gaps between the clouds. From the next ridge he saw a glow not far away in the south: the Exteca camp, with hundreds or thousands of campfires. The final touch to his disguise came to him then. He left the road and found a little grove of wind-stunted trees huddled in a gully. Quickly he filled his arms with sticks and branches, wrapped them into a bundle with his belt, and slung them over his shoulder. He would not be the only person approaching the camp with firewood.

With every step, as the fires of the Exteca grew brighter, Calindor felt his spirits rise. Whatever his mistakes had been, he would now atone for them. If this was only his greatest mistake, at least it would be his last. If he succeeded, he would buy time for Cantareans and Badakhar to learn how to live together like the people of Cadorsanbea. And they would then have to find a way to live with the Exteca.

That would be hard, and especially for the Exteca. Their way and their gods had led them from success to success; now, in half a year, they had crossed the world and seized half of Cantarea. They would not want to decide, after one setback, that they must abandon redmagic and find a new way to feed the True Gods.

And how will the True Gods themselves take this setback?

That was a fearful thought. They knew Cantarea now; they knew him. They might take a terrible revenge.

He shifted his bundle to the other shoulder. Forget the True Gods; their revenge could hardly be worse than their triumph.

Horsemen were coming north; he sensed them before he heard them, and stepped out of the road to let them pass. They were all Exteca, twenty of them carrying torches as they trotted past. One was a black-clad priest; the rest were plumed warriors.

They've taken the bait! He half ran back to the road and walked quickly up the hill. At the crest he paused.

The road ran down less than a bowshot to a stream: the Berkha, which would grow downstream into a sizable river but here was merely a wide and shallow creek.

Beyond the Berkha the whole of the next valley was a lake of stars: thousands of campfires burned in orderly rows. By their light he could see shadowy figures moving about, and through the smoke came the familiar low rumble of an army camped for the night. Horses whinnied, and other creatures answered with a strange blaring cry—no doubt the mammoths Deir and Nezaual had spoken of.

Perhaps this was the place to cast the spell. He could see almost the whole army from here, and if the spell came from the north, the invaders would flee southward. Yet he hesitated, unsure of himself. He had cast his first spell over most of Vidhumen from close to its center, but this camp covered a far greater area. Suppose he caught only the northern part, and missed the bulk of the army—and the priests?

Better to get close to the center, close to Yetecuan and whoever led this army. He gripped his staff a little tighter and walked down into the river. The bottom was hard sand, the cold water not quite knee-high at its deepest. In a hundred strides he was across it and entering the camp.

The men around the first half-dozen fires all bantered with him, demanding his wood; he ignored them at first, but then said to one group: "The high priest is to get this wood. Yetecuan, his name is. Where shall I find him?"

A stocky Badakh sprang up. "Follow me. I'll take you right to him."

He was a cheerful young man who spoke bad Cantarean with a Halamori accent. But he fended off other demands for Calindor's firewood and led him through the camp.

It felt like a festival, a strange blend of a Mod and siege and a gigantic market. Most of the people he saw were Cantareans, though their tents and clothing were Badakh. Children ran about, shrieking as they pursued one another with stick swords; women tended cooking pots and served endless lines of hungry men. Old Cantarean songs blended with the chants of the Exteca, while butchers beheaded cattle and cut up the carcasses. Smoke filled the air, and Calindor could sense the True Gods all around him.

His guide led him to a cluster of tents surrounded by Exteca bearing Badakh sabers and spears. They understood the Badakh even less than Calindor did, but at last let them pass.

Here, torches burned as well as campfires, and the air was thick with the stink of burning grease and cooked flesh. Calindor fought down nausea as he passed the reeking altar where the priests had killed the sunset sacrifices not long ago. The presence of the dead was so intense he could almost see them.

Under his breath he began to murmur the words Nezaual had taught him. When the invocation was complete he would drop the firewood, take the little knife from his tunic's inner pocket, and give the True Gods the blood they desired. After that, he did not know what would happen.

As the spell took shape he felt nausea rise again. The people around him seemed both close and far away, their voices piping and shrill as birds'. One voice, deeper than the others, almost seemed to echo his whispers.

Gritting his teeth, Calindor finished the invocation as the Badakh brought him before a tent that must once have sheltered some upermanna and his family. Several warriors and priests stood before its entrance. One priest was speaking loudly, and his words were those Calindor had heard as an odd echo of his own. But they were not the same, though they created a thickening haze of magic.

Drop the bundle. Take the knife. You know where to cut.

He lifted the little blade to his face, just as the priest mirrored the gesture only more quickly. Blood spurted from beneath one eye, then the other, and Calindor recognized him at last: Nezaual.

The spell of love engulfed him. The little knife fell from his hands. Nezaual stepped forward, blood making two vertical stripes down his face and mingling at his throat.

"I greet you, honored father, and welcome you to the service of the True Gods and their people."

Calindor felt Nezaual embrace him, heard him chuckle in his ear: "Honored father, you should not have assumed the same disguise you took when we went to drink in the tavern. I recognized you at once."

Strong though Nezaual's arms were, Calindor felt the presence of the True Gods far more intensely.

"I love you, beloved son. But I am dying."

The world tilted, dimmed, and fell silent. Even the True Gods disappeared. Darkness rose around him and he fell into it gratefully even as he yearned for Nezaual and all the Exteca.

Thirty

After three days Yetecuan sent his priests to recover back in their tents. He sat in his own tent with Nezaual, while Calindor lay open-eyed in his unchanging trance in the bed between them.

"We have a few Badakhar magicians," Nezaual said wearily.

"Beloved son, we also have mammoths and horses who would be equally useless." The old man drew a slow breath. "I am sorry. I should not snap at you—you of all people."

"Anger is the sign of a broken heart," Nezaual said. "It is an old saying, honored father, but I have come to know it is true. I grieve for your sorrow."

"You are a good boy. Help me think: have we missed a healing spell, a spell of deep sight, a spell of expulsion?"

"None."

"I think you must be right. Did we misperform any of the ceremonies, misspeak any of the invocations?"

"Honored father, they have never been done better even in healing the Tecutli. The Powers came and obeyed."

Yetecuan tapped his fingertips together, then laced his fingers into a knot between his knees. "It must be a spell of shielding, but of a strange kind. A shield should have protected him so that he could complete his own spell. Instead it left him helpless."

"We were fortunate in that, honored father."

"I know. I know. His spell would have destroyed the army before the blood reached his chin. What a great talent, wasted." Yetecuan wept silently, tears running down the scars on his cheeks. "Somehow we must revive him, break the shield, and let him recognize his true destiny."

Nezaual placed a hand on Calindor's shoulder and focused, seeking whatever it was that had thwarted the spell of love. He was no more successful than the other priests had been.

"I could try to cast a spell of healing," he said.

"Beloved son, you have no strength for it. You cast the spell of love only three days ago."

"I needed to use very little energy, honored father, since I was focusing only on Calindor. And I am thinking of a Cantarean healing spell, not one of ours."

The old man raised his hands and let them fall on his knees. "You may try. But do not try more than once. If you truly exhaust yourself, we will have almost no magic for the next few days."

Nezaual nodded. He understood how weak the army's defenses had become. Almost all of its priests had labored in desperate fear to revive Calindor, using all the strength they had gained from the mass sacrifice. Their spells had utterly failed. Some had taken to their beds; the rest shuffled about the camp, scarcely able to stand.

Colotic appeared in the entrance of the tent. His face was, as always, unreadably courteous.

"Come in, beloved son. I am glad to see you. Sit beside me and tell us the news."

The warrior entered and squatted on his haunches before Yetecuan.

"Honored father—Yaocatl has sent me to ask if we may strike camp in the morning and resume our march."

"Resume our march . . . Perhaps tomorrow evening, Colotic, if we can find a way to rouse Calindor."

Colotic said nothing for a moment. Then he looked at the dirt floor. "Honored father, we are running out of food. We have sat here for three days and four nights. The foragers are coming back with almost nothing. If we do not take some good-sized towns, Yaocatl says he will have to scatter the army all over Cantarea."

"That would be madness!" Nezaual snarled. "The barbarians would pick us off a few at a time. We must stick together."

Colotic looked levelly at Nezaual. The warrior's features were unreadable in the lamplight. "We will need to sacrifice more barbarians, then. And horses and mammoths don't eat human flesh."

"You are both my sons," Yetecuan said. "I beg you not to quarrel. Colotic, I hear your worries and I share them. Nezaual, I hear your worries also, and they burden me. But I fear that if we advance with so little magical support, the enemy will do us great harm. They have more magicians than Calindor, after all."

"You are right, honored father," Nezaual said. "But I think Yaocatl is wise to want us to move. If we stay here much longer, the enemy will have yet more time to organize. We could be in Vidhumen in a few days. Then we could examine Calindor in greater detail, and work out a cure for his trance."

Yetecuan gazed sadly at the entranced sorcerer beside him, watching Calindor's eyes move back and forth as they saw the invisible.

"Very well, Colotic. Let us go, and hope that in Vidhumen we will find the key."

"And in the meantime, honored father—"

"Yes, Nezaual."

"The Cantarean healing spell?"

"Try it if you wish, beloved son."

It failed.

Albohar sat in a farmhouse, cursing its tiny windows and his own farsightedness. He was trying to read a map of the region by lamplight and the dim gray glow that filtered in from the rainy afternoon. He did not know this land as well as he should; in the old days this had been part of Halamor, a kingdom he had rarely visited.

Standing around the table were Pervidhu, Renjosudaldor, and a half-dozen others—the captains of the ragtag army of Vidhumen.

"Here's the Exteca camp," Pervidhu said, his finger tapping a patch of prairie bounded by two rivers—the Ghrirei to the south, its tributary the Berkha to the north. "They haven't moved in three days or more, but their foragers are coming farther and farther north. We've picked off some of them."

"That means they're running out of food," Albohar said. "No wonder, with all those mouths to feed."

"It also means they'll soon break camp and move north," said Renjosudaldor.

"Why north? Why not east or west?" asked Albohar.

"They know we are north of them, that Vidhumen is the largest town within easy striking distance, that beyond the town are many farms and herds. If they turn east they must go well beyond Holy Lake before they find large settlements; to the west are forests and mountains. And if they turn, they expose their whole flank to us."

Albohar grunted. "For a man who lived in a hole most of his life, you know the country." Some of the others, less familiar with Gulyaji, shivered with embarrassment and alarm: speaking so familiarly to a Burrower seemed to them more foolhardy than fearless.

"So they'll come north," Pervidhu said. "As soon as they do, we have to break up into much smaller groups, and scatter. Otherwise they'll cast one of their spells over the whole army and we'll be finished."

"But if we do that," said Michuna, "what's to keep them from driving straight through us?"

"Harry their flanks," Albohar said. "Tie them down wherever we can, and retreat so they must pursue us east or west. If they turn back toward Vidhumen, we're on their heels again."

"And what if it doesn't work?" demanded a Badakh named Okotakh. "Then we'll have their whole army between us and Vidhumen, and our own supplies are none too large."

"We'll live off what we take from the Exteca," Albohar said. "And they won't break through. That I promise you."

After the meeting Pervidhu went back to inspect his unit's horses. The army was a half-ordered camp, with tents and shelters pitched across a couple of meadows. The local streams were already undrinkable, and the horses were scattered widely so that they would all have enough grass.

Are you seeing all this through my eyes, my lady? Do we look like a redoubtable force, or a mob on horseback? Will you come to our rescue as you came to mine in Bhadvedor?

He rode through the rain along an east-west ridge that fell away south into gently rolling prairie where every creek had its line of dark trees. Not far away out there were the Exteca and the allies, and perhaps Calindor. What would he be doing? Had he gone over to them, or was he planning some astonishment? More likely the second.

The afternoon wore away in the tedium of ensuring that men

and beasts were kept fed and exercised. Pervidhu drilled his squadrons, using Badakhar veterans to teach the Cantareans. Publicly he praised them; privately he despaired, and considered turning his squadrons into mounted infantry. If they got off their horses at the battlefield, at least the horses might be saved.

Just before the evening meal—cold porridge and hot tea—a messenger summoned him back to Albohar's farmhouse headquarters. Pervidhu was the last to arrive; he found a crowd of men standing about a rain-soaked Cantarean in ragged buckskins.

"All right," said Albohar quietly. "Tell us again, Bijandor, what Calindor said to you."

"As you wish, electman. He came to me in the camp of the invaders—"

"Excuse my interrupting," Pervidhu said, stepping closer to the Cantarean. "But what were you doing there, among the Exteca?"

"My village joined them. I went along, but I didn't want to. May I continue, sir? Thank you. He came to me, magically disguised as an older man with gray hair and a wrinkled face. He had seen, he said, that I was unhappy to be caught up with the invaders, and asked if I would do a service for all Cantarea. I said I would if I could. He told me to bring a message to the electman Albohar and his captains."

"And what is the message?" Pervidhu asked.

"Calindor has learned that the Exteca plan to strike directly for Vidhumen, at whatever cost. They will place most of their forces near the head of their column, shielding their priests and supply trains."

"And when will this happen, Bijandor?" Albohar prompted.

"They start tomorrow before dawn. At the rate they travel, they will be here within a day, and in Vidhumen in three more."

"And what does Calindor ask of us?"

"To circle around them and strike from behind. To kill every priest while he casts a spell of terror on the army. He says the best place to do it is at the ford of the River Berkha. They will reach it by mid-morning tomorrow. By noon most of the army will be north of the ford, but the priests and supply trains will still be south. By the time the army can come to the defense of the priests, it will be all over."

"And how do we know it was truly Calindor you spoke with?" asked Pervidhu.

Bijandor paused. "Are you Pervidhu?"

"I am."

"He says if you do not come, he will ask Callishandal to break your other leg."

Pervidhu laughed. As part of the army pursuing Calindor two years earlier, he had stumbled upon Calindor and Callishandal—Dheribi and Bherasha, their names had been then. They had unhorsed him, breaking his leg in the process. "That sounds like him, all right."

Albohar glanced at a guard by the door. "Take him out and find him something to eat and some dry clothes. I thank you for this message, Bijandor."

When the man was gone, Albohar looked around the room. "Well?"

"It's good to know not everyone is a slave of the Exteca," said Michuna. "He seemed to me to be telling the truth."

"I'm not so sure," said another man, a Badakh. "He could be luring us into a trap."

"But if he is telling the truth," Michuna answered, "then Calindor expects us to come to his aid—and he will be in great danger if we are not there when he needs us."

"It would also mean finishing off the Exteca in a day or two," said another man. "If we break up and fight a guerrilla war, we might be fighting for years. Will we ever get another chance to beat them so quickly?"

The debate went on for hours, until Pervidhu was weary and a couple of the others were half asleep. Finally Albohar called a vote.

"How many are prepared to strike around the Exteca at the Berkha ford?"

Most of the hands went up, including Pervidhu's. Albohar smiled wryly at him.

"You're sure? You trust this Cantarean you never met before?"

"Let me keep him close to me, electman. If he's betrayed us, I'll kill him myself. But yes, I think he's brought us Calindor's message."

"Very well, then. Go to your men and tell them to make ready. We will leave at once."

"At once?" someone echoed.

"If we sleep on this decision, we may regret it. And Berkha ford is a long ride from here anyway."

Shimmering light, of all colors. A single reverberating note that somehow changed. A wind like fire, like ice.

Brightness all around him.

This was the beginning.

A voice, or his own understanding? The same. The brightness spun away, dimmed, exploded into something brighter still.

After a long time, after an instant, stars whirled around him like the dust motes he had once played with. He found he could play with these also: move them into new paths, array them in great whirlpools and fountains, adorn them with veils of glowing dust and worlds like gleaming gems.

Their beauty made him joyous, made him joy itself. He danced within their atoms, becoming the Powers that gave life to matter; he swam among their galaxies like a great salmon in white water. Worlds beyond number stirred with the life he called from them, and he soared in their skies while creatures uncounted struggled toward his light and warmth and fell back again.

Yet some climbed high indeed before they fell, and took back with them a spark that burned upon stone and water. Their minds called him to fear, in anguish, in love, in hatred; he answered, though they rarely heard.

Each world had its own beauty, and he took from one to give to another. On one, life sought him as flowers; he plucked them and put their roots in alien soil. On another, life leaped in storm-ripped seas; he gave it tranquil lagoons under hot suns, or oceans whose only islands were ice.

From a world where the Powers had forgotten their own names, he plucked men and women as he had plucked flowers and fish and trees, and gave them new worlds to explore where the Powers still heard those who could learn to call them. Each tribe had a few magicians who could see and invoke the Powers, and these they used to build new civilizations on memories of the old world.

He knew where he was now; Obordur the dragon had shown him this place. He had stood on this same hill, with iceblink gleaming above the northern horizon and the land a vast mossy plain. He saw the little band of hunters appear beside him on the hill, gripping their beautiful flint-tipped spears, their eyes full of fear and wonder: one or two would dance forever in the Open Dream.

He had given them a part of this world, of Sotalar; it was a large world, and it would hold many more. He sowed them like seeds and rejoiced as they took root. He rejoiced even in the weeds that somehow crossed the gulfs between the worlds, the Mekhpurs who sought divinity not in creation but in destruction, not in freedom but in slavery.

Now he saw the peoples of Sotalar coming together, seeking him where he was not, and their wrath and grief were his own as well. In the same moment he turned with the first life to the warmth of long-dead suns; he screamed as obsidian opened his chest; he cried out as he drew all the light of the universes back into himself and began again.

He hovered in brightness, waiting in a realm without time.

Albohar and his son Eskel dressed each other in their tent: undergarments of fine goat's wool, tunics and trousers of tough leather, coats of chain mail. *He's taller than I am,* Albohar thought with a mixture of pride and annoyance. *Stronger too. He wears chain mail as lightly as a girl's shawl. And I, I'll be glad if this is the last day I ever have to put it on.*

"What do you think of your men?" he asked Eskel.

"They'll do well, if I lead them well."

"Then you know most of what warlore is all about."

His son looked at him, his blue eyes a mirror of Albohar's. The girlish mouth was hard, set like a crouching cat's.

"I think we are going into a trap, Father. But you and the captains chose to do so, and I will go where you command. I would like to tell you something while we have time."

"Say it."

"I grew up in Dheribi's—in Calindor's—shadow. I know you married Mother for reasons of state, and you never loved me—or her—as you loved Tilcalli and her son."

Albohar tensed, about to speak and strike in the same instant, and then contained himself.

"You thought he was your son, and even if you thought he was only half Badakh, you would have been glad to make him your heir. Now you know how Tilcalli deceived you, but you love her still, and her son, even though they brought destruction to Aishadan and all the Five Kingdoms.

"You have contented yourself with being electman of a little town, and you yearn for Tilcalli even now, though Mother still sleeps in your bed. Now you are leading us into a battle that I do not think we will survive. So I must tell you this while I still can: you are my father, and I am your son who loves you."

For a time that seemed to him very long, Albohar said nothing. Then he smiled faintly.

"Give me your arms, Eskel. I have not embraced you often enough."

The two tall men gripped each other, and Albohar kissed his son. "A trap it may be, but it will need strong bars to hold a lion such as you."

The army rode west, then south, in darkness and rain. The Gulyaji lighted the way with little pools of coldfire, keeping the

columns together. Experienced Badakhar rode on the column's
flanks and rear, herding stragglers. Few spoke, and then only in
murmurs; all concentrated on reaching the next coldfire beacon,
crossing the next creek, getting up the next hill without riding into
the branches of a tree.

Albohar kept close track of the army's progress, measuring it
always against what Bijandor had told him. Assume some delay
in even the best-run army in the field; the Exteca and their allies
would still be across the Berkha by noon. That would give him
just a few hours to deploy his column out of sight of the ford yet
close enough to strike at the priests. Exteca scouts sometimes
ranged far; he would have to put his own scouts out to track them
and kill them if necessary.

One way or the other, he reflected, by sunset he would no
longer have to fear the Exteca.

Deir rolled out a thick wool sleeping pad on the floor of
Tilcalli's room. Ghelasha, though she seemed weary, refused to
leave her chair in the corner. Dragasa stayed in his chair, beside
the bed. He seemed to have passed through exhaustion into a kind
of tranquility. Callishandal had already fallen asleep at the foot of
the bed.

Pulling a blanket over herself, Deir curled up and closed her
eyes. Strange images filled her thoughts: the sea dragon that had
risen from the bay, the roaring whiteness of the river up which
they had come from the dragons' land to Tanshadabela; the bot-
tomless pool in the cave beneath Bayodar.

Then she was asleep, and walking through the Open Dream.
The ancestors of the Cantareans still danced beneath the unmov-
ing noon sun, but Calihalingol was not among them. Nor was
Tilcalli.

But someone was walking behind her, close behind. Afraid to
turn and look, Deir walked on along the slow-moving river, past
the trees and the village and on into the forest. Still the other followed her, like a shadow. This has happened before, she thought.
These are not the woods of the Open Dream.

They were the oaks of the land of the Airn. These were the
woods between Burnbaile's fields and the eastern hills, but they
were larger than she recalled until she realized she was a little girl
again. Her left hand held a little nosegay of flowers she had
picked along the way. Her right hand was warm in the hand of her
father. She looked up at him, smiling, but his eyes did not smile
back.

They came into a little glade, well off the path, and sat at the foot of an oak. Her father spoke gently to her, but she could not hear his words. His hands stroked her, but she could not feel them. The air was cold on her skin as he drew off her smock, but she could not feel that, nor the warmth of his body as he covered her. But she felt the pain, the pain, the pain—

And now she recognized the face that swam up behind her own in the pool of the Protector: the face of Bron Mac Conal, her own father, his soul sealed within her own for all the years since that summer morning in the woods. She looked up at him as he sweated and shuddered upon her, and saw her own face beyond him, the Deir who had hidden to keep him imprisoned, who in struggling with him had grown strong beyond all measure, who had despaired in the candleboat because though his bones might return to the sea, his poisoned soul remained encysted deep inside her own.

The second Deir, the magician, pulled him away, pulled him upright, looked deep into his face; he would not look back. Her red hair burned in the sunshine, her hands tightened on his arms, and then he was a skeleton, bones that crumbled to powder as they fell at her feet. The grass blackened and died at the touch of his ashes, but then grew back again.

The second Deir came to the first one, lifted her into her arms and cradled her. *Now we are whole again. Now I am you again, and you are me. We are one, and both of us are safe.*

Naked, clad in light, Deir ran from the glade as swiftly as a young doe. The trees around her shifted, the sun's angle changed, and above the forest the tawny hills of Burnbaile were gone. Now the snowcapped peaks of the Open Dream gleamed again under the cloudless sky. Deir came out of the forest into the clearing by the river.

The dancers had stopped. All stood facing her as she approached; they were not looking at her, but beyond her. She turned.

Two women in buckskin were walking slowly, wearily, out of the forest. Deir ran to them, and as they saw her, their weariness fell from them and they hastened to embrace her.

You are whole at last, Tilcalli said. *You are my daughter, my sister, my hopes.*

Calihalingol embraced her also, but she wept as she did so. *You are beautiful, but you bring an end to Callia . . . to Beauty. You bring an end to everything.*

No, said Deir, and stroked the old woman's white hair. *I bring an end to many things, but I bring a new beginning also. And you have cleared my path.*

Yes, said Tilcalli. *We found the way. We have traveled the Open Dream to Tola and the land of the True Gods. The way is open to you.*

I will take it soon, for I have business in Tola.

Will you leave us for the True Gods? Tilcalli asked.

No. There are no gods, not even the True Gods, not even Callia. But I have a score to settle.

You will take vengeance on the Exteca? Calihalingol looked frightened. *Vengeance is foolish.*

Not vengeance, and not against the Exteca. Justice. Against my mother Sivon. She knew. She knew.

"*She knew!*" cried Deir, sitting up. Morning light was glowing in the window; they had slept late and none had dared disturb them.

Tilcalli drew a sudden breath and sat up also. Dragasa and Ghelasha sat slumped in their chairs, deep in sleep; Callishandal stirred and sighed.

Tilcalli leaned across the bed. "Deir. I do not know what you will do this day, but I ask this of you. Be kind."

The girl stood up, quickly pulling on her skirt and tunic. "Kindness. In this world of cruelty?"

"Yes, kindness, *because* it is a world of cruelty."

Deir's focus swept out in a great circle, causing Tilcalli to shudder and Dragasa to spring up and then stare about in amazement. Ghelasha and Callishandal, hearing him cry out, awoke.

"Tilcalli, I greet you at last," Ghelasha said hoarsely.

"And I greet you, my sister."

"At last," said Callishandal.

"At last," Tilcalli replied. "How far I have traveled."

"Come," said Deir. "We have farther still. Give me your hands."

They formed a pentangle: Deir with Tilcalli on her left, Ghelasha on her right; Dragasa holding Callishandal's and Ghelasha's hands. Deir murmured a word while the Cantarean magicians gasped at the power she exerted.

Light poured in as the outer wall turned to powder. Vidhumen lay at their feet; beyond its slate roofs stretched the prairie, and beyond the prairie stood the mountains shining in the sun.

The Powers of air swirled around them, rejoicing in obedience to their new mistress. They lifted the five humans like dust motes, like stars, and carried them into the clearing sky.

Thirty-one

Nezaual had no idea what had become of Bijandor; it did not matter. But the Cantarean had clearly planted the three silver pins on the persons or property of Albohar and his officers. Repeatedly through the night, Nezaual hung a knife from a thread and saw the point shift—from north to northwest to westnorthwest, coming closer all the time.

At last he had gone to sleep; another priest, physically rested though magically exhausted, could keep vigil. The enemy's progress was easy to chart now. By a little after dawn the northerners would be in position. Yaocatl would lead much of the army north across the river, leaving the priests apparently isolated on the south bank. Almost two thousand warriors, mostly Exteca armed with steel, would lie hidden a little farther east. They were to stay in reserve, and to attack only if something went very wrong with the spell of love that Yetecuan would cast upon the northerners.

How beautifully everything has worked out, Nezaual thought as he woke a little after sunrise. *The True Gods have been so good to us, and they have rewarded our faith so generously . . . We will feed them as never before.*

He looked at Calindor, who still stared blindly into his own private darkness. The sorcerer had responded to nothing—to Cantarean healing spells, to slaps and pinches, to simple speech. His face was now bruised and puffy, scabbed in the corners of his mouth by Nezaual's blows. *You will forgive me when you wake, honored father, as I forgave you for striking me on the boat. And together we will bring the whole world under the rule of the True Gods.*

He felt a tremor of joy as priests sacrificed the gifts of the morning. Calindor shuddered in the same moments, his eyes rolling. Then he lay still.

Nezaual rose and left the tent. Outside, the broad plain south of the river was trampled flat by the army's long pause here. Men and beasts had worn the grass and bushes away; latrine trenches, uncovered, sent up a great stink.

Only at a distance of several bowshots did the prairie look like itself. To the south it stretched into the haze of the horizon; to the north, not far away, the River Berkha flowed between gently sloping banks. Trees still stood at a few places along the river, but most had become fuel for campfires. East and west the land rose and then fell away again, leaving sharp-edged ridges against the sky.

The army was already striking its tents, assembling in marching order. The air was full of shouts in three languages; Exteca, Badakhar, and Cantareans all worked together as brothers.

Someday we will be brothers all over the world . . .

The reserve force had already slipped off to the east, vanishing into a nearby network of shallow gullies. To the west the land rose gradually to a long ridge climbing from south to north before it sloped away to the bed of the Berkha.

Yetecuan returned from the morning gifts, wiping his hands on his black robe. He embraced Nezaual, then pulled back and beamed at him.

"All has gone well?"

"Very well, honored father. The enemy are beyond the ridge, ready to fall upon us."

"Bijandor served us nobly. If they did not kill him, we will make him a special gift to the True Gods. And how is Calindor?"

"Unchanged. But once we are in Vidhumen, I think we will be able to undo the spell. We will have the sorcerers of the Gulyaji and the mountain Cantareans to help us—even Calindor's parents, I hope."

"Oh, I hope so too. What a pleasure it would be to meet them. Perhaps we can cure them of their inability to deal with redmagic."

"I hope so, honored father." Nezaual privately doubted that would happen. "We would gain many superb new priests."

"All has worked out for the best," Yetecuan said, "and the True Gods have rewarded our trust in them. Our destiny is manifest; we shall give them the whole world. And now they honor me with the greatest spell I shall ever cast."

"Have you decided whether it will be a spell of love or of terror, honored father?"

"Oh, of love—of course, of love. We do not want to scour the countryside looking for terrified barbarians, when we can have them marching behind us."

The old man sat on a stool outside Nezaual's tent, basking in the warmth of the morning sun. Flies crawled over his hands and buzzed around his head. Not far away, Mixnal readied the old man's favorite mammoth.

"I love that noisy beast," Yetecuan chuckled, "but my happiest journey on his back will be the day we enter Tola."

Nezaual laughed. "What a splendid day that will be! Imagine the gifts! Imagine the people staring at all their new brothers and sisters from the land of magicians."

"Indeed. I hope that Ometollin has not yet sacrificed the woman from Burnbaile. The True Gods pointed her out as a special gift, and it would be proper to make her a gift on the occasion of our return. Without that signal, we would never have imagined ourselves capable of what we have now achieved . . . and especially what you have achieved, my beloved son."

"Like all of us, I have simply done my duty, honored father. I am glad that you saw where my duty lay."

Yetecuan smiled drowsily again; he seemed a little absent-minded, as priests often were as they prepared for a great spell.

"The girl," he said.

"Honored father?"

"The red-haired girl, the sacrifice's daughter. Why was Calindor so interested in her?"

"I confess I am not sure," Nezaual said. "At first I thought he simply wanted a strange-looking slave. Then I thought he was taking her home to sacrifice just as we took her mother. Then . . . I don't know. Sometimes I think he considered her a sorcerer—no, truly, honored father!"

Yetecuan was rocking on his stool in silent laughter. "Was she really a boy after all?" he gasped at last. "Despite those breasts and hips?"

"She is indeed a woman, but among the Cantareans, women can be sorcerers. As I told you, Calindor's mother is a sorcerer, and I met other women who could practice magic. Not redmagic, however. And I have heard rumors that Badakhar women have secret magic that they keep from their men."

The old man was still laughing, hands pressed to his cheeks in helpless mirth. When he lowered his hands, his wrinkled cheeks were moistly red. "Well, we will find out Calindor's true reason before long, beloved son. Perhaps his sorcerer mother will reveal the secret!" And he bent over with wheezing laughter while Nezaual joined in despite himself; Yetecuan's joy was infectious. *May I enjoy such happiness in my old age! And may I give it to those I mentor.*

So the morning passed in good conversation and laughter. From time to time they looked in on Calindor; he was unchanged.

Meanwhile the army marched past in good order, units of Exteca interspersed among the Cantareans and the few Badakhar remaining after all the sacrifices. Yetecuan reminded himself out loud to make a similar great sacrifice of Cantareans once Vidhumen fell, and speculated on whether it might be possible to return to Tola in time for the first day of summer. Nezaual thought not, though it would be an auspicious day on which to celebrate the acquisition of so great a province for the empire.

"But end of summer would be plenty of time," Nezaual went on. "Exactly one year from the taking of Burnbaile. The greatest year in our history."

"The greatest so far," Yetecuan corrected him. "From this day forward, each year will be greater than the last. Excuse me a moment, beloved son."

He focused, and Nezaual grunted a little at the force the old man commanded.

"They are coming. They have been watching the camp for some time, and now they prepare their charge. Please ask Mixnal to notify Colotic. Without leaping up, beloved son."

With deliberate casualness, Nezaual stood and walked over to Mixnal. The mammoth tender nodded and walked—briskly but not too briskly—across the camp to where Colotic stood watching the last units crossing the ford. Meanwhile Nezaual called to the other priests sitting nearby outside their folded tents. Bearers hoisted the tent poles to their shoulders and trudged off to line up for the river crossing. The priests followed them.

A team of bearers began to strike Yetecuan's tent, while others carried Calindor in his bed out into the scanty shade of a nearby aspen. There they rigged a simple sunscreen for him and squatted beside it, awaiting further orders.

Nezaual went into deep focus. The Powers shimmered around him, dancing in the warm spring air, surging upward in the trees and grass, breathing slowly in the soil. Yes, he could sense the northern army poised close by. How few they were! How frightened and desperate! And how glad they would be to cease this pointless resistance and join the servants of the True Gods.

Yetecuan was murmuring the first words of the spell while the last of the Exteca fighting units entered the river and waded across. Now only the priests and some of the supply trains remained in the camp.

Nezaual, looking north, could see Colotic over on the right, not far from the riverbank, signaling to the mammoth tenders. They formed two lines of six each, with only Yetecuan's beast remaining tethered. The hut atop each mammoth held three or four men, their bows and spears hidden. Each beast wore armor—sheets of tough leather protecting the belly and hindquarters.

A deep sigh came from the west, like a sudden wind in trees. Even though he was expecting them, Nezaual was startled by the speed of the northerners' attack. One moment the ridge to his left was empty, a long stretch of windblown grass. The next, sun blazed on polished steel and the air sang with jingling metal and the rumble of hooves. Banners fluttered from spearheads; long ribbons rippled from helmets and bridles. This was the barbarians' last charge, and they made it a moment of splendor.

Then he leaped to his feet in alarm. They were not arrayed properly but were coming down the hillside in two, three disorganized and ragged waves. They would be too spread out for Yetecuan's spell to work properly, and hundreds of them might escape it altogether. If they did, then the reserves would have to come to the rescue—and if the northerners were desperate enough, the slaughter would be great.

Somewhere behind him he heard Mixnal call to his mammoth; turning, he saw the great beast lift Mixnal with its trunk and place him gently behind its head. Then it lumbered west, past the priests, while the other mammoths followed.

Nezaual glanced across the camp and saw Colotic's signalman waving long pennants of red and blue feathers; he had given the command to the mammoth tenders, and they were going forth.

Mixnal and two others guided their beasts southwest, toward the far right wing of the charge. Even at the present distance, at least three bowshots, the horses and their riders saw the mammoths coming. Some lost all discipline and turned off to the south, trying to avoid any contact at all. Most swung to their left, northward, as if by crowding together with their comrades they would be safer.

That was exactly what Colotic wanted, of course, so that Yetecuan's spell would seize as many as possible. Now they were funneling straight for the priests, a thickening wave of darkness and glitter rolling down the long slope of the hill. From far away Nezaual heard soldiers shouting across the river. The attackers were strangely silent.

Swords flashed—a hundred, two hundred, five hundred, ringing as they left their scabbards. Lances lowered. The northerners' faces were distinct now, grim yet foolishly confident that Calindor would appear and rescue them. Even after all this time, how strange the Badakhar seemed to Nezaual with their yellow beards and hair, the Cantareans with their gorgeously beaded buckskins.

It was growing hard to breathe; soon Yetecuan would slash his face and penis and the True Gods would fill the attackers with love. The ground trembled under the hooves of the horses and the huge feet of the mammoths.

—And somehow he was in Burnbaile again, writhing on the ground. He had always been here, moaning into the dirt and scrabbling in the grass. His body had always been on fire, his joints had always bent in agony. He flung himself over on his back; the sun blazed in his face. Five dark shapes glided across the cloud-streaked sky. They meant nothing. Only the pain and terror meant anything.

—And then it ended. He had not been in Burnbaile except in memory; he had always been here, on this trampled meadow by a northern river.

The memory of the pain was enough to keep him from moving for a long moment. Then he rolled onto his side and looked back up the hillside.

The attackers had stopped. However many of them there were, they were bunched together within one and a half bowshots. The mammoths still plodded uphill, but the riders no longer seemed to care. One by one the mammoth tenders looked back to see what the northerners were staring at; they too halted their mounts.

A man and four women hung in the air directly over Yetecuan, the height of three tall men above him. Nezaual recognized them: Dragasa, Ghelasha, Tilcalli, Callishandal . . . and Deir.

Her hair flew out behind her like a banner of fire, and when he looked at her face, he thought with dread of Cihuacoatl the Lady Serpent: *Now I have seen you, my lady*.

Dragasa, Tilcalli, and Callishandal descended to the ground and hurried to the shelter where Calindor lay. The bearers close by shrank away in horror; the Cantareans ignored them.

Another spell struck Nezaual like a club, and the other priests cried out in strangled screams. Dizzy, he pushed himself up on his elbows and saw Calindor, supported by his parents and wife, walking toward him. The sorcerer seemed fully recovered, but with a light in his eyes Nezaual had not seen before. Neither he nor his parents seemed at all affected by the enormous spells that only Deir must have cast.

Calindor is awake! The spells are not harming the Cantareans! What kind of magic can protect magicians from itself? Honored father! Yetecuan!

Nezaual struggled to his hands and knees, vaguely aware that he had bitten his tongue. The old priest was lying facedown on the grass; his extended hand still gripped an obsidian knife.

Nezaual crawled toward him, touched his shoulder, and saw him draw a painful breath.

"Honored father! Please don't die! We need you! Oh, please! They have come. Deir has come!"

Yetecuan opened his eyes and coughed. The knife slipped forgotten from his hand as he drew himself onto his side and squinted up at Deir and Ghelasha hanging in the air.

"The spell at Burnbaile," he whispered to Nezaual. "Not Calindor. Her. The girl. She was the true gift to the Gods." He frowned as if puzzled. "I don't understand, Nezaual. I don't understand."

The ground shuddered again, and a great shout filled the shimmering air. Nezaual looked to the east and saw the reserve forces scrambling from their gullies and storming across the trampled ground of the camp. Hundreds of horsemen charged, while thousands of foot soldiers raced in their dust.

Another cry went up: the army was returning across the river again, heedless of order or discipline, racing back to rescue the priests. Nezaual recognized Yaocatl among the foremost, his yellow plumes gleaming behind him as he drove his horse mercilessly through the water and up onto the bank.

From Deir came a high, thin cry that Nezaual could scarcely hear; yet in a moment he could hear nothing else. Again her magic smashed him into the ground. *Into* the ground—

The soil had liquefied around him; he was sinking into it. *She is burying me alive.*

Then it hardened again. His legs and arms had vanished into the earth; only his head, shoulders, and chest were exposed. He could not move except to lift his head a little. The Powers of earth held him in a grip he knew he could never break.

Frantically Nezaual turned his head from side to side. The soil had engulfed Yetecuan and the other priests, but not the Cantareans: Calindor and his family stood unmoving a few steps away.

Men and horses and mammoths were screaming close by. Nezaual could not lift his head high enough to tell why, but he did not need to. The ground had opened up beneath Yaocatl and Colotic and all the warriors of the Exteca, and they too were now rooted in the soil of Cantarea. He could not turn to see what had happened to Albohar's army.

If she has spared them too, they will trample us like grass.

"Be still," Deir said, and though she spoke quietly, all could hear her. Silence fell. Nezaual realized he himself had been screaming, but now he lay mute.

"The reign of the True Gods is over," Deir said. He could not tell if she spoke in Airn or Cantarean or Exteca; her words created a vision his eyes could understand but could not turn from.

"There are no gods—no Cihuacoatl, no Callia, no Great God Bha. They sprang from the minds and fears of men, and they fed on us. They were dreams only, but dreams that came alive and consumed their dreamers. Now they are gone forever. Look around you, Exteca and Cantareans and Badakhar. This is all we truly have: our lives, the sky, the earth that made us and will take us back again. And a little magic."

Nezaual saw the wind ripple through her garments, and saw above her a great gathering of birds: hawks, eagles, songbirds that soared and hovered and fluttered against the sun.

"You have no cause for war, no need for spells of love and terror. I send you to your homes, all of you. Care for your land with love, not blood. Care for your families. Or the next time the earth will swallow you up forever."

He sank deeper, felt his face sink beneath the surface, and saw the Powers of earth and water cluster round him. He opened his mouth to scream and the earth filled it. Darkness, terror—and then rising and release.

Miraculously, he could sit up, clamber upright and stagger through soil like mud. He helped Yetecuan to his feet and looked at the northerners. They too had sunk into the ground and now were pulling themselves free again. The Powers of earth and water were subsiding again; but they had shown their obedience to the magician Deir.

"Go to your homes, and I will go to mine," Deir said. "But first I go to Tola."

Ghelasha, who had hovered near her, descended gently to the ground. Without warning Deir was gone, and only the birds circled in the air.

Nezaual held Yetecuan upright and glanced around. The Cantareans were gone too—Calindor, Callishandal, Tilcalli, Dragasa. Ghelasha remained, standing in sunlight that made her hair gleam like gold. She looked contemptuously at the mudcaked priests. Insects buzzed in the silence.

The northerners began to ride slowly into the abandoned camp, while the teteuctin warriors hesitantly returned to face them. Nezaual saw Renjosudaldor gratefully dismount and stride forward while sheathing a strange and beautiful sword. Others dismounted also, but most stayed on their horses with swords or lances poised.

One horseman cantered straight for the priests. He pulled off his chain-mail hood and dropped it to the grass, then dismounted in front of Nezaual. It was Albohar.

"Hello, you little son of a bitch," he said, and knocked Nezaual sprawling. Then he walked past Yetecuan, ignoring him, and embraced Ghelasha.

The broad meadow of the camp began to fill with men and beasts who met and mingled with expressions of curiosity and fear. The Cantareans and Badakhar looked at the mammoths from a cautious and awestruck distance; the Exteca clustered around their generals Yaocatl and Colotic.

Nezaual heaved himself to his feet, sobbing softly while tears stung his split lips. Albohar came back, holding his wife's hand. "Tell your people they have safe passage out of Cantarea. But they'd better go fast and they'd better leave people's food alone."

"Of course, electman. I will tell them." He turned to Yetecuan, who squatted trembling nearby. The old man was absently picking lumps of mud from his robe. "Come, honored father. We should go and speak with Yaocatl."

The two priests stumbled across the meadow through the crowds of quiet men.

"What a strange feeling," Yetecuan mumbled.

"What is that, honored father?"

"How empty the world feels, with no Gods. How could a little girl destroy the True Gods?"

Nezaual gripped him a little harder, helping him toward the place where Yaocatl and Colotic were talking with some of their officers. Some of the teteuctin, and some of the Cantareans and Badakhar, began to dance each in their own way. They sang, each their own songs. The sound was not discordant, but it seemed to Nezaual to be very quiet and very sad.

The two priests passed a tall Badakh who stood still among his dancing comrades, looking up into the air where Deir had been. It was Pervidhu.

Nezaual followed his gaze. The birds had vanished. The sun blazed at the zenith in an empty sky.

Thirty-two

After the dawn gifts, Ometollin had spent most of the morning in meditation. He had chosen the chapel dedicated to Cihuacoatl, on the west face of the pyramid on the highest terrace before the top. Here he could sit in shade, between the Lady Serpent's scaled knees, and look out from the darkness across sunlit Tola to the sea.

A sense of great peace filled him. The empire poured its wealth and love into this city, into his hands, and he gratefully returned those gifts to the Gods. The land was tranquil, orderly—yes, a little hungry and thirsty also, but so the Gods wished it. Without hunger, without thirst, the Exteca would be no better than the barbarians. And when they really needed rain, a gift of blood would bring it.

He prayed for the success of Yetecuan and of Yaocatl's army. For a time, messengers had returned with news of the expedition; but none had come for several months now. Surely the news would be good—Calindor would take his place as a great priest of the True Gods, bringing still more barbarous nations into the embrace of the Exteca.

He leaned back against the cool stone thigh of the Lady Serpent, still sticky from the gifts of this morning. *I thank you, my lady, for this great peace you bring us.*

As if someone had shoved him, he rocked back between Cihuacoatl's legs, under her skirt of serpents, and the back of his head struck her spike-fringed vulva. Gasping, Ometollin rolled forward and tried to crawl from the chapel onto the sunlit terrace.

One great magic is an omen. Two are a threat.

He had thought that last year, when the second spell from the north had swept like storm through Tola. *And a third great magic?*

The greatest yet, a pulse of force that left him drooling and grunting between Cihuacoatl's feet like some misshapen newborn. He managed to feel a pang of sorrow for the other priests, and for the ordinary people who would have no idea what was happening.

The chapel, droning with flies, shimmered with some kind of magic he had never encountered before. It was like ... like looking at a solid door shudder under the impact of a battering ram. But this was a battering of space itself, a weakening of the world's fabric.

With more strength than he had thought he possessed, Ometollin dragged himself out onto the terrace. The shimmer, the battering, seemed to shake the whole mass of the pyramid. The sun was hot on his back. Screaming rose from the city, as shrill and inconsequential as the buzzing of the flies.

A guard in white plumes hurried to him, staggering as if drunk, and pulled him to his feet. Ometollin leaned gratefully against him.

"You feel it too, beloved son?"

"It's an earthquake, honored father! Let me guide you to safety."

Ometollin laughed giddily. "What a long journey that would be. Come with me to the north steps. I must speak with the Tecutli Itztlac."

They lurched together to the northwest corner of the terrace. To Ometollin the city below seemed normal; then he saw the streets full of running people.

How can an earthquake strike us just as we feel this magic? Have we angered the True Gods?

The shimmer stopped, and the quaking with it. Whatever had caused it, the breach in space had closed. Ometollin stepped back, startled, as he realized he and the guard were not alone anymore.

Strangers stood on the terrace near the steps, looking down at the great plaza where thousands were gathering. Two were tall men in beaded buckskin, surely father and son. Two were women, slender and beautiful. And one was a pale-skinned girl whose red hair fell like fire over her shoulders and breasts.

The younger man looked at him, smiling wryly, and spoke in Exteca: "I greet you, honored father. You must be a priest here."

"I am the Chief Priest Ometollin, beloved son."

"My name is Calindor. My father and mother, Dragasa and Tilcalli. My wife, Callishandal. And our friend Deir. We are from a land in the north called Cantarea. Deir is from Burnbaile. She wants to see her mother Sivon."

Calindor himself, the object of the expedition, present in Tola? Ometollin put the thought aside for a moment and tried to deal with something simpler.

"Sivon, Sivon ... Beloved son, the name means nothing to me."

Calindor looked impatient. "Yetecuan sent her here as a special gift to the True Gods. Have you already sacrificed her?"

"Ah, that one. That one, with yellow hair. Yes, she lives." He turned to the guard. "Beloved son, please be so kind as to go to the House of Waiting and bring the yellow-haired woman named Sivon. And please tell the teteuctin in the plaza that the Tecutli Itztlac would honor us with his presence also."

Fear in his eyes, the guard sprinted for the steps and hurried down to the plaza. The crowds below were still growing, though the earthquake had ended; the people were seeking reassurance.

"You have had a long journey," Ometollin said hoarsely. He could not think of anything else to say.

"A very short one. Moments ago we were in Cantarea. Your army has been overthrown, without a single Exteca's death. It will be returning in a few months."

"Excuse me, beloved son, but I do not understand. You were just in some other place, and Yaocatl's army is unharmed but defeated?"

"Deir has defeated all of us, and saved all of us. And now she has come to Tola to see her mother."

"Ah. How dutiful."

Other priests approached, bearing benches and even a bowl of tea. Ometollin sank gratefully onto a bench, but the strangers remained standing. They seemed exhilarated yet shocked, and they looked down at the red-tiled roofs of Tola with awe and admiration. When the breeze off the sea died, and the smell from the altars spread, they caught their breath.

Only Deir ignored the city, the stink, and the hesitantly attentive priests; she stood with arms folded, gazing north to the peaks of the mountains on the horizon.

After what seemed to Ometollin to be a long time, the Tecutli marched across the plaza within a square of the teteuctin. The warriors cleared a path through the crowds without even touching anyone. Itztlac reached the foot of the steps and paused until a small group of women joined him. One was tall, yellow-haired, and beautifully dressed. She fell in a few steps behind the Tecutli, with her own retinue of attendants. Slowly, with pomp and decorum, the Tecutli ascended while the others followed.

Ometollin tried to regain the tranquility he had felt just moments before. He could not. But the wait gave him a chance to catch his breath and consider alternatives. The girl could surely not have overthrown Yaocatl; that was a lie. Simple logic allowed no other conclusion. The strangers had not just come from the north; they had traveled south for months, eluding the army that sought them.

The girl might be a magician, though that idea also strained belief; Calindor and his father were clearly magicians, and his mother had something of the look about her as well. But they were all humans, even the redheaded girl, and a spell of love could bind them safely to the True Gods. The trick would be to begin the spell without their detecting it, and to give the blood before they could stop him.

The crowd on the steps was still far below. Evidently losing patience, Deir whispered a word. An instant later the Tecutli and Sivon soared up the white face of the pyramid like two astonished birds. They hung suspended above the terrace for a moment, and then sank gently to the pavement.

To his credit, the Tecutli Itztlac kept his dignity. He stood motionless, silently contemplating the strangers. Far down the steps, the retinue had stopped dead. Ometollin rehearsed the words of the spell of love while he groped in his robe for an obsidian knife. He wondered what Deir and her mother were saying. Perhaps he would find out after the spell had brought the strangers under control . . .

"Hello, Madhair," Deir said. It felt strange to be speaking Airn again, after all this time.

"Deir!" Her mother stared with amazement. "How have you come here? Did the Exteca bring you?"

"I brought myself, and my friends. You remember Calindor and Callishandal, who took me away from Burnbaile."

Sivon did not take her eyes from Deir. "Brought yourself? How?"

"The telling would make a long story. But I will tell you a short one instead. Long ago, when I was a little girl, my father took me into the woods looking for mushrooms. Instead he raped me. He raped me, Madhair. And he went on doing it for years, didn't he?"

Sivon's face was as pale as her fine cotton gown. "Yes."

"And you knew, didn't you?"

"Yes—no—"

A whirlwind roared around them, whipping at their clothes and tearing Itztlac's plumes away.

"Yes? No? Which is it?"

Sivon sank to her knees, her face crumpling. "Deir—Deir— We didn't know. I swear we didn't!"

"You knew. You knew."

"Listen! Daughter, listen to me! We didn't know until last year. Only then!"

"We? Who knew?"

"My brother, your uncle Simas in Kiltarra, and I. He it was who told me what your father had said to him, when they were drunk—that . . ." She fell silent and swallowed, and went on: "That your father said he had properly broken you in for your future husband, and a lusty wife you would make him."

Sivon's lips moved but she could not speak. Deir did not trouble with magic, but gripped her mother's arms and pulled her roughly upright.

"When did my uncle tell you this? When?"

Sivon drew a breath and looked into her daughter's eyes. "The night before we killed him."

The whirlwind died. The sun shone hot on the terrace.

"Your uncle Simas went into the house your father was building, and set the posts so the roof beam would roll the wrong way when your father tried to fix it in place. It flung him down and fell on him. But he wasn't quite dead, and glad I was of that, for I went in and took him by the hair and smashed his skull against the roof beam before anyone else could come in."

"You did all that?"

"More I would have done, to see him dead. And only later did I think what harm I had done you. For now you had an incestuous father and a murderer for a mother."

"Yet you said nothing bad about him—you wore the widow's shawl, you buried him, and dug up his bones and we made his candleboat and . . . and we sang him to the Happy Isles, and you said he was a funny man—"

"I thought back to what a happy, chattering little girl you had been, and how you changed and did not change again. I could tell you had made yourself forget. So I swore I would not open that wound, I would not make you remember. But oh, how long the nights were, and how I yearned to see his bones vanish in the sea. And how glad I was when the Exteca came again and carried me away, and promised that they would pull out my heart and give me peace."

Ometollin had been whispering under his breath; now he cried out, "*Cage cuel!* It is coming true!" and drew the blade from his robe. With the ease of long practice, he lifted it to his face, and with the other hand parted his robe so that the second cut, to the penis, would be easy.

Deir glanced sidelong at him and the knife flew from his hand;

for a long time it made a whirring noise as it spun far off the terrace before it began to fall.

Calindor stepped toward him and struck Ometollin's face with his open hand. The old man reeled. "You have *struck* me!"

"You are as bad as Nezaual," Calindor said. "You may make no magic without permission, honored father. And you will never have permission again."

Deir had taken her mother in her arms, embraced her. The two women wept together for a time, and kissed, and then let go.

"All will be well for us again, Madhair. My friends in the north began my healing, and you have completed it. Now I heal you of your grief and release you from the Exteca spell. Come, sit on the bench beside Callishandal and rest for a moment. I have one more task before we go home."

A rumble seemed to rise from the pyramid, or from the ground it stood upon: too deep even to hear, but strong enough to make ripples in the neglected bowl of tea on the bench beside Sivon. Deir looked at Itztlac and Ometollin, and they sank to their knees. Elsewhere on the terrace, other priests knelt also.

Deir turned to the north and looked down at the thousands crowding into the plaza, and she spoke as she had at the Berkha River: quietly, yet in the hearing of every person who saw her, and in a language all could understand.

"Hear me, people of Tola, Blood People! The reign of the True Gods is over. Never again—not tonight, not tomorrow, never— will you give blood and death to them. Never again will your priests burn hearts, never again will your teteuctin conquer other lands to feed the hunger of your gods. You created them out of your dreams and fear and greed, and now I take those dreams from you. Tend your land with love, not blood, and take nothing from it that you cannot give back.

"And when you hunger and thirst, Blood People, and you yearn for your True Gods again, remember what you are about to see."

The rumble deepened, strengthened; the tea bowl fell from the bench and shattered. Something like a heavy footfall shook the terrace.

Ometollin looked to his right, down the western terrace that ran past the chapel of Cihuacoatl, and tried to scream with a dry throat.

The Lady Serpent was emerging from her chapel.

More than twice a man's height, carved from black granite and bathed in blood for centuries, the statue of Cihuacoatl walked slowly out into the sunlight. Her skirt of snakes writhed around her hips; the bones that adorned her rattled as she walked. Her teeth were golden fangs gleaming in the sun, and her stone feet scraped on the stone pavement.

Behind her, coming from the south chapel, was Huitzil Xochitl, Hummingbird Flower; from the north chapel came Yaoyotl, True God of war, and Yolcuicatl the Heart Song came from his chapel on the east. From the temples at the top of the pyramid came other gods, their stone legs bending and straightening as they descended the steps caked with the blood of their sacrifices.

Cihuacoatl walked past Ometollin and the others and took up her place with the other gods, looking blindly out over the city and the howling multitudes below. Deir walked down the terrace until she stood beside the Lady Serpent: a small, slim girl who did not even reach to the stone snakes hanging from Cihuacoatl's waist.

"The reign of the True Gods is over," Deir said again, and raised her hand to touch the thick stone leg.

Cihuacoatl lifted her terrible face to the sky and screamed.

Fire engulfed her, spreading swiftly from Deir's hand. The statue took two steps forward, still screaming, and fell down the face of the pyramid. Cihuacoatl's limbs shattered, her torso burst apart, and her head exploded. The debris burned white-hot as it fell, trailing oily smoke, and nothing survived to reach the plaza.

Now the other True Gods turned upon one another like wrestlers or teteuctin, striking one another with stone fists and maces. They too shattered, and each fragment burned as it fell down the pyramid's white slope. In moments only smoke remained; and it too vanished in the wind.

The temples at the pyramid's top were burning now, and now the chapels. The pavement of the terrace was trembling and cracking. Ometollin, sobbing, lay curled in his stiff black robe while the Tecutli Itztlac, emperor of Tola, remained on his knees. A half smile curled his lips.

"Come," Deir said. "Let us go down to join the people."

All who were on the terrace, or elsewhere on the pyramid, rose into the air and glided down over the heads of the Exteca. Behind them the flames were spreading over the surface of the pyramid as the Powers of fire rejoiced in their sudden liberation from the Powers of earth. The sky blackened with smoke, until the disk of the sun was only a ghost of its true brightness.

Deir brought them down onto the plaza. The people nearby did not move away, though many knelt. Deir smiled at them, and soothed a crying child with a word. Then she looked back at the pyramid.

Its outline was lost now in the blaze. Like an enormous mushroom, smoke rose into the sky and spread out to mantle the city in darkness. Yet for all its intensity, the fire gave out no heat that the people in the plaza could feel—only a dazzling light and a roar as Powers gained freedom after untold millions of years.

Within an hour, perhaps less, a vast square, perfectly level and utterly empty, was all that remained. Elsewhere in the city other pyramids were burning also. Soon they too would be gone.

Itztlac had been walking back and forth, watching the destruction of a holy place that should have lasted forever. Now he turned and spoke to Deir:

"You are the new Tecutli. All Tola is yours. As your slave I would cherish the honor of showing you your palace and servants, and doing your bidding."

Deir understood him, and spoke again in her new language of images: "No, it remains yours, Tecutli. This land now is all you have. I would not take it from you. I hope you care well for your land and your people."

"But how will we live without the True Gods?" cried Ometollin. Two younger priests held him up, their faces masks of shock.

"As we live without our fathers," Deir said. She turned to the Cantareans.

"My task here is done. My mother and I are going home to Burnbaile. But I can send you home to Tanshadabela through the Open Dream."

"Can the Open Dream exist when Callia is no more?" Tilcalli asked, and bitterness was in her voice.

"For a while. But not for long. Soon your ancestors will cease their dance and walk to the mountains. Even Calihalingol. I think she will be glad to go."

Tilcalli clung to Dragasa, weeping. Deir looked at Calindor and Callishandal. "Will you return to Tanshadabela?"

They looked at each other. "Yes," Callishandal said. "Yes. I want to see the Open Dream again, and then I want to see our cabin and our friends."

"Then so it shall be."

"Wait," said Dragasa. "I don't want to go home. Not just yet."

"Why not?" Deir asked.

"Look around you. You have destroyed the gods of these people as well as our own. Their magic all sprang from blood and death, and now they have nothing. How will they feed themselves? How will they care for their children?"

"That is their concern."

"It is ours also. Tilcalli—let us stay here and teach the Exteca something of greenmagic. And let us come to know one another again."

She looked at him in astonishment, and then turned to look at the whitewashed houses around the plaza, at the roofs of the palaces rising above the trees. The Exteca—short, beautifully dressed, with feathers woven in their shining black hair—looked at them with sadness and curiosity but no anger.

"I will stay with you," Tilcalli said. "But Calindor and Callishandal must come back in a year or two. Perhaps, if we've done our work well, they might even want to stay."

"As you wish." Deir came to Tilcalli and embraced her, and then Callishandal. "We will meet again. Now I will open the path to the Open Dream."

"No need," Calindor said. "I have learned the way." He smiled at Deir. "I dreamed of teaching you; now I learn from you."

"I learned much from you, Calindor. More than you imagine."

"Someday you will have to teach me the spell of forgetting that you put on me."

Deir laughed. "And some day you will have to forgive me for doing so, and for shielding you from Nezaual's spell of love."

"You saved me, but I do not think you know what I learned while I slept."

"And what is that?"

"The gods are gone. But I was Brightness, and I saw how Bha made the worlds and peopled them. We are not quite as alone as you think."

Deir smiled. "May it be so. But we are not alone while we have one another." She embraced him and then stepped back. "Farewell, magician! Show me what you've learned."

The air shimmered around him and Callishandal. And then they were gone.

"And farewell to you," Deir said to Dragasa and Tilcalli. "You were father and mother to me, and I will always love you. Someday I will go back to Tanshadabela, and Tilcalli will too, and we'll have a sweat bath. And then I'll make it snow again."

She kissed Tilcalli and Dragasa, and then took her mother's hand.

"Come, Madhair—it's time to go home."

The two women lifted into the air and soared northward. In moments they were gone.

Dragasa turned to his wife. "Have I been a fool to keep us here?"

"No. Or am I another fool who loves you?"

The smoke that shrouded the city had turned to dark clouds. Now it began to rain. Drops pattered on the paving stones of the plaza, increased, and turned to a downpour. The thousands still standing there turned their faces to the rain.

Itztlac touched Dragasa's arm and pointed to the palace beyond the trees, inviting them to seek shelter. They began to walk through the crowds of Exteca while Itztlac waved off the teteuctin who sought to shield him from the people.

"Atl," the Tecutli said, holding up his palm to catch the rain.

"Atl. Water," Tilcalli repeated. "Well, it's a start."

Epilogue

Eastward the tawny hills shimmered in late summer heat; westward the blue waters of the Siar Bagh gleamed under the sun. The peninsulas of Donbein and Dubein still reached to one another, and beyond them the Diamuir, the Sea of Gods, lay under a bank of fog.

The house of Deir stood on the eastern side of Burnbaile, farther up the River Clachwisgy from the old home where her mother still lived and made her pots. Deir had built for herself a tower, the height of ten tall men, of stone and timber. The walls of its topmost floor were all of glass, and from it she could see the mountains, the bay, and all the towns and lands of the Airn.

They had greatly changed in the last year, and especially in this summer. Under the rule of the Exteca, the Airn had used their land too hard, trying to produce the apples, the grain, the fish and mead that Tola demanded. Many of the Airn had marched away to the north to serve Yaocatl's army, leaving women and children and old men to do too much. Exteca warriors, garrisoned in Burnbaile and other towns, had selected sacrifices almost at random; as the spell of love wore off, the Airn had come to live in dread of the plumes of the Fabarslúa.

Then Deir and Sivon had returned. Deir had sent the teteuctin home. She had restored the fertility of the fields, and called the fish back into the Siar Bagh. The granaries were full, and the drying racks held plenty of fish. Many houses had fallen into neglect; Deir had restored them and taught carpenters and masons the secrets of iron tools.

But hundreds of good people were gone, and the bay would hold many candleboats on the last night of summer.

After this year, she thought, *perhaps we should send out no more candleboats, and let the dead rest in the earth. We have thought too much about the past, we have let the dead rule us.*

But if the Airn still wished to build candleboats, she knew she would not forbid them.

She sat at the top of the tower, windows open to catch the breeze, and played the tall harp that her uncle Simas had built for her as a homecoming gift. She was not yet very good at it, and often laughed at her own clumsiness, but sometimes her fingers plucked the strings as they should. Then the notes were as lovely and clean as the Powers themselves that attended her.

This morning was not one of those times, and at last she stood up in defeat. Uncle Simas would have to give her more lessons, and him so busy as it was with the rebuilding of Kiltarra and with his trading shop in Barnachy. She walked about the wide, bright single room that was the top of the tower. Now she looked down at the town; now she looked at the tawny hills; now she looked out to the northwest at the long mountain of Dubein and the forests sheltering in its lee.

She sensed something coming, a moving magic, and looked again to the north. A dark object was moving swiftly against the sky, descending toward the Siar Bagh. Its course would bring it close to Burnbaile.

She focused on it, and encountered a strange kind of shield that reflected nothing except a sense of amusement.

Calindor! It must be Calindor. But why would he try to conceal himself when he must know I can guess it's he?

The object was closer now, leveling off and gliding not far above the water. Now it was close enough to recognize, and the recognition was a shock: it was the *Tilcalli*, the boat that had first brought Calindor and Callishandal here. Now it moved through the air as easily as it had risen through the roaring white water of the river to Tanshadabela.

Her first intent was to spring to the window and fly to greet the boat; then she decided she was now too old for such impulsiveness. Instead she walked sedately down the steps to the door of the tower, and down the new-paved road along the Clachwisgy. At her mother's house she called in and found Sivon with muddy hands, dipping unfired pots in glaze.

"Calindor is back."

"Is he indeed? And with no warning? We've little to offer him but vegetable stew and bread. Where is he?"

"He's taught his boat to fly, and it's just arriving down by the dock."

"A flying boat! Much more comfortable, I'm sure, than flying like a bird. And why did you never think of such a thing?"

Half growling, half laughing, Deir pulled her mother to a water bucket where she could rinse the glaze from her hands. Then they continued down the road and through the reeds that lined the shore. Others had seen the boat sink from the sky and were hurrying along the path as well.

Tilcalli bobbed sedately on the water alongside the dock where Yetecuan and Colotic had greeted the Cantareans almost a year ago. Calindor, standing on the rear deck, looped a rope around a piling; Deir wondered why he didn't simply use a spell, and then remembered that he preferred the simplest way to solve a problem.

"Welcome back!" she called to him. He waved and stepped onto the dock. From the boat's cabin, Callishandal came out on deck and then joined her husband. Deir and Sivon embraced them, laughing.

"A flying boat!" Sivon exclaimed. "A brilliant idea. Where have you come from?"

"From Tanshadabela, and Vidhumen, and the land of the dragons," said Callishandal. She looked almost breathless with excitement, and her dark eyes gleamed. "We have been everywhere in the last three days. We can stay only a little while before we go on to Tola to see Dragasa and Tilcalli. And we have brought another guest, if it is all right."

Deir looked perplexed, focused on the boat and found the shield still there. "Of course—but who is it?"

Calindor called back to the boat: "She says you're welcome. Come on out."

Pervidhu emerged from the cabin, looking a little embarrassed, and climbed up onto the dock.

"I feared you might be angry with me, my lady," he said to Deir. "You left the Berkha without saying good-bye."

Laughing, Deir put her arms around his neck and kissed him. "But I didn't forget you."

"You didn't?"

"I hoped you would find a way to come. I even sang an old

song about returning." And she sang it now as she had sung it on the candleboat in the darkness of the bay:

> "We summon you back, summon you back
> From dark and silent earth;
> We summon you back, summon you back
> To sail the sea and sky
> Our love will abide, our love will abide
> When sun and stars are gone . . ."

They walked together, arm in arm, back up the path through the reeds to the town.

About the Author

Crawford Kilian was born in New York City in 1941 and grew up in California and Mexico. After graduating from Columbia University in 1962, he returned to California, served in the U.S. Army, and worked as a technical writer-editor at the Lawrence Berkeley Laboratory.

In 1967 he and his wife Alice moved to Vancouver, British Columbia. Since then he has taught English and Communications at Capilano College. In 1983 the Kilians taught English at the Guangzhou Institute of Foreign Languages in China.

Crawford Kilian's writing includes eleven science-fiction and fantasy novels, among them *The Empire of Time, Eyas,* and *Lifer.* In addition he has published children's books, textbooks for elementary and post-secondary students, and three nonfiction books—most recently, *2020 Visions: The Futures of Canadian Education.* For over ten years he was the regular education columnist for the Vancouver *Province* newspaper, and he has published articles on education and the Internet in such periodicals as *Technos, Educom Review, Internet World,* and *Infobahn.* His e-mail address is ckilian@hubcap.mlnet.com.

The Kilians live in North Vancouver.

DEL REY ONLINE!

The Del Rey Internet Newsletter...

A monthly electronic publication, posted on the Internet, GEnie, CompuServe, BIX, various BBSs, and the Panix gopher (gopher.panix.com). It features hype-free descriptions of books that are new in the stores, a list of our upcoming books, special announcements, a signing/reading/convention-attendance schedule for Del Rey authors, "In Depth" essays in which professionals in the field (authors, artists, designers, sales people, etc.) talk about their jobs in science fiction, a question-and-answer section, behind-the-scenes looks at sf publishing, and more!

Online editorial presence: Many of the Del Rey editors are online, on the Internet, GEnie, CompuServe, America Online, and Delphi. There is a Del Rey topic on GEnie and a Del Rey folder on America Online.

Our official e-mail address for Del Rey Books is delrey@randomhouse.com

Internet information source!

A lot of Del Rey material is available to the Internet on a gopher server: all back issues and the current issue of the Del Rey Internet Newsletter, a description of the DRIN and summaries of all the issues' contents, sample chapters of upcoming or current books (readable or downloadable for free), submission requirements, mail-order information, and much more. We will be adding more items of all sorts (mostly new DRINs and sample chapters) regularly. The address of the gopher is gopher.panix.com

Why? We at Del Rey realize that the networks are the medium of the future. That's where you'll find us promoting our books, socializing with others in the sf field, and— most importantly—making contact and sharing information with sf readers.

For more information, e-mail
delrey@randomhouse.com